When the Buckeyes Fall

by Joanie Long

for Jim
...who taught me to love the mountains

and for Marilyn
...who taught me to love myself

thank you both for giving me life
and for making that life meaningful

A few words from some of my biggest fans...

(Thank you all so very much!)

"For all my friends who enjoy reading... A friend of mine that I grew up with wrote this book and it is so GOOD! If you enjoyed 'Where the Crawdads Sing' I think you will enjoy this as well. Captivating from the beginning. The story is about a few families that lived up on the Mulberry River and Panther Branch during the Civil War, main character being a young girl named Hannah Casey. It covers it all in this book, love, loss, perseverance and strength it took to survive during the war. This book is fiction but the places she details in the book are real, Lookout Point, Harmony, Spadra and Clarksville." ... Adera

"I enjoyed your book so very much! You, my dear, are quite talented! You have something here, a gift for sure! Keep writing and I'm hoping for more books in the future." ... Adera

"I picked up your book yesterday and was hooked in the first chapter!" ... Andrea

"Just got your book and started reading it, I could hardly put it down last night to sleep, so am reading more today! I love the book, so interesting and can relate to it because of things my grandparents used to talk about. You have done a wonderful job writing this great book! So very proud for you Joanie!" ... Anna

"Just read your book! Just wanted to tell you it was AWESOME, ready for the next one. My Mom was raised at Catalpa so it holds a special place in my heart, spent our whole summer on Bear Branch." ... Belinda

"Me and Dennis both loved your book. I vote for sequel." ... Betty

"I read it! Made me cry!" ... Cindy

"Just finished this novel. Absolutely amazing!! One of the best historical fictions. Dated during the Civil War era. Have a box of Kleenex ready for the ending! I would love to see this on the big screen one day. Thank you, Joanie Long, for writing 'When the Buckeyes Fall'. I will be waiting for your next novel." ... Dana

"I am so freaking proud and happy for you, my dear friend!! I can't wait to read it!!" ... Dawna

"I just finished your book and thoroughly enjoyed it. I laughed and cried all the way through it. Please write more." ... Debby

"Joanie, I read your book today on my Kindle. I very much enjoyed it. I felt like I was right there with them living in Buckeye! Great job! Can't wait to see what you write next!! Congratulations!!" ... Delene

"Oh, Joanie, I finished the book and we definitely need a sequel! It was great!! I'm so proud of you." ... Donna

"I read your book 'When the Buckeyes Fall', I enjoyed it, you did a good job holding my interest. I have the attention span of a 3 year old and this book kept me interested and I didn't want to lay it down. You have a talent that many of us can enjoy and wonder how you can put all of the information and thoughts into a book that anyone can enjoy! Thanks for writing it and I'll be waiting for the next one." ... Dwain

"I opened the book up and couldn't put it down! It's been a long time since I read a book that kept me into it!! I will read more of hers when they come available." ... Gladys

"I could hardly put your book down and was kinda sad to finish it. I would love a sequel. It is an awesome book!! So proud of you." ... Janice

"I've just started reading Joanie's book. It's captivating." ... Jeri

"Just from what I've read so far I love it and just started the 1st chapter!" ... Jill

"You're an excellent writer." ... Joyce

"I just bought your book last week and started reading it tonight. I've only read about 20 pages and I love it already! I know the area and I can just picture it in my mind! Keep writing please!" ... Kathy

"I don't think I ever really thought about what the families who were left behind when the men went off to fight the Civil War had to endure. The storyline builds well and comes to an ending leaving me wondering what will happen next. I hope there is a sequel." ... Katina

"I just finished reading 'When the Buckeyes Fall'. Thank you Joanie Bean Long, for writing an amazing book. I thoroughly enjoyed every word from beginning to end. These lines, 'Wait for the wagon and we'll all take a ride', brings back childhood memories for me, not only the catchy lyrics and tune, but also literally waiting for the wagon wheels to be packed and greased and horses hitched to the wagon so we could then all take a ride from Lone Pine to Woodland to Pa and Ma Houston's for a family re-union. I bought three more books to give to friends, it is so good." ... Levon

"I just finished your book, and let me say, it is so, so, so good. Thanks for posting about it so I had the opportunity of hearing about it. Y'all need to go get it. 'When the Buckeyes Fall', you won't regret it. PS... Order a couple boxes of Kleenex, too. You might need them." ... Lynn

"This book is beautifully written. I cried, I laughed and I felt all the worry, anger and love that this young girl experienced. I look forward to more from this author." ... Lynn

"I finished the book! I have to say I haven't enjoyed a book that much in a very long time. I love the families you had in it. I thought you portrayed the life of families like them during the Civil War very accurately. You covered both male and female, young and old, very well. I really like the way you ended the book on a happy and sad note. Really left a great opening for a sequel. I liked the way you went back over each person and put their names back into the mind of the reader. No one just disappeared. You brought them back into the reader's mind. You took me through every emotion I can think of except maybe confused. I was never confused. One of those books you don't want to put down. I am so proud of you. I always knew you would be an author some day. Writing a book this well is not an easy endeavor. It shows how much work you put into it." ... Marilyn

"I bought a signed copy at Rose Drug in Clarksville. I loved, loved it – didn't grab me in the very beginning, but just got better and better. Congratulations!" ... Maxine

"I like this line in your book... 'Fear doesn't stop death, but it certainly does stop life'." ... Nancy

"I enjoyed reading your book so much." ... Nina

"Hi Joanie, you are a blessing to the mountain folks that live around the part of our country you describe." ... Orbon

"This was an awesome book. Couldn't put it down. A great read." ... Pamela

"Just finished your book. It was awesome, just didn't want it to end. Thank you." ... Peggy

"My Grandpa King's place on Stillwell Mountain is called 'The Buckeye'." ... Robert

"Guys, I haven't read a book this good in 30+ years. Maybe I like it so much because it takes place in the area close to our most favorite place in Arkansas and probably the world, Ponca/Boxley Valley area. Thank you, Joanie Bean Long, for sharing this wonderful story of Civil War era Arkansas with us. Cannot wait for your next book!" ... Shane

"I wanted to thank you so much for writing this book. I've never been one to read this type of book or story. Especially about Civil War times, as it just has never peaked my interest. However, we fell in love with the area in your book about 3 years ago. I actually feel I am there with those families and Hannah as she tells the story. I'm in shock that I love this book so much! Can't wait to see what else you write. I'm going to purchase more and give to my family for Christmas." ... Shane

"I enjoyed this book so much. I would recommend it to everyone. I've read a lot of books and this one is at the top of the list. Looking forward to a sequel." ... Sharon

"Mom loves your book! Stayed up late to finish it! This is a great read. I read it in two days!! Couldn't put it down. Cried a lot as well, but that's how I am with a good book." Shawn

"So, my brother read your book and he LOVED it. He said it needs to be a movie." ... Terri

"My daughter started a private Christian school this year and she needs to read and write an essay on one book a month. Once I told her about your book she chose it as her first book and report." ... Warren

The house on the cover of this book was the actual home of my great great grandparents, Robert McKinley Baskin & Rebecca Elizabeth (Gimlin) Baskin. It was located in the community of Harmony, in Johnson County, Arkansas in the early 1900's. Bob & Lizzie raised 14 children, and had approximately 50 grandchildren who frequented this home. Sadly, the house no longer stands. As I was writing this book, I imagined that my main characters, the Casey family, lived in a house just like this one. It was an honor to be able to bring this home back to life for a brief moment in time.

Buckeye, Arkansas
a fictional community

- - - 1861 - - -

Note from the author

The following story is a work of historical fiction that takes place in Johnson County, Arkansas during the time of the Civil War. Although the story line and most of the characters are fictional, you will find that actual people, places and events in our history will pop up from time to time as you read along. The community of Buckeye, which is the main setting of my story, is completely fictional, but it is loosely based on a place called Catalpa, in the mountains of northern Johnson County. I used Catalpa as my starting point, but made subtle changes here and there for the interest of the story. You will find that as my characters go through life, they will experience the Civil War in much the same way the actual people of the area did at that time. I even use some true stories of things that happened to my own ancestors.

"It is well that war is so terrible,
or we should grow too fond of it."

~~~ *Robert E. Lee*

"I have never advocated war,
except as a means of peace."

~~~ *Ulysses S. Grant*

"In the present Civil War,
it is quite possible that God's purpose
is something different
from the purpose of either party,
and yet the human instrumentalities,
working just as they do,
are of the best adaptation
to effect his purpose."

~~~ *Abraham Lincoln*
~~~

- - - - - - -

- - - - - - -

1861

Elijah Casey stood in the front of the little one-room school to speak to the men of his community. It was a small group, because only six homes were speckled along the banks of the creek in this rural part of northern Arkansas. Not another structure existed for twenty miles in any direction. The nearest town was Clarksville, which was a daylong trek by horseback over the mountains down into the river valley below.

The little community was not incorporated, and did not have a post office, but unofficially the people living there called the area "Buckeye", because of the abundance of buckeye trees that grew everywhere. The community was centered around a spot where two creeks joined; Panther Creek, which came down from the north and flowed into Mulberry Creek, which ran in a westerly direction.

Elijah was the head of the largest family living there, consisting of his wife Emeline, and their nine children. They lived in a large two-story L-shaped home on the rise above the creek. The large home had been built out of necessity, not out of wealth, and had been a community effort. Elijah was the leader of the community. There had been no elections. There was no title. But, the others seemed to turn to him when decisions needed to be made. He was well respected and looked up to, so he usually took over and led the town meetings.

To Elijah's left sat Henry Inman. Henry was Elijah's closest friend and business partner. They ran a small sawmill together. Henry lived just across the creek with his wife Irene and their six children. The sawmill was on the same side of the creek as Henry's home. A short distance down the creek from his house there was a spot where the creek dropped off down a hill a bit, causing a rapid to form. Henry and Elijah had built a water wheel there, which was powered from the drop-off of water in the creek. They had placed rocks strategically across the creek to form a dam to help with the flow of water. The water flowed under the large wheel, forcing it to turn, and the turning of the wheel was what powered the saws to cut the boards in their mill.

Next to Henry sat William Bennett. William was only 24 years old. He had recently moved here with his young bride, Martha, and their son Thomas. A second son, Isaac, had been born after the move.

In the center of the room sat Grandpa Harris. His name was Joshua, but everyone in the community affectionately referred to him as "Grandpa". He lived up Panther Creek about a mile from the Casey's with his wife Ruth. Joshua and Ruth were both in their 70's. They were Elijah's in-laws. When Elijah and his wife came to the area, she had brought her elderly parents along, but they were independent people and chose to live separately from their daughter.

Just to the right of Grandpa Harris sat Jackson Owens. Jackson was a preacher. He and his wife were in their 50's, a generation older than the Caseys and the Inmans, who were all in their 30's. Reverend Owens and his wife had raised their children mostly back in Tennessee. When they moved to Arkansas, most of their children were already grown and married, so they only brought their youngest two with them; Abraham, who was now 18, and Lucy, who was 16. The little one-room school also served as the church on Sunday, and Reverend Owens preached to the small community. Not a soul stayed home on Sunday, unless they were sick. Religion was an important part of their lives, and Reverend Owens looked out for his flock.

The last person in the room was the only woman. Sarah Madison was a 29-year-old widow. Her husband had become sick and died after they moved here. She was left with three little girls to raise on her own. Rebecca, Rachel and Ruby were now 10, 7 and 5 years old. Sarah brought them to the little schoolhouse every morning, where she taught them their reading, writing and arithmetic, along with the other children of the community. Sarah was the teacher. Since she had no husband and was the head of her own household, and since she held an important position in the community, she was usually asked to attend the meetings along with the men.

Elijah looked out at the other five members of the group and asked for them to bow their heads first for an opening prayer. He nodded toward Rev. Owens, who closed his eyes and began...

"Dear Heavenly Father,
as we gather here today in your name
we ask your blessing upon each one
of us and our families.
Reach down and guide us
through these perilous times.
Give us wisdom and give us strength.
Bless us with understanding and humility.
Love us and protect us,
as we known you always do.
In Jesus' name, Amen."

There was a chorus of additional amens, and then Elijah cleared his throat.

"As you all know, I recently returned from a trip into Clarksville. Everyone there is full of talk of secession. When I last was there, as you remember, we had learned that seven states had seceded from the union; South Carolina, Mississippi, Florida, Alabama, Georgia, Louisiana and Texas. Well, now I've learned these seven states held a convention in Montgomery, Alabama in March, and formerly drew up a Confederate constitution and Jefferson Davis was named their interim president."

"What about Lincoln?" someone asked.

"Abraham Lincoln was inaugurated on March 4th. He reportedly was trying to hold the Union together. He said he had no plans to end slavery in the states where it already existed. But, things just kept escalating. The southern states are trying to hold onto the forts. I'm sorry to report that Fort Sumter was fired upon, and our country is now in the midst of a civil war."

The congregation sat silent for a moment or two. "War?!?"

"I'm afraid so. I heard that just a few days after the firing on Fort Sumter, Virginia also seceded. Now Richmond has been named as the Confederate capitol."

"What does this mean for us?" asked Sarah.

"I don't know," Elijah said. "Everyone down in Clarksville is talking secession. I fear our state will secede as well. I don't know what that means for Arkansas. But, I am afraid war may be coming for all of us. I don't know if it will affect us here too much. We don't live in the populated cities. Hopefully we will be safe from any skirmishes here. But, will our sons choose to sign up and serve? That is my fear. If only we could stay out of it all. There are no slaves here in our community. We choose to live our lives the way we live them, and let others live their lives accordingly. I pray to God that the struggles of people in other parts of the country don't cause harm upon those of us here. I don't know the political thoughts of everyone here. I don't know which side some of you might choose to side with in a war such as this. Maybe I don't want to know. Wars can make enemies of the best of friends. But, gentleman, if Arkansas secedes from the Union, I fear war will eventually touch us all."

"What should we do, to prepare for this?" asked William.

"I think for now we just continue on as if all is well. Tend to your crops, care for your children. No need to live in fear. When I go back to Clarksville later in the summer, I will be able to find out more. There's not much we can do until then."

Outside the window of the school, crouched down in the

dirt, sat 16 year old Hannah Casey, Elijah's oldest daughter. She couldn't stand not knowing what this meeting was all about, and didn't trust that her father would tell her everything. So, she sat under the window, listening to the words as they wafted in the breeze through the blowing window curtains. The things she was hearing were disturbing to her. She had never seen war, only read about it in school. She had a hard time believing that anything like what she'd read could possibly happen here. But, as she sat there she became more and more uneasy.

It didn't help that she was looking out toward the little cemetery that had been started when her younger sister had died at birth. Hannah was 10 years old when her mother's 7th child had been born dead. A grave had been dug behind the building that served as both school and church, and a rectangular rock had been buried standing up at the head of the little baby's grave. A few years later, when Sarah's husband had died, he was buried next to the little Casey baby, and another rectangular stone was erected. Just two lonely stones, with no markings, no fence around them. Just two stones out in the grass behind the church. Hannah began to feel sad looking at them. She started to imagine more stones, from people dying in a war, and it upset her too much. Her thoughts went to her 18 year old brother Daniel. What if he became a soldier? What if he got killed? What if he were buried in that cemetery, or worse yet, on some battlefield somewhere, alone and forgotten. She couldn't look at that cemetery any more, so she crawled out from under the window and then stood up and took off running toward the creek.

Hannah had a special place that she liked to go to down by the creek. There was a large buckeye tree on the bank that had been washed out underneath from times when the water was high. This caused some of the big roots to be exposed, and Hannah liked to sit on one of the roots, leaning back against the tree, with her bare feet hanging down in the cool water below. She ran to her special place and sat there trying to calm her fears.

"Everything will be okay. Nothing will happen here. We are so far away from the rest of the world. They don't even know we exist up here in these mountains. Everything will be okay."

She was about to doze off in the warm spring sunshine, when she heard a noise off to her right. She turned, thinking it might be a squirrel or a rabbit, but it was just Joe. She sighed to herself. She was really enjoying being alone, and wasn't really up to a visit from Joe right now. Joseph Inman was the oldest child of her father's friend Henry. Because he lived right across the creek, and because he was 16 years old, like Hannah, the two seemed to always be thrown together. She liked Joe, but sometimes he seemed a bit childish to her. Not like Abe, the 18 year old son of Rev. Owens. Oh, she dreamed of Abe! He was mature, and handsome. But, it seemed as if she didn't exist in Abe's eyes. If Abraham Owens were the one walking toward her right now on this creek bank, she would be in Heaven! But, alas, it was only Joe.

"Hey, whatcha doin'?" Joe asked as he climbed over onto the other side of Hannah's favorite root.

"Nothin'. Just sittin' here in the sun."

"I saw you listenin' in over at the meetin'. What did they say?"

Hannah told Joseph what she'd heard, and even though he got on her nerves at times, she suddenly got a jolt of fear. "You wouldn't join would you?"

"Wha'da'ya mean?" he said. "You mean join up to fight in a war? I don't know. I guess it would be exciting! I'm sure all the girls would think I was brave." He puffed out his chest and pretended to have a musket in his hand.

Hannah laughed. "Joseph Inman! No girl is going to think you are brave!" She pushed against his shoulder and he almost lost his balance and fell off the tree root.

"Hey! I bet they would," he said. "I bet even *you* would want to marry me if I showed up in a soldier's uniform."

Hannah laughed again. "I will *never* marry you, Joseph Inman. Oh my goodness! What are you thinking? You're like a brother to me."

Joe looked away because he didn't want her to see the hurt she had caused with that comment. He was very fond of Hannah Casey, and wished she could only return the feelings. But, he feared she would always see him as the little boy that she used to play tag with. If only he would fill out more and begin to look more manly. He was stick thin and had no muscles, despite the fact that he worked hard on his family's farm. He wanted to be bigger, like his pa. His mother told him that he would get there, just be patient. But, patience was a hard thing to have when you already loved a girl who wouldn't even give you the time of day.

"Look at that fish!" Joe said. He was trying to change the subject. He laid across the root on his stomach and reached down to try and catch the fish, but it got away. He stretched out across the big root and rolled over and looked up toward the sky. He squinted against the sun, then noticed the pretty red blooms above him on the buckeye tree. "This is my favorite time of year," he said. "I like when the trees have flowers."

Hannah looked up and said "They *are* pretty. But, I like the autumn time better. You know, when the buckeyes fall from the tree. I just like the feeling in the air in the fall. But, spring is okay, too, I guess."

"Girls are supposed to like flowers!" Joe teased.

"I *do* like flowers!" she said. "But, the autumn is just so wonderful.

Later that evening Hannah was in the kitchen helping her mother prepare supper. As the oldest daughter in a large family, it was just understood that she was to help her mother with everything, just as her older brother Daniel was always having to help their father. There were times when she resented it, but for the most part she wanted to be a good daughter and she liked the feeling of being needed, and looked up to by the little ones. Best of all, she liked to see the look of pride in her father's eyes when he told her what a help she was, and her mother *was* tired a lot these days. After all, she was pregnant with her *eleventh* child! She was 36 years old, but looked 50 to Hannah. She just had such a hard life. Years of working out in the sun had weathered her face. And years of giving birth and nursing had taken its toll on her body. Her name was Emeline, but most folks just called her "Emma". Hannah liked the way her father endearingly called her "My Emmy".

Elijah Casey and Emeline Harris had met in Tennessee. They had married when she was 17 and he was 19. Their first four children were born in Tennessee. First came Daniel in 1843, followed by Hannah in 1845, then two more boys; Jesse in 1847 and Albert in 1849. During this time Elijah had served his country in the Mexican War. After it was over, he received a land grant in Arkansas as part of his payment for services. Arkansas had been declared a state in 1836, but it was still mostly unsettled. The government saw these land grants to soldiers as a way to get the area settled and get people moving westward.

In 1851, the Casey family migrated to Arkansas by covered wagon, along with Emma's parents (the elder Harris couple). It was difficult to leave the only home they'd ever known, but Arkansas held promise of a prosperous future for them, and a new and better life. They were the first to settle along the banks of Mulberry Creek, and the other four families arrived in intervals after that. Hannah had been a child of 6 years old when they made the long and arduous journey. She barely remembered her home in Tennessee, or the aunts, uncles and cousins that remained back there, and only had sporadic memories of the journey itself. To her, this place was home, and this was her life. These people were her family.

Emeline Casey had been pregnant with child number five when they made the trip. After they had been settled in a few months, and were living in a small, hastily built cabin, she gave birth to Isabelle late in 1851, followed by Charlotte in 1853. Her 7th baby was due in 1855. This was the little girl who was born dead. Hannah had never heard them refer to the baby by a name. In those days babies were generally not named until days, weeks or even months after their birth. Because so many babies died, it was best not to get too attached until it was certain the baby would live, and stillborn babies were not named at all.

After this loss, Elijah decided it was time for a change, so he tore down the old cabin and built the larger, two-story house in 1856, to hold their growing brood of children. Then, Emma had two more pregnancies. In 1857 she had a son named Michael and then in 1859 she had given birth to twin boys, which she named

Jacob and Jonah, and now here she was pregnant again. Every two years she gave birth, and she had been doing it for 18 years!

When Hannah thought about a future like that for herself, she got a little frightened. She saw the pain her mother went through each time, and she saw the grief that was caused by the loss of one of the babies. She wasn't sure if this was a life she should look forward to or not. As a woman, was she just resigned to slaving away in a kitchen, sewing, and having babies? There had to be more than that! Could she be happy with just that? She wasn't sure. Ms. Sarah had told the children at school how, where she came from, women did a lot of things, including teaching, which was what she had done, and still did. So, Hannah had hope that maybe, just maybe, she could find a path for herself that was a little different from her mother's.

As she was lost in her thoughts, she heard her mother ring the supper bell. The men and boys came in from working out in the barn, and the girls helped gather up the little children. At the short ends of the table sat Pa and Ma, and sitting up and down each long side were the three girls (Hannah-16, Isabelle-10 and Charlotte-8) and the six boys (Daniel-18, Jesse-14, Albert-12, Michael-4, and the 2 year old twins, Jacob & Jonah). It was quite a family! Pa had made a very long table to accommodate them all.

Hannah loved every one of her family members, but she never seemed to have any privacy in her own home, and sharing a bed with Izzy and Lottie (her nicknames for Isabelle and Charlotte) was not always tolerable. One day she dreamed of a bed all to herself!

The Casey home had five bedrooms. The house was two stories high and shaped like an "L". There was a raised porch across the front, and directly above that porch was another porch on the 2nd floor, which formed a balcony with railings around it.

When you first walked through the front door of the home, you were in a large entry hall with a winding staircase leading up to the second floor. There was no ceiling in the hall for the first floor, so when you looked up, you could see all the way to the top of the second story, and your eyes followed the entirety of the staircase as it made it's way to the top. On the left side of the hall, downstairs, was Ma and Pa's bedroom in the front of the house, and a large walk-in pantry and storage room in the back. On the right side of the hall was the sitting parlor and beyond that was the kitchen and dining area with just enough space for the large rectangular table that sat up to 12 people. All of the ceilings were 12 feet high, giving a feeling of grandeur to the rooms.

There was no bathroom in the house. The family used an outhouse, which was a few yards from the home. They called it a "privy". It was simply a small building with a wooden seat inside, built over a hole in the ground. When that hole began to fill up, or became too putrid to stand, they would simply dig a new hole and move the little building over to it, then fill the old hole over with dirt. Sometimes Ma would plant a bush or tree in the old spot, because she said there was built-in fertilizer there, and it was true that whatever she planted always grew well and thrived.

Since there was no running water, all water was taken from the creek, and carried into the house with buckets. The kitchen had no modern sink, refrigerator or stove. It was simply a rustic wooden counter built against one wall, with a few open shelves built above it. When water was needed, a bucket or tub of water was simply placed on top of the countertop, and removed and dumped afterward.

There were six fireplaces in the home, but only two chimneys. The upstairs and downstairs fireplaces were situated in line with each other so that one chimney would serve all the fireplaces in the left wing, and another would serve all the fireplaces in the right wing. Each of the five bedrooms had its own small fireplace, and the right wing downstairs had one larger fireplace. This was because the sitting parlor and the kitchen/dining area were not separated by a wall, it was simply one large open area that served both purposes, so one large fireplace was in the center to serve both areas. The fireplace needed to be larger in this part of the house, partly because it was heating the largest area and was the main fireplace, but also because all the cooking was done in this one, and there needed to be plenty of room to put grates and several large pots and pans in it. There was even room to suspend a pot higher above the fire, if needed, by hanging it from a hook. This fireplace was so large, a small child could walk right inside it and look up the chimney, without even having to duck, as long as there was no fire burning in it, of course.

Upstairs, since each wing had two bedrooms, there were four total bedrooms in all. The two bedrooms in each wing were mirror images of each other, with their fireplaces sharing the common wall. The three girls shared one room in the wing on the right. Daniel had been given his own room in that wing, also, because he was the oldest and he was 18 now. Pa said a man needed his own room, and he had told Hannah that when Daniel left home, she would get the room to herself. Such was the reward of being the oldest child. But, Hannah knew full well that it was likely she wouldn't get much time with her own room, if any, as girls tended to marry and leave home earlier than boys. But, she held out hope.

There was a door leading out onto the upstairs balcony on the side where Hannah's room was. Sometimes she would sneak out there in the middle of the night and just gaze at the stars while the rest of the family were sleeping. The older children were always kept in the right wing, since it had access to the balcony. It was best to keep the younger ones in the left wing where they could not easily sneak out and fall to their deaths. Pa had placed hand-carved balusters all the way around the upstairs porch, to help keep people from accidentally falling, but this didn't keep little ones from trying to climb, if the idea came to them.

The middle boys, 14 year old Jesse and 12 year old Albert, were currently sharing a room in the left wing, and the other room on that side was the nursery. At the moment Ma had 4 year old Michael and the 2 year old twins in that room, but she had warned Jesse and Albert that once the new baby was born, Michael would be moving in with them.

After dinner Pa went to sit on the front porch. Ma and Hannah finished cleaning up the supper dishes, then went out to sit with Pa. He was smoking his pipe. Hannah liked the smell of the smoke as it drifted across the porch and dissipated into the night air. Soon, the other children all came outside as well. The little ones played in the yard while the oldest four sat on the porch. The sun was beginning to set, and a breeze was picking up.

Pa began telling Ma about what was discussed at the meeting earlier that day. Hannah tried to pretend she hadn't already heard all of it. She knew Pa wouldn't like it if he knew she'd been spying. After everything had been told, Ma seemed to have gone quiet.

"What is it Emmy?" Pa asked.

"Eli, what does it mean that there's a war? I don't understand. We are just fighting each other??? We all live in this country together. Why would we fight each other in such a barbaric way?"

"It's the way of man, I suppose. Men let things eat away at them, until they feel it is noble to fight it out. They think too much, and at the same time, they think too little. Each side feels strongly that they are right. Each side feels strongly that if the other side wins, life will be hell. When men unite, no one can destroy them, but when they divide, they destroy themselves from the inside out."

"If women ran the world, there would be no wars!" Emeline proclaimed.

Pa chuckled. "Well, now I don't know about that. At least men fight it out, then go home to supper. Women hold a grudge for life!"

"War is not women's history, Elijah. War is the history of men. Women are the true victims of war. Women lose their husbands, they lose their sons, they lose their homes. They lose their spirit. They become hard, because nobody asks them what they think, or how they would handle things. It's always men. Men, men, men!"

"Don't anger yourself darling. This war won't last long. It will be over in the blink of an eye and you won't have seen a bit of it. It will all take place far away."

Emeline looked at 18 year old Daniel. She knew very well what war could do to a mother, and she prayed her husband was right.

"I would join with the south!" Daniel suddenly announced.

"You will do no such thing!" Emeline cried out.

"But, Ma, I was talking to Abe and he and I both agreed that if we had to choose a side, we'd sign up on the side of the south."

Hannah's heart quickened at the image of Abe Owens in a soldier's uniform. She might have told Joe she wouldn't want to marry him if she saw him in a uniform, but she felt Abe would look so dashing, she'd want to marry him in a heartbeat. She didn't really want to think about how she'd feel seeing her brother Daniel in a uniform, though.

Pa butted in. "Now, son, there is no side to sign up with. You are putting the cart before the horse, and you are scaring your mother. The south really has no leg to stand on, anyway. Slavery is wrong, even though it has been an accepted way of life for some time in this country. Deep in your heart you know it's wrong. You cannot want to fight for the side that wants to keep slavery."

"It's not just that Pa. It's fighting for the south, the way of the south, its customs, its traditions. They would change us, and they want to change us. We are perfectly happy just the way we are. I live in the south, and I would fight for the south. And, I hope Arkansas *does* secede!"

At that Daniel stomped back into the house and slammed the door. Elijah got an ominous feeling. He had not expected that his son might feel differently about this war than he did. A new thought was coming to his mind, and he didn't like the thought at all. This war had the potential to divide families, not just people, but family units! Oh, Lord save us all.

Emeline looked emploringly at Elijah. "Eli?"

He got up from his chair and said "Let it go Emmy. It won't come to this. Just let it go." But, he wasn't sure he believed it himself.

Things had gotten a little too heated, so Hannah and her sisters decided it was time to just go on up to bed. It was warm out, so they left the bedroom window open. They could hear the sounds of the night bugs chirping, and the tree frogs croaking.

Every minute or two she heard the soothing sound of the whippoorwill's song as it echoed through the trees. Hannah had missed falling asleep to those soothing sounds. It was nice that warmer weather was here.

Hannah could hear her mother trying to get the babies settled down the hall. Jacob and Jonah were both crying. Hannah laid down in the big feather bed. She always slept on the side by the door, while Izzy slept against the wall, and Lottie, being the youngest, had to take the middle. The girls usually chatted for a bit before falling asleep. On this night their thoughts were on the possibility of war.

Izzy asked Hannah "Do you think Daniel will go to war?"

"No, the war will not last long enough for us to get involved." At least she hoped so.

"What about the other boys? Like Abe Owens? And Joseph Inman? Will they have to go?"

"Joseph is only 16, Izzy. He's too young. Abe is old enough, but like I said, that's not going to happen."

"What about William Bennett, though? He's married, but he's very young."

Hannah hadn't thought about William. She supposed all the married men in their little mountain town wouldn't have to fight in a war, but William was only 24. Would he leave his wife and two little boys and go off to war? It was just too much to think about.

"Go to sleep Izzy!"

There was a long pause, then Lottie quietly said "Hannah, do girls have to go to war?"

"Oh, sweetie! Come here," Hannah said as she put her arms around her youngest sister. "No, girls don't have to go to war. Girls just have to watch while the boys they love go off to war. But, don't worry. It's not going to come to that, okay?"

"Okay."

Hannah then quietly sang her sisters to sleep.....

"When the corn is waving Annie dear,
Oh meet me by the stile,

To hear thy gentle voice again,
And greet thy winning smile.
The moon will be at full, love,
The stars will brightly gleem,
Oh come, my queen of night, love,
And grace the beauteous scene.
When the corn is waiving, Annie dear,
Oh meet me by the stile,
To hear thy gentle voice again,
And greet thy winning smile."

The next morning the family seemed to be in a much lighter mood. Hannah rushed through her morning chores, then asked her mother if she could walk down to Rev. Owen's home. The reverend's daughter, Lucy, was 16 years old, like Hannah, and the two were fast friends. They really had no choice but to be friends, as there were no other young girls of their age living in the area. All the other girls in the community were 10 years old and younger. And, the fact that Lucy's older brother was Abe, well that just gave Hannah even more incentive to go there. As she was walking out the door, though, Daniel said "I'm going with you." Since he and Abe were best friends, it only made sense that they go together, as they often did.

As Hannah and Daniel walked the half mile down the dirt road to the Owens home, they talked on and off about various things, but avoided the thing that was most prominent in their thoughts. Hannah knew that her brother was sweet on Lucy Owens. Daniel knew that his sister was sweet on Abraham Owens. But, each went along with the charade that they were just going to visit their friends, nothing more.

The Owens home was on the opposite side of the creek, but the family had laid some large stepping stones in various spots in a low area of the creek, so that people could walk across without getting too wet. As Hannah and Daniel were crossing, they saw Lucy come running out to meet them. "Lets go riding down to the swimming hole!" She led them to the barn where they kept Biscuit and Gravy, the family's two horses. Gravy was a solid brown horse and Biscuit was brown with white splotches here and there. There were only two horses, but Lucy didn't mind, because this meant she might be able to ride double with Daniel. But, not wanting Hannah to be left out, she decided to go inside and beg her brother, Abe, to come out and go riding with them. It took some persuading, but he finally agreed to go.

Daniel and Lucy rode Gravy, while Abe and Hannah rode Biscuit. Both couples were riding bareback. The horses had traveled this path so many times, they really didn't need any instruction. They knew where to go. The pair rode east, following the creek, about a quarter of a mile, until they came to a clearing next to a spot in the creek that made a perfect swimming hole. Many times the members of the community had come here for picnics and parties, or just to swim after a hot day working in the fields.

After they reached their destination, everyone climbed down and went over to sit by the water. It was still too cool to swim, but it was nice to be away from the adults. Hannah was feeling a bit strange, because Abe had sat rather rigid on the horse with her. While she noticed Daniel putting his arms around Lucy as they rode, Abe didn't do the same with her. He kept his hands down to his sides, or behind him. He acted as if she were glass, and she might break if he touched her. "Either that, or he finds me disgusting," Hannah thought. No matter how she tried to get his attention, he always seemed to be off dreaming in another world. She tried to engage him in conversation, but he answered with quick yesses and nos, and seemed to not really want to be there with her. At one point she walked down the creek bank a bit, hoping he would follow, but he just kept sitting there, not even looking in her direction. She may as well have been invisible.

She was envious when she saw Daniel and Lucy sneak away behind a tree. She knew that Daniel was stealing a kiss, maybe. Why didn't Abe want to do the same with her? She longed for a kiss from him. She longed to finally experience her very first kiss with a boy. But, it was not meant to be on this day. Abraham was cordial, but not loving, as Daniel was to Lucy. Hannah felt like crying. Maybe she just wasn't pretty enough.

After about an hour, they mounted back up and rode home. The Owens children agreed to go on past their house and take Daniel and Hannah home on the horses, so they could get home quicker, then they would double back to their own house again. As they galloped through past the school, Hannah saw Joseph looking across the creek from his house. Then he turned and went back inside rather abruptly. She knew he probably wasn't going to like seeing her riding on the horse with Abe, but she was too focused on the fact that her time with Abe was almost over, to care what Joe was thinking right now. She was not in love with Joe, she was in love with Abe, or at least she thought she was. When she felt Abraham's body brush up against her back as they rode, she felt little shocks go through her. But, she was sure Abe did not feel the same from her touch.

At the Casey home, Daniel discreetly kissed Lucy on the cheek as they parted ways, but Abe simply said "Bye, see you at church tomorrow." Hannah ran in the house and up to her room, where she flopped down on the bed and allowed herself a short cry. Then she shook it off, and gathered herself and went down to help her mother with dinner. Her heart was broken, but she could not let any one else see it. She was too proud for that.

The next morning the whole town met for Sunday service at the church. On Sundays they called it "the church", while the rest of the week they called it "the school". The little building just served all kinds of functions, really. It had been built by the townspeople with lumber that Elijah and Henry had cut at their sawmill. It was situated in the curve where Panther Creek and Mulberry Creek ran together. A little arched foot bridge had been built across the smaller creek so that people could get across to the church.

Rev. Owens preached a good sermon about temptation and idolatry. He said "In 1st Corinthians verse 10, Paul warns the Corinthians about idolatry, the worship of other Gods, rather than the one true God. Now, you may think that you do not idolize any God but the one true God, but in this case the word 'God' does not only mean another divine being. If you idolize money, and your pursuit of money has become more important to you than your desire to know God, then you are committing idolatry. If you get more comfort from a bottle of whiskey than you do from a prayer, then you are committing idolatry. If you look upon the face of another, and put your desire for that person above your desire to know God, then you are committing idolatry. If you look to a leader, such as President Lincoln, and think him mightier than God, then you are committing idolatry. You must put God first in everything you do, and you will persevere. God will not place a temptation before you that is too much for you to bear. You can, and you must, fight those temptations. No temptation has overtaken you that is not common to man. God is faithful, and he will not let you be tempted beyond your ability, but with the temptation he will also provide the way of escape, that you may be able to endure it."

Hannah thought about what the reverend was saying. Her thoughts turned to her feelings for Abraham. Was she committing idolatry with Abraham? Was she putting her desire for him before her desire to know God? Maybe she was. But, how do you not feel what you feel? She thought "What could possibly be 'my escape' that God will provide for me, as the reverend said? How does one simply 'endure' a broken heart?" Aw, but she was young, and had not really known what true love was. She did not know what a real broken heart was. Time would take care of those things. She needed a bit more seasoning, a bit more maturing and growing. And in time, she would have more than her share.

After church the women set up a dinner outdoors next to the building. Generally, the largest meal of the day was at the noon hour, and they called it "dinner". The meal at the end of the day was usually smaller and referred to as "supper". Boards from the sawmill had been brought down and stored at the church to use as tables when needed. The men stood logs up on end and laid the boards across the logs to make tables. The women had prepared food that morning and brought everything along with them to church. They busily laid everything out and a satisfying dinner was eaten. Hannah filled her plate with a slice of smoked ham, cornbread, beans, potatoes, pickles and a big piece of apple pie. She sat down next to Joseph and Lucy underneath a tree.

"Your mom's pickles are the best, Joseph," Hannah said as they were filling their stomachs. She liked Mrs. Inman's pickles better than the other women's, because she made them sour instead of sweet. She'd never been a fan of the bread and butter type of pickles that her mom made. Mrs. Inman made what she called "dill" pickles. They made your mouth pucker, but were so delicious.

Soon the men were gathered in the shade of the church building, chewing their tobacco or smoking their pipes, and talking of politics and war, while the women sat in a circle nearby, working on a quilt together. Oftentimes, the women all worked together on a quilt. Once the original owner had pieced the quilt together, the others would gather around to help them "quilt" it, which meant attaching the backing and sewing the pieces together in a pretty pattern.

The children were playing games and running around laughing. Hannah's sisters, Izzy and Lottie, were playing "graces" with the other girls their age. In this game, each girl held a long wooden stick in each hand, and a wooden ring was placed over them. She would then toss the ring to the other girl and she would try to catch it with her sticks. Whoever caught the most rings in a set period of time was declared the winner. Hannah's sisters, Izzy and Lottie, were on one team, while the teacher's oldest daughters, Rebecca and Rachel Madison, were a 2nd team and Joseph's little sisters, Nancy and Elizabeth Inman, made a 3rd team. Some of the younger girls were playing hopscotch in the dirt by the front door.

The boys didn't care to play graces or hopscotch, so they were gathered in another section of the churchyard playing marbles. Two of the youngest boys had a wooden top that they were spinning to see who could spin it the longest.

Sundays after church were always the best times of the week. No one was expected to work hard on Sunday. It was the Lord's day. Hannah and her friends sat talking, and just watching the activities. Daniel soon came over and sat by Lucy. They became absorbed in each other, leaving Hannah and Joseph to sit and talk alone.

"Remember when my family first moved here?" Joseph asked.

"Of course! I think we were both 8 years old."

"Your family were the only ones here at the time. I remember Pa saying that he'd gotten a letter from his good friend Elijah Casey who had moved out west to Arkansas, and begged him to come join him there. Pa kept saying it was such an ordeal to pick up and move so far away, but after a few letters, your Pa had him convinced. I didn't want to leave Tennessee. I was going to school finally and had friends. I was a little sad when we started out, but after a bit it became exciting, wondering what we would find when we got here. I was 8, Harding was 6, Nancy was 2 and Elizabeth was a baby. Virginia and James weren't even born yet. Ma had lost a baby between Harding and Nancy. It was a little girl they had named Irene after Ma. She was very small and sickly from the start. I can remember holding her. She seemed so fragile. Ma was very protective of her because she was so sickly. One morning when she was about a month old, Ma went to pick her up from her crib and she screamed and fell to the floor crying. I was only 4, but I can remember that scream. They told me she had only lived a month and they buried her on a hill behind the barn. Ma was sad the day we packed up to come here, because she knew she would probably never get to visit little Irene's grave again. I can remember seeing her standing over the grave crying. Pa went to her and held her and the two just stood there. Then they came to the wagon and we all loaded up and started our journey here."

Hannah squeezed Joe's hand and said "I remember when Ma lost her baby. It was really sad. I don't know how mothers do it."

Joe said "Well, I think Ma has adjusted well here." Then he said "I have a secret that I haven't told you."

"What?! Tell me Joseph, what is it!"

"Ma is with child again. She told us a few weeks ago, but said not to tell until she was sure everything was going well. This will be her 8th pregnancy. She worries that as she gets older, the likelihood of the pregnancy taking gets less and less. So, she didn't want to get her hopes up too much."

"Oh, Joseph! How exciting! Do you hope it's a boy or a girl?"

"I don't really care. Right now there are 3 boys and 3 girls in my family. It seems pretty even."

"My Ma is about 6 months along now, she thinks. She believes the baby will be here around August," Hannah said.

"My Ma says hers will be probably around November," replied Joseph.

"Joe, when you first came here I remember thinking you were such a little bratty boy." Hannah smiled at him. "But, you really became my best friend. You were always the one I played with and told all my secrets to."

Joe shyly looked away and said "Yes, you have been that for me, too, Hannah. I used to be sad that we left Tennessee, but not any more. This is where I belong now, here with you, and my family, and all our friends. I remember at first, we arrived and there was nothing here. Even the schoolhouse hadn't been built. I thought my father had taken me to the ends of the Earth. There were no stores, no blacksmith shop, no saloon, even. Not like back in Tennessee. But, I now see that happiness doesn't come from those things. Happiness comes from the people you are with, and the feelings you have with those people. I think if I'd stayed back there, I might have gotten into trouble by now. Here, though, I work hard and I stay on the right path. I see what my Pa means when he says hard work builds character, and the results of that work bring pride."

Hannah said "I remember Father and Mother helping your Pa and Ma build their house across the creek. Back then we lived in the smaller house. It wasn't until Rev. Owens and the Madisons came here that everyone got together and helped us tear down the old house and build our bigger home that we have now." She got pensive for a moment. "It was sad when Mr. Madison died."

Joe said "Yes, I remember he was sick for a long time. He was coughing a lot and he couldn't work. He would sit on the porch in the rocker, and I would hear him coughing all the way at my house. Ma was always sending me over with food and things to help out. She would ask me to do farm chores for Mr. Madison, but she would tell me to keep my distance, because she didn't want me bringing the sickness home to our family. She told me to stand at least 10 feet from Mr. Madison when talking with him. She said to stay outside and not go up on the porch, and just talk to him from the yard. I was about 12 then. But, I did a lot of work for him. We all thought he would get better with time, but I'll never forget the day Mrs. Madison came running to our house screaming that her husband was dead. She had her three little girls with her, and they were all crying. Rebecca was about 6. She probably remembers. But, Rachel and Ruby were too little. I doubt they even remember their father. That's sad, isn't it?"

"Yes, it is," said Hannah. "But, we all adopted the Madisons, and we convinced Sarah to stay here and continue to be our teacher. I think we all started calling her 'Ms. Sarah' after that, instead of 'Mrs. Madison'. She just didn't seem like a 'Mrs.' anymore. She said she'd rather us children call her Sarah anyway."

About that time Sarah walked past and smiled and said "Hi, children!" They smiled back at her. All the children loved their teacher. She was kind and caring and made learning fun for them.

Joseph said "I have another secret I haven't told you..."

"Well, Joseph Inman, you have sure been keeping everything bottled up. Come out with it now!"

"Father is giving me some of his land. He says I am turning 17 later this year, and almost a man now. He took me to the southeast corner of our land and showed me a spot that would be perfect for putting a house. He said some day soon I might be wanting to take a bride, and I would need a place to bring her. He said I could share the barn for now, and he would start me out with a cow and a horse of my own."

"But, who does he think you would marry? Will you have to go down to Clarksville to try and find a wife?"

Joseph cringed. In all his thoughts and dreams, the only wife he saw for himself was Hannah Casey. She would be Hannah Inman. They would have children and be life partners until they were old and sitting on rockers together on the front porch, watching their many grandchildren play. Why couldn't she see that? Why was it not as obvious to her that they were perfect together? Why did she not even consider in her mind that she might be the one for him? He had seen her riding with Abraham the day before. It tore at everything inside him. He felt so much jealousy! What did she see in Abraham Owens?! He was brash, rude, thought only of himself. He obviously didn't love Hannah. He wasn't good for her at all. It was all he could do to hold that jealousy in and not lash out at her. But, he was smart enough to know that he couldn't force her to love him. It had to come from within her. But, what if it never did? What he knew was, he had no desire to go to Clarksville and find a wife. Hannah was to be his wife. If she chose not to, then there would be no other for him. God made Hannah for him, and he would wait until the ends of time to have her if that's what it took.

The next day was Monday, so Hannah and her siblings quickly did their morning chores, ate breakfast, and walked over to the school. Ms. Sarah had divided her classroom into four rows of benches. Each bench had three students. The front row closest to her was for the youngest children. In this row she sat her own daughter Rachel (7), and also Charlotte Casey and Elizabeth Inman, who were both 8. On the 2nd row back she sat Isabelle Casey, Nancy Inman, and her own daughter Rebecca. All three of these girls were 10 years old. On the 3rd row back were the younger teens, two of the Casey boys, Jesse (14) and Albert (12), and also 14 year old Harding Inman. It was interesting that the first two rows were all girls, and the 3rd row was all boys, but it just worked out that way by age. Finally, the last row was for the older teens, which consisted of Hannah Casey, Joseph Inman and Lucy Owens, who were all 16 years old. Previously she had taught two others in this group, Daniel Casey and Abraham Owens, but they were both 18 now and had left school. Daniel had completed all the courses and graduated, but Abraham simply stopped going about the time he turned 15.

Sarah normally didn't like to start students in her school until they were 6 years old, but since her own youngest daughter, Ruby, was only 5, and she needed to be able to keep an eye on her, she brought her to class with her. She had asked the Inmans if they would send their 5 year old daughter, Virginia, as well, so that the two girls could keep each other company all day. So, in a corner by her desk she had a little table set up for Ruby and Virginia as a sort of pre-school. So, all in all she had 14 students every day, the 12 regular students and the two little 5 year olds.

Sarah told the back two rows of children to begin reading an assignment while she got the younger ones started on writing their numbers. The morning went on as usual, with Hannah sometimes catching herself daydreaming and staring out the window. At break, they all went back to their homes to eat dinner, then came back for the afternoon session. This was the usual routine. The only exception was that Lucy Owens lived a half mile away, a bit far to be running home for dinner, so she generally just walked with Hannah to her house every day and shared dinner with her. This is part of the reason Daniel had become so attached to Lucy, because she was always at his home.

That day during the dinner break Hannah asked Lucy if she would go with her on the coming Saturday to see her grandparents. Grandpa and Grandma Harris lived a mile up Panther Creek. It was a rugged trek to get there, with not much of a path to follow. Hannah didn't like to go alone, because it was deep in the woods, and she was a little scared of seeing a bear or a panther, both of which were seen in the area quite often. Sometimes they heard panthers screaming in the distance. It sounded just like a woman screaming for help. It was very eerie. And, they had all seen bears off and on. Sometimes they came up to the chicken coop at night, trying to get the chickens.

After a long week of school, where all the children were beginning to have spring fever and wanting to play outside instead of sitting inside, Hannah woke up on Saturday morning to the sound of the rooster crowing out in the chicken coop. She enjoyed breakfast with the family, then went out to do the wash. They usually spent Saturday mornings washing the clothing for the week. Daniel, Hannah, Jesse, Albert and Isabelle were all given water pails to carry. They followed a path down to the creek and scooped up two pails of water each and carried them over to a wash tub that their mother kept under a tree by the creek. They turned the tub over and began dumping water into it. It took several trips to fill the tub all the way. Then, Elijah and Daniel would help Ma carry all the clothing down to the tub. It was easier to bring the clothing to the creek, than to drag all that water up the hill to the house. Ma used homemade lye soap to wash the clothing.

All winter long, every time the ashes were emptied from the fireplaces in the home, they were collected outside in a hopper. When the hopper was full of ashes, Ma would fill it with water, and the water would percolate through the ashes and drip from the channels at the bottom of the hopper and into a collection pail. This liquid was sodium hydroxide, or "lye". Emeline's mother had taught her that this mixture could be toxic to human skin if not right, so she needed to test it. The way to test it was to float an egg in the lye water. If the egg sank, or floated, the mixture was not correct. But, if the egg bobbed up and down near the surface, it was acceptable. If the mixture was wrong, it could be adjusted by either adding water, or allowing some of the water to evaporate. Once the mixture was just right, the lye was added to warm lard and stirred continuously for about an hour.

"Lard" was the fat of a pig that the family had raised and butchered in the fall. The fat was cut from the hog and "rendered". Ma did this by cutting the pieces of hog fat into small chunks and adding them to a large pot, then adding a bit of water. She would then boil the mixture, stirring it often and watching it closely, ladling out any chunks or bits of meat that rose to the top, so that all that was left was smooth melted liquid fat. She would then strain the liquid through a cloth into jars, and seal the jars shut until ready to use. She not only used this lard to make soap, but also as grease to cook food in, or to add to flour to make biscuits.

Once the lye and lard mixture was ready, it would be poured into molds and left to harden for about six weeks. Once hard, the soap was removed from the molds and cut into small square shapes and stored away to be used when needed. This soap was used to wash people, clothing, and anything else that needed a good scrub. Sometimes Ma had several batches of lye soap in various stages of development, going all at the same time. She had to make enough in the winter to get the family through the summer, since they didn't burn fires for warmth in the summer, therefore they didn't make as many ashes.

As Ma and the girls were scrubbing the clothing and linens in the tub with the lye soap, they waved across the creek to Mrs. Inman and her girls, who were also washing their clothes down by the creek. This was a regular Saturday morning ritual for both families. Hannah waved at Joe when she saw him carrying the water up for his mother.

Once the clothes were soaped up good, Ma got out her scrub board and laid it into the tub. She held onto the top part and scrubbed each of the clothing items up and down on the board to get out all the dirt. Then the soapy water was dumped and more clean water was brought up to rinse the clothing with. The rinse water usually had to be dumped and filled a second time in order to get all the soap out. Ma would then ring all the clothing dry and take it back to the house to hang from strings stretched between trees so they could dry in the breeze. Some of the heavier items would be hung from the rails of the porch, or draped along the top of a fence row. In winter, when it was colder, they would have to hang the clothing from pegs by the fireplace inside in order to dry them out, but in the warmer months they were hung outside in the sun.

Once they were through with the washing, Ma gave Hannah the okay to go with Lucy to see Grandma and Grandpa. Lucy had walked up from her house and was waiting just as the last of the clothing was hung to dry.

Hannah got a basket and went with Lucy to the strawberry patch where strawberries were ripe and red. She picked a basketful to take to her grandparents, and she and Lucy ate their fill as well. Then, they started off up the path, following the creek up to the Harris's house. It was always a scenic walk. There were so many beautiful wildflowers beginning to bloom, and the trees were all greened up now, making a lovely shaded canopy above them as they walked. They passed a waterfall that flowed down from the top of the cliff on the opposite side of the creek. It was flowing very heavy this time of year. Hannah was always impressed with the massiveness of the cliffs, and the soothing sound of the waterfall.

Grandpa Harris was outside working on something when the girls came around the bend. He was pleasantly surprised. There was no way to inform them that they were coming, so a visit was always a surprise. He called for Grandma and she came out of the house onto the porch and hugs were given all around. Lucy had been to see the Harris's with Hannah many times over the years, so they knew her well and were always happy to see her, too, and to ask about her family. Joshua and Ruth sat down in their wooden rockers on the porch, while the girls sat at the top of the steps. Hannah gave her grandma the basket of strawberries and she oohed and aahed at them. Grandpa reached in and stole a few and got his hand slapped, which made the girls giggle. Grandma then took the berries inside and came back out with a jar of homemade cookies.

After a bit, when the conversation seemed to have slowed down, and the cookies were all gone, Hannah asked her grandma a question. "Grandma, how did you and Grandpa meet?"

"Well, land sakes! Why d'ya wanna hear that 'ol story?"

"I just do Grandma. I want to know everything about it."

"Well, my, my. That was a long time ago. Ya know, yer grandpa and I are so very old. We was borned in another century even! Yer grandpa was borned in 1789 and I's borned in 1791. Oh, that was such a long, long time ago. It was a diff'rent time, truly a diff'rent time."

"You were born in the 1700's!" Lucy exclaimed. "I can't believe it!"

"Yes, ma'am. I certainly was. Well, I guess ya want me to go all the way back. When I met m'first husband...."

"Wait! What? Grandma, you were married before Grandpa?!?"

"Yes, honey. Ya didn't know that? I would'a figgered yer Ma had told that story a'fore."

"No! I don't remember *ever* hearing that story."

"Well, yer Grandpa was married a'fore, too!"

"How am I just hearing this? I'm so surprised! You must go back all the way to the beginning! I *have* to know."

Lucy sat stunned as well. She couldn't wait to hear this bit of juicy gossip. Both girls were at the age where they were beginning to think about boys, and possible marriage, so they were always up for a good love story.

Grandma rocked for a minute and then said "Well, it all started back in North Caroliny. That's where I's borned, ya know. Yer grandpa was borned in South Caroliny. I didn't know him as a child growin' up. My Pa was John and my Ma was Magdalene. They had 7 children. My oldest brother was Jeremiah. I was the 2nd child. Then after me there was Elizabeth, Cynthia, Aaron, John Jr. and Temperance."

"Temperance? What a unique name!" Lucy said.

"Yes, well, my ma thought it was *very* unique. We all just called'er 'Tempy' fer short, though. Aaron is gone now, but the others are still livin' so fer as I know. They're all still back in Wilson County, Tennessee. I don't hear from them much these days. I always figger my next news from any of'em will be that they've passed on. It's sad that I don't see'em any more, and most likely will never see'em a'gin. All of us but Tempy was borned in North Caroliny, but Father moved us to Tennessee in about 1806. Tempy was borned after we moved."

"What about Grandpa's family?"

"Well, I reckon I oughtta let him tell that part...."

Grandpa thought for a bit, took a drag from his pipe and blew a smoke ring in the air. Then he said "Well.... let's see. As your grandma mentioned, I was born in South Carolina. My Pa's name was Hugh, and my Ma was Sarah. There was five of us youngins. We was all born in Abbeville. I was the 2nd born, just like Grandma was. My older sister was Elizabeth, then came me, then the last three was Esther, Susanna and Robert. Elizabeth died at just one year old, though, so I grew up as the oldest child, really. I had no memory of dear Elizabeth, other than bits and pieces my mother told me about her. My next sister, Esther, also died young. She was 2 years old when she died. I was 6 at the time, so I *do* remember Esther a bit, and I remember her death and burial. So, really after their deaths, that just left me, Susanna and Robert growin' up. Ma was devastated at the loss of her babies, and I think she never really recovered."

"How did your sisters die?" Hannah asked.

"I don't rightly know how Elizabeth died. I don't remember hearin'. I think it was some kind of sickness, maybe. But, little Esther drowned. She drowned in the creek by our home. Ma was carryin' water up to the house, thinkin' Esther was followin' behind. When she got t'the door and turned 'round, she saw Esther floatin' in the water. She ran back but it was too late. She'd swallowed too much water."

"Oh, how awful! That's so tragic! I don't know how she ever forgave herself," Hannah said.

"Well, I don't believe she ever did, even though the Lord knows it was not her fault. These things happen. But, anyway, I grew up with my younger sister and brother, and just as we was reaching adulthood our parents both died, in the same year. We was orphaned early on. Not long after, my sister got married off, so me and my little brother Robert decided to go to Tennessee, to Wilson County, the same place where yer grandma's family had gone. But, I didn't meet yer grandma right away. Instead, I met a gal named Susannah. We married and had three children; Sally, Thomas and Abigail. My wife died in childbirth with Abigail. I was devastated and had no way to care for these three little children, so my wife's sister took them in temporarily, then I joined up to fight in the War of 1812, when I was just 23 years old. I served for the entirety of the War, until 1815."

Grandma piped in "My first husband was servin' in that war, too. I had met Arthur at 17, which was about two years after we'd moved to Tennessee, and we married right away. We had three boys in quick succession; Jeremiah, David and William. Then, Arthur left to go fight in that awful war. I went back to stay with Mother and Father while he was away. It was a dreadful, lonely time."

Grandpa took over again. "I was a sergeant in the War of 1812, in Captain Black's company. We left Nashville in November of 1814, bound fer New Orleans. We arrived there just a'fore

Christmas and made an encampment above the town. I had met Arthur Middleton (your grandma's first husband) after enlisting, and we'd been inseparable for the two years we'd been serving together. He'd told me all about his wife and boys and I'd told him of how I'd lost my wife and had three little children back in Tennessee, too. We was together all the time, me an' Arthur, the best of friends. I'm not sure I could've got through that war without'im by my side."

"We was camped together above New Orleans until January 8th of 1815, when finally we was to participate in a battle, which is now known as 'The Battle of New Orleans'. I'm sure when we marched into town we was a sight to see. A very ragged bunch we was, no matchin' uniforms, just a bunch'a rags thrown on skinny, tired soldiers. Some of us had hats made of raccoon or fox hides. In our belts we had tomahawks, knives, swords, an' all manner'a mismatched weapons. Our hair was unkempt, our beards grown out an' scraggly, we was dirty t'the core. We had rifles, or muskets, an' powder horns an' pockets full'a bullets. We didn't look like much, but we'd been trained t'pick our man, draw a bead, and bring'im down'!"

"We marched into battle thinkin' it would be quick, but it dragged on fer days and days, throughout most'a January. We was cold, hungry, weary an' lonely. We fought hard, but I watched my comrades falling day after day, until the dreaded day came when my friend Arthur was hit by a minie ball. This was the type of bullet that was used back then. It had a soft lead that would just flatten out when it hit the human body, shatterin' bones and destroyin' tissue. Many men who'd been hit had to have limbs amputated because'a the extensive damage. When Arthur was hit I ran to him. I was devastated. I helped the medical team get him out of harms way, and I went with him. I felt he could not survive, and so I wanted to be with him until the end, but t'my surprise he seemed to rally. I went back to fightin' durin' the day, but I would always have my mind on Arthur, and would go to his bedside when able. He lived fer about two weeks, seemin' to improve at first, but the wound began to get infected. One day Arthur called t'me very weakly and said 'I'm gonna die Joshua. I'm gonna die.' I pleaded with him to hang on, but I could see he was fadin'. His last words to me was that he had left the finest woman back home and the finest three boys. He asked me, as his friend, if I survived the war, could I please go back to Wilson County, Tennessee and find them and tell them of his fate, and tell'em of his love for'em. I promised him I would."

He looked down in a pensive way, as if bringing up old memories was hard for him. Grandma took this as her cue and continued on. "I just had a feelin'. Somethin' in me just *knew* that Arthur was not gonna return to me. After the war when I 'spected him to maybe come home any day, he just never came. I saw other soldiers returnin', other women reunitin' with their husbands, or their sons, but still no Arthur. With each day that went by, I just knew. Then, one day a tall, handsome soldier stood at my door."

"It was Grandpa, wasn't it?" Hannah asked with a smile.

"Yes, child. It was yer grandpa. He said 'Ya don't know me, but my name's Joshua Harris. I served in the war with yer husband.' At that, I just fell t'my knees. My world had ended. I mourned for a long time. But, Joshua kept comin' back to check on me and the boys. He had promised Arthur he would take keer of us, and he did. It was about a year inta my grief that I began to realize I had feelin's for Joshua, and he had realized he had feelin's for me as well. So, one day we shared a kiss, and I felt hope a'gin fer the first time. A week later Joshua asked me to marry'im. We got married and he brought his three children back into the home, so that we had an instant startin' family of six children, his three and my three. My boys was 3, 5, and 7. His children was 4, 6 and 8. It was a lot to handle, but we made it work, and I grew to love yer grandpa more than I ever knew I could love, and his children became my children."

Grandma continued, "A'course, I 'mediately became pregnant, and the followin' year we had a son together. We named him Arthur Middleton Harris, in honor of my first husband and yer grandpa's best friend, Arthur Middleton. Without him, we would'a never met. Then, we went on t'have six more children together; Robert, James, Emeline, Hugh, Caroline and Louisa. Our fourth child together is yer mother."

"So, you and grandpa have 13 children altogether?!?"

"Yes, three his, three mine and seven ours. We lost our boy Robert when he was 30 years old, but all the others is still livin'. They're all back in Tennessee. We came to Arkansas with yer mother, thinkin' that some of the others might be followin' shortly, but as it happened they all decided not t'come. So, we've not had the privilege of knowin' our grandchildren other than the ones through Emeline. We are so blessed to at least live close to you, Hannah, and the rest of Emma's children. But, it's sad to not get to know and see'em all. To the best of my count, there is 78 grandchildren now. We will die and they will never know us."

"Grandma, I'm sorry. I didn't mean to make you sad. But, what a wonderful story you and Grandpa have! I'm so happy to have heard it. I'm going to write it all down when I get home. I want to pass it down to my own children some day. I can't even begin to imagine what the two of you went through."

As Hannah and Lucy were walking home that evening, Hannah was full of thoughts and ideas. She told Lucy that she wanted to write down the stories that her Grandma and Grandpa had told her. Not just this one, but all the stories that she could remember throughout her life. It suddenly became very important to her to record her family's history. As soon as she got back to her bedroom, she pulled out some paper and began writing it all down.

August

All through the summer, Hannah stayed very busy. All the families in the little community had large gardens to tend. It was backbreaking labor, but with no stores around close, and not much money to be had, the only way to obtain the food they needed all year was to grow it themselves, or hunt it or raise it. It was simply understood that without this hard work, you would starve and die. There were evenings when the children all gathered to go berry picking, and the women would put up the berries for later use. There were evenings when they would go fishing and have a huge fish fry, and later all the leftover fish were cleaned and salted and stored in the barn. The main purpose of summer was to store back as much produce and meat as possible for the coming hard winter.

In addition to that, grasses had to be cut and dried and bundled to feed the livestock in the winter months. And, trees had to be chopped down and cut up into logs, enough logs to heat a house for an entire winter. Corn was harvested and stacked in barns. Potatoes were dug and laid in layers underneath the porches, with leaves and grasses covering them for protection through the winter months. Beans and peas were picked and snapped and canned in jars. Fresh tomatoes and okra were served at every meal. Each day at the garden there would be new ripened tomatoes and okra pods to pick, a continuous supply. Eggs were gathered each day. Cows were milked each day. Livestock was fed and watered. The hogs were fed all the garden leftovers possible so they could grow fat and ready for butchering in the fall.

There was rarely time to just stop and rest, and the days were so hot and long, but on rare occasions the young ones found time to go down to the swimming hole and go swimming. There were a few community gatherings, where picnics were served and songs were sang. Hannah was growing more and more fond of Joseph as the summer dragged on. He was truly her best friend, she had always known that. If she was honest with herself, she enjoyed her time with Joe more than she did her time with Lucy. Maybe because she was a bit of a tomboy, but she just enjoyed hanging around with her male friend more than her female friend. Abraham continued to ignore her and seemed to always be off alone or on the outskirts of the group when people gathered. Although she continued to find him attractive, and admired him from afar, she just kept her distance. It was better than feeling hurt by his rejection.

In early August, Elijah announced that he was making another trip to Clarksville. He had some garden produce and other items that he could sell or trade for things the family needed, but could not grow or make themselves. Henry Inman and William Bennett decided to go with him. All the men had items to sell or trade. Rev. Owens agreed to stay home to watch over the women and children.

Hannah's brother Daniel, and her friend Joseph, were allowed to go with the grown men on this trip. Hannah asked her dad if she could go, but he said "It's really not the kind of trip a girl needs to be making, and besides, your mother needs you here."

Hannah hated how she was always denied things simply because she was a girl. "One day," she vowed, "I will go wherever I want. I will travel and explore the world."

But, for now, she sat and waited until two days later when the men returned from the trip. They called a meeting at the school, once again, and Hannah snuck out and listened by the window, once again. To her dismay, this time Daniel and Abe were allowed to attend the meeting, too. It seemed unfair to her that boys were allowed to do these things when they reached a certain age, but girls could not.

As she listened at the window she heard her father say that Arkansas had, in fact, seceded from the Union. Actually, they had seceded back in May, followed by North Carolina, also in May, and then Tennessee in June. There were now eleven states that had separated from the Union. Hannah found it amazing that they had went through an entire summer in her little community without even knowing that the state she lived in was no longer part of the United States of America. How odd was that? It didn't feel any different to her. What did it matter?

Elijah continued, "There have been many battles already in this war. In July there was a big battle in Manassas, Virginia. And, just a few days ago, on August 10th, there was a battle just southwest of Springfield, Missouri, on Wilson's Creek. The south won that battle, but many lives were lost. My concern is how close the battles have come. I truly felt it would stay mostly in the East, but now we have soldiers moving into Missouri, just north of us. In Clarksville, many troops have been organized and sent out. John

Hill has organized Company C, First Mounted Rifles. Captain Basham of Clarksville was leading this group in the battle up at Wilson's Creek. Many men were killed, including Tom King, whom I have traded with in town many times in the past. I was saddened to hear of his death."

"Father, I want to enlist!" Daniel stood up and announced.

"As do I!" said Abraham.

Elijah swallowed hard, took a breath and said "Boys, please. Think of your mothers. Think of your fathers. Don't be so quick with your bravery."

"But, how can I sit here while other boys my age are fighting for the causes that I believe in?" Daniel announced. "I must! I cannot lie idly by. If *we* don't fight, who will?"

"There are other men and boys fighting this war. It will happen with or without you. Please reconsider," Elijah and the other men begged.

Just then Hannah heard the sound of feet running toward the church. She saw her little brothers, Jesse & Albert, running faster than she'd ever seen them run, making their way down the path from their house to the church. Their arms and legs were just flying, and they seemed to be in a panic. They ran across the little footbridge, then plowed through the doors of the church and stood at the back, panting and trying to collect their breath. The members of the meeting turned and stared. "Father! Come quick! Ma is having the baby, and something is wrong!"

The group dispersed quickly. Hannah ran from her hiding spot, not caring who saw that she was there. Everyone ran fast to the Casey home. Hannah burst through the door to see her little sisters huddled over their mother in her bed. A trail of blood led from the kitchen to the bedroom. Blood was all over the bed.

"Go get Irene!" Elijah yelled at the boys. They ran, splashing across the shallow part of the creek, not taking the time to step on the stepping stones, to fetch Irene Inman, who had experience with these things.

Joseph ran with his mother as they made their way back across the creek. He remained on the porch, so as not to intrude on the delicate situation, but he wanted to see Hannah. He wanted to comfort her. Hannah, however, stayed glued to her mother's side.

"I don't know what happened, Hannah", her mother said weakly. "I was in the kitchen. I felt a sharp pain, and I looked down and saw a lot of blood. I panicked and screamed. The children helped me to the bed and the boys ran to get your Pa. I'm in pain, labor pains. They are coming very close. I knew it was close to time, but this is not how it always happened before. Something is wrong!" She screamed in pain as she gripped Hannah's hand.

Hannah had never been beside her mother's bed while she delivered before, but she was a woman now, herself, and nothing was going to pry her from this spot. For the first time in her young life, she finally understood what a privilege it was to be a woman, to be able to bring life into the world, to be able to watch another woman bring life into the world, to be here like this with her mother. For once, this was something *she* could do, but her brothers could not. Oh, how she loved her mother, and how terrified she was for her!

There was no doctor in their tiny mountain enclave. Babies were born naturally with help from other women who had experienced the same. But, her mother had never had problems before. No one was expecting this after so many healthy pregnancies and deliveries.

Hannah continued to hold her mother's hand as she writhed in pain. "Oh, dear God! Is there nothing we can do!" she cried out to Irene. Irene gave her a sad look and shook her head. She examined Emeline and said she could see the head, so she needed to push. Irene told Hannah that it was happening too fast! This was not normal. After about 30 minutes of screaming and pushing and crying, a baby came sliding out into Irene's arms. Along with the baby came massive amounts of blood. Hannah grabbed sheets and other items and tried to soak up the blood. Then it occurred to her that the baby was not crying. It was covered in blood, and so still and blue. Irene spanked it on it's bottom to shock it into crying, tried to clear out its airways, massaged its chest. But, nothing worked. The little baby girl was stillborn. She wrapped it in a blanket and handed it to Hannah, so she could attend to Emeline.

Hannah was petrified! She looked at the precious baby and felt tears falling from her eyes, landing on the baby's face. She wiped them away, and felt a deep ache in her heart. "She looks like Izzy", Hannah thought. Irene was still trying to stop the bleeding. There was so much blood! Hannah realized her mother was not okay. She laid the precious baby down on a quilt in the corner of the room, then came back to her mother and grabbed her hand. She pleaded with her to open her eyes and talk to her. Emeline opened her eyes and said "The baby? It's a girl?"

"Yes, Mother. It's a beautiful girl."

"She's in Heaven now...."

It grieved her to say so, but she saw no other way. "Yes, Mother. She's in Heaven. But, Ma, you must be strong. Just breathe and come back to us. We need you here."

"Don't bother...."

Hannah jumped back. "Don't bother??? Mother, what are you saying? Open your eyes and look at me."

Emeline opened her eyes, but was extremely weak. "Elijah?"

"Pa!", Hannah yelled. "Ma is calling for you!"

Elijah came into the room and took his wife's hand. "Emmy, I'm here. Be strong, my love. Be strong!"

Emeline closed her eyes again and her breathing grew fainter.

"Irene, damn you, stop this bleeding!" Elijah yelled.

Irene burst into tears and said "I'm trying. Dear God, there is so much. Oh, God! I can't stop it!"

Hannah watched as her mother bled to death in front of her eyes. She watched her open her eyes again. She looked straight into Hannah's eyes, then smiled at her. She said "The locket...", then faded out again. She opened her eyes one more time and turned to Elijah and said imploringly "Why?" as tears fell from the corners of her eyes. She moved her hand and put it aside her husband's face. She wiped his tears with her thumb and said weakly "I can't stay awake. I'm dying Elijah. I'm afraid. But, I'm not afraid. I see Jesus. I see a light. He wants me to follow." She closed her eyes and everyone's breath caught. Then, there was one last movement. Without opening her eyes she put her hand back on the side of Elijah's face and said "My love....", then her arm went limp and fell to the side of the bed.

Time stopped. The world quit turning. The air froze in the room.

Elijah suddenly gathered his dead wife into his arms and began screaming "No!.... No!..... Not my Emmy! Oh, God, My Emmy! No!...... No!....."

Hannah couldn't take another minute. She jumped up and ran out the door. She ran until she thought her heart would burst, all the way to her spot by the creek. She fell to the ground by her buckeye tree and sobbed like she'd never sobbed. Every tree leaf could hear her cries of anguish. Every bird in the trees could feel the ache in her heart. Every fish in the creek below could taste the salt of her tears. The clouds in the sky stopped overhead because they couldn't go on floating with that kind of grief drifting upward to them. The world stopped, yet... the world kept going, and it was so unfair. How could the world keep going? How could the Earth continue to spin? How could people down in Clarksville continue to go about their lives as if nothing had happened? How could the soldiers continue to fight a bloody war, oblivious to the pain being felt right here, right now?

Hannah wanted to die, too. She simply wanted to die. Because she could not live with this feeling, like her heart was being squeezed in a vice. Like her insides were being ripped into shreds. Nothing would ever be the same again. She wanted to go back, reverse time, stop her mother from dying somehow.

Just then she felt arms around her, and just as tight as her heart was being squeezed with grief, her body was now being squeezed with love. Joseph was on the ground with her, curled up in a ball. He didn't say a single word. He just held her and held her and held her. She turned and buried her face into his chest and cried eternal tears. Joseph felt like the most useless person in the world. All he could do was hold her. He just kept holding her, for as long as it took.

After about 30 minutes, it was like a button was pushed and the tears just stopped. Hannah just stopped. She looked up into Joseph's face and with a feeling of terror and regret, she said "What am I doing? They need me." She jumped up and stood. "Joseph, I have to go back. They need me. I have to be the mother now. I can't cry!" She looked at Joe for the first time with such a feeling of love and tenderness. He felt it, but no words were said. She grabbed his hand as if to lead him somewhere, then dropped it and took off running back home.

The next 24 hours were a blur, but Hannah performed all the necessary duties and stayed strong for her father and her siblings. Her grandparents had been told of the sudden loss of their daughter, and brought down the creek to help.

It broke Hannah's heart to watch her Grandma wash her grown daughter's naked body to prepare it for burial. Ruth cried the whole time, and solemnly sang an old church song under her breath as she worked... ***"Rock of ages, cleft for me, let me hide myself in Thee"*** ... She dipped the rag into the bowl of water and gently rubbed it across her daughter's skin... ***"Let the water, and the blood, from Thy riven side which flowed"*** ... But, it must have been cathartic for her, for she had washed her baby girl when she was born, and now she washed her when she died. What a precious gift! ... ***"Nothing in my hand I bring, simply to Thy cross I cling"*** ... Hannah helped her grandmother dress Emeline in her best dress... ***"Naked, come to Thee for dress, helpless, look to Thee for grace"*** ... Grandma lovingly brushed Emma's long hair until it shined, then she carefully put it up into a neat bun, just the way Emma always liked to wear it... ***"While I draw this fleeting breath, when mine eyes shall close in death"*** ... Then, Hannah got her mother's favorite hair pin and handed it to Grandma, so she could hold the bun in place... ***"Rock of ages, cleft for me, let me hide myself in Thee"***

Elijah was in a daze. Izzy and Lottie cried all through the day. The little boys kept asking for Ma, which broke Hannah's heart each time. How do you explain to toddlers that Ma will never wake up again? How do they handle such a thing? Hannah became mother to them. She did everything she had watched her mother do. She bathed them, she fed them, she put them to bed.

The older boys, Daniel, Jesse and Albert, just tried to stay out of the way. Hannah wondered how boys handled this kind of pain. How do they sort it out on the inside? Was there anything she could do to help them? She could barely get through the day herself.

It was a sunny day in mid-August, when Hannah, her family, and the entire community of Buckeye stood in the cemetery behind the church to say final words to Emeline. The men had dug a grave next to Emma's first infant, so they could rest near each other for eternity. There was only one grave, for Elijah and his children all agreed that the sweet little baby girl should lie in rest in her mother's arms, in one shared grave.

Reverend Owens opened his Bible and said a few words. "As we gather here today to say goodbye to this cherished member of our community, we all grieve. God is rejoicing in Heaven to have another of his children home, yet we grieve. We are not sorry for Emeline, but sorry for ourselves, and that is natural. Emeline no longer suffers. Her babe no longer suffers. Yet, we suffer. Elijah and his children are forever changed. We all are forever changed."

"In Genesis 35, we learn of Rachel. Rachel was having trouble conceiving. She had begged her husband 'Give me children or I will die!' She finally got her wish. Yet, she dies in childbirth. Having children was so important to Rachel. She could not imagine living without them. Yet, having children ultimately caused her death. She gave her life in the process of having a child that she felt she would die without. The irony is not lost on any of us. Mothers are the strongest beings on this Earth. Yes, men have the physical strength. Men can lift heavy objects, fight battles, win wars. But, women..... women are the strongest sex by far. Women risk their lives to *give* life, even as their men go off to war risking their lives to *take* life."

"In a church I pastored back in Tennessee, a young mother came to me one Sunday and said 'Reverend, you will find this funny. My 5 year old son, when told he was to have a new baby brother or sister, asked me if that meant I would have to wear *eternity* clothes.' It was comical that the boy had meant to say 'maternity clothes', yet I found it to be an eye opening statement, yet another of those things that we only get 'out of the mouths of babes'. Yes, all mothers do, in a sense, have to wear *eternity* clothes, because once you are a mother, you are a mother forever. You wear that costume, if you will, until the end of time. As we lay Emeline Ruth Casey to rest today, we shall be glad that she is wearing her eternity clothes. She will forever be the mother to all of her children, whether with her in Heaven, or still down here on Earth."

"This babe who never took it's first breath, do not grieve over it's tiny soul. For God said 'I knew you before I formed you in your mother's womb. Before you were born I set you apart and appointed you as my prophet to the nations.' You see, God already had the precious baby's plan all laid out. She was not 'born dead'. She was already alive before she was even born. She was alive in her mother's womb, because God was forming her there. He loves her, and he has taken her to fulfill the plan he had for her. You see, she was never meant for this Earth. She was far more special. She was created for greater things. Now let us pray..."

"Father God,
we praise you for using us to
bring joy to your son, Jesus Christ.
In the midst of all the struggles, pressures, and
discouragement we face while in our frail,
failing bodies, please continue transforming us
into servants who are always of good courage.
Lead us by your holy spirit to find rest in the
grand promises that you've revealed to us in
your word. We confess that we are weak
and that we need your help.
Prepare us for the day when you will judge
an account of all our works and offenses.
Though we do not deserve your grace,
we cannot even begin to express our gratitude
for nailing our guilt and shame upon the cross
through your crucified son.

Lord, we earnestly long to experience the moment
when you will declare to us
'Well done good and faithful servant,
enter into the joy of your master.'
Help us this week as we continue our walk
of faith, looking forward to the day
when our faith will become sight.
It is in the name of Jesus that we pray,
Amen."

After the amens, the simple wooden coffin was lowered into the ground. Then Rev. Owens said...

"For as much as it has pleased almighty God
of his great mercy to take unto himself
the soul of our dear sister here departed,
we therefore commit her body to the ground;
earth to earth, ashes to ashes, dust to dust."

A few days later Hannah found herself standing in her father's bedroom. Her mother had a little wooden jewelry box that she had brought with her from Tennessee. Hannah and the other children had always understood that this box was off limits to little prying hands. She had seen her mother open it and take things out, but really was not privy to all the contents of it. She carefully lifted the lid and looked in.

Just then she felt a presence and turned to see her father standing there. She quickly slammed the lid and said "Father! I'm sorry. It's just...."

"It's okay Hannah. What is it?"

"It's just that when mother died, she said 'the locket', and I don't know what she meant."

Elijah walked over and opened the lid. He reached in and took out a locket on a chain. He opened it, and inside was a tiny lock of fine hair.

"What is it, Pa?"

"When your mother lost our first baby, she cut off a lock of it's downy hair before we buried her. She was always fretting about where to keep it, so she wouldn't lose it. So, one day when I went to Clarksville, I found this locket in a store there. I brought it home so she would have a place to keep the precious memento."

Then he said "I don't remember your mother saying 'the locket'."

"She did! Just before she died, she was looking right into my eyes, and she said 'the locket' and then she turned to you and talked to you after that."

"Well, I must have been so frightened, I can't remember. But, it seems obvious to me that she wanted you to have it, Hannah."

"Oh, Pa! Do you think?"

"Yes, I do. I believe that she must have been wanting to tell you that the locket should be passed down to her firstborn daughter. She loved you so much Hannah, just as I do." He then took the locket and fastened it around Hannah's neck.

"Pa, I wish we had've taken a lock of Ma's hair and of the second baby's hair and put it in here, too."

"I wish I had thought of it. My grief was just too strong. I was thinking of nothing at the time but my own heartache. If your mother had lived she would have certainly thought to keep a lock of the baby's hair. Women are just better at sentimental things than men are."

Hannah reached up and felt of the locket and began to cry. "Thank you, Pa. Oh, thank you!" She turned and fell into his arms like she'd done as a little girl. When was the last time she'd allowed a hug from her father? She couldn't remember. He was always so busy, and she was always so stubborn and independent. It was a nice feeling. She felt loved and protected and safe from all the harms of the world.

Then her father said "I think you should have this, too." He reached into a drawer and pulled out Emeline's family Bible. "I've seen how you've been writing a lot, recording stories of our family. It seems important to you, the family history and all. I think your mother would want you to have her Bible."

Hannah was overwhelmed. She didn't have a Bible of her

own yet. She had flashbacks of seeing her mother walking to church on Sundays with this very Bible in her hands. Knowing she had held it, and she had read it, and it had meant so much to her, it brought tears to her eyes again. She opened it and there was a page with writing on it, her mother's handwriting. It was all the birthdays in the family. Her father's, her mother's, and all the children. Hannah made a mental note to add the birth of the last baby, and the deaths of her mother and that baby. It was a way to preserve it for history, so her own children would never forget. She would add dates to that treasured Bible as they happened, for the remainder of her life, every birth, death and marriage.

September

In early September Hannah and Joe were hanging out under the buckeye tree again on a Saturday after the washing was all finished.

"Look, Hannah! The buckeyes are full on the tree. They'll be falling soon."

"I know. It's my favorite time."

The two of them were really quite bored. There wasn't much to do or to talk about. Finally Hannah said "Hey.... let's go see Grandma and Grandpa!"

Joe didn't really care to see the old couple, but he did like the idea of walking there with Hannah, so he readily agreed. They both ran home to let their families know where they were going, then they headed up the trail beside Panther Creek. Joe seemed quiet and pensive. They didn't talk much. When they passed the waterfall Hannah commented that it was barely flowing. It was always so much prettier in the springtime. Joe still wasn't saying much.

Finally she couldn't stand it anymore, so she said "Joseph, why are you in such a mood today?"

He blurted out "I'm probably going to enlist, Hannah."

Hannah felt her body tense up. "Joe, let's not talk about

that right now." She just couldn't bear the thought of it. Maybe if they didnt speak of it, it wouldn't come to pass.

Joe stopped and just stood there. Hannah turned to see what was keeping him.

"Hannah, we can't ignore it."

"Oh, Joseph! I know you are going to enlist. Don't you think I know? I think about it every day! My best friend is going away and may never come back. It's painful Joe! I can't think about it."

"I don't want to Hannah. I truly would rather stay here with you, running the hills, swimming in the creek. But, we aren't children anymore. Things that are happening in the world right now are important. Things that are happening now could affect the lives of any future children that we.... I mean that you or I might have."

Hannah didn't miss the slip of the tongue. She knew he was planning a life with her as his wife, and she just didn't know if she was ready for those thoughts right now.

"I just don't want you to go, that's all," she said. "I just can't bear it."

Joe said "But, the other boys are going. They would think me a coward if I didn't go."

"Do you think I care if Abe Owens is going off to war? Or William Bennett? Do you think I don't hear them talk? But, not you! And, dear Lord, not Daniel!"

She took off walking again and he caught back up to her. Maybe she was right. Maybe it was best not to discuss it right now. He wanted to enjoy the time with her, and he was afraid he had just spoiled it.

They visited with Joshua and Ruth for about an hour. Hannah could tell that Joe was getting restless. She knew he didn't like long visits, and she couldn't blame him. These were *her* grandparents, after all, not his. He didn't have the loving ties with them that she did. To him it was just a couple of old people, who didn't think like him. They were old-fashioned. He was taught to respect his elders, so he would never treat them bad or tell them he was bored. But, Hannah was able to tell. She was trying to think of a way to cut the visit short, when suddenly Joshua looked at Joe and said "You gonna go off and fight the good fight, young man?"

"If you mean 'am I gonna enlist?', then yes. I plan to."

"I suspected. Every young man has his knickers in a twist when it comes to fightin'. I remember myself at yer age. I couldn't wait to join up fer some cause. It took a long life for me to look back and wonder what it was all for."

He paused for a minute, then said, "There's absolutely nothin' to be said in favor a' growin' old. There ought t'be legislation against it. But, one thing ya do gain along with the wrinkles, aches and pains, is wisdom. Ya don't have wisdom when yer young. Ya gotta earn that."

"Grandpa, I don't want him to go," Hannah said. "It is just plain silly what these boys want to do. Why can't we just mind our own business? Nothing will touch us here if we just stay out of it. What if Joe goes off to war and gets shot and I never see him again? Tell him, Grandpa! Tell him not to go."

Grandpa said "Hannah Belle, don't let fear get to ya. Fear makes the wolf seem bigger than he is. There are some things ya cain't change, and I'm afraid this is one of'em. Young Joseph here *will* go off ta war, of that I'm sure. I can see it in his eyes. His soul is on fire. Every good man must fight a battle to put out that fire in his soul."

Joshua had always called his granddaughter "Hannah Belle", even though "Belle" was not her middle name. It was just his pet name for her. He did that with all the children. It was his grandfatherly way of showing his love. Sometimes he called Daniel "Danny Boy", or Jesse "Jester", or Isabelle "Dizzy Izzy". Grandma had told her once that Grandpa had always liked the name "Anabelle", so that's probably why he called her "Hannah Belle". No matter why, she thought that she probably had the least undesirable nickname of all of them, and of that she was thankful. She wasn't very happy with the words coming out of Grandpa's mouth at the moment, though. She felt he was just encouraging Joe.

Grandpa sat back and looked at them for a minute, then said "I'm gonna tell ya a little secret a'mine."

Hannah and Joe perked up with interest.

"Did'ya know there's a cave not far from here?"

Hannah and Joe both said they didn't know of one close by.

Grandpa said "Well, there is. A pretty big one, too. I've always kind'a kept it as my own little secret. I was out huntin' one day and came acrost it. I didn't want ta tell the young'ens because, well, it could be dangerous explorin' in a cave like that, and I couldn't be responsible for one of ya gettin' in there and gettin' yourselves in some kind'a trouble. So, I never said anythin'. But, I feel the time is right. But, now, don't you go tellin' any of the little fellers!" They promised they wouldn't.

"There's a reason I'm tellin' ya now," Grandpa said. "When war comes to a place, bad things can happen. I know from experience. People go hungry. People lose everythin' they own. Now, I don't know that the war will touch us here, but times are uncertain. I've been takin' some of your grandma's and my things up to the cave and hidin'em... some valuables, of which we ain't got much... and, some foodstuffs that will keep fer a good while... some things that a person couldn't survive without. I put some of your grandma's jewelry in there, a couple a'guns, and my old sword that I carried when I was in the war. I've stored a few quilts, some seeds fer plantin' in case gardens are completely destroyed and we have to start again. Just things like that. I've been in a war before. I know what happens. I wanted to tell ya 'bout it, Hannah, 'cause if worse comes to worse, ya might need it. And, anyway, yer grandma and I ain't spring chickens, so if we was to pass on, I would want someone to know about the things I stored there, so ya could get ta the things ya need. I would just feel better if I knew someone knew the secret."

"Where is this cave?" Joe asked. As a young boy, the thought of exploring a cave intrigued him very much. He was actually surprised he'd never come upon it before in his wanderings.

"I'm not sure ya could find it without m'help. The opening is small, barely big enough for a grown man to fit through, and it's kind'a hidden. I'll have ta show ya m'self."

Grandpa rose from his chair slowly, as his old bones cracked. He told Ruth to "hold down the fort" and he got his cane and started down the path that led away from his house. Hannah and Joe followed after him, and they walked for about a quarter of a mile until they came to a spot where two hills met and water had carved out a path down to the creek. Water only flowed there during a rain, but it had been doing this for so many years, a great wash had formed down the mountain side. Grandpa said "Ya gotta follow this holler here up a ways." Hannah and Joe fell in behind Grandpa, but it was slow going. Grandpa just couldn't make those hills like he used to. He would take a few steps, then stop and rest, then a few steps more, then stop and rest. Joe was restless and thought they would never get there at that pace, but he remained patient in his outward appearance.

Finally after about 30 minutes of slow uphill trudging, Grandpa stopped and pointed his cane and said "There she be..."

All Hannah and Joe saw was a large rock, about 10 feet wide and 10 feet tall, sitting at the base of a rocky cliff. It looked as if the large boulder had broken off at some point and rolled down and lodged where it sat. Grandpa told them to climb on up there and look behind that rock.

Joe rushed up first, and when he went around the rock and looked behind, he saw a crack in the side of the rock cliff face. It was about 5 feet high, and maybe 2 feet wide. It was just big enough for a person to fit through if he squeezed sideways a bit, but a grown man would need to duck so as not to bang his head on the rock above. Joe squeezed through, and once he'd entered about 6 feet, the crack opened up into an area shaped like a large room, but completely hidden in the mountain. If the large rock had not rolled down the hill at some time and lodged in front of the cave opening, it would have been easier to find. As it was, the rock camouflaged the entrance, making a perfect hiding place.

Hannah squeezed in and joined Joe. The light was faint inside, but they could see enough to tell the dimensions of the space. Hannah saw some of Grandpa's items that he'd carried up and stored in the cracks of the walls inside. She knew it must have been difficult for him to do in his condition.

"We will have to come back with a light, so we can see to explore better," said Joe. Hannah nodded in agreement. They agreed that as soon as they had some more free time, they would come back. It was such an enchanting place. They couldn't wait to see it in better light.

But, for now, they followed Grandpa back down the "holler" and safely back to his house, then they headed back home, because it was getting late and they wanted to get back before dark.

The next Saturday after the washing was done, Hannah ran over to get Joe. Joe rummaged around in his mother's kitchen until he found two candles and some matches, and then the two of them set off on their journey. They first crossed Mulberry Creek, carefully stepping on the large rocks that had been placed just so, then they followed Panther Creek northward until they found the hollow that took them up to the cave. Without Grandpa along, they made good time. Joe practically ran all the way up to the cave.

With the candles they were able to see everything well. The room was large enough for about 30 or 40 people to fit. It was cold and damp inside, but well hidden. There was some evidence of animals that had sheltered there, but thankfully no sign of an animal at the moment. Back in the back corner, there was another crevice, slightly smaller than the entrance one. Joe squeezed through it and saw another small room. Maybe big enough for ten people. He didn't see that the cave went any further than that.

Hannah decided Grandpa's things would be safer if they moved them to the smaller room in the back. So, they moved everything and then went back out and found a few rocks that were large, but not so large they couldn't lift them and carry them. They stacked these rocks in a pile in front of the inner crevice, so if anyone *did* come across the cave, maybe they wouldn't see that there was a second room in the back.

Afterward they climbed up and sat on top of the large boulder that blocked the entrance, so they could rest and catch their breath. It was a nice spot to just sit and view the scenery. You could see quite a long way down the mountain. Joe felt the urge to reach over and take Hannah's hand, but something stopped him. He feared she would reject him, and his heart couldn't take it. What he didn't know was that she wondered if he *would* try to hold her hand, and even wanted him to, but was afraid to ask or make the move herself. So, as young lovers have done through time, they missed an opportunity, and eventually walked back home to their families.

The next day was Sunday, so the whole town met for church. Afterward there was a dinner served outside the building. The tables were set up again. The atmosphere was wonderful, as leaves were turning colors and beginning to fall. You could hear the crunching of dry leaves as people walked around talking, and the children ran and played, trying to catch the leaves that fell and drifted back and forth in the breeze.

Hannah sat and talked with Lucy and the other women and girls. Joe was with the older boys, off away from the crowd. Hannah was curious what they were discussing. She thought she saw Abraham spitting in the dirt, and figured he had stolen some of his father's tobacco again. They all seemed so earnest and serious. "Probably talking war again..." Hannah thought.

Later that evening, after Hannah had helped clear everything at the church, she was sitting on the upstairs porch of her home when she heard raised voices from out in the barn. She laid down the sewing she was working on, then stopped to check on the children. Since her mother's death, she had been working hard from sunup to sundown, taking care of all her siblings. Sometimes on Saturday after the washing, Sarah Madison would come over and offer to watch the young ones to give Hannah some time on her own, which she usually spent with Joseph. Sometimes Hannah would take the children over to Sarah, and she would watch them at her home. Sarah was a blessing to Hannah, because without this one day a week to get away, she would have gone crazy.

Hannah made her way down the stairs and through the

house, out into the yard and toward the sounds coming from the barn, which kept getting louder and louder the closer she got. She could tell it was her Pa and her older brother Daniel, and they seemed to be arguing. She snuck around behind the barn and peeped through a crack in the boards. Daniel was standing face to face with Elijah, and words were flying.

Her father yelled "You will not disobey me Daniel! You will not enlist in this war! I forbid it!"

"Father, my convictions won't allow it!"

"You impetuous boy! Stubborn like your grandfather!" Elijah paced back and forth, hands flying in the air, anger rising with each step. "I won't allow it! Damn you boy! I won't allow it!"

Daniel looked straight into his father's eyes and yelled "Father, you would do the same...."

Elijah stopped in his tracks. He was beginning to feel defeated, and losing hope. His voice grew calmer as he said "And that is exactly why I beg you not to do this. When I was young and ignorant, yes, I would do the same."

He sighed in desperation. "Daniel... you are not as Daniel of the Bible. If you are thrown into the lion's den, I fear God will not send an angel to close the jaws of the lions."

Elijah looked toward Heaven and prayed "Lord, I pray thee....open his eyes! Open his eyes so that he may see! If thou cannot answer that prayer... then please, I beg of you, let him walk with the army of God at his side."

Daniel could see what his decision was doing to his father, but something deep inside him would not allow him to obey. He had always feared his father, but this time he didn't feel that fear. If anything, maybe the roles were reversing, and his father seemed to be the one who feared his own son.

"We are leaving tomorrow," Daniel said.

Hannah realized she'd been holding her breath. She inhaled deeply and then left her hiding spot and went back to the house to check on the children. She seemed to be in a daze. Everything was happening so fast. Everything was changing. She didn't want to see Daniel or Abe leave, but she knew they would. She was resigned to it. She just didn't have the strength to fight it.

The next morning school was called off because everyone had heard about the boys leaving. Hannah watched Daniel packing up his few belongings that he was planning to take along with him. She gathered together some food that he could take that would last him a few days; some cold biscuits, some salt pork, some jerky. She wrapped up some coffee grounds in a handkerchief, and some sugar in another handkerchief, and pushed them down inside a tin cup. Daniel tucked them into his pockets and hugged his sister.

The whole family followed Daniel down the path from the house to the area by the school. Some of the other families were already there, standing around, waiting to say their goodbyes. Abe was there with his parents and his sister Lucy. Abe had a pack slung across his back, too. Then, from across the creek she saw Joe and his family. As they got closer to the group, Hannah felt a panic in her heart. Why did Joe have a pack on *his* back? What is happening?!

Joe looked at Hannah and shrugged his shoulders. She felt the bile coming up from her stomach. She ran away from them all and down to the creek to her tree. Of course, Joe was right behind her. He caught up to her and grabbed her arm and turned her around.

"Let go!" she yelled, and yanked her arm from his grasp. "You didn't tell me you were going, too!"

"Hannah, I've been telling you all along that I was going to enlist."

"But, I thought you meant when you were older, like Daniel and Abe. I thought maybe in a year, when you are 18. I.... I.... Oh, I don't know what I thought. I just didn't think you were going *now*. I thought it was just Daniel and Abe this time."

"I didn't mean to give you that impression. I know I'm only 16, but I'll be 17 in just a couple of weeks, and I'm going. I will lie about my age if I need to. I want to do this Hannah. I *need* to do this."

Hannah felt so helpless. She sat down on one of the tree roots, because her legs felt weak. That's when she saw them.... the buckeyes. They were everywhere all over the ground. The buckeyes had started falling from the tree. She remembered how she'd told Joseph this was her favorite time of the year. She suddenly felt as if she would never be able to think so again. She picked up one of the smooth round nuts and wrapped her hand around it. She rubbed it back and forth, feeling the way it fit in her hand so perfectly, how soothing it felt to just roll it around in her palm.

She stood up and walked back to Joe. She took his hand and laid the buckeye in his palm and closed his fingers around it. "It will bring you luck. Please, take it with you. It's all I have to give you of myself."

Joe felt the smoothness, the perfection of it all, the honesty of the gesture, and tears welled up in his eyes. He put the buckeye in his pocket, and a surge of emotion welled up in him. He reached for Hannah and pulled her to him. Their lips met, and he kissed her the way he'd always dreamed of kissing her. She responded in kind, and the two of them were lost in the moment of their very first kiss.

When they finally parted, Hannah said "Well, come then. We must give you a patriotic send-off. We shouldn't keep them waiting."

They walked back to the group, and Hannah noticed Daniel and Lucy standing off to the side, having a private moment, saying their last goodbyes. She went up to Abe and told him goodbye, and that she would pray for his safety.

Then, everyone turned, and walking down the wagon trail toward them was the Bennett family. William had a pack thrown across his back, and was holding 2 year old Thomas. Martha was walking sadly by his side, carrying baby Isaac. That's when everyone realized William meant to go as well. Hannah had thought he might, but thought maybe because he had a family he would think twice about it. But, William was only 24, not much older than 18 year old Daniel and Abe, and 17 year old Joe. Hannah finally began to understand that maybe the family that she thought might keep him at home, might also be the reason he felt he had to go, to ensure their protection.

William asked Elijah and Henry if they would please look

out for his young wife and boys while he was away. They said "Of course! Of course! That is not even a thing you would have to ask."

As the four young men walked off down the rutted wagon road toward Clarksville, the rest of the small little group just stood and stared at their backs. Would this be the last image they ever had of them? Would they return some day soon? Would only some of them return, and if so which ones? Even Rev. Owens was quiet. He hadn't even thought to say a prayer. He just stood off to the side, watching his boy, his youngest boy, go off to war.

Jesse and Albert Casey and Harding Inman, boys of 12 to 14 years old, followed the older boys for a bit, envious, and wishing they were old enough to go off to war like their big brothers. They where hollering and yelling at them. The bigger boys turned and threw some pebbles back at them and said, affectionately, "Get on back home to your mothers, you greenhorns!"

As the younger boys came running back, suddenly Daniel turned once more and yelled back toward Lucy "Marry me! When I come back, will you Marry me?" Lucy, through tears, yelled back "Yes! Yes, Daniel Casey! I will marry you!" He smiled a huge smile, then put his hand to his heart, blew her a kiss and turned back around. And just like that, they were all gone, disappearing around the bend. Like ghosts that were never there.

December

The fall of '61 was a lonely time for Hannah and the others. There was a different feeling in the air. Rev. Owens still preached his sermons on Sunday, but they were weak and unconvincing. Hannah still visited her tree, but didn't get comfort there like she used to. She walked to see Grandma and Grandpa, but refused to take the detour up to the cave. It only made her think of Joe. Elijah stayed busy cutting wood and preparing for the hardships of the coming winter. Sarah Madison came over often with her three girls to help the Casey family with chores. Sarah and Hannah would sometimes cook extra food and carry it down to Martha Bennett and her two boys.

The Inmans were feeling the loss of Joseph deeply. Henry and Irene kept busy, while the other children tried to stay out of their way and out of trouble. Mrs. Inman gave birth to a baby boy in November. She named him Charles, but everyone quickly dubbed him "Charlie". It was a happy moment for the family, but they were sad that Joseph wasn't there to see his new baby brother.

Christmas that year wasn't the same, but Hannah got together with Lucy and Lucy's mother, Winnie, Martha Bennett, Sarah Madison, and Irene Inman, and the women tried to make the holiday tolerable for the children. They put up a tree down at the church and everyone made a day of decorating, stringing popcorn and beads and singing Christmas songs. They put on a play of the birth of baby Jesus, and each little child had a part to play. Little newborn Charlie had the part of baby Jesus. Isabelle was Mary and Harding played Joseph. Jesse, Albert and Michael were the three wise men. Rebecca, Rachel and Ruby played the innkeepers. Nancy was the narrator. All the other children played shepherds or angels.

The women had even made some simple toys for the children, and Grandma Harris made some Christmas candy which she brought down to the church for all to share.

It was a nice distraction, but didn't completely take away the fears and worries about their boys who'd gone off to war. And, worst of all there was no mail service that far out, so there would be no letters from the boys unless someone went to Clarksville and checked at the post office, which wasn't likely to happen until the spring.

Hannah spent most of her time that winter in the house, cooking for her family, entertaining her little brothers and sisters, and being a steadfast support for her Pa.

1862

It was late February. Hannah was covered head to toe with flour, and was busy kneading a large lump of biscuit dough on the kitchen table. She was 17 now. She felt 40, though, doing the work of a mother of seven. It was exhausting, but at least it helped to get her mind off Joseph and Daniel.

Harding Inman popped his head in the door and asked Hannah where her pa was. She nodded toward the back of the house. Harding yelled "Mr. Casey, my pa wants you to come over and help. Our cow got out."

"I'll be right over."

When Elijah got back from helping Henry with his cow, Hannah was just pulling the biscuits off of the fire. Pa said "That smells so good Hannah. I'm powerful hungry!"

"I got some fried potatoes in that skillet over there, and I cooked up the last of that ham from the smokehouse. We will have to butcher another hog soon."

"In the spring, when it's warmer. We have plenty of venison still. We have enough meat to last another month or more."

Hannah gathered the twins and young Michael and sat them in their places at the table. Then, she called Jesse, Albert, Izzy and Lottie. They sat down to supper, but first bowed their heads to give thanks. Everyone held hands and then Elijah said the prayer.

"We praise you, Oh God,
for covering our table with plenty,
and for the present opportunity
of partaking of your bounties.
Nourish our bodies with these
provisions of your hand,
and our souls with the bread of life,
for the sake of Jesus Christ, our Lord,
Amen."

March

Soon it was March, and the Dogwood trees were all abloom with their pretty white flowers. It gave Hannah a sense of renewal. The long, hard winter was almost over. The last snow had melted, hopefully. The ice in the creek had broken up and she could hear the gurgling of the water once again.

She was sitting out on the front porch enjoying one of the first warm days of the season, when her father came and sat with her. He had a book with him that he opened and pretended to be reading. But, something else was on his mind. Maybe now was the time to tell his daughter of his news. So he wouldn't lose his nerve, he just came out with it...

"Sarah and I are to be married."

Hannah put down her needlework and stared blankly at him.

He said "Now, I know how you must feel. I know that Sarah is not a replacement for your mother. Your mother will always be the love of my life, my first love, the mother of my children. But, Sarah has been such a help to me all winter, and I've grown to love her in a way I did not think I would ever feel again. I know it may seem soon to you. But, remember that Sarah has been alone for quite some time now. And, she is not trying to move in to the spot your mother held for so long. And, I assure you I had no feelings of this sort toward Sarah while your mother was alive. But, now, we both deserve to be happy, to have someone to spend the rest of our lives with. Our children won't be with us forever. Soon you will all go away, like Daniel did. What will become of me then? I need a lifetime companion. Sarah and I have been neighbors for many years. It is not as if we just met. I love her girls, just as she loves all my children. We believe we could make one bigger family unit and everything will work itself out. I can fill a void she has had in her life for a long time now, and she can fill this new void that I have in my life. Now, I know she is younger than me. I am 39 and she is just 30. But, throughout this winter she has been here at our home more than she's been at her own, and her help has been invaluable to me. It's almost as if we are already married, other than sharing a bed. I...."

Hannah stopped her father mid-sentence. "Pa! You are rambling. And, furthermore, you are preaching to the choir. There is no need for convincing. I am shocked, yes, because my mind just hadn't gone this way. But, now that I look back over the last few months, I can put the pieces together. I see that it was meant to be. I truly love Ms. Sarah. Well, I suppose if she is to be my stepmother, it would feel odd to call her Ms. Sarah, as if she were still my teacher and I her student."

Because Hannah had been needed so much at home, and all the other students her age had gone off to war, Ms. Sarah had decided she'd learned enough and could be considered graduated. It wasn't the exact way Hannah had imagined her ending to her schooling, but it was how it needed to be. She stayed home now when her younger siblings went to school each day.

Hannah continued, "I don't know that I could call her 'Ma', but certainly a simple 'Sarah' would suffice. I love Rebecca, Rachel and Ruby, too. I would be honored to have three new sisters. And, to have an older woman in the house to take over the motherly duties, what a relief that would be for me! Pa, I am very happy to hear this news."

Two weeks later, in late March, Elijah and Sarah were married at the little church. It was a simple ceremony, but everyone in the community came. Sarah wore a deep purple dress that she'd owned for years. It was her nicest one. Her girls had made her a bouquet of Dogwood flowers to hold. Her hair was in an updo with flowers entwined in it to match her bouquet. She was a very beautiful woman, very youthful and intelligent, with a clear complexion, bright green eyes, and long flowing brown hair.

Elijah wore his best suit of clothes, some "britches" without holes in them and a jacket that didn't really match. But, he did have a bow tie on, something Hannah had never seen him wear, and didn't even know he had. Hannah thought he looked dashing, with just a bit of gray at his temples, and his piercing blue eyes just twinkling. He had lost some weight since losing his first wife, so he was a bit too slim, but still a very handsome man.

There was no ring to place on the bride's finger, just simple words spoken with love by Rev. Owens.

"We gather here today for the union of our dear friends, Elijah Casey & Sarah Madison. We are honored to be present at this joyous occasion. Both Elijah and Sarah have suffered the ultimate in losses, but thanks be to God they have found each other. As it says in Genesis 'It is not good that man should be alone, I will make him a helper fit for him.' God truly works in unique ways. He has brought Sarah and Elijah together, to be helpmates to each other, to heal each other, to love each other to the end of their days on Earth."

"In Ecclesiastes we learn that two are better than one, because they have a good return for their labor. If either of them falls down, one can help the other up. But, pity anyone who falls and has no one to help them up. In Corinthians we read that if one has the gift of prophecy and can fathom all mysteries and all knowledge, and has faith that can move mountains... but does not have love... then they are nothing. Proverbs tells us that he who finds a wife finds what is good and receives favor from the Lord."

Rev. Owens looked at Sarah and said "I will close with Ephesians... Wives, submit to your own husbands, as to the Lord. For the husband is head of the wife, as also Christ is head of the church, and he is the Savior of the body. Therefore, just as the church is subject to Christ, so let the wives be to their own husbands in everything."

Then he turned to Elijah and continued "Husbands, love your wives, just as Christ also loved the church and gave himself for her, that he might sanctify and cleanse her with the washing of water by the word, that he might present her to himself a glorious church, not having spot or wrinkle or any such thing, but that she should be holy and without blemish. So husbands ought to love their own wives as their own bodies; he who loves his wife loves himself. For no one ever hated his own flesh, but nourishes and cherishes it, just as the Lord does the church. For we are members of his body, of his flesh and of his bones. For this reason a man shall leave his father and mother and be joined to his wife, and the two shall become one flesh."

"Elijah, do you take Sarah as your lawful wife, to have and to hold, from this day forward, for better or worse, for richer or poorer, in sickness and in health, until death do you part?"

"I do."

"And, Sarah, do you take Elijah as your lawful husband, to have and to hold, from this day forward, for better or worse, for richer or poorer, in sickness and in health, until death do you part?"

"I do."

"May the two of you love and honor each other all the days of your life. I now pronounce you man and wife."

Elijah kissed Sarah and everyone cheered. Hannah had tears in her eyes. She was so happy for her father to have been able to find love again.

The next few days were a whirlwind. Elijah and Sarah, with the children's help, were moving most of Sarah's belongings across the creek to Elijah's house. Hannah helped to clear space in the kitchen for Sarah's dishes and utensils. Elijah cleared room in the bedroom for Sarah's clothing and personal belongings.

For now the livestock would be left at Sarah's property. It was easy enough to cross the creek to go tend them each day, and there wasn't enough room in Elijah's pens and barn for all of them until he had time to add on.

The big question was the new sleeping arrangements for the children. Hannah had enjoyed a room of her own only briefly after Daniel left. She had to laugh because she knew all along it wouldn't last long. It was agreed, since all Sarah's children were girls, that the three of them would share Daniel's old room, and Hannah would have to go back to sharing the room with Izzy and Lottie again. Jesse and Albert would continue to share a room, and Michael, Jacob and Jonah would continue to share the nursery. The house now held eleven children, one upstairs wing containing five boys and the other wing containing six girls.

April

In early April, Jesse and Harding came into the house full of excitement. "Pa!" Jesse blurted out. "We saw soldiers!"

Pa became anxious and asked them to elaborate.

"We were about a quarter mile down the creek past William Bennett's home, and four soldiers came walking out of the trees. They saw us, and we were frightened, because we didn't know if they would be friendly or not, but then they just kept walking past us. They got onto the road to Clarksville and just started walking off that way."

"Boys, I want you to stay close to home for the time being," Elijah said.

"But, Pa..."

"No buts, Jesse! You don't know the danger you could be walking into."

Elijah went across the creek to Henry's home and after telling him what their boys had seen, the two of them walked on up to Rev. Owen's house to have a meeting and discuss what to do.

The men agreed to keep everyone close to home, until they could learn what was going on and why soldiers were in the area. They needed to scout out and see if there were other soldiers, and what regiments they were with. They agreed that the three of them would arm themselves and keep a gun near them at all times, even if working in the fields or the barn.

The next morning the three men, taking Jesse and Harding along, went back to the spot where the boys had seen the soldiers. They scouted about in the forest for a bit, but saw no sign of any other soldiers. There was no evidence of where anyone had bedded down for the night, or where a campfire had been built.

But, just to be safe, on their way back, they stopped at William Bennett's home and told his wife, Martha, to pack up a few things and bring the two babies. It wasn't safe for her to be there alone. Her home was a half mile down the creek from Elijah and Henry's homes, and could not be seen from that distance. In order to protect her and the boys, the men felt it was best if she moved in to Sarah's old home temporarily. It was better to have her closer to the others. William had made them promise to look out for her, and they knew this would be what he would want.

The men kept their weapons on them, and kept their eyes open at all times. The next day Elijah was in the barn when he heard a commotion by the chicken coop. He saw two soldiers and grabbed his gun and aimed. "Stop!" he yelled.

"Don't shoot, sir!" the first soldier said, putting his hands up into the air. "We are no harm to you. We are just passing through."

"Lay your guns down on the ground and step away."

The soldiers did as Elijah asked. He then motioned for them to come toward him.

"Sir, we are just trying to find our way to a town. We're lost from our unit. Can you point us in the right way?"

"What side are you fighting for?"

"We are in the Confederate army, Sir."

Elijah asked them if they knew of soldiers named Daniel Casey, Joseph Inman, Abraham Owens or William Bennett, in hopes he could get some news about them. But, the soldiers said "We don't know of those men."

Elijah told the soldiers it would be best to move on. He pointed them toward the trail that led to Clarksville and told them to follow it. It would take a good day to reach the town, though. He asked them if they had food. They said no. He felt sorry for them. What if this were his boy? These boys looked no older than Daniel. He would want a stranger to help Daniel if he were in need. So, he told them to wait while he went into the house and got them a little food to take along, enough to last the day.

The soldiers thanked him and continued on down the trail and disappeared around the bend.

Elijah felt strongly that more soldiers would be passing through. If there had been a battle, they could be from either side. Some could even be injured. There could be conflict. He decided it was time to go up Panther Creek to warn Grandpa Harris and Ruth. Joshua was old, but should be able to still handle a gun and protect himself if need be. But, he needed to know what was going on.

Two more days passed with no sign of soldiers. Just as everyone was beginning to relax a bit and feel safer, one evening, just before dusk, some of the children who had been playing near the creek saw something in the distance and started yelling "Soldiers! Soldiers!"

Everyone came running out in a panic, telling the children to run back to their homes. The men grabbed their guns and ran in the direction the children had been looking. With guns aimed at them, they cautiously approached.

"Pa?! Don't shoot! It's me!"

Elijah and Henry paused, and it took a second for it to register. Then Elijah lowered his gun and ran to his son and hugged him so ferociously he almost suffocated him.

Henry ran back toward the middle of town and yelled "It's Daniel and William! They've come back!"

Martha ran out and met her husband with a flood of tears. It was such a relief to finally see him again, to know he was alive. It had been 6 months since they'd gone, with no word from any of them. Hannah ran to her brother and hugged him. The relief that he was okay was a wonderful feeling. But, her mind was in a headspin. Where was Joseph? Where was Abe? The questions came pouring out of everyone. Where are the other two?

Daniel and William were a sight for sore eyes, but at the same time, they both were so skinny and haggard looking. They looked beaten, exhausted. Sarah realized that they must be starving. She suggested everyone go to her home, where they could all listen to their stories of the past six months, and get them something to eat, and a place to sit and rest.

After they'd all gathered, Hannah again asked "Where's Joe & Abe?"

"We don't know where Joe is," William said. "He got separated into a different company a couple of months back. I know he was alive and well when we parted, but have heard nothing since."

Daniel continued "We were in a battle at Pea Ridge a few weeks back. It lasted 2 days. The Yanks really routed us good! We lost a lot of men. They killed General McCulloch and General McIntosh. We thought we had'em. By that first night we got control of Elkhorn Tavern and Telegraph Road. But, the next day the Union rallied and pushed our forces back. We ran low on ammunition and they ordered us to retreat. Now the Union army is in control of the Missouri-Arkansas border, and soldiers are dispersed out all over these mountains. Mostly it's Rebs trying to flee, but there are some Yanks out there, too. Daniel and I found each other and decided to try and make our way back home. Our company is so dispersed right now, we don't even know where to go."

Hannah was so concerned about Joe, but it was better to hear 'I don't know where he is' than to hear 'He's been killed', so she felt somewhat better.

Someone then asked if they had news of Abe. Daniel looked down and William seemed to be stalling. Hannah felt a sense of dread creeping in. She kept thinking "I don't want to hear it! I don't want to hear it! Just don't say it!"

But, William said it anyway. "Abe is dead..."

The whole crowd let out a gasp. "Was he killed? Was it in battle? What happened to his body?" So many questions were being thrown at them.

Finally Daniel spoke up. "He died during the battle at Pea Ridge." It was very difficult for Daniel to speak about the loss of his best friend. But, he found a resolve hidden somewhere down deep and continued on. "I was with him. I saw it all. We were running, fleeing the Union forces. I turned and he wasn't behind me anymore. They shot him in the back! He was down. I couldn't stop or I'd be dead, too. Everyone was yelling 'Run, Run!' and grabbing at me and pulling me along. But, later, after they had retreated back, I went to see if I could find him. They were picking up the bodies and putting them in a mass grave. I found him....and I prayed over him. I cried, because I knew he was going in that mass grave and not coming home to Rev. Owens and Mrs. Owens. I was the last one to see his face. I will never forget his face."

Elijah stood up and said "I'm going to see Rev. Owens." Oh, the horror of having to tell him about his son! That was a job nobody wanted. Hannah wanted to go, too, to support Lucy, but she had been away from Daniel for so long she was afraid to leave him for fear he would disappear again. So, she stayed behind and let her Pa and Mr. Inman go do the terrible chore. Oh, how Winnie and Lucy were going to cry when they heard! Hannah just didn't think she could handle being there to see it.

They had a service for Abe. But, there was no body in a coffin, no grave to dig. It didn't seem real. Jackson, Winnie and Lucy Owens were so full of grief. Jackson couldn't even speak at the service, even though he was the town preacher who normally performed this type of function. He just sat and stared. Elijah was the one who stood up and spoke.

Hannah felt sad for the loss of a boy she'd grown up with and attended school with, but it wasn't the type of sadness she might have felt a year ago. She had lost her romantic feelings for Abe during the time he and Joseph were away. Her thoughts had only been on Joe, and nothing else, and she felt a little ashamed of the way she had brushed him off in favor of Abe so many times in the past. But, even so, how could Abe be gone? He was so young. It didn't seem fair at all.

After the service Hannah went down to the creek and sat under her tree. She clasped her hands in prayer and closed her eyes and prayed:

"Dear Heavenly Father,
I know that you know every thought
within me before I even think it.
But, even so, I feel the need to ask
your forgiveness.
I feel ashamed that I have
fleeting thoughts that
I know are wrong.
When I heard Abe had been
killed in battle,
for a brief moment I thought to myself
that if one of them had to die,
I was glad it wasn't Joseph or Daniel.
If I am honest, it wasn't just
for a brief moment.
I still have those thoughts.
I know they are wrong,
and I ask you to help me
to control them.
I don't understand why
any of them had to die.
My head hangs low today.
I know that the Owens family
is shattered, and for that
I feel so much grief.
I ask your mercy for their family,
and I ask your mercy for me
and my sinful thoughts.
I pray that your love for me will bring
the grace that I do not deserve.

I pray that there will be
no more carnage and death.
I pray for an end to this war!
I pray for healing.
In Jesus' name,
Amen"

Since William was back home, he took his wife and two little boys back to their house. He told Martha that he wasn't going back to the war, that nothing was worth going through that again. He had not been dismissed from duty, but he was resigned to not go back.

Surprisingly, Daniel pulled his father aside and told him the same thing. "Pa, the things we saw! The horror of it all! I can't go back. I don't feel that the things I was fighting for are worth the deaths of so many. I saw boys my age with legs shot off, with arms shot off! I watched them bleed to death, with fear in their eyes! I saw one boy with his intestines hanging outside of his body, and he was staring at me with the eyes of a ghost. I heard soldiers crying for their mothers. And for what? Nothing makes sense in this war. I can't be a part of it anymore. It wasn't at all what I thought it was going to be."

Although Elijah was ecstatic to have his son back, he also knew that what he and William were choosing to do was a dangerous thing. He knew that if they were found, they would be arrested and court-martialed. He knew that harboring them was a dangerous thing for all involved. But, he could not do anything other than just that. He loved his son. He had not wanted him to go in the first place, so why would he send him back now?

"Do you think me a coward, Father?"

"No, Daniel. I think you have gained the wisdom that I wish you'd had six months ago. The last thing I would call you is a coward."

June

Throughout the rest of that spring and into the summer, the little mountain community harbored their fugitives. Occasionally a soldier or two would stumble through the area, but William and Daniel would hide out until they were gone. Usually one of the families would feed the soldiers, all the while praying they would hurry and move on out before anyone was found out.

Daniel and Lucy resumed their love affair, and the proposal of marriage that he'd yelled out so impulsively all those month ago still stood. They were just having trouble agreeing on the best time to do it. Daniel spent most of his time at Lucy's house, when he was not doing the necessary chores at home. Elijah and Sarah had pulled him aside and told him that in the event he and Lucy were married, they would like for the two of them to move into Sarah's old home across the creek, since it was sitting empty anyway. Daniel was looking forward to that, and had been over at the house fixing it up somewhat and preparing it for the arrival of his bride.

One day in early June, Daniel left to go see Lucy. Hannah had finished her chores and had told Sarah that she was going down to the creek for a bit to cool off. She was sitting on her root under the buckeye tree, cooling her feet in the water. She'd brought her journal with her and was jotting down some thoughts about Joe. It had been so long since she'd seen him, close to nine months now. Where was he? What was he doing at this moment? Was he thinking of her? Then her mind would go a different way and she would wonder if he was dead. Maybe he died in a battle long ago and was buried in a mass grave like poor Abraham. Maybe she would go her whole life never knowing what happened to her dear Joseph. She was wishing that he would just come walking back to her, any day now.

Suddenly she was jolted from her reverie by a loud bang, then another! She was startled. Whatever could that be? Thunder? No, it sounded like a gun. Who was hunting, and so close by?

Then she heard a rumbling that she recognized as horse

feet, galloping quickly. It got louder and louder and she realized they were coming her way. She hid behind the tree and waited until the thundering hooves passed by. She watched as they made their way past the church and on down the road toward town. She recognized them as soldiers, most likely Confederate soldiers. She wondered what they were in such a hurry for. And, why were they shooting? She felt a bit uneasy, but didn't know what to make of it. By now she had gotten used to soldiers randomly making their way through. It seemed like the mountains were just full of soldiers. But, she didn't get too worried unless they were Union soldiers. Since William and Daniel had fought on the Confederate side, she felt only the Union soldiers would be likely to do them any harm.

She was about to sit back down on her root when she heard a blood curdling scream. It was coming from the way the soldiers had come, from the direction of the Owens house. It was a woman's scream. Lucy?!? Hannah didn't even stop to pick up her journal or her shoes. She just took off running barefoot up the dirt road toward Lucy's house. Her feet were flying, and her heart was pounding.

She rounded a bend and saw something in the middle of the road. Somebody was laying there. Was that Lucy bent over them? She kept running and came up on the scene and her heart plummeted when she saw it was Daniel laying on the dirt road. She fell down next to him and cried "Daniel! What happened?" Daniel wasn't responding. Then she saw the blood. She stared up at Lucy, whose face was white with fear.

"They shot him!" Lucy cried out. "Those men on the horses! Did you see them?"

"Why? Why did they shoot him?"

"They called him a coward and said he was a deserter and then they just shot him!"

"Lucy, get your Pa!" Hannah yelled. Lucy jumped up and ran to her house. Hannah sat next to Daniel and put his head in her lap. He wasn't responding at all, but his chest was still moving up and down. He was still alive! But, Hannah was terrified that at any moment his chest would stop moving. She prayed and prayed and tears were rolling down her face. "Oh, God! Please don't take Daniel. Please!!!" She kept thinking "Why is it taking so long to get Rev. Owens?" She just kept talking to Daniel and asking him to please hang on, please keep breathing.

Finally, Lucy and Rev. Owens came back with a horse and wagon. Rev. Owens took one look at Daniel and said "Oh, no! Oh, Dear God, no!" He ordered the girls to help him get Daniel up in the wagon. They then took off quickly back to Hannah's house.

Upon arrival Elijah and Sarah and all the children came running out. "What happened?" Sarah cried.

"He was shot!" yelled Hannah. "Hurry, get him in the house."

Jesse ran up and when he saw the blood on his brother, he said "Who? Who shot him?"

Lucy said "Some soldiers. They came riding by on their horses."

"Where did they go?"

"Toward town. They just kept going."

Jesse, believing his brother was dead, took off running toward the barn. He untied one of the horses and jumped on bareback and tore out of there in a cloud of dust, chasing after the soldiers.

Hannah saw him and yelled out "Jesse! No!", but he was already gone and out of sight. All Hannah could do was turn back to Daniel and try to keep him alive. Everything was out of control and she felt so useless. She couldn't save Daniel, she couldn't stop Jesse. She had no power and the world around her was crumbling at her feet.

As all these thoughts were going through her head, Hannah was helping to carry Daniel into the house. Elijah told them to just lay Daniel on his bed on the main floor, so they didn't have to try carrying him up to his own bed. Hannah sent 13 year old Albert to fetch Grandma Harris, because she knew a lot of natural remedies and cures that could maybe help save Daniel's life. Albert started running toward the trail to his grandparents' home, but then Hannah yelled "No, not on foot! Take one of the horses! You can get her back quicker!" So, Albert went to the barn and got a horse and took off to get Grandma. In the meantime, Sarah and Hannah were washing and cleaning Daniel's wound. The wound was in his left shoulder. Elijah said he was hopeful that nothing major was hit.

The Inman family came running across the creek after hearing the commotion. In the middle of it all, with people running everywhere, fear in everyone's hearts, some crying, some asking "what happened?", all at once there was a loud booming sound. It sounded like another gunshot, coming from down the road to the west. All the talking and crying stopped abruptly, and the people all turned to look toward the direction of the loud noise. There was an eerie quiet, and nobody was moving. Then, softly in the distance, the sound of horse's hooves. It grew louder and louder. At first Hannah thought "Oh, thank God, Jesse is coming back", but then from around the bend came Jesse's horse... with no rider. It ran past them all and straight to the barn, the one place it felt safe.

The powerful realization of what just occurred swept through the crowd. Hannah screamed "Jesse!" and led the crowd as many of them took off running down the road in the direction the horse had come from. They ran around the bend and down the road until they were almost to the Bennett's home. Then, in the settling dust up ahead in the road they saw the most heartbreaking sight. William Bennett was standing in the road facing them, holding Jesse in his arms. He had one arm under Jesse's back, and the other under his knees. Jesse's head and arms were hanging down, lifeless. William was walking toward them, fear in his eyes. They all ran up and took Jesse from William's arms. But, it was too late. Jesse was gone. Hannah screamed in rage.

"This is madness! This is complete and utter madness! Make it stop, God! Make it stop!"

Hannah was broken. She had never felt more helpless in all her young life. How easily a life can be taken, and for what? He was just a boy! Just a 15 year old boy! So much life ahead of him. So much promise. Now gone. Just gone forever!

She felt anger. She wanted revenge. She wanted to run through the hills tearing up every tree, throwing every rock and smashing them into a thousand pieces, cursing at God until there was no voice left inside her.

But, all those feelings were stuffed down into a place that was becoming very crowded. She walked along as William and Henry carried Jesse's body down the road back to his father. As they walked, William explained what had just happened.

He said "I heard horse riders go past my house. They weren't running, just going along at a slow pace. I didn't run out because Martha was afraid they could be coming after me. I watched from behind a window curtain and saw Jesse coming behind them. Before I could even have time to understand what was going on, Jesse caught up to the riders and started screaming 'You killed my brother!' I was so confused! His brother? Which brother?"

The others explained that Daniel had been shot, but wasn't dead... yet.

William was stunned. "Oh, my God! Now it makes sense."

He continued and said that the soldiers pulled their horses to a stop and turned to face Jesse. They laughed in his face and said "You will be next, boy!" Jesse didn't even have a weapon on him. He was just angry, yelling words of revenge. Then, one of the soldiers said "He will grow up to be a coward and a deserter just like his brother. Might as well take him out now." And he just pointed his gun and shot! Jesse fell off the horse, dead immediately. The horse was scared and took off running for home. The soldiers turned and trotted off, laughing.

"I ran out and saw that Jesse was dead," William continued. "All I could think was that I had to get him home, home to his family. I was just trying to carry him home," he said, as he broke down in tears.

About that time they rounded the bend and the others came running out to see what was going on. When Elijah saw his little boy, it was as if something snapped inside him. He changed in an instant. Hannah saw it. Everyone else saw it, too. Elijah Casey was no longer passive. Elijah Casey became a man with a cause. Elijah Casey would never be the same again.

Two of Hannah's brothers now lay wounded, one dead, one who might die at any moment. Jesse was laid out on the front porch and covered with a sheet. Hannah cried every time she walked past, but right now it was Daniel who needed her attention. She knew the task of cleaning up Jesse for burial would come soon enough, and it was not a task she ever thought she'd be called to perform.

She and the other women cleaned Daniel's wounds as best they could. Now it was just a waiting game.

Hannah was defeated, exhausted, numb. She saw her father sitting on the porch and she went to him. She fell into his arms and cried like she was a little girl again. Izzy and Lottie saw them and they came over and they just piled themselves together and bawled. They had been through so much loss. When would it stop? How much more could they take?

Elijah held his three daughters, knowing there was nothing he could do to stop their pain, but hoping just being there was enough. He knew that holding them in his arms was a healing balm to him, so he hoped they felt the same. He didn't know how he was going to comfort his young sons. Sarah was keeping the little boys out of the way for now, but Albert still didn't know, for he had went to fetch Grandma and Grandpa. Oh, how devastated he was going to be when he came home to see his closest brother, his lifelong roommate, dead on the porch. Elijah wasn't sure he had the resolve to deal with it all, but somehow he did.

Everyone in the little community was now at the Casey home. Grandma had arrived and was using various natural herbs to make a poultice for Daniel's wound. She had learned many healing secrets throughout her long life. Hannah was watching and paying close attention. When Grandma explained what she was mixing together, Hannah made a point to write it down in her journal. She was beginning to understand the importance of many things in life that she'd only taken for granted before.

Throughout the rest of that evening and all night long, a watch was kept over Daniel, and someone was always sitting with Jesse's body, as well. In those days, it was believed someone must always be sitting with the body, up until the time it was buried. Hannah took her turn and sat on the porch holding her dead brother's hand and crying. His hand was already hard to the touch, but it was still little Jesse's hand, and she wanted to hold it, because somehow it comforted her, and she hoped that if he hadn't quite made his journey to Heaven yet, then maybe it was comforting him, too. She would have sat there all night in order to keep him from being alone, but around 3 a.m. Albert came and said he would take a turn. Hannah walked away and felt crushed, knowing how hard this was for Albert, but also knowing that he needed to do this. He needed to do this to help with closure, to help with the process of his grief. "Oh, Albert..." she thought. "You are such a brave and strong boy."

Lucy stayed by Daniel's side throughout. She helped Grandma Harris and did everything she was told to do, in hopes that they could save the life of the man she loved. Lucy continued to sit with Daniel the next day when the other women were washing and cleaning Jesse's body and preparing it for burial. That evening Lucy again stayed with Daniel while everyone else solomnly carried Jesse's body down to the cemetery and held a small ceremony. He was laid to rest next to his mother, the 4th grave in the little cemetery.

Once again Hannah found herself feeling the unfairness of it all. It didn't seem right that life just continued on for everyone else, while little Jesse's life was snuffed out. The void she was already feeling because of his absence was shattering. She would never again hear the sound of his footsteps running through the house, or the sound of his voice, so full of exuberance. She looked at her mother's grave and for once was glad she wasn't here to witness this loss of yet another child.

That evening Daniel finally awakened. He was in terrible pain, but he seemed somewhat lucid. No one told him of the death of Jesse. It was best to wait until he was stronger. Lucy held on tight to him and nursed him constantly. Hannah was in and out, checking on him, but with Lucy by his side, she knew he was well taken care of. Grandma, also, was still there, tending to the wound, trying to keep infection from setting in. Hannah spent most of her time helping with meals, and taking care of all her siblings.

There was a constant fear among the townspeople that more soldiers would come through. The men and older boys took turns keeping lookout at the road and along the creek banks.

Albert was struggling, dealing with the loss of his brother Jesse. Suddenly, he was alone in his room at night. Harding Inman offered to come stay nights with Albert for awhile, to help him get through. The three boys, Harding, Jesse & Albert, had always ran around together as a trio. They were rarely seen apart. It was hard for them to have lost one of their group. It left a huge, gaping hole. Harding knew he could not replace Jesse, but it truly was a help to Albert having him there. It gave him someone to talk to when the loneliness and grief snuck in in the deepest depths of the night. Harding felt Jesse would have expected him to step in like he did. It was the least he could do for his dearly departed friend. Truth be told, Harding was also struggling. Now, not only had his older brother gone off to war, but now his best friend was gone, too. Albert was just as much a help to Harding as Harding was to Albert. The two boys clung to each other for support in the days and weeks ahead.

After a few days, Daniel had enough strength that he was moved upstairs into the room with Albert. Harding was able to go back home, and Daniel and Albert kept each other company. By now Daniel had been told about Jesse. It kept him sick to his stomach and he couldn't eat, but everyone was urging him to eat to keep his strength up. He just kept thinking how unfair it was. If only Jesse had waited to see that he was not dead. It wasn't worth this loss. "Dear, dear Jesse. You always were so impulsive, but so protective of those you loved. You paid the ultimate price."

After eight days, Daniel was finally strong enough to come out onto the porch and sit for a bit. Lucy felt the fresh mountain air would be good for him. They were sitting together, watching some of the children playing in the yard, when Daniel suddenly looked over at Lucy and said "Marry me."

She said "Of course, Daniel. I already said I would."

He said "No, I mean, now... today. Marry me today."

She thought he had lost his mind, but at the same time, she thought of how quickly life can be lost, how fleeting time could be. The last few days had taught her that. She realized that she didn't want to wait one more day, either, to become Mrs. Daniel Casey. So, she said yes. She called out to Hannah and told her of the plan. She asked Hannah if she could go get her pa so he could marry them.

It wasn't safe to walk alone, so she took Harding and Albert with her. They fetched Rev. Owens and his wife Winnie, and brought them back to the Casey home. And, right there on the porch, Rev. Owens married his 17 year old daughter to 19 year old Daniel Casey. It was almost a solemn occasion, rather than a celebratory one.

Four days later, Daniel was feeling much better. It seemed Grandma's poultices had staved off any major infection. It still hurt to move his left arm, but Daniel was on the mend, and feeling very trapped inside that house. Also, being newly married, he was anxious to begin his life alone with Lucy. So, he told his Pa he was ready to move across the creek to Sarah's old house.

Although he was concerned it was too soon, and that Daniel might try to do too much too quickly, Elijah felt resigned to allow Daniel to move. So, everyone helped them move some things across the creek. Some of Sarah's old furnishings were still in the home, so they had a good start. All they had to do was bring over a few linens, and some kitchen items, which the other women donated to the newly married couple. Lucy's mother gave her quite a few things. Elijah and Sarah agreed to give the couple one of their cows and some chickens.

As the last load of items was being carried over, Albert cautiously asked his older brother if maybe, just maybe, he could come stay with him. He promised he would be a help to him while his arm healed. He could do most of the heavy work at first. Daniel wanted to be alone with his new bride, but at the same time, he thought of Albert all alone in that room again at night, and he couldn't tell him no. He felt Albert's place was with him. Elijah, surprisingly, agreed to the plan.

So, Daniel, Lucy and 13 year old Albert moved across the

creek. The Madison home had been built as a small one-story home with three bedrooms. Daniel and Lucy took the largest room, and they strategically put Albert in the room furthest from theirs, so he couldn't hear any noises coming from their room at night. The third room, in the middle, would just be used as storage for now. Lucy had not felt comfortable, after her marriage to Daniel, sleeping with him in the bed in his parents' home, so she had continued to live with her parents a half a mile away, knowing that it would only be a few more days until Daniel was healed enough that they could move in together. So, despite being married for four days, the two had not had their actual wedding night yet, and both of them were anxious to finally consummate their marriage.

This move left an empty room at the Casey home where Daniel and Albert used to sleep, so Sarah did some rearranging. She moved the youngest two girls, Rachel and Ruby, to Albert's old room in the left wing. So, now they were on the same side as the three little boys, who were still sharing the room that they always called 'the nursery'. Then, in the right wing of the house, she kept the oldest two girls, Hannah and Izzy, together in one room, but had Charlotte move out and go share a room with Rebecca, since they were the two middle girls out of the six. Hannah was glad to have a little more room in the bed now, since she was only sharing it with one girl instead of two, but it took her a few nights to get past this unexpected feeling of loneliness, not having little Charlotte there to talk to as she drifted off to sleep. She missed her just being there.

July

Somehow the world kept turning and the sun kept rising each morning. Most everyone was still grieving over Jesse, and several times a day Hannah found herself feeling as if she'd been stabbed in the heart, because something would make her think about her brother. It was so difficult. Would this feeling ever go away? She tried to stay busy so she wouldn't think about him as much. There was plenty of work to be done in the gardens. It hadn't rained in awhile, so everyone was having to carry buckets of water to the plants to keep them alive. Berries were ripening in the wild. Hannah and her sisters had started picking blackberries from the thickets down by the creek. Hannah and Sarah wanted to make blackberry jam, but they were running very low on sugar. So, Sarah told her husband that maybe it was time for a supply run to town.

Elijah didn't like the idea of leaving, but things had been quiet for a few weeks. No soldiers had been wandering through. He and Henry talked and agreed that Henry and the Reverend would stay to look out for the women and children, while Elijah went to town, taking young Albert and Harding with him. After the loss of Jesse, it would be good for the two boys to get away from the memories for awhile and experience something new.

Hannah begged her Pa to let her go with him, too. She had never been to town, and she could be of so much help to him. Elijah said no, out of habit, but then Sarah pulled him aside and said "Elijah, dear... Take Hannah with you. Do it for me. Hannah needs a change of scenery. You can't treat her like she's a helpless girl. She will be as much a help to you as those boys, I can promise you that."

Hannah had never loved her stepmother more than at that moment. When Elijah reluctantly agreed to take her, Hannah ran and hugged Sarah.

The next morning, the wagon was loaded up with a few items that Elijah wanted to trade in town. The horses were tied to the wagon and ready to start out. There was a small seat big enough for just two people, meant for the driver of the wagon. Most of the time, Pa would be driving the horses while the other three walked alongside. Pa said they might ride in the wagon some on the flatter parts of the road, but going up or down the mountainside, it was easier on the horses to have less weight to pull. Pa would even get down himself in the roughest parts, and just guide the horses with their reins.

Hannah was amazed at everything they saw along their journey. She had lived in these mountains most of her life, but had no idea just how far away from everything they truly were, because since the age of six she had never left the mountain. Her memories of the trip up here had mostly faded from her brain. Being only six at the time, she probably wasn't paying that much attention to her surroundings, anyway. She had not remembered what a perilous trip it was, and how steep the trails were that her father had always taken. In some places, the drop-offs on the sides of the trails were amazingly steep, and seemed to disappear into an abyss. One misstep of the horse and all would go over to their deaths. It made Hannah's heart race with fear! But, it was exhilarating just the same. And, beautiful! The views were astounding! It seemed she could see forever from the top of the mountain.

About mid-day they stopped to rest and eat. The horses had been allowed to drink at each stream or creek that they crossed, and at one point they had stopped to drink from a natural spring that was running out of the side of the mountain. It was the coldest, clearest water Hannah had ever tasted. But, now that they were stopping for a longer rest, the horses were given some oats that Pa had brought along. Hannah, Elijah, Harding and Albert sat down in a spot where the trail curved back onto itself as it made it's way down the mountain. There was a worn out place where it looked as if others had stopped to rest in the past. After they ate, the boys were walking about exploring and they came running back saying they found some sort of trail leading off down the side of the mountain. Elijah said "Yes, that trail goes down to some rocks that hang out over the ledge. I've been down it before." Well, of course, he now had to take the children down to see it, too.

It was a steep climb down, but when they made it to the rock overhang, Hannah knew it was worth the trip. She could see forever! Pa pointed to a spot way, way down at the bottom and off in the distance and said "Clarksville is down there." Hannah squinted, but couldn't see anything. She commented that they must be close then, but Pa said "Oh, your eyes are deceiving. We have many hours to go, still." Hannah watched a hawk flying across the huge chasm spread out before her, and thought how free that hawk must feel. If only humans could fly like that!

The remainder of the day was not as exciting as the first part. Everyone was getting extremely tired, and impatient to finally see the town. Once they made it to the bottom of the mountain, the land flattened out and they were able to speed up a bit. After another hour or so they began to see signs of civilization. They had not seen a soul all day on the road, but now they saw a house here and there, with people milling about outside, or working in their gardens, or sitting on their porches having a glass of lemonade. Occasionally someone would pass them walking on the road, or riding on a horse. As they passed, the men would tip their hats and say "How do?" All of the people seemed so friendly, and some of the women and children would stop what they were doing and wave at them in greeting. Hannah always waved back. She had been so sheltered all her life. It was exciting to see all of these new people.

Hannah asked her pa if they were in Clarksville now. He said "Not quite. This little area here is called Harmony. A little further on we will pass through Woodland, and then after that is Clarksville."

"What a pretty name!" Hannah said. "I would like to live in a place called Harmony. I wonder why they call it that?"

Pa said "Well, I heard once that it was named Harmony because when the settlers first came here, they were all of many different religious denominations, but they wanted a church, so they all met and worshiped together, in harmony, despite their religious differences. So, they decided to simply call the place Harmony."

"What a wonderful story!" Hannah exclaimed.

Pa told her that they were in the river valley, because the Arkansas River ran through here, very near the town of Clarksville. The town was situated north of the river, on the banks of Spadra Creek, which drained into the river.

Hannah said "Spadra is another unique name. I wonder why they call it Spadra."

Pa said "Well, as it happens, I heard a story about that, too. If you liked that last story, you'll really like this one. You see, there is a community called Spadra, too, which is past Clarksville, on down Spadra Creek a ways, closer to the river. I reckon the creek and the community were named after the same thing. What I heard was that many, many years ago, when it was mostly only Indians living here in this part of Arkansas, a Spanish settler landed in Florida. He was told by the Indians in Florida that there was gold farther to the northwest, so this settler set out, probably going up the Mississippi River, and then following the Arkansas River until he came to this area. The story goes that he met an Indian maiden here, and fell in love with her. But, the Indian maiden had been promised in marriage by her father to another Indian from their tribe. The girl didn't love that man, though. She loved the Spanish explorer, so she agreed to run away with him."

Hannah's eyes lit up. She loved a good love story. "Did they live happily ever after?"

"Well, no," Pa said. "As they were running to the river to escape, the girl's pa found out and got a group of braves together to go after them. When they caught up to them, a battle ensued. The Spanish explorer was fighting valiantly for his love, but at one point she saw a man coming toward him, and fearing it would be a fatal blow, she jumped in front of her love to save him. The blow meant for the explorer hit the Indian maiden instead, killing her. When the explorer saw this, he became enraged and began swinging his sword and fighting with everything he had. But, somehow, one of his thrusts sent his sword into a rock, where the point of it stuck fast, and the blade broke off. Without his weapon, he was defenseless, and he was also killed."

"Oh, no!" Hannah said. "This is not a happy story at all, is it?"

"No, it's not," Pa agreed. "However, the legend lives on. Because many years later, another party of Spanish explorers came through, and one of them saw the sword, still stuck in the rock, and yelled out 'Spadra!', which some say was the Spanish word for sword, or possibly what the people heard and remembered as the Spanish word. Anyway, the name stuck, and the area began to be referred to as Spadra from there on out."

"What a romantic story!" Hannah said. "I think I'll write that story down later in my journal."

"Well, I can't guarantee you that it's true. It's just a story that was told to me. But, it's an interesting story, regardless. No one has ever told me any other reason why Spadra got its name."

As they pulled into town near dusk, Hannah's mouth just dropped open with amazement. She had tried to imagine what town was like, but it was far more than she had pictured in her head. Before her were several buildings. The biggest one seemed to be in the center. Pa told her that was the courthouse. He explained that the town had been designed and laid out so that the courthouse would be in the center, with other buildings built in rows on each of the four sides of the courthouse, forming a town square. She could see that a square was beginning to form, as a few buildings had already been erected, and some were in the process of being built, but there was still a lot of work to be done. Pa said that the town had been incorporated in 1848, so it was only officially 14 years old. It would take time to get it looking like a real town square.

Elijah drove them around town a bit so they could see everything. He took them past a beautiful Methodist church with pretty stained glass windows. Hannah wondered what it looked like on the inside. He took them to the East side of town and showed them the bridge that crossed over Spadra Creek. On the opposite side of the creek was a bluff line, and Hannah could see a few homes built up on the bluff, where they had a commanding view of the courthouse and the town.

It was getting dark, so Elijah pulled the horses off to a grassy area behind one of the buildings and stated that they would stay there for the night. They would sleep in the wagon, or make beds on the ground near the wagon. They got some food out and ate a quick supper. A night of sleep sounded so welcoming after such a long day. Hannah made her bedding and laid down, but it was extremely hard to sleep in such a new and fascinating place.

The next morning they woke and had a meager breakfast, then cared for the horses. Pa looked around in the wagon to see what he had that he might be able to trade that day. There were people beginning to mill about, horses and buggies here and there clopping along on the dirt streets. On the courthouse square there were some men standing around a table with a Confederate flag hanging from it. As they passed by the men yelled toward Pa "Come join the southern army!" Pa tipped his hat, but kept walking.

Hannah saw a man opening up a shop, standing out front sweeping with a broom. He nodded toward them. After awhile, she began to notice women walking around in very poofy dresses, some carrying strange sticks over their heads with material stretched out at the top. She'd never seen anything like it. Up on the mountain, the women wore very simple dresses, and they just hung straight. Hannah could not understand why the women here would want their dresses to stick out so. Wouldn't it be hard to sit, or to do your chores? And, what was that stick they held in their hands? What was the purpose of that?

"Pa, why do the women's dresses stick out so?"

Elijah explained that they had a hoop underneath, and many other layers of things that he wasn't quite sure of. "I think there's something called a petticoat, and something called a bustle. I'm not sure to be honest. They have layers and layers of things under there."

"I don't understand. I suppose it's pretty in its own way, but not very functional, now, is it?"

Pa smiled. "Well, these women have a much easier life than you, my dear Hannah. Some of them have slaves to perform their chores for them, so they have a leisurely life of just sitting around in the shade reading books and fanning themselves."

"Hmmmm. That sounds good in theory, but seems rather boring."

"Hannah, my dear, some would say *they* have the better life, but if you ask me, *you* are the lucky one."

"What is that stick thing they are carrying?"

Pa laughed when he realized just how remote Hannah's

upbringing had truly been. "You have never seen a parasol? Well, the idea is to keep the sun off their delicate faces so they can retain a pale coloring. The paler the better. You see, the poorer you are, the more likely you are to work out in the hot sun all day and get tanned and burned skin. Slaves have dark skin. So, the whiter your skin, the more proof that you are of higher class, and you don't have to work outdoors. And, maybe it's just a bit of a fashion statement as well. The well-off woman wouldn't be seen without her parasol when outdoors!" Pa rolled his eyes as if the "well off" woman didn't really impress him all that much.

Hannah said "It would be impossible to get *anything* done with two hands, if one was always holding that, what do you call it?...Parasol? What silliness!"

Pa said he agreed wholeheartedly!

But it didn't stop Hannah from reaching up and touching her own tanned face and wondering what these women must be thinking about her.

As they walked around a bit more, Hannah noticed several of the men wearing hats that were really tall. Pa said it was a stovepipe hat. He said President Lincoln wore them, so the men wanted to be like him and copied him. "But, much like those poofy dresses, I don't think those hats are very functional either," he said, as he winked at Hannah.

One of the first things Pa did that morning was go to the edge of town where it looked like someone was building a new store. Pa asked the men if they needed some boards, because he'd brought down a few boards from the mountains that he had cut in his sawmill. They were good strong pine boards. The men looked them over and agreed to purchase them. So, Pa now had a little money in his pocket.

Pa then took the children to the general store where they traded for all the sugar, salt, flour, baking powder, matches, coffee, sewing thread and candles that Sarah had said they needed for the house. Sarah had also suggested that if he felt it in his heart to do so, Daniel and Lucy did not have a coffee pot for their new home. So, Pa picked up the cheapest one they had for sell, a simple tin one that could be placed on top of the coals to heat, with a strainer in the top to place the coffee grounds in.

At the counter there was some candy. Pa had brought candy treats home to the children before, but Hannah and Albert had never actually been in a store and seen it all for sell in one place like that. Pa allowed them to each pick one piece, and one piece to take home to each of the other children. For himself, Pa chose some nice fragrant cigars for a treat. For Sarah, he asked Hannah to pick out her favorite print of fabric so that Sarah might make herself a new dress.

As they were about to go pay the man at the counter, Hannah noticed a table with some very pretty journals and books on it. She was looking through them, longing to have something so pretty to do her writing in. One journal was so beautiful, with flowers etched on the front and a gold clasp that folded around and hooked to keep the pages closed. She picked it up and flipped through the clean, crisp pages, and imagined what a thrill it would be to fill those pages up with stories and thoughts.

Elijah came up behind her and said "You should get it."

"No, Pa. I know there are more important things that you need to trade for."

"Hannah..." he said. "Why don't you go and get some of your canned goods and see if you can make a trade?"

Hannah said "But, Pa, I brought those for you to trade with."

"*You* made those things yourself," Pa said. "All the effort was yours. You put in the time, and you had the wisdom to know how to do it. That makes these things worth something. And, when an item is worth something, you can trade it."

With much excitement, Hannah ran out to the wagon and dug around to find the items she had brought. Carefully packed in wooden crates that Pa and Henry had crafted at the sawmill, with hay stuffed all around so the jars wouldn't break, were some canned goods Hannah had made that summer. There were twenty jars of dill pickles and a dozen jars of purple hull jelly. She lifted them out, examined them to see if any were broken, which thankfully, none were, and she carried them into the store.

The proprietor of the store looked at them and said "I have plenty of pickles and jelly," and he motioned toward a shelf to his left that was loaded with various foods in jars. Hannah felt disheartened. She was about to say "okay" and give up, but something inside her stirred and she grabbed a jar of pickles and said "But, sir! These are not just any old pickles. These are *dill* pickles. My neighbor, Irene, taught me how to make them. If you ask me, they are ten times better than the sweet ones. I bet you don't have any dill pickles in your store."

The man picked up a jar and said "Dill pickles, huh? Well, I suppose you're right. I only have sweet pickles here in the store. But, I don't know... I have so many pickles."

Hannah grabbed a jar and opened it and said "Try one! If you taste it, there is no way you will say no!"

The man tasted one and said "Well, I declare! These are really good! And, different! Ok, you talked me into it. But, what else ya got?"

Hannah showed him her purple hull jelly. The man said "It looks like grape jelly."

She said "And it tastes like grape jelly, too! But, it's not made from grapes! My grandma taught me how to make jelly from purple hull peas!"

The man looked at her quizzically, as if he didn't believe her. She said "No, really! Grandma said when times are tough you have to make do with what you have, so she learned to make jelly from pea hulls. See, after you pick your peas from the garden and take all the peas from out of the hulls, instead of throwing the hulls to the hogs, you take them and put them in a big pan of water and boil them. Soon, the water turns purple. Then, you strain the water out and add sugar and pectin and cook until it gets thick. I promise, you would never know it wasn't made from grapes!"

The store owner was enchanted by Hannah and her spiel. He told her that if she would give him all her jars, she could have the fancy journal she liked so much. Hannah agreed and squealed with delight, but as she reached for the journal, she had a second thought. "Mister, if I were to take the plainer journal instead, the plain brown one without the fancy gold clasp, then could I take a few of those empty jars over there, so I can make some more pickles and jelly?"

The man liked her entrepreneurial spirit, so he agreed. Hannah picked up the plainer journal, telling herself that the pages inside were the important part, not the fancy outside. She could write the same words in a plain journal as she could in a fancy one. And, best of all, she now had more jars so she could make more canned items and trade for more things.

Elijah had stood back and watched his daughter the whole time, and he was very impressed. "Hannah, you might make a fine businesswoman some day. I didn't know you had it in ya. Maybe I should be letting you bargain for *my* goods, too!" Hannah beamed! To see pride in her father's eyes, and knowing she put it there, it was the best feeling in the world.

As they were about to leave the store, the store owner said "What was your name again?"

"Hannah. My name is Hannah Casey."

"Well, I think I'll make a special table for these and put a sign on the front that says 'Hannah's Specials'. If these sell good, I might be interested in buying more."

"Did you hear that Pa?!" Hannah said. "Oh, thank you, sir! Thank you so much!"

Elijah then went to another store where he traded some raccoon and rabbit skins that he'd tanned for some lead alloy that he needed to make bullets for his guns. He also got some black powder that he would need in order to shoot those bullets. He looked longingly at some muskets that were for sell, but knew he could not afford such a thing.

Finally, they made their way to the post office. Hannah had been waiting all day to find out if there was any news of Joseph. She was so nervous as she listened to her Pa asking the man at the window if there was any mail addressed to "Casey". The man said he had one item. He showed it to Elijah and he said "Yes, that's mine."

The letter was addressed to Emeline Casey. Hannah said "Pa, why would it be addressed to Ma? She's been gone almost a year now."

Elijah said "Well, I wasn't able to get a letter off to her family until two months after she died. I sent one down with Henry when he came to Clarksville last fall. Most likely this letter was mailed before they ever received my letter. It's been sitting here for months because no one had been here to pick it up." Hannah thought it was extremely sad that someone was writing to Ma, not even knowing that Ma wasn't even alive to receive the letter. She asked her Pa who it was who had written and he said "Your aunt Caroline, your mother's sister. From back in Tennessee."

Hannah then asked the man to check again, surely there was something for Hannah Casey. But, he insisted there wasn't. Hannah had so hoped for a letter from Joe.

Elijah then asked if there was any mail for "Harris", "Inman", "Owens" or "Bennett", because any time one of the mountain folk were able to make a rare trip to town, they always checked to see if anyone else had mail.

The man at the counter looked through his slots of mail and pulled out two things for Jackson Owens, and one for Mrs. Henry Inman. He said he didn't see anything with the names Harris or Bennett on it. Elijah took them all and handed them to Hannah. Hannah questioned the man if he was sure there was nothing for her Grandma and Grandpa Harris, but Pa reminded her that they couldn't read, so generally their other children had always just written to Emeline, who would then read the letters to her parents. Hannah then said "Pa, should you not ask for 'Madison', too, since Sarah's family doesn't know she is Sarah Casey now?" Pa thanked Hannah for thinking of it, because it hadn't crossed his mind. And, sure enough, there was a letter for Sarah, too.

Sarah's letter was from her mother, and was very fancy, on pretty stationery that was sealed with red wax and had an "H" stamped into the wax. Hannah remembered that Sarah's maiden name had been Huff, and that her mother, still having that last name, would have an "H" for her letter seal. The rest of the correspondence was just written on simple, crude paper, folded over into thirds. Writing was squeezed in in all directions all over the paper, so as to get as much on the sheet as possible, and after it had been folded, the name and post office of the intended person was simply written on the part of the fold that was facing out.

Hannah and the others went back to the wagon to sit down and have a bite to eat and read some of the letters. She handed Harding the letter addressed to his mother so he could read it. Then, she opened the one from her aunt that was addressed to Emeline. She read it out loud to all of them, although it was a bit difficult because Aunt Caroline had not had much schooling and her spelling was not the best.

Dearest Sister,

I take the opertunity of riteing you a fiew lines to let you know that we ar all still in the land of the living and ar faring as well as can be ecspected. Philip has bin sick but is better now thanks be to God for his mercy. I am hopeing when this comes to your loveing hands it may find you injoying the same like blessing of God. I hain't got mutch to write but I want to see and hear from you mighty bad. I want to no how you are doing and how you like that country or if you think you will ever come back to your old home. The war is bad here. I see fragements of redgements dayly. I pray that you have peace and you must guess how lonsom I feel that you ar so very far away. I want you all to rite to me. Tell Ma and Pa I miss them somethun feerse. Do take down sum words from them and send my way. James Calhoun is dead. He died of small pox the 26 of October. I hain't had narry a letter from

Arthur or Hugh since they goed off to war. Louisa lost her baby. God bless hits little soul. I fear you may be on suferance due to war. Rite to me to ease a worried mind. Give my love to Eli and the children. Tell them I hain't forgot them. Kiss Hannah for me and let her laff a holy laff like she did when I kist her last and kiss Daniel too. Tell him not to marry and never come back to see his dear old aunt Caroline. I wish to be remembered by all your children. Farewell for awhile. We'll soon meet again if kind providense will smile. We have suffered long and we suffer still but blessed is the one who perserveers for that person will reseev the crown of life that the Lord has promisd to those that love him.

My love to you all,
Caroline Perryman
to Emeline Casey, Elijah Casey,
Joshua Harris and Ruth Harris

Hannah laid the letter down in her lap. "Uncle Calhoun is dead, and Uncle Arthur and Uncle Hugh are off to war. And, poor Aunt Louisa, losing her baby like that." Louisa had been a teenager when Hannah and her family left Tennessee. She had a vague memory of her, and a vague memory of her aunt Caroline. But, she really couldn't remember the uncles that where mentioned in the letter. She only knew of them by hearing her mother and grandmother talk about them. But, she knew her Pa could remember them all.

Hannah tucked the letter into her new journal and told Pa she would read it to Grandma and Grandpa as soon as they got back home. But, she wasn't looking forward to being the one to bring them the news that their grown son was now dead of small pox, and their daughter had lost a baby. It seemed the only news anyone got any more was bad news.

Hannah knew it wasn't polite to read someone else's private correspondence, but the Owens mail was practically falling open, and she couldn't keep her eyes from straying. She saw that the letters were from Rev. Owens' oldest son, Alexander, who still lived back in Tennessee. She couldn't help but see that Alexander, in both letters, was pleading for his parents, and his little brother Abraham and little sister Lucy, to come home. He would even come fetch them if need be. Surely they were tired of living that experiment in the mountains of Arkansas. All their children missed them, and the grandchildren, too. It was foolhardy to be living so far away and in such a remote place, when all their family was in Tennessee.

Hannah felt a sickness in her stomach again when she realized that Alexander didn't know yet that his baby brother had been killed in the war, and he didn't know yet that his baby sister was married. Things changed so quickly and mail was so slow. It was impossible to keep a family informed in a timely manner.

Later that afternoon Elijah wanted to go around and see what news he could find out about the war. He told the children to stay with the wagon while he did some investigating. He made his way over to the soldiers who were sitting at the court house trying to get men to enlist. As he walked up he heard "...that skirmish over at Cotton Plant. Ol' Rust failed to stop them damn Yankees." When the men saw Elijah they stopped and said "You signin' up mister?"

Elijah said "No, just lookin' to get any news."

"What's yer name fella?"

"Elijah Casey's the name. I'm from up yonder in them mountains." He motioned toward the peaks off in the distance to the north. "I don't get much news up in them parts."

Elijah noticed some young soldiers standing off to the side, whispering and motioning toward him. One of them finally said "You related to that Casey boy they shot up?"

Elijah bristled and said "Yes, he's my son." He felt his anger rising. Were these the boys who did it?

He came toward them in somewhat of a threatening manner. One of them said "Hold on now there! Ain't my fault your boy's a deserter. Cain't expect no sympathy for a coward."

Elijah had heard enough. He grabbed the boy and threw him to the ground and began pummeling him with his fists. The other boys jumped in and started punching Elijah, but he was holding his own pretty good. Finally the other men standing around grabbed ahold of them and began pulling them apart. Elijah was ready to kill that boy. As another man held him back he yelled out "You killed my younger boy, too! He didn't do a damn thing to you! He was no deserter! He wasn't even old enough to enlist!"

Then the boy said "I didn't kill him! I just heard about it. I know the man that did it, but it wasn't me."

Elijah shook his arm loose from the man who was holding him. He said "Who was it then? Give me his name."

The boy said "No, I won't do it. I'd a done the same, truth be told. Any damn coward that won't fight for our boys must be favorin' the other side. Or he's a damn girl!" Elijah lunged again but was held back by two burly men. He yelled out "It doesn't look to me like *you're* out there fightin' either! Are *you* a coward? What are you doin' just standin' around at the courthouse? By your definition, I'd say that makes you a coward, too!"

A crowd was forming and Hannah and the boys had left the wagon and ran over. Elijah began to realize that he did not have the numbers for this fight, so he backed off. He had fire in his eyes as he made his way to their horses and wagon, with Hannah and the boys right behind him. He said "Let's go" and untied the horses. Hannah had understood they were to stay one more night before heading home, but she could tell Pa was serious about leaving, and besides, if they stayed, she wasn't sure that Pa could stay out of trouble. She wasn't sure they were safe.

"We can't go in the dark, can we?" she asked Elijah.

He said "No, but we'll go as far as we can, then camp somewhere safer tonight. I can't be anywhere near those sorry excuses for men."

They got as far as the foot of the mountain, then stopped and made camp for the night. The boys collected wood for a fire. After the fire was going good, Hannah got out the iron skillet she'd brought along, and mixed up some batter for johnny cakes. She made several of them and served them with some dried jerky meat and some tomatoes and cucumbers that she'd picked from the garden just before they left.

Albert and Harding seemed excited about the fight they'd witnessed. Albert said "Pa, you had them good! You still got some fight in ya, for an old man." Elijah just grunted. Truth be told, he was hurting all over from the beating. He wasn't proud of the fighting, but he would do it again in a heartbeat if he could find the man, or men, who did this to his boys. At 39, he didn't think of himself, necessarily, as an "old" man. But, he had to admit, he probably couldn't have taken them all on if the fight hadn't been broken up. It would be hard for any one man to take on several at a time.

Hannah had felt a touch of pride, as well, seeing her father stand up like that for his children. But, more than anything she was just worried for his safety. She was happy they had moved out of town before camping for the night.

"Pa," she said. "I don't know that I like Clarksville."

"Well, it's not always like what you saw today. The war is making everyone act a fool. I think you might like it more during normal times. Maybe I shouldn't have brought you."

"No, I'm glad you did, Pa. But, I really didn't feel like I fit in. I don't know if I could ever get used to those big poofy dresses. I suppose I felt rather backward among those pretty women."

Elijah said "Hannah, you have more beauty in your little finger than those women have in their whole bodies. Beauty comes from within. But, that being said, you are also beautiful on the outside, but you don't know it, and that's the best kind of beauty. You have a naturalness about you. If you were fixed all up and dressed like any of those women, you would blow them out of the water. Of that, I have no doubt."

Harding said "Well, I know my brother sure thinks you're pretty." Hannah layed back on her quilt and looked up at the stars outlining the shape of the mountains. "Joseph...." she thought to herself. "Where are you? Are you laying on some battlefield, looking up at these same stars that I am seeing tonight?"

The next day was spent going back over the mountain toward home. It wasn't nearly as exciting on the way back as it had been on the way over. They didn't even bother to stop and look out at the overlook rock this time. They just kept trudging onward, stopping once at the top of the mountain for a break to eat and rest the horses. Then they continued on.

When they reached home they were weary and exhausted. They parked the wagon in a shade under some trees, then unhooked the horses and took them to the barn. As they were walking toward the house, Sarah and the children came running out to meet them.

As Sarah rushed out to hug Elijah, he walked purposely toward her with a serious demeanor, then suddenly assaulted her with the words "I'm joining the Union Army!"

Sarah stopped short, thinking she'd mis-heard. Then she looked at Hannah for confirmation, but Hannah just looked back and shrugged, because this was news to her as well.

"Elijah Casey! Whatever are you talking about?" Sarah asked, as she turned to follow behind him on his way to the house. He climbed the steps to the porch, then turned around and looked down at her.

"Sarah... I can no longer just sit here and allow this war to go on any longer than it has. To sit here and do nothing, is to have no say in the matter. A man who does not participate has no right to complain about how it all turns out in the end. I saw men today..." he stopped and swallowed back a knot in his throat that threatened to turn into tears. "I saw men today that were supposed to be fighting on the same side as our Daniel. Yet, they talked of him as if he were the devil himself. I fear that this war has become such that no man even knows what he is fighting for. No man knows who is his enemy and who is his friend. When even men of the same regiment must watch their backs while they sleep at night, the sense of it all has become lost to me. I believe men are fighting just to fight, as if their brains have been overtaken and they have no thoughts of their own any more. All they know to do is kill, kill, kill, with no thought of what they are even killing for. If I am to have any part in stopping this Godforsaken war, before another son of mine is old enough to run off and be killed, then I must join the cause."

"But, why the Union Army?"

"Because I cannot fight with the side that produced the kind of men who killed my son. And, because I truly believe that the Union must be preserved. What interest do I have with wanting to keep slavery alive? Slavery does not benefit me whatsoever. And, a country divided against itself surely cannot survive. The states must find a way to reunite again. I truly believe that the north will be the ultimate victors in this fight. I am tired, though. I am tired of it all. It is dragging on too long. We have boys from both sides running all over these mountains, up to no good. They no longer care about fighting on the battlefield. They fight whoever comes along in their path. There is chaos, too much chaos. If more men like me will simply take up arms and put a stop to this, then the quicker it will all be over and we can go back to the kind of lives we used to enjoy."

"Eli, you realize that this puts a target on our backs?" Sarah reminded him. "The majority of men in these parts are strongly aligned with the south. You may cause us to be looked upon as enemies. I love you and I support you in any decision you make, of course, but I fear for our safety."

"Jesse was killed when I had not made a move to take a side," Elijah said. "Our safety was gone long before now. And I realize, finally, that we may never get it back. It's a helpless feeling, Sarah, when a father cannot even protect his child. It's a helpless feeling, when a father watches the suffering of his wife and children, while he sits and does nothing to prevent it. It should have been *me* who went after those men that day, not Jesse. *I* should have been the one. It's time Sarah. It's time I took a stand."

Hannah had been watching this whole exchange, not knowing what to say or do. Her father had not mentioned this to her all day as they made the long trip home over the mountain.

How the thoughts must have been running through his head as he walked in the hot sun! She had not realized the torment he was putting himself through.

A year ago, she would have screamed and yelled and protested, not wanting her father to go. But, so much had happened in the past year, so much water had passed under the bridge. Her heart had become hard, her tears had receded. Nothing surprised her anymore. Nothing scared her. Nothing tormented her. She had built a high wall around her heart so as to protect it.

Her father going off to war was just a fact of life, something she had no control over. She was resigned. She had given up the fight. At the moment, she simply had no more stamina. She was exhausted from the trip, and she just wanted to go crawl into bed and pass out into oblivion. Maybe somewhere in that oblivion she would find a place where wars did not exist.

The next morning Hannah took Izzy and Lottie with her, and they walked the mile to Grandma and Grandpa's house so they could read them the letter from their daughter. It was very hard for the girls to sit and watch the emotions that they went through when they heard of their son's death. It's one thing to think you may never see your son again, but at least knowing he's still alive somewhere, so there is still a chance, but another thing to know that chance has been snuffed out. Through tears, Grandma said "Blessed are they that mourn; for they shall be comforted." Hannah was amazed at Grandma's strength, and her never-failing faith in the Lord.

The girls stayed for an hour or two, not wanting to leave until they felt their grandparents were going to be okay. As they were walking home, Hannah began telling her little sisters all about what it was like in town. She talked about the dresses, the soldiers, the stores. She talked about how far it was to get there. She described all the candies, and bolts of material, and books and dolls and other toys that she saw. She described the courthouse and the beautiful Methodist Church with stained glass windows. The more she talked, the more Isabelle and Charlotte were jealous and wished they could go there, too, some day.

When they passed the hollow that led up to Grandpa's cave, Hannah didn't mention it. It was her and Joe's special secret, and besides, Grandpa had asked her not to tell the younger children.

When they got back to their home, Hannah decided to cross the creek to see Lucy and Daniel. When she arrived she saw Daniel sitting on the porch with bandages wrapped around his shoulder still. Sarah had ripped up some old pieces of cloth to make bandages for him. Although he was much better, he still had some healing to do, but Hannah thought his coloring looked great, and he'd begun to gain back a bit of the weight he'd lost while off fighting in the war. She was so happy to see him home, but she knew in her heart of hearts that Daniel was not the type of man to sit around for long. Most likely he would go back again, especially once he knew their father was joining.

Hannah first read aunt Caroline's letter to Daniel and Lucy, then she reluctantly told them of Elijah's declaration yesterday that he was joining the Union Army. Daniel seemed more concerned that he was joining the Union side than he was that he was joining the war effort. He loved his father dearly, but could not understand his insistence on standing with the Union. He tried to ease Hannah's fears by saying "Don't worry so much, Hannah. Father is almost 40 years old. They most likely will assign him a leadership position, maybe even a captain. The younger boys generally get sent in first to battle, while the older men stand back and tell them what to do."

Hannah was smart enough to know that older men died in wars, too, but she tried to let Daniel's words settle her nerves a bit. She tried to remember Grandpa's words... "Fear makes the wolf seem bigger than he is."

At Church that Sunday, Elijah announced that he would be going off to join the army. Most everyone had already heard about it by then. But, what most people had not heard was that Henry Inman planned to go with Elijah. Henry stood up and made his announcement, and the congregation began to stir and murmur among themselves. Henry had told his wife and children the evening before, but no one else was expecting it.

Hannah was not surprised. Her Pa and Henry had been best friends since childhood. Henry had followed her Pa here to these Arkansas mountains so they might raise their families near each other. It was natural they would want to be together at a time like this, when faced with difficult days ahead.

The other men and women discussed the fact that with them gone, the only men left in the little mountain community would be Daniel, who was injured, William, who was hiding out because he'd ran away from the army, Grandpa Harris, who could use a gun, but otherwise was too old and frail to be much of a protection, and Rev. Owens, who just did not have a fighting nature. These four men would be left to look out for and protect seven women and seventeen children. Elijah and Henry were concerned about that, but they felt they had no choice. They truly thought if they just joined, then the war would be over that much quicker.

They left the following Saturday. Everyone gathered to make their farewells and to watch as the two men walked off down the road to an uncertain future. Sarah thought "I already lost one husband, I can't bear to lose another." And, Hannah thought "I already lost my mother, I can't lose my father, too."

August

Two weeks later, in August, there was another announcement at Sunday gathering. Reverend Owens said an opening prayer, then told the congregation that this would be his last time to preach to them. Only Lucy and Daniel had been made aware of this news, so everyone else began to talk and ask questions. Reverend Owens asked them to settle down a bit and he would explain. "Ministering to all of you has been one of the greatest joys of my life. This decision was not an easy one. Winnie and I have been receiving letters from our grown children ever since we came here, begging us to return to them. We have resisted up until now. We felt like this was our home. But, then we lost our dear Abraham, and Lucy is now married to Daniel and they are starting a life of their own. More and more Winnie and I are starting to understand how much we are missing. We have six married children back in Tennessee, and nineteen grandchildren. We're getting older each day, both in our late fifties now. If we don't take this opportunity to get to know our grandchildren, we may never have it. Our biggest regret is that we will be so far away from our dear Lucy, but our hope is that we may convince her and Daniel to come live near us some day. This decision was extremely hard for us, and our hearts are broken, but we feel it is the best thing to do, especially now, in these uncertain times."

Two weeks later, with some of their things packed away in their horse-drawn wagon, and some of their things given to Lucy, Rev. Owens and his wife left their empty house for the last time, traveled the half mile, then stopped near the church to say their goodbyes to everyone. Lucy cried. Hannah cried. Mrs. Owens cried. It seemed as if everyone cried. Who would preach at Sunday service now? A huge hole was going to be left in the community, with no one to fill it. They already suffered for lack of a doctor, and now they would not have someone to tend to their spiritual health, either.

Hannah walked over to their horses, Biscuit and Gravy, who were tied to the wagon, and ran her hands along their necks. She realized that she was even going to miss the horses. She remembered how she and Lucy had rode them on many occasions. She remembered riding bareback with Abraham, down to the swimming hole. Oh, what a young and immature child she was then, she thought. It seemed a lifetime ago. How times had changed! How her heart had changed!

As Mr. and Mrs. Owens made their final turn and disappeared from sight, Hannah felt a sense of envy in a way. They were escaping. What a sense of freedom they must be feeling! Escaping from what, she wasn't sure. She just knew it felt as if they were escaping, and Hannah had imagined escaping so many times. But, here was where Joseph would know to find her, and here she would wait.

October

For the next few months, Hannah just went through the motions of day-to-day life. She helped Sarah at home as much as she could. The older children didn't require a lot of looking after, but six year old Ruby, five year old Michael and the three year old twins, Jacob and Jonah, were enough to keep any two women busy.

They had finished putting up all the remaining garden produce and with the help of the men and boys, killed a hog and butchered it and smoked it in the smokehouse. It was October now. The leaves were turning and the nights were getting cooler. Hannah knew there was a war going on out there somewhere, but they hadn't seen a soldier in quite some time. Daniel was almost completely back to normal. His arm and shoulder only seemed to give him trouble on rainy days. He was able to do all the chores that needed to be done at his home, and some of the things that needed done at Hannah's home, since his father wasn't there.

One evening after all the children had been put down to bed, Hannah and Sarah sat talking on the porch, as the sun was slowly going down behind the mountains. Hannah had brought up the subject of her trip to town a few months back. Sarah told her that she really had only seen a glimpse of what a town was, by seeing Clarksville. She said "Where I am from it is so much larger than Clarksville. Clarksville probably has a few hundred people, while the city I'm from has thousands, like tens of thousands. You would not believe it if you saw it."

"Where *are* you from? I don't remember ever knowing for sure. I just knew you were from far away to the East."

"I was born in Richmond, Virginia. My Pa and Ma were very well off. We had a large plantation with many slaves. We had a big house, and there were fields as far as the eye could see. We grew mostly tobacco, but also some cotton. In that last letter I got from my mother, she said she feared what would happen if the north wins the war, because without their slaves, they couldn't possibly continue to operate as they have. She fears they will lose everything."

"How do *you* feel about that? I mean, Pa is off fighting to end slavery, yet if he is successful, that means your parents may suffer greatly!"

"I am not sure how I feel, Hannah. I don't wish to see my parents struggling, but since I've been living here, I have done nothing *but* struggle, and I'm surviving. There is always a way. I loved our slaves. There was Esther, who took care of me when I was a child. I loved Esther more than anything, and I know that she loved me, too. But, when I think of it from her perspective, I don't know that she was so happy to be forced to take care of a white man's children, and not be free to live her own life the way she saw fit. I do feel in my heart that it is not right to own a person, but at the same time I wonder what will happen to all the slaves once they are freed. Will they be able to survive? How will they get their own places to live? In Ma's letter, she said some of the slaves were begging her not to make them go if they were freed. But, I feel like it's more of them just being scared of doing something different and unknown, not really that they don't want to be free. They just never knew any different. Ma says if they keep them on, they'd have to start paying them for their work, and it would be impossible for them to pay them all, so they would have to let some of them go."

Hannah said "I don't remember ever seeing a black person. I'm sure maybe I did back in Tennessee before we came here, but I was so young when we moved, I just really don't remember. I can't imagine what that is like, to have someone to just do all your work for you. I just can't imagine a life like that. I'm not sure I would even want that kind of life, to be honest."

"Well, Richmond, Virginia is very different from the mountains of Arkansas," Sarah said. "There, women have a lot more freedoms to do things. When I was there, we didn't have to do very much of the housework, because we had slaves to do it for us, so we had time to pursue any leisure activities that we might desire. Also, girls could attend school much longer and receive a better education. Some women could even work in jobs and receive pay. I was teaching there, but then when I met Mr. Madison, I quit my teaching job so we could move here. I was happy when I learned there was no teacher here, so I was able to continue my profession. Although, there really was no pay to speak of. But, I did it anyway, because I enjoyed it. It was especially helpful to me after my first husband died, because it kept my mind occupied so I couldn't wallow in grief all day."

"You know..." she continued. "Not many children growing up in such remote places are able to receive the level of education you and your brothers and sisters received here. Most of the time there is no teacher around, and you must learn to read and write from your parents, but your parents are so busy they hardly have time to spend on such things. And, many parents don't even know how to read and write themselves, or very poorly at best, so how could they even begin to teach their children how to? I wanted my own girls to have an education, and it made me feel very good to know I was teaching all of you children at the same time. It just gave me a sense of accomplishment, and I want to continue doing it as long as I am able."

"Your Pa told me how you traded at the general store down in Clarksville," she said. "He said you did very well and made a good trade. It's a good feeling, as a woman, to be able to do what a man usually does. Not many women are able, or even allowed, to do that, especially in a place like this. But, in Richmond it's more common. I think you, Hannah, have that spirit about you. You could make it in a place like Richmond. I don't know that you are the type of woman who would be content to just sit at home and raise a bunch of babies, and never have something you can call your own. You are like me in that respect."

Hannah felt proud to hear Sarah say she was like her. She admired Sarah. Not that she didn't admire her own mother, but she always envied Sarah, and the fact that she got to do things that her own mother never did, like teaching school, and attending important community meetings.

Then a thought popped into her head "Sarah? Did you wear those big fancy dresses back in Richmond?"

"Oh, yes! My Ma made sure of that! I had several of them. I brought some with me, but quickly realized they were impractical here. I cut most of them up to make dresses for my girls over the years. The only one I still have is the purple one I wore when I married your Pa. But, I didn't put the hoops under it, so it didn't look quite the same as it would have back east."

Just then, with the sun about to completely fade from view, Sarah and Hannah heard a noise coming from down the hill by the road. It was getting too dark to see. They squinted to try and make out what was making the noise. Was it an animal? No, not an animal. A shape of a person began to form in the distance. Was one of the boys from across the creek coming over to tell them something? No. Wait! A soldier!?

Sarah jumped up from her chair and grabbed Hannah's arm. "Get in the house!" The women were hurriedly heading to the front door when they heard a faint "Wait...."

Hannah stopped and thought "I know that voice!" but it wasn't registering in her mind why she knew the voice.

"Hannah, is that you?" There it was again. She turned and as the figure stepped into the glow of the moonlight through the trees, her heart soared.

"Joseph?"

"Joseph!"

She picked up the bottom of her dress and pulled it up so she could run without tripping, and she practically flew as she ran across the porch, down the steps, and down the hill. She fell into Joe's arms and hugged him with everything she had. They were both so filled with emotion.

Joe finally let go of her and stood back and said "Let me look at you. Oh, Hannah! You are a sight for sore eyes!"

She said "Joe...." then reached up and touched his beard. "You have a beard now. You don't look like yourself. You're different somehow. You seem taller. Your shoulders are broader.

You seem ten years older, yet I know it has only been a little more than a year since I saw you."

"Come into the light..." she said, and they walked up onto the porch, where a candle was burning in the window. "Could this be my Joe? It can't be! You are.... Well, you're a man now!"

"I suppose war has aged me. I hope I'm not a disappointment."

"Oh, no!" she quickly said. "Not at all. It's just, I can't get over how different you are. It must be the beard. You are not the smooth-faced little boy I once knew."

"And you, Hannah... you have changed, as well. You seem so grown up now. What happened to that little tomboy I used to run around with? I imagine times have been tough and you have had a lot to deal with."

"Oh, Joseph, so much has happened. But, I will tell you everything later. Right now, let's get you into the kitchen. You must be starving! Have you been traveling long?"

"I've known nothing *but* traveling for the past year. I feel like I've never stopped walking."

Hannah watched Joe in the flicker of the fireplace light as he ate some food that she'd made for him. He was wearing his uniform, ragged as it was. She remembered a time not so long ago when he'd teased her that if she saw him in a soldier's uniform, she might want to marry him. She'd insisted that she wouldn't. But, sitting here looking at him now... she couldn't think of anything she wanted more.

As much as Joe was enjoying being with Hannah, he was anxious to also get home to see his family, and it was getting late. He knew how happy and surprised his Ma and Pa would be to see him. He couldn't wait to see the looks on their faces, and to feel their arms around him. Oh, just to be home, in familiar surroundings, with people who loved him. So many nights he had yearned for this. But, Hannah then informed him that his father was not going to be there. He and Elijah had went off and joined the Union Army.

It was then that Joe made the realization that Elijah had not made an appearance yet. Why had he not thought to question where Elijah was? He must have supposed he was off asleep in bed, much like some of the children were. Truth be told, he hadn't been able to focus on many things lately.

Hannah thought it was best to just get everything out, get the hurt all over with at once. So, she told Joe about how Daniel & William had returned and informed them that Abe was dead. She told him how Daniel had been shot, and Jesse had gone after the men, and also been shot. How poor little Jesse did not survive, but Daniel did. She told him of the marriages of Sarah and Elijah, and also of Daniel and Lucy. She told him that Rev. and Mrs. Owens had left to go back to Tennessee. And, for some good news, she told him that he had a new baby brother at home.

Now it made sense to Joseph why Sarah was sitting on the porch with Hannah so late at night, and not home with her children. She lived here now, and her children were upstairs asleep. It was a great deal to take in, and Joseph was exhausted. He said good night to Hannah and Sarah and made his way in the dark across the creek to his home. The women stood on the porch and listened until they heard the faint sounds of excitement and elated voices when Joe's family realized he was home.

The next day Hannah rushed through her morning chores. She couldn't wait to see Joe and learn more of what he had been through the past year. She knew his family wanted time with him as well, but she couldnt help feeling like Joe was hers, and she wanted him all to herself. Every hour that passed she wanted to race across the creek to see him, but Sarah told her that was unbecoming of a lady, and maybe she should wait for him to come to her. It was extremely difficult, but finally, after the noon meal Joseph escaped his mother for a bit and came to call on Hannah.

They talked on the porch for awhile, but then felt they needed privacy, so Hannah told Sarah they were going for a walk. They naturally headed straight toward Hannah's favorite spot by the creek. As soon as they got out of sight of the others, Joseph reached for Hannah's hand, and they walked in silence, with their hearts full of young love.

They sat under the buckeye tree, huddled close together. As long as they were touching, it felt like all the troubles of the world had gone away. Nothing else mattered at that moment but that they were sitting together, holding each other.

It was that time of year again. The buckeyes were all over the ground, laying at their feet. Joe reached down and picked up some of them. "Funny how it seems we always manage to meet here when the buckeyes fall. I'll never forget how you told me it was your favorite time of year," Joe said.

Hannah told him that having him there only reinforced her opinion. It truly *was* her favorite time of year, because her best friend had returned to her. Her mind was full of plans, plans of a future with Joe. Maybe he would ask her to marry him. She couldn't see any other future for her than one with Joseph Inman in it.

At some point in the conversation Joseph realized that Hannah thought he was home to stay. "Oh, Hannah... I can't stay long. I'm sorry if you thought so. I'm only here for a short visit. I have to go back to my company. I was not discharged, only given a pass to visit home. I'm supposed to return in two weeks."

Hannah felt her heart plunge. Tears were welling up and she was trying to hold them back. Joe felt the same way. Leaving her again in two weeks would be one of the hardest things he ever had to do, even harder than leaving her the first time.

"Hannah," he said, as he placed his hand under her chin and lifted her face up to his. "Let's not focus on what will happen in two weeks. Let's focus on each day, and make the best of it. I want to make memories with you. I don't want sad memories. I want happy ones!"

Hannah felt so much love going through her as she looked into Joseph's eyes. This was her Joseph, the little boy who annoyed her at times, but whom she always seeked out when she wanted to play or explore, her best friend through her teenage years, the one who knew all her secrets, the man who had returned to her and stolen her heart. The two had been lost in each other's eyes for what seemed like an eternity, until Joe leaned in and kissed her. It was only their second kiss. The first one had seemed a lifetime ago. Hannah lost herself in that kiss, and the many more that followed as they sat among the buckeyes in the fall, with the leaves swirling all around them.

That evening Joe's mother invited everyone over for a celebration of Joe's homecoming. She was there, along with Joe and his six younger siblings. The entire Casey family came, including Sarah and Hannah and the eight younger children. Daniel, Lucy and Albert walked over from their new house which was just down from the Inman's on the same side of the creek. William and Martha Bennett walked down, with their two babies, and someone even went and got Grandma and Grandpa Harris and brought them down. Everyone but Elijah and Henry, who were off to war, was there. It was a true shindig.

Tables had been set up outdoors in the cool autumn air. Food was brought by everyone, and there was more than enough to go around. Everyone ate until they couldn't eat any more. Then, some of the young children began dancing around, acting silly. Isabelle, Rebecca and Nancy, all girls of 11 years old, were holding hands in a circle and spinning around, singing silly children's songs and getting dizzy. They began singing "Ring around the Rosy, a pocket full of posies" and laughing and falling down, then getting up to do it again. The younger girls, Charlotte, Rachel, Ruby, Virginia and Elizabeth, begged to join in, so the older girls took their hands, and now they had a large circle of eight girls. There was much merriment, and everyone else was watching and laughing.

Suddenly, from off to the side came a few strands of music. Everyone turned. Joe was standing with one foot up on a tree stump, and holding something to his mouth. "What was that?" one of the girls said.

Joe put his hands behind his back and said "I don't know what you mean. I didn't hear anything." The girls began to dance around and sing again, until once again the magical musical notes floated through the air. They turned again, but Joe had quickly put his hands behind his back. This time the girls weren't fooled. Joe's three little sisters, Nancy, Elizabeth and Virginia, ran and tackled him, trying to see what was behind his back. He laughed and ran around a tree as they chased him. "I don't have anything!" he yelled. But, the girls didn't give up, until finally Joe said "Okay....okay." Then he showed them what he had.

"What is that?" the girls asked in unison.

"This is a harmonica." He blew a few chords. "A bunch of the soldiers have these. At night in camp we play songs. Some of them have other instruments, but a lot of them have harmonicas. One of the soldiers taught me how to play his, and I was able to pick up one in a little town we went through. I've learned to play a lot of songs on it. I'm gettin' pretty good at it actually."

Joe was in true form. He was the star of the show. All the young girls were gathered around him yelling "Play us a song Joe!" Hannah sat back and smiled. She was proud of Joe. She was impressed at how everyone was looking up to him and admiring him. She loved to see the adoration that the little girls were giving him, and was feeling it too, only she was too old to be running around acting so silly.

Joe said "Okay...here's the first song I learned. It's called 'Dixie'. " He blew a few chords to get the tune right, then sang, then blew a few more chords, then sang. Between each line he would stop and blow a few chords.

"Oh, I wish I was in the land of cotton
Old times there are not forgotten
Look away, look away, look away Dixie land

In Dixie Land where I was born in
Early on one frosty mornin'
Look away, look away, look away Dixie Land

I wish I was in Dixie, Hooray! Hooray!
In Dixie Land I'll take my stand
To live and die in Dixie
Away, away, away down south in Dixie

Away, away, away down south in Dixie"

By now the girls, and even some of the others, were beginning to pick up on the lyrics. Joe sang the next verse...

"Ole Missus marry "Will the Weaver"
Willum was a gay deceiver"

Everyone else joined in with...

"Look away! Look away! Look away! Dixie Land"

Now they waited for Joe to sing the next verse....

"But when he put his arm around her
He smiled fierce as a forty pounder"
And again they all joined in....

"Look away! Look away! Look away! Dixie Land

I wish I was in Dixie, Hooray! Hooray!
In Dixie Land I'll take my stand
To live and die in Dixie
Away, away, away down south in Dixie
Away, away, away down south in Dixie"

This continued with the next verse, with everyone picking up on the part they knew was coming, but this time Joe would stop singing himself during the repeating parts, and instead would play the harmonica along while the others sang...

"His face was sharp as a butcher's cleaver
But that did not seem to grieve'er
Look away! Look away! Look away! Dixie Land

Ole Missus acted the foolish part
And died for a man that broke her heart

Look away! Look away! Look away! Dixie Land

I wish I was in Dixie, Hooray! Hooray!
In Dixie Land I'll take my stand
To live and die in Dixie
Away, away, away down south in Dixie
Away, away, away down south in Dixie"

Joe plopped down on the ground and said he was worn out from playing, but the girls begged him to play another. So, he got up and started dancing a funny jig. A campfire had been built to stave off the cool night air. Joe began dancing around the campfire, and soon the girls were following him and imitating him. Hannah was laughing and having so much fun watching Joe. He was in his element, and just eating up the attention.

He put his harmonica to his lips and played another song. It was a rolicking one, and when he was done, the girls asked him if their were words to it....so he taught them the words.

"Sittin' by the roadside on a summer's day
Chatting with my mess-mates, passing time away
Lying in the shadows, underneath the trees
Goodness, how delicious, eating goober peas

Peas, peas, peas, peas
Eating goober peas
Goodness, how delicious
Eating goober peas

When a horse-man passes, the soldiers have a rule
To cry out their loudest "Mr. here's your mule!"
But another pleasure, enchanting-er than these
Is wearing out your grinders, eating goober peas

Peas, peas, peas, peas
Eating goober peas
Goodness, how delicious

Eating goober peas"

Little six year old Ruby suddenly began giggling so uncontrollably it made everyone else laugh, too. She said "That song is sooooo silly!" She kept giggling as he gave her a goofy look and stuck his tongue out and continued dancing silly, kicking his legs up high in the air as he danced around in circles. He sang the rest of the song...

"Just before the battle, the general hears a row
He says "The Yanks are comin', I hear their rifles now"
He turns around in wonder, and what d'ya think he sees?
The Georgia militia, cracking goober peas

Peas, peas, peas, peas
Eating goober peas
Goodness, how delicious
Eating goober peas

I think my song has lasted just about enough
The subject's interesting, but rhymes are mighty rough
I wish the war was over, and free from rags and fleas
We'd kiss our wives and sweethearts, say goodbye to goober peas

Peas, peas, peas, peas
Eating goober peas
Goodness, how delicious
Eating goober peas"

The little girls kept singing "Goober Peas", even after Joe had stopped. It was so catchy to their little ears. Finally Hannah said "Oh, my word! Can you stop singing that song?!" but she was smiling and covering her ears at the same time. "Thanks a lot Joseph! They'll be singing it for days!"

Joe came and sat by her and said "Maybe you'd like to hear a slower one? Maybe a song about a sweetheart?"

Hannah blushed, but the little girls squealed "Yes! Sing a

song about a sweetheart!" They sat down finally and grew quiet as they waited.

Joe said to the girls "This song is called 'Jeannie with the light brown hair'." Even the adults moved in closer as a group so they could hear this song.

First, Joe played the tune on his harmonica. It was slow and sweet, and almost brought tears to the eyes of the women. "What are the words, Joe?" one of the little girls asked. He began singing...

"I dream of Jeannie with the light brown hair
Borne, like a vapor, on the summer air
I see her tripping where the bright streams play
Happy as the daisies that dance on her way

Many were the wild notes her merry voice would pour
Many were the blithe birds that warbled them o'er
Oh! I dream of Jeannie with the light brown hair
Floating like a vapor on the soft summer air"

Joe then paused and stood up and reached for Hannah's hand. She had a questioning look on her face, but she took his hand and let him raise her to her feet. He then began to dance slowly with her around the edges of the fire. He began to sing again. He had a twinkle in his eye when he sang...

"I long for *Hannah* with the day dawn smile"

Everyone oohed and aahed when they noticed that he'd substituted Hannah's name into the song in place of Jeannie. The women smiled and the boys rolled their eyes, as he continued...

"Radiant with gladness, warm with winning guile
I hear her melodies, like joys gone by
Sighing 'round my heart o'er the fond hopes that die

Sighing like the night wind and sobbing like the rain

Wailing for the lost one that comes not again
Oh! I long for *Hannah* and my heart bows low
Never more to find her where the bright waters flow

I sigh for *Hannah* but her light form strayed
Far from the fond hearts round her native glade
Her smiles have vanished and her sweet songs flown
Flitting like the dreams that have cheered us and gone

Now the nodding wild flowers may wither on the shore
While her gentle fingers will cull them no more
Oh! I sigh for *Hannah* with the light brown hair
Floating like a vapor on the soft summer air"

"Well, my, my, young Joseph, you are givin' this old woman the vapors, I do declare!" Everyone laughed at Grandma Harris's sudden outburst. Hannah was glad of it, though, because all the attention had been on her and she had begun to feel uncomfortable, not quite knowing how to react. While he sang and danced her around, she had almost forgotten everyone was there, but once the singing stopped, she didn't quite know what she was supposed to do next.

Irene was sitting quietly. She hadn't realized her boy had such a romantic side. She realized that the war had changed him in many ways, mostly not ways she was happy with, but this one... this one was nice. Her oldest boy was in love. It was a side of him she had never seen.

As the party began to wind down around midnight, the people began filtering back to their homes, carrying candles for light as they walked along in the dark. Sarah and the children escorted Grandma and Grandpa back to the Casey home, where they were to stay for the night. Hannah walked slowly behind them, with Joe as her escort. They didn't talk much, just held hands and stared at the pretty stars that were twinkling bright in the sky. Hannah quietly said to God as she looked up "Thank you, God. Thank you for bringing our Joseph home safe." Then she smiled when she heard her sisters up ahead in the distance singing "Peas, peas, peas, peas, eating goober peas."

Soon a week had already passed. Joe and Hannah were together for a bit each day. They would go walking, as they talked and made plans for a future. Sometimes, in the midst of her happiness, she would feel guilty... for how could she be happy when there had been so much loss? But, then the happiness would come back, if only briefly. She tried to hold onto each of those fleeting moments, for with each day that passed, she was one more day closer to having to say goodbye to Joe again.

Then two weeks had passed. The smiling, happy Joe had begun to show himself less and less, and a more moody, quiet Joe was emerging. Oftentimes Hannah caught him just staring into the distance, not listening to a thing she'd been saying. She knew he was worried about going back to war.

On his last afternoon home, she went to look for him and couldn't find him anywhere, so she decided maybe he was down at the buckeye tree. "Her" spot had naturally become "their" spot now. As she got closer she saw him sitting there on her favorite root, staring across the creek. She slowly approached, trying not to spook him. She stopped and tried to memorize his profile, the way he looked sitting there.

"Oh, I didn't see you there!" Joe said as he turned around.

"Oh, it's only me," she said, as she remembered all the times the roles had been reversed and she'd thought to herself "It's only Joe." How far they had come, and how much they had changed.

Joe moved over and gave Hannah space on the big root and motioned for her to come sit next to him. She scooted up close to him and they just melted together as they sat, not knowing quite how to handle the upcoming goodbyes. They sat quietly for a long period of time, occasionally reaching down and picking up a fallen buckeye, or a twig, and tossing it into the creek. It was as if they were simply soaking each other up.

Then, Joe broke the silence when he said "Hannah... I want you to marry me." He turned to face her and said "Will you marry me? Will you be here waiting when I come back again, so we can marry? I'm 18 now, and you are almost 18. I think we are old enough, and I'm ready. I want so much more from you than just kisses. I long to be intimate with you."

Her heart raced at the thought of being "intimate" with Joe. She had imagined it so many times, herself, but it wasn't proper for her to talk of such things. "Yes, Joseph, I will. Of course I will! I'd marry you right now, if Rev. Owens hadn't left. There's no one here to marry us, though."

"When I come back, I will take you into town, and we will find a preacher to marry us."

"When will that be Joe? How long?"

"I don't know Hannah. I just don't know. I hope the war will end soon, maybe in just a few months, then I can return. There's just no way to know for sure how long that might be. But, knowing I have you here, waiting for me, it will give me so much to look forward to. I will be longing every day to get back."

"I wish you would at least write to me. If only I could receive a note from you now and then, it would help so much."

"I'm sorry that I didn't write to you," he said. "If only you knew how many nights I lay on the ground trying to sleep, writing you love letters in my mind. The beautiful words would just flow out of me, but then in the daytime, I would sit and look at a piece of paper and nothing worthwhile would come. I'm just not a writer, Hannah. I can't think of anything to say but that I saw so much blood and death all day, and that is not the type of letter I want you to read."

"I understand, Joe, but maybe you could just try. It would mean so much to me."

"I will try. If only I could just make up a song to sing to you instead."

"Then, do it! Make up a song, and write down the song lyrics and send that to me instead. Anything will lessen the burden of worry off my heart."

"I will try Hannah. Oh, I do love you so.... If I could give you the world, I would."

There had been murmurings that Daniel might return to

war with Joseph, and Hannah was saddened to find that it was true. Daniel's shoulder was healed now, so he couldn't use that excuse for not going back into the battle. Once he had said he could never go back, but he'd had another change of heart, and he now felt it was cowardly for him to continue sitting at home while the other boys and men were off fighting. He had spoken with Lucy the night before, and young Albert, as they sat in their kitchen. Albert had promised to stay on living in the house with Lucy, and to help her with all the chores. Daniel told his brother that he was proud of him, and he knew he had went through a lot the past year. He said knowing he would be there to look out for Lucy eased his mind a great deal.

William Bennett was asked if he might have the desire to return to war, as well, but he said he just could not do it. He would continue to stay with his wife and two young sons. He used the argument that he would be the only man left, other than 73 year old Joshua, to look out for the women and children. In some ways this made Daniel and Joseph feel better, knowing he would be there, but in other ways it made them think William was taking the easy way out. But, nothing was said to that effect. This was a hard time, and each man had to make up his own mind, and deal with the consequences later.

It was a late October day when Joseph Inman and Daniel Casey dressed in their ragged Confederate uniforms and said goodbye to their family and friends.

Joe stood kissing Hannah goodbye, and he reached into his pocket and pulled out a buckeye. "Remember when you gave me this, and you said it was for luck? Well... I believe it did bring me luck. It got me through some tough moments, and it brought me back to you. So, I will continue to carry it. I have no doubt it will keep me safe and bring me back to you again. I will probably carry it all of the days of my life." He put it back in his pocket, and with tears in his eyes he said his final farewells to everyone.

Daniel was also struggling with his goodbyes. Hannah hugged her big brother so tightly, and realized how much he had filled out since being home, how hugging him now was like hugging her father, because he had the body of a man now, not a little boy. She admired her big brother so much. He was 20 years old now, and he was married. So much had changed in such a short amount of time.

As the two young men disappeared around the bend in the road, Hannah stood for a moment and tried to fight back her tears, and mostly her fears. She had no way of knowing if she'd ever see either of them again. Besides her Pa, these were the two most important men in her life, and she was heartbroken.

She turned to look at the gathering crowd, what was left of her little mountain village. She saw two old people, only one grown man, and a whole bunch of women and children. Oh, what was to become of them all?

1863

Hannah climbed the stairs for what felt like the one hundredth time that morning. Sarah and some of the children were sick. It was January. The winter had been particularly hard, and now sickness had made it's way into the mountains.

That morning Hannah had trudged through a very deep snow to get down to the creek, where she had to break ice to get to the water. The wind was blowing briskly and snow was blowing into her eyes. She could barely see, and the cold was biting straight to her bones. She brought the buckets of icy water back to the house to melt on the fire, so she could make a hot broth for the sick ones to drink.

If only she could get to her Grandma, to ask her advice about ways to treat the sick, but Grandma and Grandpa were snowed in a mile away. Hannah looked through her journal and found a few notations she had made about cures her grandma had told her about in the past. She did her best to treat everyone, but felt like she was failing miserably. It seemed they all just got sicker and sicker.

The worst was the cough. They all were coughing

constantly, and nothing Hannah tried seemed to ease it. There was rattling in their chests when they breathed, and most of them were running fevers. Hannah had no way of checking temperature, but she could just tell by feeling them that they were burning up.

Sarah seemed to be the sickest, and Hannah was worried, because Sarah was with child. About a month after Elijah and Henry had gone off to war last summer, Sarah had realized that she was pregnant. She thought she would be due in about April. She was about 6 months along now, and Elijah still had no idea.

Sarah was very excited about the pregnancy, hoping that maybe she would finally have a little boy. She had thought, after the death of her first husband, that she would most likely not have any more children, so the hopes of having a son kept her going through the long, cold winter months. But, now she was sick, and she prayed that her baby would be okay.

All three of Sarah's daughters, who were now 7, 9 and 12 years old, were very sick, as well. Hannah had them all in beds in their rooms. She was on her way up now to bring them some broth that she had prepared. Hannah's sister, twelve year old Isabelle, was also laying in her bed. She had been up and about some, but was not feeling the best. Ten year old Charlotte seemed to be the only one in the house besides Hannah who hadn't shown any symptoms. Charlotte was doing her best to help Hannah. Currently she was sitting in the room with her three little brothers. Six year old Michael was coughing incessantly and crying. The four year old twins, Jacob and Jonah, were not as sick as Michael. They were coughing some, but seemed to be feeling a lot better, for they were up running around and playing. Charlotte was having a time keeping them corralled. Hannah had said it was best to keep them in their room, so they didn't disturb Sarah or the other sick girls.

Hannah had tried to keep anyone else from visiting their home, for fear of spreading the sickness further. Lucy had come to the porch a few times to talk to Hannah from a distance, just to make sure everyone was okay and ask if there was anything she could do to help. She told Hannah that her Ma had always baked some onions, then boiled them, then made her and Abraham drink the onion juice to treat a cough. She said she wasn't sure if it really worked, but maybe it was worth a try. She also gave Hannah two bottles of muscadine wine that her mother had made from the wild grape-like fruit. She told Hannah to boil the wine and serve it warm in small amounts. It would help to calm the cough.

Hannah also remembered something her mother had done to help with fever. She got two pans of water. She heated one up, but left the other cold. She would then put the sick person's feet down in the warm water for a few minutes, at the same time soaking a pair of socks in the pan of cold water. Then, as soon as the feet came out of the warm water, she would take the cold wet socks, wring them out, then put them on the warm feet. Then she would take a dry pair of socks and put over the wet pair. This was thought to draw the blood to the feet, which would get the blood circulating, hopefully helping to reduce the fever. Hannah had been doing this routine at least once a day to all of them. This meant she was constantly hanging wet socks by the fire to dry. There were socks everywhere!

More than once Hannah had wished for a doctor in their community, but none more than she did now, when the care had fallen solely on her shoulders. She had no way of knowing if this sickness was a life threatening one, or simply a winter cold. She had no way of knowing if what she was doing was helping or not. But, she just kept trying, praying that she would not come down sick as well, not for her own sake, but simply because there would be no one left to care for any of them if she were to also get sick.

The next day Hannah's 14 year old brother, Albert, who was still living across the creek with Lucy, came to the porch and called for Hannah. She told him to not come in. She opened the door and peeked through the crack to talk to him.

He said "Hannah, Lucy is sick now, too. What do I do?"

Hannah felt defeated. She had hoped and hoped that the sickness would stay in her household and not travel. How could Lucy have caught it, when she was never allowed in the house, and only talked to Hannah through the crack of the door, from several feet away? The worst of it was, Lucy was also expecting a baby. About three months after marrying Daniel, Lucy had become pregnant. She also had not known for sure that she was pregnant when Daniel had left to go back to the war, so Daniel had also left not knowing he had a baby on the way. Elijah and Daniel, father and son, were both off fighting in a war, and each had a pregnant wife back home that they didn't know was pregnant.

It seemed the pregnancy fairy had flown through the mountains spreading her dust, because Martha Bennett was also expecting her 3rd child with William. In this case, William *did* know his wife was expecting, since he was still at home.

With three pregnant women, no doctor, sickness running rampant, freezing cold weather, and most of the men away at war, it was a trying time in the little mountain community of Buckeye. Hannah sometimes asked herself why did women just have to keep having babies every two years, until they had 10 or 12 children. Was there not some way to lessen this burden just a bit? She hadn't even had children herself, yet her entire life had seemed to revolve around taking care of children. She loved them all, and was resigned to her fate, but at the same time, she dreamed of just going away, with no responsibilities, no children to look after constantly.

However, if she married Joe soon, children would start coming for her as well. There was just no way around it. God made women to bear children, to be fruitful and multiply. Hannah knew that women generally had children up until their early 40's, but she wished that God had designed them to only have them until their early 30's instead, then they would have less total children. But, then, Michael, Jacob and Jonah would not have been born, so maybe she didn't really wish that at all. As much as she wished she had freedom from caring for her little brothers so much, she couldn't help but feel an overwhelming love for the little rascals.

Hannah had no choice now but to run back and forth across the frozen creek to care for sick people in two different homes. She would have brought Lucy to her house, but asking a very sick pregnant woman to trek through deep snow and cross a frozen creek, did not seem like the best plan. So, she simply went back and forth several times a day to check on everyone. Soon, Albert was also sick, so she put him to bed in the same room as Lucy, so they could keep each other company, and she told Charlotte to stay with them. Poor Charlotte. She was only 10 years old, but she was really such a huge help to Hannah. Thank God at least one other person seemed to be healthy.

Hannah soon learned the Inman household had been hit hard, too. Irene and four of her six children were sick. Irene told Hannah to not worry about her family. As sick as she was, she would manage. She felt Hannah had enough to handle as it was. But, at least once a day, when Hannah crossed the creek to check on Lucy, Albert and Charlotte, she would go and peek in the door to the Inman home and ask if everyone was okay and did they need anything. She would sometimes carry some firewood in for them, or at least stack it on the porch where they could get to it easier.

Hannah was glad her grandparents were far away and snowed in, so they would hopefully not be exposed to this, and she was thankful that the Bennett family was also far enough away that maybe they would also stay safe.

It was five long, exhausting days before Hannah began to see improvement in some of the children. The twins seemed perfectly normal now, other than an occasional coughing fit. Most of the girls were up and around for a good part of the day, but they still got tired easily. Sarah was still in bed, and Hannah worried more and more for her each day. But, the baby was still moving, and Sarah was beginning to stay awake for longer periods. Lucy and Albert were much better, and somehow Charlotte still did not show any signs of sickness.

Hannah, however, had known for a day or two that she was beginning to get sick, but she didn't tell anyone. She just kept taking care of all of them. She kept going out in the cold and crossing the creek. Soon, she could not keep it hidden any longer because she began coughing, too. Thankfully, by this time, Isabelle and Rebecca were well enough that they made Hannah go to bed, and they said they would take over from here. They were both 12 years old now, and with 10 year old Charlotte's help, they managed well enough.

Hannah became very sick, but about 2 days into her confinement, Sarah began to feel well enough to get up and help the other girls. Soon, most everyone in the house was better, except for Hannah. Sarah chastised her for going back and forth in the cold like she did, all the while knowing she was sick. She most likely made herself worse by doing that. But, she was also proud of her, of the way she had taken over and handled everything, and she told her so.

After about a week of being bedridden, Hannah began to feel much better, and it was such a relief. She hadn't been that sick in a long time. She still had a terrible headache, but she got up and went downstairs for the first time in eight days, and sat by the fireplace. Everyone else seemed to be all back to normal. She was happy to see that. They all said she looked a hundred times better. Hannah asked about the neighbors. Sarah told her that she, or one of the girls, had been to check on them each day. Everyone was much better. Two of Irene's children had managed to never catch it, and the rest of them were on the mend.

So much housework had been neglected while everyone was sick, and Hannah soon was up and about trying to catch up on things, but Sarah insisted she was doing too much too soon, and made her sit and rest for a couple more days.

It seemed they had all weathered this ordeal, there had been no loss of life, everything was back to normal, and for that Hannah was grateful.

March

Somehow they all got through the remainder of that winter with no more sickness. It was now March, and the sun was peeking through the clouds at times, bringing a promise of warm days to come. One morning Hannah opened the door to find William Bennett approaching. He was looking around a lot as he walked, and moving rather quickly. Then, he came inside and closed the door behind him.

"Hannah... Sarah... " he said as he tipped his hat at them. "I felt it my duty to warn you. There was an event at our home earlier today. Some men came up to the house and asked Martha where the man of the home was. Luckily, I was up on the hill behind the house at the time and they did not see me. They said they had heard a deserter was in these parts. They then brushed past Martha and came in the house. She said they were acting very rough in manner. Thomas and Isaac were crying and they told Martha to shut them up or they'd give them a reason to cry. Martha said they rummaged around in the house, looking under things and behind things, thinking I was hiding somewhere. When they didn't find me, they simply stole from us. They took some of our food and they took my tobacco box from the fireplace mantel. Then, thanks be to God, they left without harming Martha or the boys. But, I fear they may return."

"Did they come this direction when they left your house?" Sarah asked.

"No, they went the other way. But, I don't know that they might come back, and there may be more of them. I don't think these men were soldiers. I think they were just up to no good, thinking with most of the men away at war, they could easily go to houses and take advantage of the women and children. I believe they asked for me first to make sure there was no man about. If I had been home, they may have tried to harm me, but since I wasn't, they were able to steal without retribution."

"What should we do, William?" asked Hannah. "How do we protect ourselves from men like these?"

"I don't rightly know. I have no easy answers. My best advice is that if you have any valuables, you may want to hide them somewhere, in case they come back stealing again."

With that, he bid them goodbye and said he was going across the creek to warn the other familes.

The only things that Hannah owned that had any real value to her were her journals, and her mother's locket and Bible. She searched for a long time, trying to find a good hiding place for them, but nothing seemed safe enough. Finally, she remembered a floor board in her bedroom that was loose on one end. She had placed a rug over it so she wouldn't trip, until she had a chance to fix it. But, in all the craziness of late, she had forgotten all about it. She moved the rug aside and got hold of the loose end of the board. She pried until she got the board up enough that she could reach under it. She felt around, and was able to tell that there was a space between the floor of her upstairs room, and the ceiling of the downstairs part of the house. It was a small space, but big enough she could slide her journals, the Bible and the locket into it. She then pressed the board back into place and put the rug back over it.

After that she went through the house, seeing if there was anything else of value that someone might want to steal. She asked Sarah what she thought. Sarah said maybe they should hide the silver. By this she meant the silver utensils that they ate with. Hannah wondered what a bunch of grown men would want with their forks and spoons, but Sarah told her that the silver they were made out of was worth money. If anything, they could sell it to a silversmith, who would melt them down and make other things out of them.

Sarah also gathered up a silver baby cup that had been hers as a child, a silver pocket watch that had belonged to her late husband, a cross necklace that she owned, and a gold wedding band that she'd worn during her first marriage. In Elijah's belongings she found two pocket knives and a flask that she felt might be valuable. She got the two candleholders off the fireplace mantel and hid them as well. All of these things were small, and fit in the hiding spot under Hannah's bedroom floor.

Now they all just sat each day, living in fear that at any moment one of these marauding bandits could show up. With each day that went by, they would count their blessings and let their guard down a bit more and a bit more. Soon, they were beginning to feel more confident and Hannah began leaving her current journal out some and not putting it back in the hiding place, because it took a lot of extra time and effort to hide it each time and she wrote in it almost every day.

One day, toward the end of March, Hannah took her journal and her little bottle of ink and her pen and she went down to her tree by the creek and sat down to write. It was the first day in months that it was actually warm enough to sit outdoors without being chilly. The sun felt so wonderful on her face, and she could feel her spirits lifting. Her thoughts were on Joe. She wondered where he was, what he was doing, and if he was thinking about her the way she thought about him. She wanted to write some words about Joe and how she was feeling, but she just sat their staring at the water of Mulberry Creek as it gently flowed across the rocks. She was in a bit of a daze, what some might refer to as 'writer's block'.

After a bit she began to feel a mist of wetness in the air. She looked up and saw a small dark cloud gliding over and a very light spring rain had begun. She placed her journal under her dress and hunched over to protect it and keep it dry. But, just as quickly as it had started, the rain moved on out. It had lasted less than a minute. It hadn't even been enough to soak her clothing through. "What a gentle rain!" she thought.

As she retrieved her journal and sat back down in position to write, the words "gentle rain" kept running through her brain. She found herself saying "Fall down gentle rain, wash away my pain." She smiled. "Sounds like a good beginning to a poem. But, I've never really been a poetry writer. Let's see.... What rhymes with 'rain' and 'pain'? Hmmmm" She began going through the alphabet. "Bane? Cane? Dane? Gain? Oh, I've got it!"

She jotted down the first four lines of a poem. She sat back and thought about it. She felt it needed more. What else could she add that would make sense?

Her mind began to go back to some of the events of her life in recent years. She thought of the tears she'd cried, of the fears she'd developed. "Hmmmm, Years, tears and fears. I could make something with that."

She began to feel the rhythm of the poem that was forming in her brain, and she dipped her pen in the ink and began writing again. She didn't stop until she'd completed her thoughts. When she finally looked down at the paper, the poem that reflected back at her seemed like something that someone else had written. She hadn't known she was capable of writing a poem that she actually thought was very good. She read it out loud....

"Fall down gentle rain
Wash away my pain
Clear away the worries
From my ever weary brain

Take me back in years
Before I cried the tears
Before loss instilled in me
A multitude of fears

Clean the stress away
And upon my spirit lay
A calming understanding
That will last me all the day"

Hannah felt something stirring inside of her. The creation of this poem had brought her a sense of peace, a very healing sense of peace. It was like she took all the pain she'd been holding inside of her and transferred it to the paper, through her pen, and now it was on the pages of her journal, and no longer festering away on the inside of her body. It gave her a sense of release like none she'd ever experienced.

She looked up at the little rain cloud, which was now far off in the distance. She wondered if maybe, just maybe, her late mother had sent her that cloud from Heaven, to poke and prod her creativity to the surface. She told herself she was being ridiculous, but then again, anything was possible. There was so much that human beings just didn't know about. The world was full of miracles. Like for instance, this tree she was sitting under, at one time it had simply been a tiny little seed, blowing around on the ground. The chance that it would land in the right place and take hold, was probably one in a million. The chance that she herself was even here, was one in a million. Her father and mother had to be born first, they had to meet each other, they had to have relations at just the right time. Every little decision made for thousands of years had led up to the fact that Hannah Casey was even here. What was her purpose? Why was she here? What were God's plans for her?

She was deep in reverie, when she got that feeling again. "I once was but a seed...." she thought. She picked up her pen, dipped it in the ink again, and began to write. She would stop occasionally and look off into the distance, then pick up her pen again. When she was done, she read the words she'd written out loud, to see if the rhyming all matched up and flowed evenly....

"I once was but a seed
Blowing 'cross the land
Touching blades of grass
Grazing bits of sand
Never knowing where I'd land
What the future held for me
Would I dry up and die
Or bloom into a tree
I thought I found a place
I sat waiting for the rain
But all I got was baking sun
Cracking the terrain
Then one day a dark cloud
Brought worries of its own
And a brittle gust of wind
That blew me 'neath a stone
I waited there... lost
What would happen to me now
But little drops of rain
Found a path somehow
I still desired to grow
But couldn't see the sun
My branches knew the way
As they grew out one by one
They wrapped around the rock

Branches on each side
The pattern of my growth
Could not be denied
It wasn't always easy
With the burden that I carried
But I just soldiered on
I guess I wasn't worried
Twenty years down the road
I stood tall as all the rest
But, ten feet up a boulder
Was lodged within my breast
Instead of growing straight
Like every other tree
I was meant to lift a rock
So high that it could see"

Hannah knew that what she'd written was beautiful. It brought tears to her eyes. She read through it again, and still was madly in love with her creation. What had brought this on? This talent for poetry? She wasn't sure, but she was willing to embrace it, because the way she felt now, after writing her first two poems, was such a freeing, light, peaceful feeling. She longed to feel it more often.

She decided then that maybe it would be wise for her to hide her journal again. She didn't want to risk losing something that she had created from the deepest depths of her soul, something beautiful that came from pain. What a wonderful thing! She knew she would continue writing in her normal way. She knew she would continue to record family history, stories that her grandma told, little hints and recipes, funny things her little brothers said that she wanted to remember always. But, from here on out, she knew that there would be poems sprinkled into her writing, as well.

Hannah packed up her things and went back to the house. She hid her journal in the floor boards, then went down to help Sarah with supper. Sarah had been cooking a big pot of beans all day, and now was mixing up the batter for cornbread. Hannah gave Michael a bowl and told him to go under the house and fill the bowl with potatoes. When he got back she began peeling them and slicing them into small pieces. The potatoes were all growing eyes now. After sitting all winter, they were becoming shriveled and growing little roots which protruded out of the potatoes like arms and legs, which everyone referred to as "eyes". Hannah carefully cut off each eye, leaving a bit of potato attached, and put those in a separate bowl. It was about time to start planting the garden, and they would need these potato eyes to plant so they could grow more potatoes for next winter. A new potato plant would grow from the potato eye, as long as it had dirt, water and sunshine.

After she'd cut all the potatoes up, Hannah put them in a pan with a bit of lard and began frying them. By the time they were done, so was the cornbread and beans. Sarah and Hannah called the other children to the table. Since Elijah wasn't there, Sarah and Hannah sat at the short ends of the table now, while four children sat down one long side of the table, and the other four sat down the other side.

There was a bowl of clean water sitting on the wooden counter, with a bar of homemade lye soap sitting next to it. Each child went by the bowl and washed his or her hands first, then dried them on a rag before seating themselves at the table. Sarah wanted to keep the children clean, and hold back on the amount of germs they got into their bodies, but changing the water between each person was unthinkable. Everyone just washed their hands and rinsed them in the same water, and then they all used the same rag to dry with. By the time the last person took their turn, the water was turning brown. It wasn't ideal, but it was the best they could come up with at a time when all water had to be carried from the creek. Some families didn't make their children wash their hands at all before they ate. Sarah felt she was at least making an effort.

Sarah asked Rachel if she would say the prayer this time. She liked to call on a different child each night, partly as a test to see if they had memorized some of the prayers she'd written down for them.

"Father, we give our thanks
For food that stays our hunger
For rest that brings us ease
For homes where memories linger
We give our thanks for these
Amen"

Sarah said "Very good Rachel!"

Just as they were beginning to fill their plates, they heard a commotion outside. Sarah and Hannah looked across the table at each other, and they each had a look of fear on their faces. They jumped up in unison and looked out the window.

"Soldiers!" Sarah said. "Four of them. Union, I think."

Hannah could see the four men standing out in the road. They had most likely been walking along the road, maybe trying to make their way to Clarksville, when they came upon the little village in the mountains. From where the men were standing, they could not see the Harris house, or the Bennett house, and they had probably already passed the empty Owens home. From the view they had now, they could only see three homes; the Casey home on the north side of the creek, and the Inman home and Daniel's home, which were across the creek on the south side.

Since the road was on the north side of the creek, Hannah figured they had not been across the creek yet. She hoped that they would keep moving along, but they had stopped, and appeared to be talking among themselves. Finally, they looked toward the Casey home and began walking toward it.

Hannah's breath caught in her throat. What should they do? What is going to happen? She was more terrified than she could ever remember being. Sarah was terrified, too, but she calmly said "If we just give them some food, maybe they will be on their way."

The soldiers came up on the porch. Sarah and Hannah didn't open the door to them, but waited to see what would happen. The men didn't wait for an invitation, though. They just barged right in, with their weapons pointed. The two women screamed and grabbed for the children, herding them into a corner of the room.

One of the men spat his tobacco right on the floor near the table, then looked at the food, which had hardly been touched, and said "Looky here boys! What a fine supper they've laid out fer'us." Seeing no sign of a man about, they put their weapons back in their belts, and they sat down at the table and started eating. Hannah felt anger welling up inside her, but Sarah grabbed her arm and squeezed, as if to say "Don't do anything! Stay quiet!"

"Where's your man?" one of the men asked, with a mouth full of food. He was looking at Sarah.

"He's enlisted."

"Hmmph! Confederate, I reckon," the man snorted.

"No, he's in the Union army."

Even though it was the truth, the men didn't believe her and one of them said "Ain't nobody livin' round these parts in the Union army. You just tryin' to lie to save them young'ens over there."

Hannah was growing more and more angry, as she watched the men devour all the food meant for her family, the food she and Sarah had worked so hard to prepare. But, Sarah kept a tight grip on her arm.

When the men were done eating, they got up and began roaming around the house, rifling through things, turning over things, looking for valuables. One of them walked over to Hannah and, looking her up and down, said "You sure is a fine lookin' piece 'a woman. Look at 'er fellas! Bet she'd scream real good if we took a turn at 'er." He looked hungrily at Hannah and came toward her. She screamed and ran across the room. The man grabbed her and started making lewd movements toward her, and laughing. He grabbed her hand and tried to make her touch him between the legs. She yanked back and slapped his face hard! The man seemed excited by that and said "Oh, you like it like that, do ya?" His friends started laughing and urging him on.

Sarah was shielding all the children, but she couldn't stand to watch this display so, against her better judgement, she yelled out "Leave her be!"

Now the man turned to Sarah instead. "Oh, jealous, are ya?

Well, don't worry ma'am, I got enough for both of ya." Then he came toward Sarah. Hannah yelled again and ran toward the man to stop him from attacking her step-mother. The man then turned and grabbed Hannah and threw her onto the ground. She tried to scramble up, but he grabbed at her legs and held her down. He pinned her on the floor, and began trying to undo his pants. Hannah was a virgin, but she knew enough to realize what he was intending to do to her. Sarah also knew, and was not having any of it. She grabbed an iron that was used in the fireplace and started swinging it at the man. The children were all screaming and crying and huddling in the corner. The other men were laughing as they watched their comrade trying to fight off two very spirited women.

"These two ain't gonna take it lyin' down like the last ones did, are they?" one of the men asked. "Guess they make'em tough up here in these parts." They watched as the other man kept trying his best to rape Hannah, but with Sarah swinging at him, and Hannah fighting back, he was not making much progress. Then, suddenly, one of the men said "Stop it Jeb! Come on! Let's go see what's goin' on in them other houses across the crick."

"Damn it, Rube! Always spoilin' my fun!" Jeb said.

Then, as quick as they had entered, the four men went running out the door. Sarah, Hannah and the children watched out the windows as the men ran down the hill and splashed across the creek. They saw Harding come running out onto his porch with a gun in his hand when he heard the commotion. Hannah felt a sick feeling in her stomach. "No! No!" she said out loud. "This is not happening! No! Oh, God, please don't let them hurt Harding!"

The women watched, helpless, as the men came up to Harding, laughing at him, as if the sight of a 16 year old boy with a gun was humorous to them. Harding yelled "Stop right there! I'll shoot!" But, Harding had not had time to actually load the gun, so he knew it was an empty threat. He hoped that just maybe it would work.

But the men just continued laughing at Harding, and one of them said "Look at this young whippersnapper! Tryin' ta do his Pa proud." Then, as a group, they just charged right up to Harding, grabbed the gun from his hands and then held him down. From inside, Irene let out a scream, and Harding's three little sisters all started crying uncontrollably. Little Virginia was screaming "Don't hurt Harding! Leave him alone!"

The men dragged Harding across the yard to a tree with a low hanging branch. "Wha'da'ya think fellers?" one of them said. "This looks like a good hangin' limb to me." The others got excited and nodded their heads in approval. Two of them went running toward the barn, looking for some kind of rope. The other two held onto Harding while they waited. Irene ran out screaming "Take me instead! Please! I'll do anything! I've got food! I've got silver! Anything you want, you can have it! Just take it. For the love of God, please don't hurt my boy."

The one named Jeb yelled "Shut up woman!" and slapped Irene so hard she fell to the ground. Harding couldn't stand seeing his mother treated that way, and he began fighting even harder to get loose, but it was a futile effort. He was only making himself so completely worn out, he had no energy left.

By then the other men had returned with a piece of rope they had found. Two of them continued to hold Harding as he fought against them, while the other two made a noose and were fitting it over Harding's head. Irene was still laying on the ground, crying out in anguish for her boy.

Hannah had seen all she could stand. She ran out of her house and down the hill screaming "Stop it! Stop it!" Her heart couldn't bear to watch Joseph's little brother being murdered. She splashed across the creek, but the men paid her little attention as they continued their task. She ran toward them, slinging her arms and trying her best to hit them, but they kept grabbing her hands and laughing. One of them yelled "Get her out of here!" and another grabbed her and flung her to the ground next to Irene.

By now the other men had the noose around Harding's neck and they'd thrown it up over the tree limb. One began pulling down on it and trying to raise Harding up. Harding began making a choking sound. The men kept pulling and were laughing.

Suddenly a loud report rang out, and Hannah felt the whiz of a bullet as it flew just above her head in the direction of the men. They dropped Harding and he fell to the ground. They were looking frantically around to see where the bullet had come from. Hannah's 14 year old brother, Albert, had run out the back of his brother's house a few yards away and hid around the corner of the porch and aimed at the men and shot. But, he kept himself quiet as he reloaded his gun. Then he snuck around to the opposite corner of the house and shot again. This time one of the men yelled out that he'd been hit in the arm.

Another of the men yelled "There's two of'em! Let's get on out of here!" They all took off running as fast as their legs would carry them, through the trees. Albert had loaded again and shot one last time as they ran off in the distance.

Everyone sat stunned for several minutes. No one dared to move. Then, Hannah broke the stillness when she jumped up and ran to Harding. She pulled the noose from his neck and said "Are you okay, Harding?" He weakly said "Yes" and then Hannah looked down and saw that her hands were shaking uncontrollably. In fact, her whole body was shaking. She sat down in a heap on the ground next to Harding, and just started crying, partly from relief, and partly from complete and total fear.

Albert came running over. He ran around checking on everyone. The children all ran out of the house, and Lucy finally felt brave enough to come out of the house next door. She was big and pregnant and had been terrified to come out and have the men do something to her unborn baby. From across the creek, Sarah ordered Charlotte to stay with the little ones, while she and Isabelle and Rebecca ran down to comfort the others.

There was a fear that the men would return, so everyone composed themselves as quick as they could and got back into their homes. Harding suggested that everyone barricade their front doors by pushing furniture up against them, just in case. Lucy and Albert ran back to their home. Irene and Harding and the other Inman children ran back into their home, and Sarah, Hannah, Isabelle and Rebecca ran back across the creek and up the hill to their home. Hannah, with the help of Sarah and the older girls, quickly began pushing all the chairs and the kitchen table over against the front door. Then they put some more furniture against the back door. They went around making sure the sticks were in position at each window to keep the window from being opened from the outside. Then Hannah and Sarah huddled around the children and they all sat facing the door. They just sat there, for what seemed like hours. It grew dark outside, and the children began, one by one, falling asleep on the floor next to them.

Hannah finally began carrying the sleeping children up to bed. Then, she made the rest of the children go up, too. They cried for Hannah not to leave them, for they were terrified of the bad men returning. Hannah promised she would be right back. She went down and got Sarah, who was still sitting, facing the door, as if she were in a trance. She said "Sarah, come upstairs with me and the children. We can all sleep up there tonight. We will barricade the door at the top of the stairs so no one can sneak in on us."

So, they did just that. They pushed a large chest-of-drawers in front of the door at the top of the stairs, then the two of them sat against the wall facing the door, just watching and waiting. They sat that way all night, each of them only dozing off for minutes at a time, then jerking back awake.

The next morning Hannah could hardly move. Sitting on the hard floor all night, tensed up like she was, and after the way those men had thrown her around, every muscle and bone in her body was aching. She had never known such a night of fear in her life. She was afraid to go out of the house, even though it was daylight again, and the soldiers surely were long gone by now. But, she needed to use the privy so badly she thought she would burst. She ran for it and then came back in as quickly as possible. After that, they all took turns going, two at a time. Then they barricaded themselves back into the house.

They were all starving, because after the men had eaten their supper, and all the terrible frightening things had happened, no one had thought to eat again. So, Sarah began going through the motions of making breakfast. She asked Hannah if she were brave enough to go out and get the eggs from the henhouse. Hannah wasn't brave enough, but she did it anyway.

As they were eating and discussing what had happened the evening before, Hannah said "Albert was so brave, and so smart, too. The way he moved locations before shooting the second time, so the men would think there were two different people shooting at them. I don't know how he thought of that in the heat of the moment. And, also, the way he stayed hidden, that was smart, too. If they'd seen he was a boy, they would have simply ran after him like they did Harding. But, since they couldn't see him, the men just assumed it was two grown men shooting at them from different sides of the house. I'm so proud of Albert! I can't wait for Pa to return so I can tell him what a fine job Albert did of protecting us all. He truly saved all of us. My heart could just burst with pride for that boy!"

"Yes," Sarah said. "I was so impressed with him. Your Pa will be so proud." Then she paused and sighed. "Oh, Hannah... how I wish your Pa were here. I just don't know how much longer we can go on like this. I need him now more than ever."

"I wish all the men were back home. Why they felt they must go off and fight in a war, I'll never know. We need them here. I pray every day for their return," Hannah said.

Sarah reached down and felt her stomach. "I felt the baby move this morning. It was a relief! I was terrified that in my fighting with those men last night, I may have hurt the baby. I didn't feel him move all night. I didn't tell you, but I was so scared. I didn't want to worry you. But, this morning he has finally moved. I know he's still alive. I am so thankful."

The women and children were still too frightened to leave their homes, but Harding and Albert finally ventured out to make rounds and check on everyone. Albert took Lucy over to Irene's house and left her there so she wouldn't be alone, and then the two boys armed themselves and set out to check the area. It took Hannah and Sarah a minute or two to move the furniture out from in front of the door so they could let the boys in. They assured them they were okay, although shaken up quite a bit. But, Hannah said she was worried about Grandma and Grandpa. So, the boys said they were heading up that way next.

Since Joshua and Ruth were a full mile away, up a different creek, they had not heard any noise the day before and did not know anything had happened. They told the boys that they had not seen a single soldier at their home the entire time of the war. Harding and Albert discussed whether they should bring them down to stay with the others, but they finally agreed that they were safer staying where they were. They were a mile off the road that most of the soldiers were taking when they traveled, so most likely their tiny little home would never be discovered. Joshua said he agreed with them, but at the same time, he was very concerned about terrible things going on with his family when he wasn't around to protect them. Albert said "Grandpa, I'm afraid there was nothing you could have done with this group last night. They would have strung you up and killed you. I'm glad you were not there."

The boys didn't stay too long, partly for fear of leaving all the women alone, but also because they still had one more house to go check on. They made it back to the center of their little community in quick time, then went back to the Casey home to tell Hannah that her grandparents were safe and sound. They then said they were heading down the creek to check on the Bennett family. Their home was also far enough away that it couldn't be seen from the main section of town, and far enough away that noises usually couldn't be heard.

As Albert and Harding came into view of the Bennett home, they began to have an eerie feeling. There was a strange stillness to the air. They yelled out "William! It's Albert and Harding. Come out!" But, nothing happened. They wondered if maybe William had gone off hunting. "Mrs. Bennett? Martha! Are you in there?" Still nothing. The boys began to get very nervous. This was the direction those men had ran yesterday when they took off into the woods. Did they find the Bennett's home and do something terrible to them? Harding motioned for Albert to follow, and they snuck around to the barn. "Let's check out the barn first," he whispered, "In case those men are hiding out in there."

The boys did not find anyone in the barn, but there was an eerie quiet in there. "Where are the horses?" Albert wondered. "Do you think the Bennetts went on a trip or something without telling us? I don't see the cow either. Okay, now I'm getting very concerned."

They were almost afraid to go up to the house, but knew they had to. They went up onto the porch, in a very guarded manner, and called out for someone, anyone, to answer. Still nothing. Then, they heard a faint cry.... the cry of a little child.

Without hesitation the boys barged through the front door, weapons aimed. They saw nothing in the main room. They then walked toward the back of the house where the cries seemed to be coming from a bedroom. They carefully stepped through the door, weapons aimed, but immediately laid them down and ran across the room when they saw Martha lying on the bed with her children sitting next to her. At first they thought she was dead, but as they got closer, they saw she was just laying there staring at the wall, not moving, not talking, as if she was completely in shock from something.

Albert gathered up 4 year old Thomas and 2 year old Isaac and led them out of the room. Meanwhile, Harding took this as his cue to try and rouse Mrs. Bennett. But, it seemed she was refusing to talk. Something terrible must have happened to her! Harding kept asking questions, but getting no answers. He asked Martha if there was anything he could do for her. No answer. He asked her if her unborn baby had been harmed. No answer. He asked her where William was. No answer. He asked if men had come to the house and done something. Still no answer.

Harding came back out into the kitchen, where Albert and the little boys were, and said "Something really bad is wrong. She won't talk." Then he looked at little Thomas and said "Thomas, do you know what happened?"

Thomas said "Those bad men did it."

"Did what, Thomas?" Harding asked.

"They hurted Ma, and they were mean."

He asked the little boy if he knew where his Pa was.

"The bad men took him!" Thomas said, and then he started to cry. Harding didn't want to upset the little boy any more, so he stopped asking him questions. What awful thing had these poor little boys witnessed? He was going to have to find a way to get Martha to talk.

His next thought was that maybe she would talk to one of the women, so he told Albert to take the two boys and go back to get Hannah. "Take the boys over to my house and leave them with Ma and Lucy, then go get Hannah and bring her back here. I'll stay with Martha until you get back."

Somehow, in the absense of Elijah and the other men and older boys, everyone had begun to turn to 18 year old Hannah as their leader, the one to make important decisions, the one to go to in a crisis, the one who seemed to have all the answers. Hannah projected a strength about her, and an intelligence, that the others picked up on. She was wise beyond her years. Sarah was that way, too, but being big and pregnant at the moment, most people didn't want to put too much of a burden on her. So, Hannah had unofficially become the decision maker of the group. Unbeknownst to Hannah, Sarah had been sort of grooming her for that position. Sarah saw in Hannah the same qualities Elijah had, and Sarah was not one to think a woman couldn't do just as much as a man, or be just as important as a man. So, she had never led Hannah to believe she couldn't do something.

Martha Bennett and Irene Inman were both the sort of women that Hannah's own mother had been. They were happy to step back and let their husbands lead and make all the decisions. This was the life they wanted for themselves, and as long as they were happy, that was okay. But, women like Sarah and Hannah just would never be content with that.

When Albert showed up at Hannah's door, all the fear she had of going outside completely vanished, and her leadership role re-surfaced. She left Sarah with the children, and she and Albert ran as fast as they could run, all the way back down the road to Martha's home. They burst through the door to find Harding pacing the floor, saying that Martha still had not moved or talked.

Hannah sent the boys outside and told them to look around a bit, and see if they could see any sign of William, or any hints as to where they might have taken him. But, she warned them not to go too far. However, her real reason for sending them away was so she could talk to Martha in private. Martha was only 22 years old, only four years older than Hannah. They had never been particularly close, because Martha was married with children, and was at a completely different point in her life than Hannah was, and also her house sat a bit further apart than some of the others, so they didn't see each other as often. And, Martha was a newcomer to the area, and had not grown up there as a child, playing with Hannah and the other girls and going to school with them. Martha was already grown and married when she came here three years ago, and she was the type who kept to herself a lot. But, looking down at her now, laying there so helpless and obviously damaged, Hannah felt so much sympathy for her.

"Martha..." she said calmly as she sat next to her on the bed. "It's Hannah."

Martha didn't respond at first, but Hannah just kept talking. "Martha, did someone hurt you? Did four Union soldiers come to your home?"

Still no answer.

"They came to our homes yesterday, and I thought maybe they came by your way as well."

Still nothing.

"Did they hurt you, Martha? Because they hurt me...."

Martha suddenly turned and looked into Hannah's eyes. "They hurt you Hannah? Did they...."

Hannah said "They threw me down, they hit me..."

Martha suddenly began to sob hysterically. "One of the men had his way with me! Oh, dear God! One held me down, while the other had his way. He didn't care that I was with child. He didn't care that my husband was right there in the room."

"William was in the room!?"

"Yes, the other two men were holding him and making him watch. I saw the look in his eyes. He was dying inside, not being able to stop what was happening. My boys were crying in the corner. Oh, Hannah! I think my babies saw what those men were doing to me!"

Hannah put her hand on Martha's stomach. "Do you think they hurt the baby?"

Martha said "I don't know. I feel numb inside. Wait! Where are my children?!?"

Hannah put a calming hand on Martha and said "It's okay. Irene and Lucy are with them. They are safe."

Martha relaxed a bit, then said "They took my William..."

Hannah didn't know what to say or what to do to ease the pain of a wife who had been through such an ordeal. She said "We are going to try to find William. Try not to worry." But, in her heart she feared the worst.

"Martha, until we find William, I would like for you to come back with me so we can look out for you. It's not safe for you to stay here. It seems the men stole your horses and your cow, and I don't know what else. Please, come stay with someone closer in to the center of town so we can watch over you and the boys."

"Just leave me here..." Martha said very weakly. "I'm damaged now. I feel so violated. I feel so dirty. I will never want another man to touch me, ever again! *Ever*! Do you hear?!" she finished off in a loud scream.

Hannah could understand her pain, at least she thought she could. She had felt glimpses of it when that horrible man was trying to attack her, ogling her with his eyes.

"Don't you dare let those men win, Martha! Do you hear me? If you give up, you let them win. I know it's hard, but your boys need you. You must find some strength inside you somehow."

Martha finally gave in and allowed Hannah to lead her down the road back toward her home. She was met by Lucy and Irene, who had been watching and waiting for them. Lucy was holding the hands of Martha's two boys, and when they saw their mother they ran to her. She hugged them, but with little passion. She was still in shock.

Lucy said "It's been decided! I want you and the boys to come stay with me, Martha. Please, I won't take no for an answer. Hannah and Irene have so many people in their homes already, but all I have is Albert right now. I would like you and the boys to come stay in our extra room. It would be nice to have another pregnant woman to talk with, to go through this experience with. Please say you will."

Martha nodded weakly, and so the other women helped to get her across the creek on the slippery wet stones, without slipping and falling and hurting her baby, and they got her into Lucy's house. Hannah said she would take her sisters later and they would go back and get some of their clothing and other belongings for them.

For the next 3 days, the boys would go scouting about, trying to find William, but with no luck. They finally decided maybe the men had taken him all the way to Clarksville, maybe he was being held as a prisoner of war. Martha continued to remain in her weak and defeated state. She barely ate, and barely payed attention to her boys. No one could seem to snap her out of her depression. But, Lucy stepped right up and began mothering Thomas and Isaac, and she was doing a very good job of it. Everyone felt she was trying to prove to herself that when her own baby arrived, she had what it took to be a mother.

On the evening of the 3rd day, Hannah and Isabelle were outside carrying pails of water up from the creek, when Hannah looked up to the sky and saw a circle of birds flying around in the distance. She didn't think too much of it, for she'd seen them before. Pa had said they were buzzards, and they feed on dead animals. When you see them circling like that, he had said, it means they have located a carcass, and are about to go down and feast on it.

"Ugh, nasty birds..." Hannah thought. Then, she stopped in her tracks because a thought came to her mind. "Do you think? No, you're being silly, Hannah." She convinced herself it was nothing and continued to carry the water to the house.

But, all evening, each time she was outdoors, she saw the birds, still circling, in the same spot. She had an uneasiness in the pit of her stomach. A nagging thought just kept coming to her mind, so she finally went to get Harding and Albert to tell them what she was thinking. She took them out in the yard so the others couldn't hear. She pointed to the birds in the sky. "They're after something," she said.

Albert said "Probably a deer."

She cautiously said "What if it's William?"

Harding looked back up at the birds. "I suppose it's possible."

"Should we go try to see for ourselves?" Albert asked.

"I feel like, if it *is* William, at least we would have an answer for Martha. At least she would know, as horrible as it would be. It's probably not a person, but everything is so crazy any more, I just keep getting this awful feeling in my gut."

Harding said "Well, it's getting late. I say after breakfast in the morning, if we can still see the birds, we will at least try to see if we can find what they are after."

Hannah said "Come and get me before you go. I want to go along."

In the past, two teenage boys would have balked at having to take a girl along, but after everything that they had been through, it sort of seemed natural that Hannah should go. They were a little creeped out about possibly seeing a dead body, but being young boys, they were also a bit intrigued. Hannah, on the other hand, was praying that they would only find an animal, nothing more.

The next morning the birds were still circling, so the three of them set out. It didn't seem possible that they could find anything in this vast wilderness, but they were determined to try. They just kept walking in the direction of the birds. They followed the wagon road for a good deal of the way, until it began to veer away from the creek as they got closer to the Bennett home. It became apparent that the longer they followed the road, the more they were veering away from the direction of the birds. So, they decided to leave the road and follow along the creek bank instead. The path of the creek continued to lead them right toward the birds, so they began to think whatever the birds were after must be close to the water, or maybe even in the water.

After a few more minutes, they begin to notice a smell, an unmistakable smell of death. It was so strong it was hard for them to want to continue on and get closer to it. It was repulsive, and made them want to gag. They would take a few steps, then stop and put their clothing up over the faces so they could try to filter out the smell. They knew they were close, but were not pinpointing the source of the smell. They were looking all along the bank, and in the trees.

Then, suddenly, a large buzzard was startled and flew up into the air. They turned to see where it had been, and that's when they saw it. On a large flat rock that stuck out into the water, lay a body. It was definitely not a deer. It was human. But, it was rancid and mutilated. Harding got a little closer, then came back, gagging, and trying to breathe cleaner air.

"It's William," he said.

Hannah felt a sickening bile coming up, and it wasn't only because of the smell. Poor Martha! And those poor little boys!

Harding said "It looks like they shot him multiple times. There's blood splattered all over that rock. I think they must have made him stand up there, and then they just all started shooting. Let's hope he went fast. What an awful way to die."

"We have to get away from this smell," Hannah said. They began backtracking until finally they could breathe freely again. Once they got away from the creek and back onto the road, Hannah found herself crying. There had been so much senseless death the last few years!

"Albert..." she said. "If you had not done what you did, shooting at those men and scaring them off, it could have been any one of us, or all of us, in that same situation as William. You truly saved us. I will be forever grateful."

"I just did what my instinct told me to do," Albert said. "But, I wasn't able to save William, or Martha or their boys, from a lifetime of sorrow."

"You couldn't have known," Hannah said. "I just don't understand this war! Those men were Union, and Sarah told them that Pa was off fighting for the Union side. The sides don't even matter any more! Once these soldiers get a taste for blood, they just want to kill anyone who comes in their path, regardless of which side they are on. I just don't understand what is happening to our country. If you disagree on some issue, you have to murder each other? Why? What good does it do? What does it solve? How many more lives have to be lost before we end this damn war?!"

When they got back, Hannah went straight to Lucy's house, before she lost her nerve, and told Martha that she had something awful to tell her. "We found William," she said.

Martha simply looked down at her hands and asked "How did they kill him?" She just seemed to have already known that if he was found, he would be dead.

"They shot him. We found him by the creek, down a ways from your house." She decided to save her the horror of hearing that buzzards had been eating on her husband's flesh.

"Did you bring him home?" Martha asked.

Hannah wasn't sure how to answer that question. She finally said "No, Martha. His body is in bad shape, and the three of us had no way to get him back."

"But, you will. I know you will. We can't leave him out there like he is. I want him to be buried in our little cemetery."

Hannah didn't have the heart to say anything other than "Of course we will!"

Later, she and the boys sat out in the yard discussing how they could possibly manage this feat.

"First off," she said. "We can't just bring him back and lay him around with that stench. We will need to have the grave already dug so we can put him right in it. And, we don't have a coffin."

"There may be some boards at the sawmill that I could use to build a box," Harding said. "It won't be a very nice one, though."

"Well, I don't think we can be choosy," Hannah said. "It's a crude box or *no* box at this point."

So, it was agreed that Harding would go nail some boards together into some kind of box, while Albert, Hannah and some of the older girls would get shovels and do their best to dig a grave.

Hannah said that four graves was enough for a row, so it was time to start a new row. So, she chose the spot at the foot of Mr. Madison's grave, and they began digging.

Hannah had never realized how difficult it was to dig a grave. They dug and dug and dug for two hours, yet still had barely made a two foot deep hole in the hard ground. Finally she took a break and went to see what progress Harding had made. She almost laughed when she saw the miserable excuse of a coffin that Harding was trying to build. She didn't mean to laugh, because it was such a sad occasion, but she could tell immediately that carpentry wasn't a skill Harding possessed. And, when she saw how big the box was going to be, she realized how much bigger the hole they were digging was going to have to be. It seemed impossible that they were going to be able to get it done. So, she told Harding to stop. She had another idea.

She went to speak to Martha again. She could tell Martha had been crying, and understandably so. She was laying in her bed at Lucy's house, and didn't seem to have the energy to even sit up. So, Hannah just sat on the edge of the bed and came right out with it.

"Martha, without the men here, we simply are not able to make a proper coffin. I know it may seem cruel, but I think we are going to have to just wrap William up in a sheet and bring him home and bury him wrapped in that same sheet, with no box."

Martha feebly said "Is there no other way?"

Hannah replied "I can't see any other way. And his body is very decomposed Martha. I'm sure you must realize that. And, it smells. We will need to be quick about getting him in the dirt once we get him back. There will be no time to view the body or say any words. We will have to quickly get him in the ground and covered up. I'm sorry to sound so awful, but I'm only telling you the truth."

"I don't want to see him anyway," Martha said. "I want to remember him how he was, not how he is. I want you to bring him back and get him buried, then come and get me and we can say some words after he's in the ground."

"Okay, Martha. We will do that for you. You just lay here and rest and keep that baby healthy."

Hannah went and told the others the plan. They finished digging the grave. They could not make it 6 feet deep, it was just too daunting of a task, so they made it about 4 feet and stopped. And, the hole was not very wide at all, since they were not burying an entire coffin.

Hannah now had to decide who to take for this awful task. She couldn't take any pregnant women, of course, so the group she assembled consisted of the only two males of any size, 16 year old Harding and 14 year old Albert, and the three 12 year old girls; Isabelle, Rebecca and Nancy, and herself. What a ragged group! Six teenagers, basically, going to do a job they should never have to do, seeing something they should never have to see, and being supervised by an 18 year old girl who had no clue what she was doing.

They decided to take one of Hannah's horses and walk it up to the Bennett home and use their wagon. Thankfully the soldiers had not stolen the wagon. Their reason for choosing this wagon was so they could bring it back after and park it far away from everyone, because they felt the smell of the dead body would probably stay in it for weeks, and no one wanted that smell in one of the wagons parked closer to home. Hannah also gathered up an old sheet, and asked the other women if they could spare an old sheet, too. She felt she would need three or four to wrap around the body.

Once they had the sheets and the horse, the six of them set off for the Bennett home. Once there, Hannah had an afterthought and ran inside the house and tore some curtains off the windows. She brought them along with her. Then they hooked up the horse to the cart, then led him as far as they could down the road, until they were about even with where the body was. At this point they tied the horse to a tree and left him there while they cut across through the woods to the creek. There was no way to get the horse and wagon through the thick undergrowth, so they were going to have to carry the body a little ways from the creek back up to the road.

When they began to start noticing the smell, Hannah took

the curtains she'd torn down, and ripped them into six even pieces of cloth. She had them each fold the cloth into several layers, then tie it around their faces to block out some of the smell. Then, they continued on.

When the body came into view, the three younger girls gasped upon their first sight of it. Hannah and the boys saw that the buzzards had picked at William's face and eaten out his eye sockets since they had seen him last, and swarms of flies were buzzing around it. Hannah knew the flies were laying their eggs in William's flesh, and soon the body would be teeming with maggots. She was glad they had found the body before the maggots had taken over. She didn't think she could have handled that.

They tried to be mature and handle the gruesome scene like adults, but all of the sudden Nancy felt the bile rising in her stomach. She yanked off her curtain mask and began to violently vomit all over the place. When Isabelle saw what Nancy was doing, it sent her into waves of convulsions, as well. She ran off a ways and started vomiting, too. Soon, all of them were gagging and trying to fight off vomiting. Harding ran off behind a tree and tried to gain his composure to keep himself from throwing up. It took a good 10 to 15 minutes for all of them to finally control the gagging enough to get back to the job at hand.

Hannah had them spread out a sheet right up next to the body, then lay a second sheet over that one, for a double layer. Then, they stood back and wondered how they were going to get this putrid body onto the sheet without touching it or having it fall to pieces. Hannah said "As terrible as it sounds, we are going to have to get some tree branches or something, so we can push him over onto the sheet." So, they each broke off a tree branch and they all six stood along one side of the body, placed their sticks underneath it, and lifted and pushed the body toward the sheet, rolling it as they went. As they lifted the smell intensified, and the body began to tear and open up. It was the worst thing Hannah had ever had to do in her life! And, she felt like the cruelest person ever for asking these 12 year old girls to be a part of it. Yet, without them, she didn't see how she could manage.

Finally, after several tries, they had the body over onto part of the sheet. At this point, they grabbed the ends and rolled the body up tight in the sheet. Now, Hannah had them lay two more sheets down, in a double layer, and they rolled the already wrapped body up in the 2nd layer of sheets. Now it was held down good and tight with four layers of sheets. But, the smell was still just as horrendous.

Now, the two boys each grabbed an end of the sheet and they carried the body through the trees back toward the wagon. It was heavy, and they had to stop and put it down several times. The girls took turns, too, but being so small, it was hard for them to lift that kind of weight. Hannah was able to hold one end of the sheet, with one of the boys on the other end, or sometimes with two of the girls on the other end, but it was slow going. No one wanted to touch the center part where the body was, because it had begun to leak fluids out and the sheets had wet spots here and there. So, they simply grabbed the extra material that was at the head of the body, and the extra at the foot, and lifted the body that way. For the most part, the boys did the carrying, because they were able to cover more ground, and at a faster rate, than the girls. Thankfully it wasn't too far and they finally got the body to the wagon. Now, getting it up in the wagon was another task that was difficult to figure out, but they managed it. By the time they were done, that poor body had been dropped, twisted, mangled and mutilated, but it was still inside the sheet.

Even the horse was flaring its nostrils as they headed back toward the cemetery, as if he could hardly stand the awful smell, either. But, he walked and pulled, as he was directed to do. Harding led the horse by the reins out front. No one wanted to be anywhere near the body, so rather than ride in the wagon, the others walked several steps ahead of Harding.

Some of the younger children were waiting for them as they came back down the road, and they gasped when they smelled the body. One of them wanted to see it, but Hannah said it was not an image she wanted them to remember, so she wouldn't allow them to unroll the sheet. Instead, as quickly as they could they lowered the body into the slim grave, then began covering it with dirt. Once they had the dirt mounded up and the body was completely buried, Hannah told the boys to quickly take the wagon back to the Bennett home and leave it there so they could get the smell out of the air.

They all went back to their homes to let the dirt and smell settle some. Hannah said to Sarah "I could have insisted we leave the body where it lay. I could, and maybe should, have insisted upon it. I don't know if I was right to make such a promise to Martha, or to force the children to help me and participate in such a thing, but I just think if it had been Pa, or Daniel, or Joseph, or anyone I loved, I would not be able to stand knowing they were laying on a rock being eaten by birds. I would have wanted to bring them home, too. I did what I had to do, but Lord help me, I hope I never have to do something like that ever again."

"I don't know where you found the strength, Hannah, truly I don't. I continue to be amazed by you with each day that passes. I could not love you more if you were my very own daughter, and yet I know I am only 13 years older than you. But, I am your stepmother, and I once was your teacher, and I have watched you grow and become... just this amazing creature."

Hannah blushed and ran to hug Sarah. "You are more than my teacher or my stepmother. You are my Sarah. You are part of me, and you are my partner in life right now. Without you, where would I be?" She smiled and said "I can tell you where I'd be! I'd be watching all these children alone, that's where I'd be! And, I'd be bald because I'd done gone insane and pulled out all my hair!"

They both laughed and then wiped away a tear or two. "Now," Hannah said. "What words to say over William's grave? We have no preacher, and I know my Pa would have said something inspirational if he were here. But, he's not. So, I feel it's up to me. I will be in my room for a bit trying to think of something."

Later that evening, just before the supper hour, everyone gathered at William's fresh grave to say a few words. Everyone except Grandma and Grandpa Harris, that is, because Hannah just didn't have the heart to drag them into this sadness. Maybe it was better they just live in bliss for now, not knowing about the horrors taking place.

After everyone was gathered around, they admired the good job Harding had done of finding a perfect rock to bury at the head of William's grave. It matched perfectly with the other four rocks sticking up on the first row.

Martha made her way to the front of the group and sadly looked down upon her husband's grave. Everyone was quiet, waiting to see if she wanted to say something. She seemed as if she might want to, but then she feebly said "I just can't. I don't know what to say. I just feel like my life is over." Then she started crying. Lucy went to her and put her arm around her to comfort her. Hannah decided maybe it was time for something to be said, and obviously it was going to fall to her. So she began...

"I don't have the words, really, to know the proper way to conduct a funeral. If Rev. Owens were here, he would know. I am no preacher, but I will do my best. I don't know what it is like to lose a husband, or a father, as you and the boys have. I know what it's like to lose someone you love and to grieve over them, though. It is the worst feeling one can ever feel. I tried to find a passage in my mother's Bible that would be appropriate, but nothing seemed right. I can't think of a decent sermon, or even a prayer, to utter at a time like this. But, there is one thing I would like to read aloud, if I may." The others were listening attentively, so she kept going. She was holding her journal and she opened it up to a particular page that she had marked. "I want to read you a poem that I wrote not too long ago when I was missing my brother Jesse. Writing the poem helped me in my grief, so I hope hearing it will help you in yours." She looked down at the page and began...

"If there was no such thing as Heaven
Then my grief would overtake me
What puts the breath into my chest
Is knowing God will not forsake me

If death on Earth is the end of all
Then what's the point of living
How can peace be in your heart

When you're fraught with such misgiving

If there really is no Heaven
Then I suppose I'll never know
But, I won't have fear of death
For I chose to let my spirit grow

If loved ones are truly waiting there
Then I know the tears I'm crying
Are tears of joy and wonder
Not the fears of really dying
When you live your life for God
Then you can truly sing
"Oh, grave, where is thy victory?
Oh, death, where is thy sting?"

"That was beautiful, Hannah. Thank you! Thank you for bringing William home," Martha said. "Could someone maybe sing a song for him?"

Feet shuffled and no one could think of what to sing. Without Rev. Owens to tell them what to sing, everyone's minds were going blank. The silence was beginning to get uncomfortable, but then the soft, childlike voice of little 7 year old Ruby Madison began with...

"Amazing Grace
How sweet the sound
That saved a wretch like me"

Everyone else joined in and finished with a beautiful chorus of voices that rang out through the trees...

"I once was lost
But now I'm found
Was blind, but now I see"

It was short, and it was simple, but somehow it was

enough.

April

Martha and her boys continued to live with Lucy and Albert as the weeks went by. She didn't want to ever go back to the home she'd shared with William. It was just too painful. At times Albert wondered if maybe he should go back home to live with his stepmother and siblings again, but then he'd remember his promise to his big brother to look after Lucy, and he would decide to stay. The women were happy to have a capable young boy around to help out.

Things began to get back to a semblance of normalcy. Each household was planting their gardens and tending them. There was much work to be done. Without any men around, the task seemed insurmountable, but the women did the best they could manage. There was no time for schooling because every waking moment was spent working. Sarah hated the fact that the children were not learning, but she kept telling herself when the war was over, she would make up for lost time and start the school back up. Losing Sunday church services had been bad enough, but now not having school either, the little school/church building just sat empty most of the time.

Many of their supplies were running out, but there didn't seem to be a way for them to make it to town to restock, and they had no money that they could buy with, and very little of value to trade with. In the past, they had depended on Elijah and Henry's sawmill to bring in some money throughout the year. They would cut a load of wood and haul it to town and make enough money off of it to buy needed supplies. But, they did not have that source of income now. The women were beginning to ration some of the things, like sugar and flour. They tried to go to bed as soon as it was too dark to see, so they didn't have to burn as many candles, or use as many matches. They didn't serve as many options at meal time, keeping it simple. Some meals they would not serve meat at all, for all of their smokehouses were almost empty of meat. They all lived in the hope that the war would end any day now, and the men would come home. With Elijah, Henry, Daniel and Joseph back home, everything would be so much easier. They just had to get by for a little bit longer.

One morning in mid-April, Hannah was coming downstairs to head outside to work in the garden. As she passed Sarah's room, she heard her name called. "Hannah, can you come in here please?" It was Sarah. Hannah walked into the room, expecting Sarah needed help doing up the back of her dress or something, but instead, she saw her holding onto the bed post and bent over in pain. "Hannah, it's time," she said. "The baby is coming..."

Hannah helped Sarah to lie down on the bed, then she went to get Irene. After Irene had examined her, she said that she thought it would be awhile still, so she went back home to finish up some chores and care for her children. She told them she'd check back in in a few hours, but in the meantime, all Hannah could really do was sit by Sarah and hold her hand when the pains came, and give her water to drink and keep her as comfortable as possible.

After several hours of labor pains, Sarah was beginning to tire a great deal. At one point she looked at Hannah and said "What was I thinking? Getting married again and having more children?" She half smiled when she said it, because she didn't really mean it, but she was reaching a breaking point and was just ready to get this baby out of her.

Irene returned and checked on Sarah again. She said maybe they should leave the room for a bit and let her try to close her eyes between contractions and rest. So, she and Hannah went into the kitchen for a bit. They also decided to send all the children across the creek to Lucy's house for the duration. Once they were gone, it was just Irene, Hannah and Sarah in the house. Irene said she didn't think it was a good idea to ask Lucy or Martha to come help, because each of them was due to have a baby soon, too, and if something were to go wrong with Sarah, or if they were to sit and watch her struggling with so much pain, it might just give them anxiety about their own impending labor.

Hannah was amazed at the strength that women had to have to get through something like this. She wondered how a woman found the courage to go through it again, and again, and again. One would think once was enough! But, Irene told her that God has this amazing way of making a woman forget how terrible it was, and the love they feel for their children makes them willing to go through it again, just to feel that love once more.

"But, don't some women just get tired of having babies?" Hannah asked.

"Oh, absolutely! Some women pray their husbands will not want relations each night, for fear of getting pregnant again."

"Why don't they just tell them no?"

Irene laughed. "If it were only that easy. Part of the vows of marriage are that you will be available to fill those needs for your husband. If you don't want to fill those needs for a man, then you must never get married. That is the trade you make for the security of being taken care of."

"That seems so unfair! I feel like the woman gets the bad end of the deal."

"Well, it's not always bad. Believe it or not, many women enjoy the relations with their man, and look forward to it, even. At least at first. But, with each baby that comes along, many women begin to come up with all sorts of ways to keep their man at a distance."

"Relationships are so complicated," Hannah said. "Everything is simpler when you're a child. I'm finding that out more and more. I didn't know how easy I had it when I was younger. I didn't appreciate it until it was gone."

"I think you'll find most people feel that way, even the men and boys."

Just then Sarah called out from the bedroom. The other two women got up and went to her. It had been ten hours since her first pains. She had been struggling along all that day, in a constant cycle of pain, but with not much sign of change. But, now she said "I feel the urge to push all of a sudden."

Irene took a look and said "I think it's time. Hannah, please go boil a pan of water, and make sure you have some clean rags close by. And, give Sarah another drink of water."

For the next two hours, Hannah dutifully performed every chore Irene asked her to do. She watched in amazement as her stepmother continued to find the strength to push, then push again. She began to see the head crowning. Even though it was a traumatic experience, Hannah couldn't help but compare it to the experience of watching her own mother die giving birth. This labor and delivery was much different. She supposed this was what a normal delivery was like. She prayed silently the whole time that nothing would go wrong and Sarah would have a healthy baby, and that she would not start bleeding profusely and die, like Emeline had done.

At dusk that evening Sarah made one final push and a little slippery baby came shooting out into Irene's hands. It was immediately crying, which was a good sign. It was so different from the eerie quiet of Emeline's baby when it came out.

Hannah wrapped a cloth around the baby and kept it warm while Irene cut and tied the umbilical cord. She then told Hannah to carefully take the baby and clean it up. "Now, don't submerge him in water, just take a cloth and dab him clean. And, don't use water that is too hot or too cold, just lukewarm."

Hannah realized suddenly that Irene had said "him". Just to be sure, she took a peek under the cloth. She turned to Sarah, whose eyes were closed, and said "You got your boy, Sarah." Sarah opened her eyes and smiled, then closed them again. She was exhausted.

Hannah took her new baby brother into the kitchen, and carefully cleaned him off, talking to him the whole time. He was so perfect and beautiful, with good coloring, and a small bit of dark hair. When he cried, his little face scrunched up in such a cute way. Once he was clean she wrapped a cloth around his little bottom, and then swaddled him tightly in a small blanket that Sarah had made for him. She then took him in to meet his mother for the first time.

A week later, Hannah and Sarah and the baby were sitting out on the porch after supper. The children were playing in the yard. Some of the neighbor children had come across to play, and they were really enjoying the warm spring evening. Sarah had gained most of her strength back, and was finally getting up and around a bit. As the two women sat on the porch, Sarah rocking the baby, she suddenly turned to Hannah and said "I think I'll call him Jasper. That is my father's name. It is a good, strong name, and my father is a good, strong man. I will name him after his grandfather and his father, so he will be 'Jasper Elijah Casey'."

"I think that is perfect," Hannah said. "But, I thought you might pick an 'R' name, since all your girls have 'R' names."

Sarah smiled. "Well, if I were still married to Robert, this little boy would probably have been 'Robert Junior', because Robert always said he wanted his first son to be named after him. So, in that case, I would have had another "R" name. But, Robert did not get to have a son. I honestly didn't even think about continuing with the "R" names this time. It didn't even occur to me. It's a new life, time for a new way of doing things, I suppose."

"You know," she continued. "I never really planned to have all 'R' names. It just happened that way. I named Rebecca and Rachel without really even thinking about it. Then, when I was pregnant the third time, after we had moved here, I had this wild idea that I wanted to name a little girl after a gemstone, because I thought that meant she'd be both pretty and strong at the same time. I had narrowed it down to either 'Opal', 'Pearl' or 'Ruby'. It was actually your mother who decided on 'Ruby' for me. We were sitting talking after church one day and when I told her the three names I'd been considering, she said 'Well, you have to choose Ruby, because it starts with an 'R', like your other girls' names.' What she said kept sticking in my head. So, when the baby was born, I went with your mother's suggestion."

"I didn't know that! What a wonderful story! So, Ma had something to do with little Ruby being named 'Ruby'? That makes me happy inside."

Hannah thought about how baby Jasper was her 7th

brother. There had been Daniel born before her, and then after her it was Jesse, Albert, Michael, Jacob, Jonah and now Jasper. But, only two sisters. She thought about how there would have been two more sisters, only they didn't survive their births. She thought about dear Jesse, who was no longer living. This was her father's 12th child, if you counted the three who were buried in the little cemetery behind the church. And with his marriage to Sarah, he had acquired three new step-daughters, as well, so that brought the total children to 15, with 12 living. And, with Sarah only being 31 years old, it was possible he could still have several more.

Hannah loved them all, but she didn't want to have 15 children herself. Maybe three, or four at the most, she decided. It seemed like the more children you had, the harder your life was. Hannah thought her life had been hard enough already!

May

Hannah woke up to the sound of rain and thunder. It had rained all night. She had been startled awake several times to the sound of loud thunder cracks, and bright flashes of lightning. She went downstairs to find Sarah already in the kitchen starting breakfast.

"It's really storming out there!" she said to Sarah.

"Yes, I barely slept."

"I know, me either," Hannah agreed. "I guess we won't be getting any garden work done today."

"Most likely not," Sarah agreed.

The women had all been getting their gardens started over the past few weeks. Sarah and Hannah, with the help of the children, had planted several rows of things in their garden on the hill. On the lower side of the creek, Irene and her children had begun planting their family's garden. They had all planted their corn, carrots, cucumbers, peas, onions, cabbage, okra, potatoes, tomatoes, watermelon and cantaloupe.

Sarah said "Well, we have most of the things planted. I

suppose the rest can wait another day or two."

"What are you putting in the eggs?" Hannah asked, as she watched Sarah chopping up something green.

"Oh, I found some wild pokeweed yesterday, and a few wild onions. I'm just chopping them up in the eggs for flavor, and nourishment. My Ma always said anything green was 'good for what ails ya'. She believed it helped build your body up and make it stronger, so you wouldn't get sick as much."

Hannah could smell the aroma of the wild onions as Sarah was chopping them, and it brought back memories of sitting in the kitchen while her own mother did the same. It was a nice, homey feeling.

After breakfast Hannah went out on the porch and just sat watching the rain. She sighed, because she knew it was going to be a long, boring day, with not much to do to keep the children all occupied.

In the afternoon, after the children had driven her and Sarah crazy, Hannah came up with an idea. She got her journal and said "Children, come help me make up a fun story!" So, they all gathered around her and as they all threw out ideas, they came up with a cute little children's story. Hannah tried to make sure each child got to participate and come up with ideas for the story, so no one felt left out. One child said they should write a story about a family of deer who lived in the woods. So, Hannah then asked each of them to think of names for the deer, and she made sure each deer was named by a different child. Then, she had them all brainstorm and think of ideas for story lines for the deer family. After several hours, they had a nice story written down. Hannah read it outloud to them and they all liked it. Hannah thought it was cute, and she had enjoyed the time with her little brothers and sisters on that rainy spring day.

Sarah commented afterward "Hannah, I think you would make a good teacher. You really held their interest and got them to thinking."

All that night it continued to rain. The next morning was a repeat of the morning before. Hannah woke again to the sounds of rolling thunder, echoing through the mountains. She got up and went out onto the porch and commented that the creeks had risen quite a bit overnight.

Sarah went out and said "Oh, my! They sure have! It better quit raining soon, or we may have a flood."

The women kept watch all day as the rain continued to fall. About halfway through the day the water in the creeks began to rise above the level of the banks. Hannah could see her brother Albert across the creek, standing on his porch, and she knew he was getting concerned. She wanted to yell over to him and console him, but the water was rushing so fast now it was making an awful roaring sound, and she knew Albert would never hear her over that noise. She also saw Harding and Irene standing on their porch, watching the rising waters.

By dinner time, water was making its way across the lower areas, getting closer and closer to the church, and also to the Inman home, and Daniel & Lucy's home.

"I'm worried, Sarah," Hannah said. "What if the water gets up into their houses? What if they get washed away?"

"I'm worried, too," Sarah said. "The worst part is, I see no way of getting them across the creek now. The water is too high and swift. If we could get them over here to our home, we are much higher up and we, hopefully, could all be safe up here."

The adults didn't sleep much that night, at any of the houses. All night long, the roaring of the water just seemed to get louder and louder, and no one was sure how high it was rising. It was too dark to see. Every now and then they would here loud cracking noises, which they all assumed were trees being uprooted and washed downstream.

The rain just kept coming. By morning, when there was enough light for Hannah to see again, she was shocked at the image that lay before her. Mulberry Creek had become Mulberry River! The waters were so wide, it was impossible to tell where the original pathway was. It looked like a giant lake spread out before her. The church was sitting in the middle of water, as if it were an island.

Across the way, she saw that water had made it up to both houses. Later, she would learn that both families had spent most of the night moving their household items as high as they could move them, because water was about to get into the houses. She now saw them all standing on their porches, not knowing what to do next.

"Oh, Sarah! What can we do? How can we help them get to safety?" Hannah asked.

"I don't know," Sarah said. "That water is way too swift. They'd be washed away if they tried to cross it. We should have brought them over sooner."

They watched, helplessly, as one of Irene's wooden flower pots was picked up and washed downstream, breaking into pieces as it bumped into rocks. Then, a watering trough that had been beside the Inman barn also began to move, then eventually washed downstream, as well. Hannah watched, helplessly, as little bits and pieces of their lives began to wash away.

She saw Harding and Albert at the edge of the water, walking along downstream, as if they were looking for something. A little bit later she saw them return, and then they began rounding up everyone from that side of the creek, and they all started walking downstream. Hannah was curious what was going on, so she went out into the rain, herself, and began following the edge of the water on her side, keeping pace with the ones on the opposite side, to see what they were doing.

Soon, she learned what they were planning. Down below the sawmill, a large tree had fallen across the water in an area that was deeper than the rest, therefore, the water hadn't spread out as wide there. The tree had gotten lodged there and was stuck, sticking up out of the water, which was rushing fast underneath it, making a sort of bridge across the deepest part. As Hannah watched, she realized that they were planning on trying to cross the creek by using that downed tree.

She waited on her side as the first of them began to make their way across. First, Harding came across with his mother. She was holding little 1 year old Charlie, and Harding was holding 4 year old James. Hannah's heart was in her throat as she waited until they finally made it across. They had to wade knee high water for the last few feet, but they made it to dry land. They then turned and watched as Albert was making his way across with the very pregnant Lucy. He knew it was up to him to protect his big brother's wife and unborn child, so he was doing his best. Lucy had insisted he carry one of Martha's children as they went, so he had grabbed the youngest one, 2 year old Isaac.

After Albert, Lucy and Isaac were safely across, the two boys, Harding and Albert, made their way back over again. This time Albert got pregnant Martha and her older boy, 4 year old Thomas, and brought them across. Right after him, Harding was coming with his 7 year old sister, Virginia. Hannah got the children from them and watched as they went back yet a 3rd time.

The only ones left on the other side were Harding's two oldest sisters, 12 year old Nancy and 10 year old Elizabeth. Albert grabbed the hand of Nancy and Harding grabbed Elizabeth and they began crawling across the downed tree, holding on for dear life. When they were almost across, they all heard a loud cracking sound, and then the big tree began to move.

"Hurry!" the ones on the shore yelled. They felt panic rising in their chests as they saw the tree begin to break lose on the far end. Harding and Albert saw what was happening, so they each grabbed on tight to the girl they were helping. They were rushing them across, but feared they would not make it. Hannah had never felt so helpless! Rain was pouring down on her. She could barely see. And, the noise of the water was so deafening! If she tried to jump in and save them, she would surely drown right along with them.

Suddenly, there was one final loud crack and the tree broke lose. The far end flipped around with a jerk, and all four of them were thrown into the water. Harding and Albert kept a tight grip on the girls, but they all began floating downstream at a fast rate.

Hannah and the others screamed and began running downstream, trying to see if they could help them, but the water was too fast, and within seconds they had floated out of sight. The other women couldn't keep up with Hannah, she was soon far ahead of them and out of sight, so they stopped and huddled the little ones together, as Hannah continued running down the side of the creek, not knowing what to expect, or how far she would have to go. She just knew she couldn't stand there and do nothing. She knew that all of them could swim, but the power of the water was just too much, even for a good swimmer. Even though Harding and Albert had played the heroes, in all reality, they were still children themselves. Harding was only 16, and Albert 14. These were four *children* floating away from her. Hannah may have been only 18, herself, but she felt a strong compulsion to save them. So, she kept running and running, through the rain, glancing across the water as she went, trying to find them, and praying that they wouldn't drown and disappear forever.

She ran for what felt like hours, tripping sometimes and falling over broken tree branches on the ground. But, each time she would jump up and continue on, oblivious to any injuries she might have received. She was in panic mode. She just ran and ran, screaming out their names "Harding! Albert! Nancy! Elizabeth!" even knowing full well that they could not hear her over the deafening roar.

She ran until she'd reached the spot where William's body had been found on the rock. She knew she was at that spot, but the water was so high it had covered the rock and there was no evidence of it. She knew "blood rock" was under the water somewhere. She and the other children who had witnessed the horrible tragedy there had taken to calling the spot "blood rock". They thought of it as a forbidden, cursed spot, that nobody was allowed to go to. She had a quick, fleeting thought as she ran, that she hoped the flood waters would wash "blood rock" away, so there would be no evidence of it any more.

She kept running, until finally, after she'd ran about a mile, she saw something in the water up ahead, a flash of color. "Oh God! Please let them be okay!" She ran to the edge of the water, and saw that all four of them were clinging to a tree that used to be on the bank, but was now in the water. They were alive, but extremely worn out. One of the girls was coughing, because she'd inhaled some water. Hannah frantically looked around and found a long tree branch that had fallen from a tree. She stretched it out toward them. Elizabeth grabbed onto it and Hannah pulled her out of the water. Then, she did the same for Nancy, and then Albert and Harding. Then, the five of them collapsed on the ground in an extreme state of exhaustion. Hannah and the girls all started crying. Elizabeth just laid there, holding onto her brother, and Nancy held onto Albert. It was as if they thought they were still in the water and if they let go they would die. They all just laid there, gasping for breath, for several minutes, trying to recuperate from the ordeal.

Hannah knew the others would be so worried and concerned, so she finally urged everyone to sit up and try to get their bearings. Just about that time she looked up and saw Isabelle and Rebecca running toward them. They had been sent by the others to try and help. They hugged them all with a feeling of relief, then began helping them to their feet. It took a few more minutes for them all to get their legs back.

As they slowly made their way back toward home through the pouring rain, trudging through mud and muck, Hannah was watching Harding up in front of her, and she couldn't help but get emotional over all he had been through. First, he had started the year very sick, possibly almost dying, then he had been strung up from a tree, again, almost dying, and now, he had almost drowned! It seemed he had an angel on his shoulder, protecting him and keeping him alive.

Hannah knew that all of them had been through so much already this year. She was tired and weary. They were all tired and weary. But, for some reason, her thoughts were on Harding at that moment, maybe because he was Joseph's little brother, and he reminded her of Joseph. At that moment, for the first time, she realized that she deeply loved Harding, not in a romantic way, but in a brother-sister kind of way. She just really loved and admired and respected the person that he was. With all the men gone off to war, Harding had become the one she went to for help in everything that needed to be done, and he had stepped up and never failed her. He had been steadfast and true, beside her through it all. If she had of lost him, it would have broken her.

Harding was just as much a brother to her as Albert was.

The seven of them finally made it back home. The minute Irene saw her three children were safe, she ran to them and hugged them all for dear life. She had feared the worst, and thought her world was ending. She said a silent prayer to God and thanked him for his mercy.

Everyone gathered in the Casey home, which stayed safe from the raging waters. During the night the rains finally stopped. The next day they all watched as the waters crested, then began to go back down. But, it wasn't until three days later that the creek was finally shallow enough that they could make it safely back across to the lower houses.

They found that the water had been about a foot deep inside the houses. Everything was in disarray, and mud was everywhere. Thankfully, most of the smaller items had been placed up high or in the attic, so only a few things got ruined. Everyone spent the next few days cleaning the houses and airing them out, and the boys rebuilt a new rock pathway across the creek, because the force of the flood had washed the old rocks all away. Some of the gravestones at the cemetery had been washed down, so they fixed those back up as well, and opened up the church doors and cleaned and dried out that building, too.

Irene stood looking at her garden and commented "Everything we planted is ruined. It was completely covered in water. I'm sure all the seeds got washed away."

Sarah told her that they would gladly share what they could from her own garden. Not to worry, they would manage.

Irene said "At least we still hadn't planted the sweet potatoes, squash, pumpkin and beans. At least we will have some semblance of a garden. But, I don't know how we are going to make it through without potatoes and corn, and all the other vegetables. I suppose the Lord will provide, but I don't see how. I'm just thankful my children are safe. I can go without potatoes and corn for one winter, as long as I have my children."

Sarah said "And, thankfully, all your animals survived in the barn. I'm sure they were terrified, standing in water like they were, but thankfully they didn't drown."

"Yes, I'm grateful for that."

June

The springtime flew by that year, and soon it was almost summer. Little Jasper was 2 months old now, and Lucy and Martha were both due to have their babies at any time. Both believed that June was the month they most likely would be full term, going by the dates of their last periods. It was now June, and each day Hannah visited Lucy & Martha's home to see if anything was happening yet. Some of the children were taking bets on which woman would have their baby first. They were making a game out of it. Rachel said she thought they would have their babies on the same day. Elizabeth argued that that was almost impossible. Bets were also going on between the children on whether it would be two boys, two girls or one of each. Little Virginia even made an outlandish bet that both of them were going to have twins and so there would be FOUR new babies!

Lucy was extremely excited to meet her baby. It was her first baby, and she couldn't wait to hold that special little miracle that was part her and part Daniel. She missed Daniel, and prayed each day for his return from the war. She had hoped he would return in time to be there for the birth of his first child, but she was beginning to realize that was not going to happen. She was excited at the thought of surprising him with the baby when he did come home.

Martha was not showing outward signs of excitement. It was hard for anyone to really tell how she felt about it all. She was still in a depressed mood most days after the tragic loss of her husband. She and Lucy had become close once they'd begun living together. But, even Lucy didn't hear Martha's innermost thoughts and feelings. Lucy hoped the new baby would be just the thing to finally snap Martha back to reality. But, she was worried, because she was becoming more and more distant with her boys, and it seemed that Lucy was doing most of the caregiving in recent weeks. Martha stayed in bed all day sometimes while Lucy was up doing most of the chores and caring for Martha's children. She didn't mind, but she worried about what it would be like once the two new babies were born and there were four children to be cared for in the house, instead of just two. Would Martha expect Lucy to do everything still?

The other women had noticed Martha's morose behavior, too. She seemed quick to anger, and quick to suddenly break out in tears. She was argumentative at times. Other times it just seemed she had given up on life. Without her husband, it seemed she had just lost the will to live. Everyone was worried about her, but nobody really knew what they could do to help. How do you deal with a woman who's been forcibly raped? No one really understood how deeply it had affected her. Just the rape alone was enough to throw anyone into a mental state, but then add to that the brutal murder of her husband by those same men, and it just sent her over the edge, and it was beginning to look as if she could not, or would not, recover.

It was the the evening of June 6th when Hannah and Sarah went to check on the women and found Lucy acting different than usual. She was walking around, organizing things, moving things to one place, then moving them back to the same place they'd been to start with. She was dusting and sweeping. Hannah noticed that she couldn't seem to stop fidgeting, and wouldn't sit down for more than a second 'til she jumped right back up again. Sarah smiled and said "She's about to have that baby."

Hannah asked her how she could tell. Sarah said "Because she's nesting. Her body is telling her it's about time, so subconsciously she's getting everything ready for the arrival, doing everything that she might not have time to do later. She's fidgety and can't sit still."

Hannah wasn't quite sure if she believed that, but it turned out Sarah was right. By dark that evening Lucy was beginning to have pains. It lasted through the night. Hannah stayed with her, sleeping in the bed next to her, and woke each time Lucy woke with pains. She did her best to comfort her and ask if there was anything she could do. Early the morning of the 7th Irene came over and said it might still be hours, especially since this was Lucy's first baby. Sometimes the first ones took the longest.

By the noon hour all the women had gathered at the house to wait and watch. Older children were left at home to watch the younger children for a bit. The women were gathered around Lucy's bed. They were chatting away and trying to keep Lucy's mind on other things besides her pain. As women are known to do, they began to compare stories about their own pregnancies and births. When one would talk about how she had been in labor for two days with one of her babies, another one would say "Oh, that's nothing! One time I was in labor for *three* days!" When one would say their baby was a whopping 9 pounds, another woman would say one of her babies was a 10-pounder, for sure. Each had to outdo the others and prove that they had suffered more than any woman had suffered in the history of the world!

They also shared some 'old wives tales' that some were skeptical about, but others truly believed. It started when Lucy said she had a headache, and Irene said "Oh, that means you are having a boy!"

Then, Martha said "No, she's having a girl, because her pillow is facing south."

Sarah piped in with "She's been craving a lot of sweets, that usually means it's a girl. If you crave salty, it's a boy."

Hannah said "But, she was carrying very low, and Ma always said carrying low means a boy, and high means a girl."

Then Irene said "Here's the surefire test.... Lucy, show me your hand." Lucy was confused, but she lifted up her hand toward Irene. "It's a boy, just like I said," Irene announced.

"How do you know?" Lucy said.

"Because, when you ask the expecting mother to show you her hand, if she shows it palm up, it's a girl, but palm down, like you just did, it's a boy."

Lucy rolled her eyes and said "I don't believe any of that nonsense."

Sarah said "Well, you could always try the needle test."

"What's the needle test?" asked Hannah.

Sarah asked Lucy where she kept her sewing needles. She took one and threaded some thread through it. Then, she dangled the needle by the thread, just over Lucy's tummy. "If the needle goes side to side, it's a boy, but if it goes in a circle, it's a girl."

They all held their breath and watched as the needle slowly began to move back and forth just a bit, then suddenly it began to go around and around in a circle. "It's a girl!" they all announced.

Just then Lucy let out a loud moan. "Oh, that one really hurt!"

The women grew quiet, but when Lucy calmed down and seemed to almost close her eyes and sleep for a bit, they began to talk about the war and their husbands and sons who were off fighting. They all agreed that this war couldn't end soon enough. They were tired, and they wanted their men and boys back home.

Sarah said "Well, I don't see how it can last much longer. I don't think the south really has a chance against the north. I wish the north would just hurry up and win so we can get back to a semblance of normal again."

Suddenly, Martha became very angry. She loudly said "I'd rather see this war last until my own boys are old enough to fight, than to see the Union win!" All the other women sat stunned at the sudden outburst.

Finally, Irene said "But, Martha, how can you say that? You'd have our men and boys gone for years, they'd all be dead before it was over!"

Martha said "It was Union soldiers that killed my William. I'll be damned if I want them to win this war!"

"Martha..." Irene continued. "You can't blame the whole army for the actions of four men."

"To hell I can't!" she screamed. "All them Yankees are is a bunch of murdering bastards!"

No one had ever heard Martha use profanity like that. It was disconcerting. They could understand her anger at losing her husband, but the sudden outburst just didn't seem appropriate.

Hannah then tried to calm her by saying "Martha, it was *Confederate* soldiers that shot my brothers. Surely you can see that there are bad men on both sides. Wishing that the war would last for years and years doesn't make any sense. The sooner it's over, the less killing we will have to endure."

"Don't tell me what I should or shouldn't wish for!" Martha yelled out.

"But, Martha, my father and Mr. Inman are in the Union army, and you just called them 'murdering bastards'! I know that my Pa is a good man. I can't allow you to sully his name in such a way."

At that point Sarah could feel that the tension in the room was becoming so thick you could cut it with a knife. She said "Ladies.... Ladies.... We mustn't fight amongst ourselves. It's not the time or place. Irene has a husband and a son who each are fighting on opposite sides. Think of how this must tear her apart inside. She can't very well root for either side, without rooting against someone she loves. And, Hannah has a father and a brother who are fighting on opposite sides. This war is difficult on all of us, but let us not forget that we, as women, must not allow ourselves to turn on each other. We cannot let the actions of our men tear us apart."

Then, Lucy screamed "Stop it! Just stop! I'm hurting so bad. Please, everyone just go away, except Irene. I can't deal with so many of you here right now."

Hannah was a bit hurt by that rejection, but Sarah said she understood completely. When you are in the throws of labor, so much can agitate you. It probably was best if the two were alone, so Lucy could focus and Irene could concentrate on what was going on.

Sarah and Hannah went back across the creek and up the hill to their house. It was very hard to wait and not be near enough to hear what was happening. But, they wanted to respect Lucy's wishes. They tried to busy themselves with housework. After a bit Sarah looked out the front door and asked Hannah "How many times are you gonna sweep that porch? I think we could eat off it now."

Hannah stopped sweeping and looked down at her feet. She turned to Sarah with a sheepish grin and said "I can't help it.

I'm trying to see if I can hear a baby crying, or some sign of what's going on over there."

"I know what you are feeling Hannah, but staring at a thing doesn't make it happen any quicker. Come help me clean the ashes out of this fireplace."

Finally, as Hannah and Sarah were cleaning up the supper dishes, they heard a voice calling from out front. They ran to the door and saw Albert running up the hill toward the house. He was grinning from ear to ear. He looked at Hannah and said "We got a little baby niece!"

Hannah squealed with delight and hugged Albert. "What about Lucy? Is she okay? Is the baby okay?"

Albert assured her that both were fine. He said Lucy was feeling bad for chasing them away and wanted them to come right away.

When Hannah walked into the room and saw Lucy propped up with pillows and holding her precious little bundle, tears just started pouring down her face.

"Why are you crying Hannah?" Lucy asked. "It's not a sad occasion!"

"I know Lucy, I know! But, all the sudden I looked at you and remembered that little girl I used to play dolls with under the tree by my house. I remembered all the times we went swimming at the swimming hole and had contests with the boys to see who could stay underwater the longest. I remembered two young teenage girls sitting around talking about how many children we wanted to have some day, and what we were going to name them. Back then, I never imagined you would one day become my sister-in-law. Oh, Lucy! We've grown up! How did it happen so fast?"

Lucy smiled and said "Well, time marches on, I suppose. Why don't you quit reminiscing and come hold your little niece."

Hannah gently took the baby from Lucy and sat down next to her on the bed. "Oh, Lucy! She is so pretty! Look at her! I think she looks like Daniel so much! Oh, Lucy, how I miss him. I know you must miss him, too. I'm saddened he didn't get to be here for this wonderful occasion."

"I have faith that he will be home soon. In the meantime, I have already decided on a name," Lucy said.

"Oh, do tell!"

"Well, Daniel and I had talked not long after we married. He told me ideas he had for both boy and girl names. He said that if we had a little girl, he would like to name her 'Emma', after his mother. I want to honor him with fulfilling that wish. Won't he be surprised when he comes home to little 'Emma'!"

"Is it 'Emeline', like Ma, or just 'Emma'," Hannah asked.

"We want it to be just 'Emma', because that was what most people called her, and we like that better anyway. And, I was having trouble with the middle name, but I've decided, since she was born in the month of June, I will name her 'Emma June Casey'. What do you think?"

"Oh, Lucy, I love it! Ma would have been so honored to have her first grandchild named after her. Thank you for honoring Daniel's wish."

Then Hannah let out a giggle.

"What are you laughing at?" Lucy asked.

"Oh, I'm just glad you didn't name her Bathsheba! Remember when we were about 12 years old, and you said you were going to name your first daughter Bathsheba, and I was going to name mine Zipporah."

"Oh, Lord!" Lucy cringed. "What were we thinking?"

Lucy was a wonderful little mother to her baby, and she was up and around in no time. Motherhood suited her perfectly. Hannah was impressed by how she could cook dinner, or dress Martha's boys, or go collect the chicken eggs, all while carrying her baby around in her arms. By the time little Emma was a week old, Lucy seemed completely back to her normal self, and one would not have known she'd been big and pregnant just seven days ago. Sarah commented that mountain women were just stronger, because back where she was from the women would have a 'lying in' period after giving birth, which meant they would lay in bed for several weeks and do very little. Sarah had done the same when she had her first two babies back in Virginia, but after moving here and having her third daughter, she quickly saw how lazy and impractical that seemed. In two days she was up and about, doing most of her usual chores, although not overdoing it too much. It was just a different time and place, and different rules applied.

It was the morning of June 17th when Albert once again was sent to Sarah and Hannah's home. This time it was to report that Martha had been in labor since the middle of the night, and Lucy had sent for Irene. After a quick visit, Sarah and Hannah left and came back home again, much like they'd done last time. Maybe too many hens in the henhouse was not a good thing, best to let Irene and Lucy manage. They helped the best way they could, by bringing Martha's boys, Thomas and Isaac, back home with them to keep them out of the way.

In the early afternoon, Albert came back to report the good news, that Martha had also had a little baby girl. The girls rushed over to see, but when they walked into the house, there was a strange feeling in the air. Lucy looked sadly at them and said "Martha is not doing well."

"What do you mean? Is the baby okay?"

"Yes, the baby is fine. She seems perfectly healthy. But, Martha just gave up at some point. We would ask her to push and she would just lay there and do nothing. She wouldn't try at all. The baby probably would have come sooner if she would've got into a squatting position like Irene kept asking her to, but she just refused. And, after the baby was born and we cleaned her up and brought her back, Martha refused to hold her."

While the women were still there visiting, Martha's baby began crying and wouldn't stop. Lucy decided maybe she was already hungry. She took her to Martha, but Martha refused to try to feed her own baby. She was physically pushing the baby away. The women could not understand what was going on in Martha's head. How could any mother refuse her baby that way?

Lucy couldn't take the crying any more, so she simply let the baby latch on to her breast. She was already nursing little Emma, but hoped she had enough to give the new baby, too, or else it might not survive. Thankfully, once the baby figured out what was going on, she latched right on and stopped crying.

This went on for two days. Lucy did all the nursing. Every time she tried with Martha, Martha would say she didn't feel well. Lucy was concerned Martha's milk would dry up if she didn't start feeding her baby soon, but Martha continued to refuse.

On the third day, Martha began running a high fever. Irene came over and said she thought Martha had developed an infection, possibly something had torn or ripped up inside her during birth, and it wasn't healing right and had become infected. She had no way of knowing for sure, but that was her best guess. But, it was also possible that she had developed milk fever because she wasn't nursing and allowing the milk to flow through her milk ducts like it was supposed to.

Martha's fever was worse by day four, and she was completely delirious. The other women tried, but for two days they had not been able to get her to eat or drink anything. It was beginning to look hopeless.

On day five Martha died.

Lucy sat holding both of their babies and cried. She told Hannah "Martha died of a broken heart. I truly believe that she just didn't want to live anymore. I just don't think she was made of strong enough stuff to handle the tragedies that had befallen her."

Once again the women and children had to dig a grave. They buried Martha next to William, wrapped in a sheet, the same way William had been. Their two little boys stood by the grave and cried. Thomas was 4, and might somehow retain a bit of a memory of his parents' deaths. But, little 2 year old Isaac would most likely forget, and that was a blessing for him. Sadly, their new baby sister would never have a chance of even being held once in either of her parent's arms.

But, God knew what he was doing when he placed Martha in Lucy's home. He knew what he was doing when he made both women become pregnant at the same time. Lucy had fallen in love with little Thomas and Isaac. And, after 5 days of nursing the new baby alongside her own baby, she had fallen in love with her, too.

She looked down at the little orphaned girl and said "Don't worry, sweet girl. I am your mother now, and you will have all the love due to you in this life. If I have my way, you will never know grief like your mother knew."

When Hannah next visited Lucy, Lucy told her that she had named Martha's baby. She said "Martha never really discussed with me what she might want to name the baby. I think, in her heart of hearts, she didn't really believe she or the baby would survive, so she just didn't bother thinking of a name. She had been robbed of that joy. So, I sat here and thought about how these two little girls will grow up together. They were born 10 days apart, both in June, one on June 7th and the other on June 17th. I decided I would give Martha's baby a name that would match in some way with Emma's, because I think of them as twins, in a way. So, I want to call her Ella. Emma and Ella. They will grow up as sisters. I thought if I gave Ella the middle name of 'Jane', it would tie in nicely. I heard Martha say once that her middle name was 'Jane', so it would be nice for her baby to have her same middle name. So, it's Emma June and Ella Jane."

"Will they have different last names?" Hannah asked.

"Well, I thought about it, and with both parents gone, I feel I should truly adopt her and just give her our last name. Both of the girls will be Caseys. And, if I'm going to adopt and raise the boys, too, I will probably just use Casey as their last name. I feel like if you have a different last name than the rest of your family, you might feel like an outsider. I feel like everyone in my house should have the same last name, and everyone should be treated as if they are all an equally important part of the same family.... the Casey family."

She continued by saying "You know, I never remember hearing what the boys' middle names are. Since I have no way of knowing, I suppose I could just use their old last name as their middle name. They could be 'Thomas Bennett Casey' and 'Isaac Bennett Casey'. At least that way they hold onto some semblance of their old life. I certainly don't want to hide their true identity from them."

Hannah said "But, wouldn't Martha or William have family

that might want the children?"

Lucy said "Most likely... but how would we ever find them? I wouldn't even know where to look! I never heard either of them talk of their family, or even where they were from. It's almost as if they ran away from something when they came here, like they didn't want to be found. I don't know Martha's birth name, so I wouldn't know what name to even look for to find her side of the family. I have no names to go by from William's family, either. I don't even know what state his family is in, and I don't have the means to be traveling around searching, anyway."

Hannah said "Now that I think of it, when mail was brought back from town, there was never anything for Martha or William. I think you may be right, and they fled something and didn't want anyone to know where they were. Maybe that's why they kept to themselves so much. Or maybe they simply didn't have any family. It sure makes me curious, wondering what their story was. No matter, we don't even have a piece of mail with a name on it to help us find the children's blood family, so they are Caseys now."

Lucy said "I know that the children will be raised in a loving home with me and Daniel, and with you as their doting aunt, and Sarah and Elijah as their grandparents. I can't imagine they'd have a better life with anyone else than us. I feel as if this is how it was meant to be for them."

Hannah was so amazed at her sister-in-law's compassion, and how easily she was willing to take on so much. Only a few short months ago she was not a mother at all, and here she was now a mother of four. And, just a few short months ago Hannah was not an aunt yet, but now she was an aunt to two little boys and two little girls. How quickly things can change. Nothing is ever certain in this world.

October

Sarah sat bouncing six month old Jasper on her knee. He was giggling, the first time the girls had heard him do that. They were enjoying the sweet sound of a baby's laugh, and trying to get him to do it again.

There had not been much to laugh about in recent months. There wasn't a bit of sugar, flour or corn meal left in the house, which meant no cake or pies or breads could be made. They had used the last of the sugar making jellies and jams and preserves. The girls had put up as much garden produce as they could that summer, but the smokehouse was empty. Harding and Albert had gone hunting some, but were inexperienced hunters and had not brought back much more than a squirrel or a rabbit. Hannah and the girls had tried fishing. They caught a few little fish, but they just didn't have the knack for it. They didn't know Pa's secret for catching the big ones. But, whatever they did manage to catch, they cooked up and divided between all the family members. They were only managing to come up with meat for dinner maybe once a week, if that.

Hannah and Sarah still had one hog left, and several chickens, and two cows. Hannah knew they would probably have to butcher the hog soon. She didn't want to kill her cow or it's calf. Without the cow, they would have no milk. If it weren't for the Inmans having a bull that her cow could mate with, she wouldn't have even had that. And, the chickens were needed for the eggs they layed, so she didn't want to kill them for meat, either.

That afternoon, as she sat watching Jasper laugh, she suddenly jumped up and slapped her leg and said "That's it, Sarah! I want some meat! Let's cook up one of those chickens tonight."

Sarah thought it was a fine idea. Her mouth was watering already. She called for Isabelle and Rebecca and told them to go catch one of the chickens, they were going to have a feast tonight. The girls were excited, so they ran out immediately and went straight to the hen house.

Hannah could hear a lot of cackling noises coming from outside, but minutes were going by and still no chicken. She finally went to the porch to see what was going on, and she started laughing when she saw Izzy and Becky running around all over the yard trying to catch this one particular hen. The hen was running in a zigzag pattern all over the place and cackling loudly. The girls were following in a zigzag pattern, and yelling at the chicken and calling it all kinds of names.

Hannah watched as Izzy tripped on a tree root and fell, then got up fighting mad, determined that she was going to catch that chicken. Hannah was in tears, she was laughing so hard. Soon, Sarah and the other children came out to see what all the commotion was about. They all began laughing and yelling out things like "Come on, Izzy, you can get'er!" or "I'm rootin' for the chicken! Go, chicken, go!" or "That's not the way to do it! Chase her the other way 'round the tree!"

Finally, Rebecca ran across in front of the porch, breathless, and said "Can someone please help us catch this Godforsaken chicken!"

Hannah gave her a hard time then, and said "Oh, my goodness, Becky! You can't catch a little ol' chicken?! We are all gonna starve to death because you can't figure out how to catch a little ol' tiny bird."

Izzy, who was still running after the chicken, yelled "You couldn't do any better! She's a crafty one!"

Hannah decided it was time to show them up, so she hitched up her skirt and ran barefooted across the yard. She told the girls to chase the chicken one way around the henhouse, and she would go the other way, and they'd get her for sure. But, the old hen truly was crafty. She sidestepped all of them and took off a different way. Hannah chased her around a tree, then back around the other way. Izzy and Becky fell in a heap on the ground and started laughing so hard they were crying. Hannah was not going to let that bird get the best of her, so she kept trying. She said "Sorry ol' girl, but it's either you or me." The bird led her clear around the house and back again. Hannah yelled "You are going in that pot tonight if it's the last thing I do!" But, soon Hannah had tripped and fell, and she was rolling on the ground laughing, too. It was a nice release of emotions that they all needed. Finally, Hannah said "I guess you win this round 'ol Henrietta. Guess we'll have potatoes and peas again tonight."

Just then, as Hannah was getting up and dusting off her

dress, from down at the bottom of the hill they all heard a male voice say "You need help catchin' that chicken, ma'am?" Then they heard the laughter of men.

The way things had been going this year, their first thought was one of fear, and Hannah was about to grab the girls and run for the house. But, then she heard Charlotte from up on the porch say "Daniel! Daniel! Look, Daniel's home!"

Hannah whipped around to see, and sure enough, it was her brother Daniel standing there, and right beside him was another soldier... wait... that was Joseph! Joe!

She screamed "Daniel and Joseph are home! Oh, thank God! Sarah, they're home!"

Everyone went rushing down the hill at once, and Daniel and Joe were catapulted with hugs and kisses. The little children were jumping into their arms, and the women and girls were weeping with relief to know they had not been shot dead on a battlefield somewhere.

After a bit Hannah felt a shyness creep over her, and she found herself standing back from the others and just watching. She couldn't take her eyes off of them. They both had changed so much in the year they had been gone. Her brother seemed so much like a man now. He seemed a little more hardened around the edges than when she last saw him. He was 21 now. Time and circumstances had removed all the boy from him, and what was left was a remarkable replica of their father. And, Joseph... he had become much more handsome than she could remember. His shoulders were broader. His beard was even longer and fuller than before. The muscles in his arms and legs seemed more defined. Hannah knew he'd just had his birthday and he was now 19 years old. What a difference a year had made! What a difference war had made in both of them.

Hannah almost felt sick to her stomach. Could this be real? Or was she dreaming? It would be a cruel trick to open her eyes right now and realize it had all been a dream. She was almost afraid to get too excited, for fear of being let down.

The other children were busy filling them in on everything that had happened since they left. They told of the soldiers coming to the house, and of how they ate all their supper and how they pushed Hannah and Sarah down, and how they tried to hang Harding, but that Harding was okay because Albert shot at them, but then they went to Martha and William's home and took William away and killed him, and then Hannah and the others had to go get the dead body because they saw buzzards, and boy did it stink, and then Martha had a baby but she died.

It seemed the children were talking all at once, and non-stop. It was a lot to take in.

Daniel said "Martha and William are both dead?"

Sarah said "Yes, it has been a very rough time since you left."

"Has Father or Henry returned?" Daniel asked.

Sarah said "No. We have not seen or heard from them since July of '62. It's been over a year now since they left. But, enough of this sad talk! There have been good things happen here, too. For instance... Three new babies were born while you were away."

"Babies?" Daniel said. "How could that be? Who had babies?"

Sarah said "Wait right here..." She went into the house and got little Jasper from his bed and brought him outside to meet his big brother.

Daniel was amazed! "You mean... you and Pa have a baby now? But, when? I mean, how? I mean... well you know what I mean. Does Pa know?"

"How would he know, Daniel?" Sarah said. "He's been gone for a year and three months with no way to get word to him. He has no idea. I did not know I was expecting until after he left."

"But, you said three babies were born..." Joe said.

"Well, yes, Martha also had a baby, a little girl. Even though Martha died, her baby was very healthy and is alive and well."

"If Martha and William are both dead, then who is taking care of her baby, and her boys?" Daniel asked.

Sarah looked at Hannah with a wink and said "Well, your lovely wife is looking out for them. She is looking out for all *four* of the children."

Daniel didn't catch what she'd said at first, but then said "Wait, *four* children? Oh! You're talking about Albert. I suppose Albert is still staying with her."

"Well, Albert *is* staying with her still, but I'm not talking about Albert. Maybe it's best you get on home now before I spoil too much."

Daniel didn't even take a second to say goodbye because the wheels had started turning in his head and he was beginning to realize what they were trying to hint at. He turned and ran as fast as his legs would carry him toward his house. He practically scaled the creek in one jump!

Joseph watched him run off, then turned back with a smile. "Are you telling me Lucy had a baby while we were gone?"

"Yes, Daniel has a little girl now."

"That is such great news! I suppose Lucy didn't know she was expecting either when we left, because Daniel had no idea. I imagine he is over the moon right now."

Sarah said "He went away a newlywed, and came home a father of four."

"So much has happened." Joe said. "I have a lot to take in. I'm very unnerved to hear that Harding was almost hung by soldiers. I'm enjoying seeing you all, I truly am, but I feel I must go and see my family now. I know Ma is gonna be so happy to see me. And, I want to hear Harding's version of everything that has happened since I've been gone. I've thought of him a lot while I was away. I've seen some boys his age out on the battlefields, and every time it made me think of him."

Joe looked longingly toward Hannah, but she was standing off to the side, and something felt odd to Joe, so he said "Hannah, we will talk tomorrow?"

Hannah said "Yes, Joe. I would like that."

Her heart was pounding and she couldn't understand why she was feeling so odd and shy. She had never been shy around Joe before. It was just that he had changed so much, she almost felt like she didn't know him anymore.

The next day after the noon meal, Joe came calling on

Hannah. Both of them felt so different. In the past, Joe would have just come running in the house hollering for Hannah to come out and play with him, or go to the creek with him, no different than if he'd been coming to get one of Hannah's brothers. But, something had changed in the past year. They felt like two different people now, almost like strangers, and he felt the need to treat her differently, with more respect, and to call on her like a real gentleman, not just assume she wanted to go running around with him like he'd always done in the past.

Hannah called down from the upstairs landing and said she would be right down. She brushed her hair a bit more and pinched her cheeks to make them rosier. She picked up her mother's old hand mirror and looked at herself. She frowned. She thought she looked like a poor mountain girl, not like one of those pretty women she'd seen in Clarksville, with the pretty dresses and the fancy parasols. She was afraid Joe had seen prettier girls during his time away, and maybe wouldn't find her to be his best option anymore. But, she put the mirror down and told herself there was no sense sitting there worrying. Might as well get it over with.

She came down and walked past all her siblings and Sarah, and felt as if they were all staring holes through her. It felt awkward! She didn't like this. She didn't want things to change and become so serious. She just wanted to run out and play with Joe, like the old days.

The two began walking away from the house. Behind them they heard some of Hannah's sisters singing...

"Hannah and Joseph
Sittin' in a tree
K-I-S-S-I-N-G
First comes love
Then comes marriage
Then comes Hannah
With a baby carriage!"

Hannah was mortified! She felt too old to be treated in

such a fashion, but at the same time, she felt too young to be courtin' with a boy. She just wanted to run away and hide. She felt like everyone was forcing her to become involved with Joe. She wanted it to be her choice, not everyone else's. Even Joe seemed to be forcing her, and she was feeling a little trapped.

Joe said "You wanna walk up to the cave?"

Hannah nodded, and the two set off down the trail beside Panther Creek, up north toward her grandparents' house. She told Joe that she hadn't seen her grandparents in several weeks, and she felt guilty for that. They were getting so old that they couldn't make the one mile walk as easy as they used to, so they didn't leave their home much at all. Hannah had meant to see them several times, but she was always so busy. She told Joe that while they were up there she wanted to stop and see them, too. He said that was fine with him because he also would like to see them.

As they walked along in the quiet of the woods, they both felt a bit awkward, not really knowing what to say. Hannah finally asked him to tell her what the war was like, what he had been through this past year.

He sighed and said "It's hard to talk about it, really. I can't even begin to describe the horrors of war. I've seen so much blood, so many dead bodies, so much anger, pain and loneliness. I hope you never have to see anything like what I've seen."

"How many battles have you been in?" she asked.

"Too many to count. There are always little skirmishes going on. We mostly do a lot of walking, going from one place to another, where they say we are needed. Some of the main battles were 'Arkansas Post' back in January, 'Chalk Bluff' in about May, 'Honey Springs' in July and then the last one before I left to come home was 'Devil's Backbone' at the beginning of September."

"Why were you fighting these battles? I mean, what causes the men to say 'this is where we are fighting'?"

"Well, they sent us to Arkansas Post to disrupt the Union's shipping of supplies on the Mississippi River. When the Union retaliated, we were overpowered and retreated to Fort Hindman. They fired upon us, and we just didn't have the manpower to hold them back. It was an awful, bloody battle. I heard we lost over

5000 men, to the Union's 1000."

"At Chalk Bluff we were trying to cross the St. Francis River, but the Union tried to stop us. We got across but not without losing about 200 men. The Union lost around 100."

"At Honey Springs Depot, we were trying to gain control of Indian Territory. We had planned to try and march into Fort Gibson to overtake it, but the Union army got word and sent troops to stop us. They crossed the Arkansas River and began firing on us. It was wet and rainy, though, so our powder was wet. Our guns were misfiring because of the wet powder, and the rain was intensifying, causing even more problems with visibility and the like. We had to retreat to try and obtain better ammunition. But, we just couldn't get back into control. There were command issues, and finally we had to full on retreat and give up any hopes of taking Fort Gibson. We lost a good 600 men in that battle, some of them men I had grown close to. The Union only lost about 70."

"Devil's Backbone is a ridge in the Ouachita Mountains, southwest of Greenwood. Again, we were trying to get control of Indian Territory. We halted the Union forces for a time, but eventually they overpowered us and we retreated into Waldron. I think we lost about 40 men that time, and the Union lost less than 20."

"It's getting hard to keep a good moral, because we just keep losing. The men still have some hope, and we've developed this rallying cry. They call it the 'rebel yell'. When we are heading into danger we just do the rebel yell and it gives us courage to head into the uncertainty."

"What does the rebel yell sound like?" Hannah asked.

Joseph threw his head back and let out a loud primal scream, unlike any sound Hannah had ever heard. She imagined Joseph among a group of other soldiers, making this noise as they went into battle. It almost seemed comical to her. In her mind, she imagined this was how wild Indians acted when they attacked. It just seemed so strange to her. In some ways, the man walking next to her down this well-worn path seemed like a stranger. Had she really walked this same path with him many times before? It didn't seem possible. Why did things have to keep changing? Why did Joe have to go off and be around other people and learn new things and just... well, just become so different?

Suddenly, Joe stopped walking and stopped talking about the war. She turned to see why he stopped.

"Hannah, do you still want to marry me?"

There was a brief silence as Hannah recovered from this sudden change in topics. She then said "Of course I do, Joe!"

He said "You paused. You didn't answer as quickly as I'd hoped. Are you having second thoughts?"

"No, Joe, really I'm not. It's just... You've been gone so long, and I feel like I'm having to get to know you all over again. But, you are still my Joseph. I do still want to marry you. But..."

"But, what, Hannah?"

"It's just that... You will go off again, for who knows how long this time. And, maybe this time you won't come back. You will be one of the 5000 men that die in the next battle. You won't come home to me. I'm afraid to let myself love you because it will hurt too much if you die!"

Joe took her hand and pulled her closer to him. "Hannah, fear doesn't stop death... But, it certainly does stop life."

Hannah took in the meaning of his words. He was right. She knew he was right. Even her grandpa had always said that fear only makes the wolf seem bigger than he really is. She knew if she lived in constant fear she would miss out on so many wonderful things, that, even if short-lived, were still wonderful things worth going through and remembering. But, it was so hard to convince her heart of what her mind already knew.

Joe leaned in and kissed Hannah, and they stood there holding each other for a long time. Then, he took her hand and said "Come on! Let's go see our cave."

Inside the cave they saw that Grandpa had brought a few more items up. He had placed a few tools inside, and some more preserved foods. There was a container of what looked like dried deer jerky. Hannah was amazed at the agility of the old man, being able to navigate the hills and carry these things. She knew it was hard for him and it took him twice as long to get up to the cave and back as it took her and Joe. She wondered what kinds of horrible things he had seen in the war he had been in, things so bad that he felt the need to stash away so many items. She had seen some horrible things herself, in this current war, but thankfully her grandparents hadn't physically witnessed most of the bad. Since they lived a mile off the main road that most of the soldiers traveled, their home had not been discovered by any of them. No soldiers had come to their door, or even passed by, that they knew of. Hannah had thought of trying to bring them down to live with her, but something in her gut told her that they were safer up here, away from where most of the skirmishes with soldiers had taken place.

When she commented on the eccentricity of her grandfather, hoarding away all these things, Joe said "Well, if you think about it, once you've been through something bad, you don't forget it. He's been through a war before, so he has that wisdom to know what *could* happen and he just wants to be prepared, because maybe last time he wasn't prepared. You may think it silly and unnecessary, but after what I've seen the last two years, I can kind of understand what is making him do this."

Joe and Hannah climbed out of the cave and sat up on top of the rock that covered the entrance. Joe was feeling amorous, and began kissing Hannah again. She was enjoying it, but then he began to touch her in ways he had never tried before. He began caressing her breasts through her dress. She began to get a bit uncomfortable, but at the same time she was imagining what it would be like if his hand were underneath her clothing. After a bit more kissing and touching, Joe began to undo some of the buttons on Hannah's dress. She was lost in the moment, wanting to go further, wanting to experience the feeling of being skin to skin with Joe, wanting his hands all over her.

But, suddenly she jumped back! Did she really just want his hands to be all over her!? What kind of thought was that for a proper young lady to be having?

"Joe... stop!" she said. She began to do her buttons back up.

"Did I do something wrong?" he asked.

"No! I mean.. Yes! I mean... Oh, Joe. I'm sorry, I just can't do this. I can't let this go any further unless we are married."

She was almost kicking herself for saying that, because she truly wanted to keep going. She wanted to find out what it was like to be with a man in such a way. But, then the image of her mother with all those children clinging to her skirts made her once again realize that her decision was correct. She did not want to end up with child, not now.

Joe said "If Rev. Owens were still here, I would marry you today, right now. But, he's not. Times are different now. I don't think the old rules apply."

"Oh, Joseph, you know that you don't believe that. You know in your heart that God would not look down on us and approve of us sinning this way. We must be married first."

"Then go into town with me, Hannah! We can go to Clarksville and get married there!"

Hannah had a fleeting thought that maybe he only wanted to marry her so he could have sex, but she quickly convinced herself that Joe was not like that, and so she said "Okay, Joe. We will. We will go to Clarksville and get married. But, not yet. Not until the war is over, because I can't marry you and then have you go off to war and leave me a widow. When the war is over, you come back to me, and we will marry."

She almost hated herself for saying that, but she knew she could not marry him until he could truly be home with her and not running off to fight battles. She did not want to find herself raising their children all alone, because he was dead, the way she'd seen Sarah do for so many years.

Joe was a little hurt, but with the promise that she, indeed, still wanted to marry him, he composed himself. "Let's go see your grandparents," he said.

When they arrived at the Harris house, things were quiet. No one was out in the yard, or came onto the porch to greet them. Hannah called out to them as she opened the front door. The house was very small, only built for the two of them. It had two rooms. The larger of the two served as the kitchen and sitting area, while the smaller room was their bedroom. Like most of the homes at that time, the bathroom was a simple outhouse behind the main house.

Joshua came out of the bedroom to greet them. "Hi, Grandpa!" Hannah said.

"Hi there Hannah Belle, what brings you my way? And, is that young Joseph with ya! You back from the war?" He went over and gave him a hearty handshake and a slap on the back. "My, if you don't look ten years older. War'll do that to a man. So, tell me, what was it like? What kind of battles ya been in? Is that ol' Confederate army about'ta crumble yet?"

As the two men began their war talk, Hannah said "Where's Grandma?"

Joshua said "She's in bed, Hannah dear. She's not been feelin' well of late. You can go see'er."

Hannah was concerned to hear that her grandma wasn't well, especially at her age. She quietly walked into the room and saw her laying in bed looking so small and frail. She was already a small woman, but she looked like she barely weighed 90 pounds, all skin and bones.

"Grandma, it's Hannah."

Ruth turned and opened her eyes and smiled. "Well, if it ain't my favorite girl."

"Grandma, are you not feeling well? What are you sick with? I could try and help..."

Ruth said in a weak, gravelly voice "Oh, it ain't no sickness like that. I ain't got no cough or fever. But, somethin' is wrong in my insides."

She reached for Hannah's hand and took it and moved it toward her stomach. She pressed Hannah's palm down on the left side of her abdomen. "Feel that knot in there?" she asked.

Hannah pulled her hand back quickly when she felt it. It felt like a hard rock was under her skin. She carefully put her hand back and felt it again. "What is that Grandma?" she asked, with fear in her voice.

"I don't rightly know honey, but there's somethin' growin'

inside a'me, and I know that cain't mean I have much life left in this ol' world. I been hurtin' some, and I don't seem ta have any appetite these days. I suspect there's some kind'a tumor inside a'me."

Hannah was angry at first, for why hadn't Grandpa come to get her so she could help? Then she was ashamed because she, herself, should have been to visit before now, then she would have known. She felt helpless, because she knew there wasn't a thing she could do to help her grandma. How could she, when she didn't even know what this was.

"Grandma, you and Grandpa need to come down and stay with me, so I can take care of you."

"Oh, now child. I know you can take care a'me, but Grandpa is doin' a fine job, and I would feel more com'terble right here, dyin' in my own bed."

Hannah began to cry at those words. "Grandma... don't talk of dying!"

"Hannah, dyin' is a part a'life. If old ones don't die, new ones cain't be born. It's just the way God planned it all out. I've had a long life, and I'm not afraid to go meet my maker. My only regret is that I don't wanna leave Joshua alone, so promise me that when I go, you'll look out for yer Grandpa."

"Of course I will Grandma!"

On the walk back home Hannah told Joseph everything her grandma had said, and she cried a lot. Joseph kept telling her how sorry he was, and that he would do anything he could to help. Hannah swore she would come check on Grandma at least every other day, and asked Joe if he would come with her each time. He said "You know I will, Hannah."

Each day, Hannah feared Joseph would announce he was going back to war again, but each day he kept staying. He told Hannah there were things that needed to be done here first, before he could leave. Daniel, also, was staying around to help Lucy with the new baby and the three adopted children. He hadn't got used to saying "my children" when talking about them, but that would come with time. There was no part of him that wished to turn those children away. He wanted to raise them with Lucy. But, coming home from war thinking you only had a wife, and finding out you had four children, was quite a surprise to one's system. It was a bit overwhelming.

The main concern when Joseph and Daniel had returned, was finding the women and children in such a poor condition. They decided the first thing they needed to do was make a run to town for some things that the women had completely run out of. They couldn't very well make it through the winter without some of these things. They decided to do a little work at their fathers' sawmill, and cut enough building lumber to make a load to take to town to sell. They also had each received some pay from the army, so they had a bit of cash on hand.

It took Daniel & Joe two weeks to cut enough trees to make a load of lumber, but with the help of their little brothers, Albert & Harding, they got it done. It was hard work, chopping down trees with an ax, and using horses to pull the trunks back to the mill. Thankfully, Henry and Elijah had made the boys help enough when they were younger, that they remembered how to run the mill.

The two Casey brothers and the two Inman brothers loaded up all the items they needed to trade in town, and enough food to get them through the trip. As they left the women were calling out last minute orders... "Try to get five large bags of flour!" "A bottle of whiskey so we can make more cough syrup!" "Plenty of salt so we can butcher the hogs!"

"And don't forget to check at the post office!" Hannah yelled. "Maybe there will be a letter from Pa or Henry." The girls had given them a stack of letters to be mailed off while they were there. Lucy had written to her parents to let them know of the new grandchild, and also of the three new adopted children, and the sad events leading up to that. Irene had written back home to some of her and Henry's family. Sarah wrote to her mother back in Virginia to let her know about little Jasper, and Hannah wrote to her aunt Caroline back in Tennessee. They also wrote letters to Elijah and Henry, in hopes that somehow they might receive their mail.

Hannah was upset that she wasn't getting to go to town, too, but she knew it wasn't her place to go this time. So, instead she performed her chores and tried to keep her mind occupied, until three days later when the boys returned.

Everyone came out to help them unload the wagon. All of the flour, sugar, cornmeal, salt and other food items needed to be put into dry storage places. Joseph handed three little piglets down to the children. Since they were about to butcher their hogs, they felt each family should have a new piglet to raise, so they would be able to butcher again next year. Sarah told Charlotte to put all three of them in their barn for now. She thought it was best to keep them together until they got a little bit bigger. Through the winter they could huddle up together for warmth. Come spring they would take one pig over to the Inman's barn, and another over to Daniel's barn, and each family would spend the spring and summer feeding their pigs and fattening them up.

The children all gathered 'round the wagon hoping for a surprise of candy, like their fathers always brought them. Daniel let them think, for a bit, that there was no candy, but then he finally gave in and pulled out a piece for each child from his pockets. Hannah smiled, because Daniel so reminded her of their Pa, the way he teased the children about forgetting to get candy, and then even the way he went about handing the candy out to them. She had begun to see her brother in a different light. He was not the little boy that she once knew. He was a grown man now, a husband and a father. He was dependable and knew how to take care of people.

As they were unloading the wagon, Daniel told everyone how they'd come upon three men on their way out of town that were walking along down the road in their same direction. So, Daniel, being kind, had asked them if they would like to hop up in the wagon and ride for a bit, to give their feet a rest. So, the men said they were much obliged. They hopped aboard, and introductions were made.

Daniel said "Two of the men were brothers, named Michael

& Thomas Bean. Michael was older, maybe in his 30's, and his little brother said he was only 19, the same age as Joseph. The third man was Solomon Martin, who was married to one of the Bean brothers' sisters. We rode along with them for about an hour, and we were all getting along just grand. I really liked all three of them."

Daniel continued talking as he was handing items down off the wagon. "All three of them said that they'd enlisted on the same day, along with several other men from their community, and they were supposed to meet in Ft. Smith in December to muster in. Michael and Solomon were both married, and they both had 6 children at home. Solomon said his wife was due to have his 7th real soon. He was hoping she would have the baby before he had to muster in. The men had hoped to stay out of the war, but had come to realize this war was not going to end any time soon, so they would have to do their part."

Joseph picked up a bag of flour and handed it down to Albert and then said "Thomas Bean and I got along well, because we were both 19. I really liked him. We talked about all sorts of things as we rode along. Since I'd already been in the war, he was picking my brain, asking me what it was like, what did they feed us, how were we treated, was it hard being away from home. I could tell he was a bit worried about what was in store for him. I told him about you, Hannah, and he said he had a girl that he loved, too. He told me that there was a place near there called "King's Canyon" that a lot of folks went to to have picnics and go swimming. He said there was a big rock there that was shaped just like the state of Arkansas, and everyone called it the Arkansas Rock. It stood up several feet high out of the water. He said it was a right of passage, of sorts, for people to get up the nerve to jump off the rock into the water. He said the local teenagers liked to hang out there, and if I ever got a chance in the summer time, I should come down and visit him and we could go there. He said I should bring my girl and we could all get together." He looked at Hannah and she smiled at the thought that she was 'his girl'. He then continued on and said "I also invited him to come up to the mountain some time and go hunting with us. I told him about the big look-off rock on the way up the mountain, and he said he'd like to see that some day."

As Harding was getting the last item out of the wagon and handing it down, he stood up and looked down at the others and said "You know..... it's odd how people are, how political things can change how you act or how you treat someone."

"What do you mean?" Hannah asked.

"Well, we were all getting along so well. It was great making new friends, and meeting new people. Until suddenly something was said that made us realize that these three men had enlisted with the Union Army. I suppose all along, we had assumed that they had enlisted with the Confederate Army, like Daniel and Joseph had. And, I guess they had all along just assumed that Daniel and Joseph had signed up with the Union Army. For some reason, when the discussion about war had been going on, with all the talk of enlisting and fighting, no one had actually said what side they were on, so a bunch of assuming was going on. I found it interesting how, as soon as it was realized that we were supporting different sides, it was like the air changed. The demeanor of each man suddenly changed. The talking subsided and we all were just riding along in silence. No one said anything ill toward anyone else, but everyone could feel the difference of opinion in the air, an uncomfortableness. We had just been getting along so well, and one word, one sentence, changed everything. It was almost a relief when the three of them suddenly said 'This is where we get off', and they got down off the wagon and walked away. I'm not sure that was really where they had meant to get off, but it just seemed like it was the best thing for all involved."

Joseph said "I could have been friends with Thomas Bean. We were getting along so well! But, just the mention of us fighting on different sides in this war, and any chance of that seemed to vanish. It's a shame. It's just a damn shame what this war is doing to people."

Harding said "Yes, it is. I was thinking about it all the way home, how we were all fast friends, getting along perfectly, until political differences were discovered. I'm not sure why it took so long for us to realize that we were on different sides. Maybe it was

God's way of teaching all of us a lesson. Maybe he wanted us to see how our enemy could be our friend in a different circumstance. Maybe we all learned something today."

As they were handing the last of the purchased goods down, Sarah said "It looks like you were able to get most everything we needed. You did good, boys."

Daniel said "It was difficult, though, because some stores didn't want to take our money."

"What do you mean?" Sarah asked. "Why wouldn't they want your money?"

"Well," Daniel said. "The Confederate Army paid us with Confederate money. The Union side uses greenbacks, which are different from our money. They call ours 'greybacks'. Some of the stores said they were afraid to take the greybacks, because the south appeared to be losing, and so they feared the greybacks might not be worth anything if that happened. Luckily, we found one place where the proprietor was so staunchly in favor of the south, that he refused to take greenbacks, and only took greybacks. So, we purchased most of our goods there."

"I can't believe they would turn down your business over which money you had!" Sarah said.

"Well, who can blame them?" Daniel replied. "They were quick to tell us that they supported our side, but that they had to think of things with a business mind. They were happy to trade with us, but they just didn't want to trade for greybacks. Some of them said they took Confederate money in the beginning of the war, but as things progressed, and it appeared the north might be winning, they became nervous about taking that kind of money any more. It seemed too risky."

Once the wagon was completely unloaded, and the horses put back in the barn, everyone in the little community gathered around to see if there were any letters. Receiving the mail was no longer a private thing with the group. Each person wanted to hear what was going on in the world by hearing all of the letters. So, they all sat around on the porch and in the yard of the Casey home, while Daniel got out the letters.

It had been over a year since anyone had been able to go to town to bring back the mail. So, there were several things. Daniel handed Irene a few letters that had been sent by members of her family, and one or two from Henry's sisters. She read them all aloud to the group. In some of the letters there was news of the war, which everyone was curious to hear about.

Then, Daniel handed Lucy three letters from her parents. She read those aloud, too. Since the Rev. Owens and his wife had lived with all of them for so many years, it was wonderful for all of them to hear that they made it back home and were enjoying life with their other children and grandchildren. Of course, they were begging Lucy and Daniel to come back and live with them in every letter. It was only natural they wanted all their children and grandchildren in one place so they could see them all.

Daniel then handed Sarah some letters. Most were from her Ma, but there were two from her sisters, and one from an aunt, as well. She read them all out loud, and Hannah was amazed, as usual, at how different life was for a family that had money. How less of a struggle their life seemed, compared to Sarah's life here in the mountains of Arkansas. Hannah wondered why Sarah hadn't simply went back to that life of ease after her husband died, instead of staying in Buckeye where life was so hard. Maybe having money didn't necessarily mean life was better, or happier. She knew Sarah had her reasons, and now that she was married to Elijah, it seemed she was always meant to stay here. Hannah had been living her life thinking that Sarah had given up so much to be here, but suddenly she saw things differently, and realized that in Sarah's mind, if she left Buckeye, that is when she would feel she was giving up so much. Hannah was starting to see the world in a different way, and realizing that value was not always tied to money.

Daniel then handed Hannah a few letters that had come from their Aunt Caroline. They were meant mostly for Caroline's parents, the elder Harris's. Hannah read them out loud, then tucked them into her skirt so she could take them up to read to her grandparents later.

Daniel began to act like that was all of the mail. The women began to have fallen looks upon their faces. Was their nothing from Elijah or Henry? No news to let them know they were still among the living? Daniel was teasing them, much as he had teased the children about the candy. Hannah saw the way his mouth was turning up at the corners, trying to hide his smile.

She yelled out "Daniel Casey! Give me those letters!"

He laughed and handed Irene a few letters from Henry, and Sarah a few letters from Elijah. Hannah's heart jumped! Just knowing there were letters meant that at least they had been alive when they wrote them, so she had hope. It was such a relief to know there was hope.

Sarah opened the first letter from Elijah. She read it quietly to herself at first, then said "I'm going to leave out some of it, but I'll read the rest to you all. Some of it is private, from a husband to his wife." She had tears in her eyes, and Hannah knew there must have been some deep expressions of love and longing in that letter.

Sarah began...

September 21st, 1862

Dearest Sarah,

Henry and I are together. They have put us in the same company. I have been made a captain, and Henry was placed under my command. I was happy for that, for we can watch out for each other. It is good to have my friend so close at hand. We have not been in a battle, so please do not worry. We have been preparing, learning drills, gathering supplies. We are in Little Rock at the moment. How are the children? Please send me word of Daniel. I fear he is back in the midst of battle. It pains me to know we fight on opposite sides. Kiss all the children for me. Please write to tell me how they fare. Hannah, Izzy & Lottie, remember to treat Sarah as if she were your own mother, and help her as much as you can. Give my little boys my love. Please write, I may not receive it, but I may. Some mail has been making it's way to the troops.

With my deepest love, Eli

Sarah opened the next letter...

December 18, 1862

Dearest Sarah,

I am camped with my troops near Fayetteville. On December 7th we participated in a battle at Prairie Grove. There were some casualties, but do not worry, for Henry and I are both safe. The Union Army is doing well, winning most of our battles. Troops have been brought in from other states, however. As you know, Arkansas has seceded from the Union and for the most part aligns with the Confederates. I was told that Arkansas has around 70,000 Confederate enlisted men, but only about 9000 Union. I may be in the minority, but with help from other companies, we are holding our own. We do not eat well. I miss your cooking, my dear Sarah. Oh, how I long for a pile of your biscuits smothered in a good white gravy. We soldiers are rationed out a portion of food each day. Each of us receives a pound of meat a day, usually salt pork, and a pound of bread, and a little *coffee. I don't know if you receive my letters. I write at least once a week. I have received nothing from your way. Maybe you could not make it to Clarksville, and that I understand. Give all the children my love. Write me of what you know of Daniel, Joseph and William.*

With my deepest love, Eli

As Sarah opened the next letter, she commented on how sad it was that she was missing so many letters. He had said he wrote once a week, yet she only had four total letters here. He'd been gone about fifteen months, he must have written at least sixty letters by now. So many of them were lost somehow and didn't make it through. She continued on with the 3rd letter...

February 9, 1863

Dearest Sarah,

I think of you daily, and the children are always on my mind. It has been a long, hard, cold winter. I am concerned of how you all have fared through this winter. I only hope I had cut enough firewood for you to last. Albert, you may have to cut more wood to keep the other's warm. My company has had to march all the way across Arkansas this winter. It was not a pleasant march. Many nights I wished I was home in the warm bosom of my family. We marched east all the way to the Mississippi River. The rebels were causing a stir over at Arkansas Post, trying to stop our supply lines on the river. We joined other companies there and fought the Rebels back. They retreated to Fort Hindman. Our artillery then fired from across the river so that the infantry could move in for the attack. We got them to surrender, but lost much life. Please do not be concerned as Henry and I came out unscathed. You may not have heard that President Lincoln has introduced an executive order called the 'Emancipation Proclamation'. It went into effect on Jan. 1st. It states that all slaves in the rebellious secessionist states are now free. They are encouraged to flee their masters with the aid of Union soldiers. The freed black men are being offered paid service into the Union Army. My hopes are this will be the thing to end the war. Tell me how everyone is doing. How are the Inman, Owens and Bennett families? Are our boys home from war? Give Grandma and Grandpa my love, and kiss the children for me.

With my deepest love, Eli

Sarah folded up the letter and said "It breaks my heart that he doesn't know so many things. He doesn't know that Rev. Owens and Winnie have left. He doesn't know that William and Martha have died. He doesn't know that Daniel and Joseph are home safe from the war. He doesn't know, even, that he has a new baby boy at home, or that he has his first grandchild."

Daniel said "I didn't know that when I was stationed at Arkansas Post, Pa was there as well! We were fighting against each other. I didn't see him, or Henry. I didn't know they were there. Oh, what if I'd shot my own father? I can't even think of it!"

"This war makes no sense to me whatsoever, what with fathers and sons fighting each other and brothers going against each other. It's tearing families apart, and with no sign of anything being accomplished by it," Sarah said. "Here is the last letter...."

July 11, 1863
Dearest Sarah,
My love, I miss you deeply. When I return there will be no greater joy upon our reunion than any two people have ever felt. I have been gone the good part of a year now with no word from you or my children. It is a difficult cross to bear. As for the war, my company has moved north up the Mississippi River to a place called Helena. We set up fortifications around that town, but the Rebels attacked on the 4th of July. We were able to hold them off, so we still have control of Helena. The Union has captured Vicksburg, Mississippi, therefore giving us complete control of the Mississippi River, which limits the Confederate supply lines. The next step of action is to take Little Rock. The army is struggling to keep us all fed. There are many days when we are issued only a little salt pork and some hard tack. If you don't know what hard tack is, you are blessed, because it is the worst thing, simply a tasteless, hard-as-a-rock cracker of sorts. One day the hard tack they gave to all of us was full of bugs! But, we persevere. I am told the Confederates have it much worse, which causes me many sleepless nights worrying about Daniel. I worry about you, Sarah, and each of my children. I pray you are not suffering in my absence. Please give my love to Hannah, Albert, Isabelle, Charlotte, Michael, Jacob and Jonah, and to

your sweet little girls, Rebecca, Rachel and Ruby, whom I love as my own. Each one is special to me. I fear I will not recognize them when I come home, because they will have all grown so much.
With my deepest love, Eli

Sarah folded her final letter up and listened as Irene read the letters she had received from Henry. By now all the letters had been read and shared and everyone went back to their respective homes. As Joe was walking away, Hannah asked him if he would walk with her to her grandparents' house in the morning so she could check on her grandmother and also read her the new letters.

The next morning Joe and Hannah set off up the creek to the Harris's house. They were walking along, holding hands, chatting about various things, enjoying each other's company. When they got to the waterfall and the pretty rock cliffs that Hannah liked so much, Joe asked Hannah to come sit down beside the creek, because he had something to show her.

Hannah sat down near the water and looked across at the beautiful view. There was just something so majestic about those cliffs. She always felt drawn to them. She wondered how many years it took for them to form, and what secrets they held in all their cracks and crevices. She watched a hawk swoop down and land on a small tree that was growing way up high on the side of the cliff, barely hanging on in a small crack.

Joe sat down with Hannah and said "I wanted to give you this in private, not in front of the others." He handed her a small beige-colored card. It felt thick and had something inside it. She noticed that one side opened up, so she lifted the edge of the card, and inside she saw an image of Joseph in his uniform with the buttons all down the front, with his hat on and his gun proudly held across his chest. She touched it. It was an image on a piece of hard tin. She turned it over and over and marveled at it.

"It's called a tintype," Joseph said. "A lot of the soldiers get them to send home, you know, just in case they never return, so they can be remembered. I had sent this to you and it was at the post office when we picked up the mail yesterday. I didn't know if I'd make it home to you, so I wanted you to have an image of me to remember me by."

Hannah held it close to her chest and said through tears "I love it Joseph!"

He said "Well, I know you wanted me to write you, and I just am not very good at writing, so I had thought to at least send you this."

"Oh, this is even better than a letter Joseph! I will cherish it always."

She turned it over and saw where he had written her name and location on it so he could mail it, and below that he wrote "To my best friend, and the woman I hope to grow old with."

Now that the boys had brought back the supplies, it was time to butcher the hogs. Hannah and Sarah had a hog, and the Inmans had a hog, both huge and fat and ready to be butchered. They had wanted to preserve them in salt, but there was none left. Now that the boys had brought plenty of salt back, the task could not be put off any longer, and everyone was starving for some good, fresh pork.

The first thing that had to be done was the killing of the hogs. This was not something Hannah had ever been able to stomach, so she never watched. Thankfully, Daniel and Joseph took on the task. Hannah cringed when she heard the two gunshots, and was thankful to not hear any more, because that meant the first shot had done the job and the hogs had died quickly.

Both hogs had been brought up to the Casey home before being killed, because this was going to be a community effort. Daniel and Joe got Harding and Albert to help them with skinning the hogs. While that was going on, Sarah and Hannah went with the girls to bring out some barrels and wooden boxes from the barn, which would be used to store the meat. As the older girls were digging around searching for the barrels, the youngest two,

Ruby and Virginia, went to the enclosure where the three piglets had been placed when the boys got back from town. They picked the squealing piglets up and were carrying them around like they were toy dolls. Sarah told them to put those things down so they would quit squealing.

Ruby then said "But, Ma.... We are playing with them."

"I know you are playing with them, but that squealing is a little much for my nerves to handle. Put them down!"

Ruby sighed and lowered her piglet back into the pen. "This one is Dixie," she said.

Virginia put her two down and said "This one is Yankee, and that one is Rebel."

Sarah said "What in Heaven's name are you girls talking about?"

"We named them! They are Yankee, Rebel and Dixie. Isn't that cute?"

"Oh, my word!" Sarah exclaimed. "Don't be naming them! They are gonna be dinner some day. You're not supposed to be getting attached to them."

"But, they are so cute!" the girls chimed in.

Finally the girls got all the barrels and boxes that they needed brought out into the front yard where the boys were skinning the pigs. Then they went over to the Inman's house and got their barrels, too. Sarah put Isabelle, Rebecca and Nancy to work rubbing lard all along the insides of the barrels. This was so when they put the meat in later, it would keep the air from getting into the barrel and spoiling the meat. Hannah then went inside the house and brought out a large washtub and sat it by the hogs. "Here, put all the fat in here," she told the boys. Later, once all the fat was cut off, they would have to render it to make lard.

After the hogs had been skinned and all the fat cut off, the boys began cutting the meat into small chunks. As each chunk came off, they handed it to one of the children, who then carried it over to the women and girls who were sitting around the empty barrels. The girls had covered the bottom of each barrel with a layer of salt. As each piece of meat was cut off, one of the girls would take salt and rub it all over the outside of the meat, until it was completely covered in salt, then they would lay it in the bottom of the barrel on top of the layer of salt that was already there. Once a complete layer of meat was placed, another girl would come along and pour another layer of salt on top of the meat until it was covered. Then, a second layer of salted meat would be placed, then another layer of salt, and so on, until the barrel was full.

It took several hours to finish the task. At one point, when the girls had touched so much salt their hands were drying out and cracking, Sarah smiled and thought of a story from her past, which she shared with all of them.

She said "I remember when I was a girl, my mother asked our neighbors if she could borrow a little salt. I was confused, because I knew we had plenty of salt at home. I asked Ma why she did that and she said it was because our neighbors were poor. I thought that answer did not make any sense at all, and I told her so. It didn't seem right to ask a poor family to give up some of their hard-earned salt, when we already had plenty at home. I thought my mother was being selfish. But, then she reminded me of all the times when these same neighbors had come begging at our door. Ma said that no matter how rich or poor you are, it makes a person feel very bad to have to beg others for help. So, occasionally she would ask the neighbors for a bit of salt, so as to make them feel needed, to make them feel like they were giving back just a little. Ma said she chose salt because that would be something they would most likely have enough of to share without it burdening them too much. She said 'Don't you see, Sarah? I gave them back a little of their dignity by asking.' I didn't really understand as a child, but now that I have experienced being on the poorer side of life, I understand what Ma was trying to do."

When the backbreaking labor was about to get to all of them, Joseph began humming a song under his breath to break the monotony. The song wasn't familiar to the rest of them, but Daniel knew it, and he began humming along, too. Hannah finally asked them what that tune was they were humming.

Daniel said "Oh, it's a song that the soldiers sing sometimes at camp at night. It's about a soldier marching home at the end of the war, and how everyone is celebrating."

"Sing it for us!" all the children begged.

So, Daniel and Joseph began singing as they continued to work.

"When Johnny comes marching home again
Hurrah! Hurrah!
We'll give him a hearty welcome then
Hurrah! Hurrah!
The men will cheer, the boys will shout
The ladies, they will all turn out
And we'll all feel gay when
Johnny comes marching home

The old church bell will peel with joy
Hurrah! Hurrah!
To welcome home our darling boy
Hurrah! Hurrah!
The village lads and lassies say
With roses they will strew the way
And we'll all feel gay when
Johnny comes marching home

Get ready for the jubilee
Hurrah! Hurrah!
We'll give the hero three times three
Hurrah! Hurrah!
The laurel wreath is ready now
To place upon his loyal brow
And we'll all feel gay when
Johnny comes marching home

Let love and friendship on that day
Hurrah! Hurrah!

Their choicest treasures then display
Hurrah! Hurrah!
And let each one perform some part
To fill with joy the warrior's heart
And we'll all feel gay when
Johnny comes marching home

When Johnny comes marching home again
Hurrah! Hurrah!
We'll give him a hearty welcome then
Hurrah! Hurrah!
The men will cheer, the boys will shout
The ladies, they will all turn out
And we'll all feel gay when
Johnny comes marching home"

Joseph then said "I'd play it for you on my harmonica if my hands weren't covered in pig blood. I learned how to play it because they sang it almost every night at camp."

After the larger barrels had all been filled up, the remainder of the meat was layered into the smaller wooden boxes. Finally, all the meat had been salted except for the best cuts which had been put aside for dinner that day. The salted pork was carried and stored away, the majority of it split between the Inman house and Hannah's house, because they had the most mouths to feed, but Daniel also took home a fair share for he and Lucy to have.

Two days later everyone got together again to harvest the corn. The women had done the best they could and planted a crop together that they agreed to all share when harvest time came. They hooked a wagon on to the back of one of the Inman's horses, and pulled it along as everyone pulled the ears of corn off and threw them into the wagon. They then stored them all away in the barns, some in the Casey's barn, some in the Inman's barn, and some in the barn at Daniel and Lucy's house.

The following day some of the children walked down the creek about a mile to a spot where a few wild pear trees grew. It was near the end of harvest, but they picked quite a few pears and brought them home with the horse and wagon. The women divided them up and began peeling and slicing them. They made pear preserves with them, since they finally had some sugar.

Hannah added her family's jars of pear preserves to the other items they'd put up that summer. Neatly in rows in the pantry were jars of beans, peas, tomatoes, okra, squash and two kinds of pickles made from the cucumbers they'd grown. Hannah had made some of the dill kind that Irene had taught her how to make, and some of the sweet kind her mother had always made.

Under the house and in the barn were stored onions, Irish potatoes and sweet potatoes that the women had grown. The women had done fairly well with the garden produce. It was meat that they had run out of and suffered without for most of the summer. Now that Daniel and Joseph were back home, they were hoping to send them out hunting to add some more meat to the salt pork that they now had stored away. Maybe the winter wouldn't be so bad after all. Especially now that the boys had brought back flour and corn meal, so they could have bread again.

Since they had salt now, Sarah got some of the cabbages that they had recently picked from the garden. She chopped the cabbage up and salted it. She then pounded it and squeezed it until it made juice. She then put the cabbage into jars and poured the juice over it until all the cabbage was submerged in the juice. She then set the jars aside and covered them to let them ferment. In about a week, she would have sauerkraut. She was excited, because she loved sauerkraut, and had thought she was not going to have any this year because they had no salt. Once again, she said a silent prayer of thanks that the boys had come home when they did.

It was now late October. Daniel and Joseph had been home for a few weeks. Everyone was beginning to feel a lot better about their prospects for surviving the coming winter, especially after Joe and Daniel had told them they planned on staying around for awhile. If the war was still going on by the spring, they might consider going back and re-enlisting, but for now they felt it was more important to stay home and take care of everyone, at least until Elijah and Henry returned. Daniel had felt very uneasy when he came back and saw what little his stepmother and siblings and wife had left. He shuddered at the thought of what winter might have been like for them if he had not returned when he did. They might have starved, or even froze to death. The thought of them freezing to death had prompted him to gather the other three boys and start cutting down trees for firewood, so they could stock up before it got too cold.

Hannah had taken some of the salt pork, a few jars of the canned foods, some ears of corn and a few onions and potatoes up to her grandparents' home, with the help of Joe and some of the other children. She had also ground a bit of coffee beans so Grandpa could make coffee, and she had thrown in two loaves of bread that Sarah had made the day before, some fresh milk, a few eggs and one of the butter molds she and Sarah had made. Hannah was afraid they weren't getting enough to eat, and she knew Grandpa couldn't really cook much.

Grandma was still in bed, and still sickly. Each time Hannah went, she feared she would find her grandfather hovering over a corpse. It was dreadful to think about, but she knew it was coming, like it or not. She knew her grandmother was dying. Each time she visited, she begged them to come back with her, but Grandma insisted she wanted to stay in her own home with Grandpa. Hannah wasn't sure how she would get Grandma back to her house, anyway, since she couldn't walk on her own. She probably wouldn't survive the trip.

One evening Hannah and Joseph were sitting under the buckeye tree, cuddled up close because the air was a little brisk. Joe was leaning back against the tree and Hannah was leaning back againt his chest. She had her journal with her and was reading out loud to Joe some of the poems she had written while he was away at war. They were just doing what young lovers do, taking any opportunity to sneak away and just be close to each other. Joe was stealing kisses and Hannah was smiling. It was so good to have him home. The buckeyes had fallen. Joe had picked a few of them up and was rolling them around in his hands as Hannah read.

Just then Joe said "What's that?"

Hannah turned in the direction he was looking. She saw a thin trail of smoke coming up off to the east. She sat up and began to get nervous. "That's coming from Rev. Owens' empty house."

Joe said "Someone is burning a fire at their house. Someone must be staying there."

He stood up and helped Hannah up. "Hannah, I want you to go back home. Stay in the house. I'm going to get Daniel and go see what's going on."

"Oh, do be careful Joseph. Don't let them see you."

Joe and Daniel were gone about an hour. When they finally returned they first went to the south side of the creek to tell Irene and Lucy and the children what they'd seen. Then, they both crossed the creek to come tell Sarah and Hannah and the other children what was going on.

"It's a gang of bushwhackers," Daniel said. "About a dozen of them, I'd say. They are camping at Lucy's old house up the creek. They have a fire going in the fireplace. I have a feeling they came from the east and were walking down the road when they came upon the empty house and decided to stay for awhile. They probably don't yet know that there are houses just another half mile down, but they will soon enough. Don't anybody start a fire in the fireplaces tonight. We don't want them seeing the smoke and being drawn this way. I fear they will find us anyway, but let's hold them off as long as we can. And, all of you children need to stay close to home and stay quiet, no running around screaming and yelling and playing. I don't want to take a chance on them hearing you. If we are lucky, they'll decide to go back the way they came."

"What is a bushwhacker?" Hannah asked.

"Nothing but outlaws!" Daniel said. "They are men too

cowardly to fight in open combat, so instead they run around all over the woods, hiding out, breaking into homes, stealing, attacking people, even killing. They claim it's all in the name of the war. If they attack a family of Union supporters, they will say they are with the Confederacy. If they attack a Confederate soldier's family, they will say they are on the side of the Union. If a man ever had a thought of doing something evil, now would be the time, when they can do it in the name of war and get away with it."

"Do you think the men who killed William and tried to hang Harding were bushwhackers?" Sarah asked.

"Most likely," Daniel said.

"But, they had on uniforms!" said Hannah. "Union uniforms."

"I don't doubt it," Daniel continued. "There have been many deserters who left the real army, but go around pretending as if they are still in it. With the uniform on, they can gain people's trust at first, and then rob and steal from them. Wearing the uniform gives them a sense of righteousness. But, then again, they could have simply been part of a company that got separated and were trying to find their way back. Either way, what they did was wrong. This war seems to be bringing out all the criminal element. From what I've heard from the other soldiers, this part of northern Arkansas where we live, and up into southern Missouri, is running rampant with bushwhackers right now. The mountains are full of them. No one is truly safe."

Sarah had a worried look on her face as she asked "Will they steal from us?" She was thinking about all the food that Daniel had brought back, how precious it was for them. She thought of the hogs they'd just butchered and stored away, and how important that was to their survival.

Daniel said "They might, and most likely will if they discover us. It might be a good idea for us to hide some things, and quickly. But, I don't know where a good hiding place would be."

Joe and Hannah exchanged glances. They knew it was time to give up their secret. Hannah turned to Daniel and said "There's this cave...."

She explained to him how their grandpa had showed it to them, and how he had stored some things in the cave already. Joe told Daniel that it really was hidden well, and would be a perfect place to hide things for safe keeping.

Time was of the essence, so they quickly went to all the houses and explained the plan. They got the horses and loaded them down with as much as they could, then Daniel, Joe, Harding, Albert, Hannah, Isabelle, Rebecca and Nancy led the horses as quickly as they could up the mile long trail to the cave. They then tied the horses at the part of the trail where they needed to turn off and go up the hollow. The horses couldn't make it up that steep incline, so everyone just carried as much as they could and took a load of items up to the cave, then came back and got another load, repeating until everything was carried up.

Those who hadn't seen the cave yet were amazed. They all agreed it was perfect. Harding even admitted that he had been up here before hunting, and had passed this very spot, not realizing there was a cave there.

Once they were done they stood back and inventoried. In the little small room at the back, next to the items Grandpa Harris had already brought up, there was now also a basket of corn, two boxes of salt pork, about two dozen jars of canned vegetables, some dried fruits, several fresh eggs, some lard, a sack of Irish potatoes, a sack of sweet potatoes, a basket of onions, a large bag of flour, another of sugar, another of salt and another of corn meal. Sitting next to that were a few cooking pots and pans, some utensils, some matches and candles and several blankets. They had also brought up a few valuables that each family did not want to be stolen. There was some jewelry, some silverware, and a few sentimental items. Hannah placed her journals, her mother's locket and Bible, and the tintype Joe had given her next to the other things. Then, they stacked the rocks back up in the crack leading to the smaller room, so if an animal got in there, maybe it wouldn't get to the food.

Daniel said he would feel better if they could hide more, but it would be dark soon and they just didn't have the time. They went back down the hollow to where the horses were, but just as they were about to untie them to bring them back, Daniel suddenly had an afterthought. "I think we should leave the horses here. If they find them, they will take them." The others agreed, so they left the horses tied to the trees for the night.

When they got back to their houses, the boys went and got all the cows and took them out in the woods a bit and tied them to trees and left them.

That night no one slept much. The women and children stayed inside the houses. Hannah and Sarah paced back and forth all night, worrying. Inside the Inman home Irene was pacing. At Daniel's house Lucy was sitting by the beds of the children, watching over them, worried to death about what might happen.

Daniel sat out on the porch of his house, watching and waiting in case trouble arrived, with his gun loaded and ready. Harding was doing the same at his house. Albert was pulling that duty at his home across the creek. Joe was back and forth all night, sometimes helping Albert to guard Hannah and the others, and sometimes helping Harding to guard their mother and siblings.

It seemed the sun would never rise, but finally a faint orange glow began to appear at the horizon. All night long, these four young men and boys, ages 14, 17, 19 and 21, had protected their families. They had taken over in their fathers' absence and done the duties of men.

At first light, Daniel and Joe set off up the road again to go spy on the bushwhackers. Joe came back to report they were still there. Some of them were up moving about. Daniel was keeping watch in case they started moving closer. Joe said he was going back to watch with him, but for everyone to be alert and prepared.

The women didn't want to start any fires, for fear of giving away their position, so for breakfast they gathered the children around and cut slices of bread and had them put butter and jelly on the bread. Just as they were finishing up with the breakfast, they saw Joe and Daniel running very fast back down the road.

Daniel ran across the creek to warn everyone on that side, while Joe ran up the hill to Hannah's house. Breathlessly, Joe yelled "Get all the children in the house!"

Joe and Daniel had worked out a plan as they were sitting spying on the men. It was time to put that plan into action, and quickly.

Joe said "The men are packing up their horses, and are probably about to head this way. Sarah, keep the little ones in the house. Hide them under beds, upstairs, wherever you can find a place, and stay down and stay quiet. Hannah, Izzy, Lottie and Becky, come with me, quick!" He grabbed all the guns that were in the home and ran with the four girls out to the barn.

Meanwhile, Daniel had done the same across the creek. He told Lucy to grab Thomas, Isaac, Emma and Ella and run across to the Inman home. He told her to hide out with Irene and Irene's youngest three children, while Daniel grabbed all the guns he could find and took Irene's older children, Harding, Nancy and Elizabeth, and also his own little brother Albert, and they all ran to the Inman barn.

Once inside the barn, Daniel began loading a gun for each of his group, while Joe did the same for his group across the creek. Their hands were shaking, because this was not a quick process, and time was of the essence. Hannah could feel the urgency in the air as Joe loaded each gun by grabbing a paper cartridge, ripping the paper with his teeth, then dumping its contents down the barrel of the gun. Then he would place a bullet in the top of the barrel, grab his ramrod and push the bullet down into the barrel to pack it. Next he placed a percussion cap on the nipple of the gun, the place where the hammer strikes when it falls. Hannah was amazed at the speed in which Joe performed this task.

Once Joe had finished loading all the guns he placed each of the children in a different spot around the barn with their weapons aimed out cracks big enough for them to see out of. The girls all had big eyes and looks of fear on their faces. Joe didn't give them time to think, he just went around and made sure all the hammers were fully cocked and ready to go. He told them to just hold their position, and don't fire unless he gave the order to.

Hannah's hands were trembling, but she did as she was told. She was terrified! She looked across the barn and saw little Charlotte, trying to be brave as tears rolled down her face. She looked the other way and saw Izzy pointing her gun and shaking like a leaf. Up in the loft she saw Becky, pointing her gun out a crack, and sitting as if in shock. Joe was also in the loft, peering around the edge of the little window up there, watching and waiting. She saw him make some kind of sign toward Daniel, who was up in the loft across the creek. Now, they all just sat and waited.

Lottie began to whimper "I can't do it Joe! I can't shoot nobody! I don't know how!"

Joe looked down at her and sternly said "Yes, you can Charlotte! You can and you will if you have to! Now, stop crying right now and be strong."

It was hard for Hannah to see her ten year old sister having to go through this, but at the moment there was nothing she could do to comfort her. Everything was completely out of her hands. All she could do was sit and stare down the barrel of that gun toward the road, watching and waiting, for what she didn't know.

Across the creek, Daniel, Harding and Albert were showing little twelve year old Nancy Inman, and ten year old Elizabeth Inman, how to hold their guns and point, and where to pull when and if it was time to shoot.

From their two positions on each side of the creek, the ten armed children sat and waited. Daniel and Joseph had sat in rifle pits with armed men many times during the war, but to be sitting here with armed children was not something either of them were truly prepared for.

Just then they heard the sound of hooves pounding on dirt, and a cloud of dust appeared in the distance, followed by ten or twelve men on horseback.

Joe and Daniel each told their group to just hold and not make a sound.

Hannah watched as the men came to an abrupt stop when they saw the houses. They gathered in a group and began talking, but Hannah couldn't hear what they were saying. She saw one of them point toward her house. Her heart raced! The men began to dismount. A few of them began walking toward the creek, as if they were heading toward Daniel and Joseph's homes. The rest of them started walking toward Hannah's house.

"Hold...." Joseph whispered to the girls.

One of the men went up onto the porch. He yelled out for the occupant of the house to make themselves known. "Make yourselves known or I will burn you out!" he yelled.

From inside Sarah yelled out "Please go away. There are little children here."

Joe aimed his gun right at the back of the man's head. "Hold...." he still kept whispering.

Hannah and the girls each had their gun aimed at a different man, just waiting for the order to shoot. They knew they would only get one shot, then they could not shoot again unless Joe was able to come and reload their guns with powder.

Hannah was trying to watch her man, but also watch what was going on up on the porch at the same time. The first man motioned for another man to come up on the porch with him and they began kicking the door down. Sarah screamed from inside the house. Joe then yelled "Now!" and all five of them pulled their triggers. One of the men on the porch went down. The other ran for cover. All of the shots that the girls had fired missed their mark, but they scared the men enough that they all ran and hid, and some of them began shooting back.

From across the creek, Daniel and his group had also fired. Daniel, Harding and Albert were reloading their guns while the two girls just put their guns down and started crying and shaking with fear. "Go hide in the stalls!" Daniel yelled to them. Daniel had seen the man he was shooting at go down but the others were running about trying to figure out what to do and where the bullets were coming from.

Two of the men took off running toward Joe's house. He saw them run up and bust through the door. Daniel and Harding hadn't been able to fire at them because they were still reloading. Joe heard his mother scream. Without thinking his instinct kicked in and he ran out of the barn and towards his home, thinking he had to protect his mother and siblings.

For the rest of her life Hannah would always see what happened next in slow motion. Whenever she remembered it, the scene would always play out in her mind in such a slow and excruciating way, so that every detail of it was etched into her brain forever.

Joe was running down the hill. She was yelling "No, Joe!" but it was coming out in slow motion. Joe ran across the creek and then hid behind a tree in his yard. Hannah's head turned in slow motion and she saw Joe's seven year old sister, Virginia, come running out onto the porch. She was just standing there. Why was she standing there? One of the men, ever so slowly, was bringing his gun up as if to shoot little Virginia. Hannah's head slowly turned back to Joe and she saw him running in slow motion across the yard and he jumped through the air and grabbed Virginia, just as a deafening slow-motion sounding shot rang out, and the two slowly rolled across the grass, just as Harding, from the loft of his barn, pulled the trigger of his gun and shot the man who had aimed at his sister. The man fell dead. Little Virginia jumped up screaming, but in Hannah's mind all sound had stopped after the gunfire, and even though Virginia's mouth was moving in slow motion as if she were screaming, no sound was coming out.

Joe didn't move.

Hannah realized later that all of this happened in about ten quick seconds of time and that all the movements had happened very quickly, but in her mind it played out as if it were ten slow, long minutes of agony. She was replaying it now, even, as she sat motionless in the barn. People were running toward Joseph, she saw their mouths moving, but everything was muted for her. No sound. Just an eerie quiet pause in time. She kept seeing the man's gun fire, the slow-motion moment that the fire exploded from the end of his gun. It was almost as if she could even see the bullet as it slowly pierced the air and made a path straight to Joe, and then he was down.

Joe didn't move.

The bushwhackers jumped on their horses and rode off fast as lightning, leaving their three downed men behind.

Everyone came running out of the houses and barns. Irene screamed and fell down next to her son. Hannah sat frozen in the barn, looking out the crack where her gun had been.

"Move Joe!" she said to herself, as her voice came out in a whisper. "Move! Come on Joseph, get up!"

Then she very loudly screamed "Noooooo!", and suddenly there was sound again and time sped back up. She ran out of the barn and down the hill and across the creek and fell in a heap next to Irene.

"Nooooo, not Joseph! Oh, my God, nooooo!"

1864

Hannah sat in the little graveyard behind the church, bundled up against the January cold. She was looking at Joseph's grave, and her thoughts were running wild. Again, as she'd done so many times in the last two months, her thoughts were replaying the awful incident. As soon as she saw Joseph go down in her memory, that ever-present ache came back into her chest, and she felt like she couldn't breathe. There was something about that moment, that instant when the bullet hit Joe. It was as if it hit Hannah, too, and she could feel it traveling through her body and lodging right in her heart, where she would forever have an ache.

She had been afraid to visit the grave, afraid of the feelings she would endure if she did. But, something gave her just enough courage on this day to finally embrace her fears. She clutched the tintype photo that Joe had given her, and ran her fingers across it. Her tears fell on it, and she wiped them away. She flipped the card over and read the words he'd written... "To my best friend, and the woman I hope to grow old with."

It was all Hannah could do to not jump up and run, just run

away and never come back. Where she would go she didn't know, but she would run and never stop running. How unfair was it that Joe would not get his dream of growing old with Hannah! How unfair! Why was God being so cruel right now? What had anyone done to deserve the pain that had been inflicted on her little community the last few years? The pain that had been inflicted upon *her*!

Hannah had always been a believer, always full of faith, but she was having a hard time as she sat by Joseph's grave on this cold January day. She was mad at God. She was mad at the men that came into their lives so abruptly and took her best friend away. She was angry at the world!

"These men! These men and politicians! They stir up the storm clouds, then the rest of us stand back and wonder why it's raining!" she cried out.

For two months she had closed her heart up and felt nothing. She had tried to close off her feelings and suppress them. It was the only way she could get out of bed in the mornings.

As she sat there that morning by his grave, she was finally allowing herself to process some of her emotion, but it was so painful. She cried what felt like rivers of tears. Then she began talking out loud to Joe.

"Oh, Joseph! How I miss you!"

She thought back to the hours after it all happened. She knew she'd been in a daze most of that first day.

"Your funeral was the next day. I'm glad we didn't have to wrap you in a sheet, like we did with Martha and William. Daniel and Harding and Albert made you a wooden box and they were able to dig a hole deep enough to put the box in. I'm thankful for that."

"The thing that stands out the most, is that it was a dark and dismal day, and there was a distant roll of thunder. We were standing here, about to place your coffin in the grave, and suddenly it started raining. We were trying to say some words, but we were all becoming drenched. Even so, nobody thought to run back to the houses to get out of the rain. We just kept standing here. In my mind, the raindrops were tears from Heaven. It was all the combined tears of you, Ma, Jesse, and all the others, as they looked down upon the scene. For some reason we all just stood here, and let ourselves be soaked through with the rain, and the sadness. Our clothes became heavy with rain, much like our hearts were heavy with grief. It seemed fitting somehow."

"But, then I saw the water gathering in the bottom of the grave, and I didn't want you to be sitting in water. It was breaking my heart to think of you drowning in that water, even though common sense told me you were already dead, you could not drown. But, my heart was shattered, thinking of you having to rest in the water. Your ma saw it, too, and began crying for someone to please scoop out the water. Several of the boys ran and got buckets, and jumped down inside the hole and began scooping the water out. It was difficult, because the rain was attempting to fill the hole back in as fast as they could scoop it out. But, finally they got it down low enough to satisfy Irene and me, and then they quickly put your coffin down in the hole and we began filling the dirt back into the grave before the water could get any deeper."

"I will never forget helping your mother prepare your body. It was the most heart-wrenching thing I have ever witnessed. I know how deep my pain is, Joe, but I don't think it compares to what your ma was going through! I have never seen anyone so racked with grief. There's nothing worse than the primal scream of a mother who's lost her child. You were her boy, her first born. She truly has not been the same since. I think your death has broken her. I feel like it's broken me, too. I feel like so many hopes and dreams are gone now. There is so much you will never get to experience or do, that I will, God willing, and that doesn't seem fair. You were such a good person. Why does God always call the best ones home? Sarah said that if I was walking along and saw a field of flowers, would I bend down and pick a wilted one, or go to the most beautiful one of all? She said God does the same. I know she was trying to comfort me, but I can't help but being angry with God, because I wanted you here."

She stopped talking for a moment to catch her breath and stifle her sobs. Then, she continued on...

"I didn't want to bury those men... the ones that killed you. I wanted to kick them, throw rocks at them, toss them off the highest cliff. Harding wanted to burn them. But, Sarah said as evil as they were, they're still somebody's sons, somebody's brothers, and those people were never going to have the closure of knowing why their loved one didn't return, not knowing if they lived or died, so the least we could do was bury them with dignity. But, Daniel and Harding wouldn't agree to digging three graves, so they took them about a half mile off into the woods, dug just one hole, and threw them in it. Daniel told me that Harding spit on them before he threw the dirt on. Oh, Joe! Harding is so angry that you died! He looked up to you so!"

She blew her nose and turned to block the cold winter wind from blowing right into her face. When she turned, she was facing her brother's grave.

"We buried you beside Jesse. I thought you would want that. Oh, Joseph! I had to go through your pockets. Your Ma couldn't do it. She stood and watched as I pulled your things out and laid them on the table."

Hannah let out a long shudder, the kind that comes only from the most heart-wrenching of cries. She was hyperventilating and struggling for breath.

"I found the buckeye in your pocket, the one I gave you when you first went off to war. I didn't know you'd kept it so long. I have it now. I will keep it always. I know I've seen a million buckeyes, and I'll see a million more, but this one is the only one that will be with me always. Just knowing that you carried it with you for two years, and touched it so many times... it is the most special thing to me. When I'm holding it, I'm holding you."

A new round of sobs came. Hannah wasn't sure how she had any more tears left to sob, but they just kept coming.

"I also found your harmonica in your pocket. Oh, Joseph! How I remember the times you played it and we all sang the songs you taught us. Your Ma and I decided that Harding should have it. You had taught him how to play 'When Johnny Comes Marching Home', and so he played it at your funeral. It's funny how it had seemed like such a happy song the first time you and Daniel sang it for us when we were butchering the hogs. But, this time, with him just playing the tune, slowly, with no words, it became the saddest tune I'd ever heard. Instead of it being about a soldier marching home from war, it became about a man marching home to Heaven. It broke my heart."

"I wrote a poem about my grief." She picked up her journal which had been laying on the ground beside her, and she began to read...

"There were a million flowers growing
In the field that day
But, only one that I had planted
In the middle of the fray
I cared for it and watered it
And made sure it had sun
There were many flowers in that field
But, to me there was only one
It was just beginning to bloom
With colors, oh, so bright
When an angel came and plucked it
In the middle of the night
By morning it was gone from me
My hard work done in vain
I yelled and screamed and lost my heart
My tears fell hard like rain
Of all the flowers in that field
Why did you pick mine?
I'll never plant another seed
My sun will never shine"

Hannah felt something hit her nose, then another hit her cheek, but this time it wasn't tears. She looked up and saw that it had begun to snow. She sat there for a few more minutes, until the snow began to get thicker. She was standing up to head back home when she saw a flicker of color out of the corner of her eye. She turned and saw a bright red Cardinal sitting on a tree branch that was hanging out over the edge of the graveyard. It just sat there staring at her, a splash of red against the backdrop of white snow. Hannah felt like maybe it was Joe sending her a sign. She put her hand to her heart and looked up to the sky, blinking as the snowflakes fell against her eyelashes. She felt a peaceful feeling go through her, if only for a moment.

February

Hannah walked across the creek to visit Lucy and the children. Thomas and Isaac were thriving in Lucy's care, and the babies, Emma and Ella, were beginning to be so much fun. They were both 8 months old now, and sitting up. Lucy really had her hands full. Daniel had built a little pen in the corner of the kitchen, so Lucy would have a place to put the babies while she cooked and did household chores.

Lucy and Daniel had taken to calling the girls their little "June Bugs", because they were both born in June. It was so adorable when Daniel would come in from working outside, and the girls would reach for him, smiling, and he would grab one in each arm and swing them around and say "How are my little June Bugs?"

Hannah said "I don't know how you do it, Lucy! I'd be pulling my hair out raising all these children!"

"What are you talking about, Hannah? You *have* been doing the same thing as me your whole life! While I was the baby of my family, with no little brothers and sisters to take care of, you had lost your mother and you were taking care of all those little babies, even the twins! You may not realize it, but you have been doing the same as me, but for much longer."

Hannah sighed and said "Maybe you're right, but at least now I have Sarah, and the children are really *her* responsibility now, not mine, and that takes some of the load off my shoulders."

Lucy smiled and said "Well....."

"Well, what?" Hannah asked.

"Well.... there's going to be another one."

"What!? Another baby? Are you serious?!"

"Yes, I'm very serious."

Hannah was astounded. "But, Lucy! What are you thinking?"

"There is no 'thinking' about it, Hannah. It just happened. When Daniel came back from the war, well, we were just so happy to see each other, and to be together again. It just happened."

"Oh, my goodness! I don't know what to say!"

"I know what you mean. I feel that way, too, but I'm also happy. The new baby will be here probably in about September, if I figured right, so it will be fifteen months younger than Emma and Ella. I know it's awful close together. I wasn't expecting it. I thought I couldn't get pregnant again so quickly, but God had other ideas."

Hannah was thinking back to just three short years ago, when she and Lucy were just two teenagers running around full of freedom and dreams, and now here Lucy was a mother of four, with a fifth on the way. It was enough to boggle the mind. She was happy for her, and delighted to know she would have another niece or nephew, but she couldn't help also feeling glad she wasn't in that same predicament. She just wasn't ready, yet, for all that responsibility. Maybe it was because she already had that responsibility with her own brothers and sisters. She wasn't ready to start doing it all over again with her own children. She knew if she had married Joe, babies would have come soon enough. But, now she just figured she wouldn't marry for a long, long time, if at all. She was resigned to her fate, and she was okay with it.

After visiting Lucy and the children, Hannah began walking up the trail to her grandparents' home. There was a time when she was afraid to walk alone this far, a mile through the deep, dark woods. But, now it just didn't seem to bother her any more. As a matter of fact, she actually relished the time alone. She had been making the trip several times a week because her grandma was so sick.

On this day when she walked through the door she saw that her grandpa seemed to be in despair, much more so than usual. He said "Your grandma's not long for this world, Hannah."

Hannah knew her time was short, but she still was not prepared to hear that on this particular day. She went into the bedroom to sit with Ruth. For a brief moment she thought she was already dead, because her breathing was so shallow. She sat and held her hand, but Ruth wasn't responding.

"Grandpa, I'm going to go back and tell the others that I am staying here with you. I don't want you to be alone when Grandma goes. I'm going to bring Izzy back with me and we will take care of Grandma."

Hannah ran most of the way back. She explained to Sarah what her plan was. She and Isabelle gathered up a basket full of foods and medicines and told the others they would not be back until after Grandma passed. Grandma wanted to die in her own home, and that's how it was going to be.

So, the two girls sat with Grandma night and day. They cleaned her when she soiled herself, they tried to get her to at least drink broth from a spoon. They comforted Grandpa. They kept a fire going, and cooked meals for him. Grandma slowly withered away. She mostly just slept, and when she wasn't sleeping she was moaning in pain. She rarely talked to anyone.

But about a week into their vigil, there was a day when Grandma seemed more alert. Hannah was sitting by her bed reading a book out loud to her, when suddenly Ruth turned and opened her eyes and looked at her. Then, plain as day, as if she wasn't sick at all, she said "Hannah, you sure do read good. That Sarah sure did teach you well. I never learnt t'read. That's one of my regrets in this life."

Hannah yelled into the other room for Izzy and Grandpa to come, because Grandma was talking. They all gathered around and talked with Grandma for about an hour. She held Grandpa's hand and they talked about memories from their early life. She told her two granddaughters stories from her youth. Hannah was making mental notes so she could jot these stories down later in her journal.

Then, suddenly Grandma turned to Hannah and said "I know yer strugglin'. I know yer sad about the death a'young Joseph. I see it in yer eyes. It's normal t'grieve, but I want ya t'know that you will overcome this grief, and you'll move on t'the life God meant for ya."

"Oh, Grandma, I know you mean well, but I don't see how that can be true, not for me anyway."

"Don't think I don't know where ya stand. I was in yer shoes one time. When my first husband died, I thought my life was over. I grieved, just as you do. But, then yer grandfather came inta m'life. If ya were to ask me now if it was possible to go back an' change things, make it t'where my first husband didn't die, and I didn't feel that grief, I wouldn't wish it t'be so. Yer Grandpa is my life. I was meant to spend my life with him. When my first husband died, I prayed and prayed for God to take it back, to bring him back to life for me. But, God sometimes gives us the gift of *unanswered* prayers."

"I just don't see how my life will go like yours did Grandma. There are no boys my age anywhere near here. I don't see how I would even have a chance of meeting someone, and I don't see how it would even be possible for me to love again the way I loved Joseph."

"The Lord will provide, Hannah. The Lord will provide," Grandma said.

"I feel like all the Lord has done lately is take away."

Then her Grandma stunned her when she announced "Hannah, you are gonna marry a preacher man!"

Hannah erupted into a laugh. What a funny thing to say! "Grandma, you are delusional!" she laughed. "A preacher man...." she laughed again. "Oh, my word! Where am I gonna meet one of those?!" Grandma even smiled a bit, and Grandpa and Izzy laughed. It was good to be laughing again, even if it was only for a brief moment.

"Mark my words!" Grandma said. Hannah just shook her head.

Then, Grandma changed the subject when she said "At my funeral, I want you all to sing 'Angel Band'. It is my favorite hymnal. Promise me?"

Hannah looked at the others and the laughter stopped. "Of course we will Grandma," she said.

"I'm tired now. Best to let me sleep."

They left the room and went to the kitchen to have a bite to eat. After they finished, Hannah cleaned up and stoked up the fire good and hot. Grandpa sat up in his chair until late. He just didn't sleep much these days. Hannah and Izzy went and crawled in bed with their Grandma, one on each side. They each took one of Ruth's hands and held it as they drifted off to sleep.

Hannah awoke with a jolt. She looked around in the dark. For a moment she forgot where she was. Then she remembered. It must be the middle of the night. She was still holding Grandma's hand. Her skin felt so cold. The room was cold. Maybe the fire was dying down. She began to raise up from bed to go tend the fire, but as she pulled her hand loose from her grandma's grip, something didn't feel right. Then, the realization hit her. Her heart raced with sudden fear!

She groped in the dark to find the candle. She stumbled into the main room to light the candle in the fire place. She stopped to also add more wood to the fire. She was finding any little chore to keep her from having to go back and learn the truth. She saw Grandpa sitting in his chair with his head forward, sleeping. She quietly took the candle and slowly walked back into the bedroom. She let the faint glow of light fall across Grandma's face. And, then she was sure of it. Grandma was gone. She had died in her sleep, holding the hands of her granddaughters.

Somehow Hannah found strength she didn't know she had. She didn't start crying. She just gently pulled Izzy's hand from her grandmother's and woke her to tell her that Grandma was gone. Izzy began sobbing. This woke Grandpa, who came to the door of the room. He just stood there. How are you supposed to react when your lifelong partner is suddenly gone? He just stood there. Whatever was going on inside him, Hannah couldn't tell.

Hannah stepped up and took over. She told everyone what to do. She sent Izzy back to the house to tell the others, and told her to send the boys back with a horse so they could get Grandma's body moved. They wrapped her in a blanket and gently laid her over the back of one of the horses. Daniel and Albert walked on each side of the horse, holding onto their grandmother, to make sure she wouldn't fall off. Hannah carefully led the horse down the path, and Grandpa just walked behind them all, enveloped in his grief. He was a shell of a man.

Once they got her back to the house, Hannah and Sarah and the girls laid her out on the kitchen table and cleaned her and dressed her. The boys went to start the backbreaking job of digging a grave in the cold February ground. That afternoon they buried her in the hole dug next to Martha Bennett's grave. The boys shoveled the loose dirt back onto her. Everyone stood for a bit, some crying, some just in sad shock. It was so cold. Everyone was miserable. Without a preacher, no one really knew what to say. But, Hannah had not forgotten her promise, so she began to sing, and the others joined in with her, for a beautiful chorus that echoed through the snowy mountains.

"My latest sun is sinking fast
My race is nearly run
My strongest trials now are past
My triumph has begun

Oh, come, angel band
Come and around me stand
Oh, bear me away on your snow white wings
To my immortal home
Oh, bear me away on your snow white wings
To my immortal home

I've almost gained my heav'nly home
My spirit loudly sings
The holy ones, behold they come!
I hear the noise of wings
Oh, come, angel band
Come and around me stand
Oh, bear me away on your snow white wings
To my immortal home
Oh, bear me away on your snow white wings

To my immortal home

Oh, come, angel band
Come and around me stand
Oh, bear me away on your snow white wings
To my immortal home
Oh, bear me away on your snow white wings
To my immortal home"

Hannah forced her grandpa to leave his home and come stay with her and Sarah. She just could not bear for him to be all alone a mile away. He fought it and did not want to do it, but in the end she won. He seemed to give up after Ruth died, after the light of his life had gone out. He stopped eating. He wouldn't talk to anyone. He just simply stopped living. And, two weeks later, when Hannah went to wake him up for breakfast, he was gone. Everyone said he died of a broken heart, because he couldn't bear to be without his Ruth. He was 75 years old. Ruth had been 73. They had shared a long life together.

Everyone went through the motions again, digging a grave next to Ruth's grave, and laying Grandpa out and then burying him. As Hannah helped to dig, she said "I am so, so tired of digging graves! Dear God, have we not buried enough? How much more will you put us through? I fear there is not enough strength in me to do this again. Please, if you have any mercy at all, make this be the last time! I will give you what little I have today, but after this, I don't have anything left to give."

Hannah found it hard to cry. She knew they were both in a better place. Grandma was no longer suffering from her illness, and Grandpa was no longer suffering from a broken heart. She was almost glad he had gone to join her so soon. It wasn't right that they not be together. As much as she loved them, she almost felt relief that they were gone. There had been so much sadness in the last few years, it was wonderful to know they didn't have to suffer through any of it any more.

April

Hannah rose from bed and went downstairs to the kitchen to start breakfast. She put the last of the salt pork into a pan with a little lard and began frying it up. She heard baby Jasper crying in the downstairs bedroom that he shared with Sarah. Sarah soon came out with the baby and sat down in a chair and began to nurse him.

Hannah got the bowl of eggs off the counter. There were six of them. The hens hadn't been laying very well. They would have to make do. There were eleven people, not counting Jasper, who would want eggs. They would have to be divided into a half an egg apiece.

"That was the last of the pork, Sarah," she said. "And, I'm not making biscuits this morning because the flour is getting so low. I think we must go back to eating bread only on Sunday again, like we did last year. Even then, we won't make it much longer."

"We will have to send the boys to town again, maybe next month. The strawberries will be ready in May. We could send them down with a load of fresh berries, and maybe they could cut another load of lumber. It's hard to think of things we could trade with. It's been so long since I've been able to get some of the things I need. Baby Jasper has had no clothing to speak of for his entire life. I've simply wrapped him in blankets most of the time, but he is walking now. He needs clothing. I have no more things I can cut up to make him a suit of clothes, without using clothing that you older children are wearing. I've already took down all the curtains and made more diapers for Jasper and Emma and Ella. They have all been soiled so many times and rewashed so many times, they are about to fall apart."

She looked down at her baby. "You are gonna have to learn to use the privy soon, my love." He cooed back at her from the comfort of her breast.

She suddenly realized what day it was. She said to Hannah "Jasper is one year old today!"

Hannah looked off in the distance as she counted up the days in her head "Oh, you're right! He sure is! Well, happy birthday little brother!"

"He is one year old, and I don't even know if Elijah knows he exists! Isn't that sad? I sent him a letter last fall by the boys, but who knows if he even got it."

After breakfast, the entire family walked out to the garden. It was time to start some of the planting. There was much work to be done, breaking up the soil and plowing rows to plant seeds in. Charlotte and Rachel were put in charge of watching little Jasper. They were to also keep an eye on the 5 year old twins, Jacob and Jonah. But, everyone else, from seven year old Michael up, had to help with the work.

After a meager dinner, Sarah asked Albert if he would go down to the creek and see if he could catch some fish for supper, since they'd run out of pork. Albert was happy to be able to escape the garden work, so he went willingly. He tried to get Harding to go with him, but Irene said she really could not spare him. She had so much garden work to do herself, and with Joseph gone and Henry away at war, Harding was the only male of any size left in her household who could do the heavy work. He knew Daniel couldn't go, either, because he was the only male in his home who could work, and it was hard for Lucy to help him because she had four little children to take care of. Daniel was out in his garden by himself working, so Albert just passed him by and went on down to the creek with his pole. After two hours he had only caught five fish, but it was enough to give everyone a little bit of meat at supper time. He took his catch back home and began cleaning it out in the front yard, while the others continued to work in the garden.

At supper time, Hannah and Sarah fried up the fish and made some potatoes to go with it. They were getting low on potatoes, too, and most of what they had left would be needed to cut the eyes off of to re-plant the garden for this year's potato crop.

Michael asked for a glass of milk. Hannah said "I'm sorry

honey, but we don't have any milk. You know that. The cow quit making and she won't make more until she has her calf."

"Why did she quit making milk?" Michael wanted to know.

"Well, after a cow has a baby cow, she makes milk for it, and we take some of that milk for ourselves. But she only makes milk for about as long as her baby would need it, so usually about nine or ten months, then she dries up. We put our cow in with the Inman's bull last year, and she is now carrying a baby cow, but it will still be a few months before she births, so we just have to wait."

"But, how did the baby cow get in her belly?" he wanted to know.

Hannah looked at Sarah as if to say 'Uh oh, I've said too much.' She turned back to Michael and said "Oh, God puts it there." Thankfully that answer seemed to satisfy him.

They were all just sitting around the table, about to say the blessing, when they heard the sound of horses' hooves outside. This sound always struck fear into them. Albert was the first to jump up. He ran to look out the window.

"Soldiers!" he said. "Union soldiers."

They had learned to fear the Union soldiers more than the Confederate ones, simply because Arkansas was mostly a Confederate state. Union soldiers were more likely to harass the women and children, believing them to support the opposite side. But, like Daniel said, they didn't always need a reason to harass, be they for the north or the south.

Sarah told Albert to stand back. "They are more likely to harm men and young boys than they are the women and girls. Best they don't see you, Albert."

But, Albert, being the 'man of the house', found it hard to listen to his stepmother. He felt he should be the one to go out on the porch and confront these men. But, at fifteen years old, he was still on the cusp of being a child. He still felt he was supposed to listen to his elders, so he did as Sarah asked and ran up the stairs to hide. He found a window to peek out of to keep watch. If need be, he would run back down.

The men came up onto the porch and just opened the door and came in. Hannah was appalled at their lack of manners. She was repulsed by these horrible men.

Some of the children were still seated around the table, with their plates of food in front of them. The soldiers roughly grabbed the children and pushed them out of their chairs, then they sat down themselves and began to eat the food. The children all huddled next to Sarah and Hannah in the corner of the room. Hannah saw Albert peeking down from the top of the stairs, and she made a silent motion for him to stay put.

Something inside Hannah was building and building. She had never felt so much anger in her entire life. Here they were, just innocent women and children, barely scraping by, while her own father was out fighting for the same army these men were fighting for, yet they had the gall, no the *audacity*, to come in her home and take food that her little brothers and sisters needed to survive. She watched as one big, burly man scooped up a big bite of food and shoveled it into his mouth. And, then she snapped!

She ran across the room and grabbed the ash shovel, scooped up a big shovel full of hot ashes and coals from the fireplace, then ran over and began pouring hot ashes over all the plates of food. If her family was not going to eat, then neither were these worthless examples of humanity! The men all jumped back to keep from getting burned. They all began laughing. It was a wonder they didn't become angry and retaliate! Maybe it was simply the shock of something happening that they didn't expect, or maybe somewhere down deep inside they were a bit impressed by this young woman, but for whatever reason, the men just got up, still laughing, and left the house. As they crossed the porch one of them turned and said "Best be cookin' up some more vittles, 'cause there's plenty more soldiers comin' behind us." Then, they roared with laughter again.

They got on their horses and left, and that's when she saw Daniel standing behind a tree in the yard, with his gun cocked and ready. He had seen what was going on across the creek and come to protect his family.

Hannah ran to Daniel and told him what had just

happened, and what the man said about 'plenty more' soldiers coming this way. They decided to gather everyone together at the church for a quick meeting.

All 25 members of the little mountain community gathered inside the church. From Hannah's household there was Sarah (32), and all her children and stepchildren, including Hannah (19), Albert (15), Isabelle (13), Rebecca (13), Charlotte (11), Rachel (10), Ruby (8), Michael (7), Jacob (5), Jonah (5) and Jasper (1). From the Inman home there was Irene (37) and her children, Harding (17), Nancy (13), Elizabeth (11), Virginia (8), James (5) and Charlie (2). And, from Daniel's home there was Daniel (21), Lucy (19), Thomas (5), Isaac (3), Emma (10 months) and Ella (10 months). Only three households held people at the moment, because the Owens home, the Bennett home and the Harris home were now all sitting empty.

Of all these 25 people, Daniel was the only grown man. He stood up to try and take control and lead the meeting. As they were all discussing what to do, Hannah suddenly spoke up.

"The cave! We all have to go to the cave! We will be safe there," she said.

Daniel hated to admit that his sister was right, and he hadn't been the one to think of it. But, it was the only idea that made sense.

He said "We don't know how soon these other soldiers may arrive, so we must be quick. I want everyone to go back to your homes and gather what you can carry and go to the cave, as quickly as possible."

Hannah ran back with Sarah and the children and she began loading each child's arms with things. There wasn't much left to even consider taking, but she took what little bit of food was left in the pantry and divided it out among the older children. Sarah wrapped Jasper tightly to her body so her hands would be free, and then picked up some blankets to carry. Hannah grabbed the journal that she was currently writing in. Her older journals were already stored away at the cave, along with her other sentimental items. Something had told her to keep them there until the war was over.

As everyone began walking up the trail alongside Panther Creek, Hannah looked back and said to Daniel "The animals..."

Daniel said "There's no time!"

All 25 people crammed into the cave just as the sun was beginning to set for the evening. It was dark and cold, but they had candles and a good stock of food in the little back section of the cave. They would not be able to build a fire, for fear the soldiers would see the smoke, but at least they had a good supply of blankets. At one time there had been salt pork stored away in the cave, but as they ran out in their homes the boys had been sent to retrieve what was left in the cave. Hannah had been worried at the time, about them not having any stocked away, but as she sat in the cave huddled up with everyone, she realized that the pork wouldn't have done them much good, anyway, without being able to build a fire to cook it with. Thankfully, there were still several jars of canned food items stored there, and a basket containing beets, sweet potatoes, irish potatoes, cabbage, onions, carrots and squash. Because they had kept it stored in the cool cave, the vegetables were still edible. And, Irene had just baked six loaves of bread the night before and brought them with her.

The little group of people spent a cold and dark night huddled together, barely sleeping.

The next morning Daniel said he was going back to take a look around. He told them all to stay in the cave and for no reason were they to come out, or try to go look for him, even if he did not return.

"Daniel, please don't go..." Lucy begged.

"Don't worry, I will stay out of sight."

Daniel was gone for a couple of hours. When he returned he told them that there were soldiers at the Owens house. It would just be a matter of time until they came on down to the other homes. There was nothing they could do but sit tight and wait for them to move on out of the area.

Sarah asked Daniel if they might consider just staying in

Grandpa Harris's old house. But, Daniel was afraid that they might notice the faint trail leading to the house and follow it. It was best to stay in the cave.

The group sat in the cave all that day. It was very difficult to keep the children all occupied and quiet. But, the women did their best to come up with games, and to tell stories. Many of the children got so bored they just fell asleep and took naps, which was a blessing for the women. When they were hungry they opened a jar of something, or ate a little bit of Irene's bread. It was so hard to come up with a meal when you couldn't build a fire and cook something.

Later that evening Daniel went back outside and said he could smell something that smelled like smoke. He decided to go back and spy some more. This time when he came back he said to Lucy "I'm sorry, but they have set your old house on fire."

"Ma and Pa's house is burning?" she exclaimed.

"Yes, they set it on fire and they have now moved down to where the rest of the homes are. There are soldiers all around. They are looting everything. It makes me so angry, but what can one man do against a large troop of armed men? I can only watch and feel helpless."

The group had another restless night in the cave, but finally a streak of morning light found it's way through the crack at the entrance of the cave. Some of the children began to complain of being hungry, so the women dug around in the stash and found a little food for them. "We must ration our food and not eat until we are full, children," Irene said. She unwrapped two of her loaves of bread and broke off chunks for each person. She then opened a jar of pear preserves that had been stored in the cave, and allowed each of them to dip their chunk of bread into the preserves. When the two loaves and the jar of preserves were all gone, Irene said they must stop and not eat any more for the time being. No one knew how long they might have to stay in the cave. They couldn't risk running out of food.

Daniel took Harding with him this time when he went

down to see what was taking place back at their homes. Albert wanted to go, too, but Daniel said the more people that went, the more likely they would be seen. Maybe he could go next trip.

The boys stayed hidden well back in the trees as they watched the soldiers. From what they could tell there were about fifty of them. There seemed to be a commander that the others were taking orders from. The commander had moved into the larger Casey house with some of his men, while other men were inside the church, and across the creek in the other two houses. It seemed as if they'd set up to stay awhile.

Daniel saw that they had killed one of their pigs. He didn't know if it was Yankee, Rebel or Dixie. Then, he silently chastised himself for thinking of the pigs by the names his sisters had given them. The men were roasting the pig on a fire. It was hard to watch as they carried up handfuls of the firewood Daniel had cut for his family, to use on the fire.

Daniel and Harding went back to the cave, where they told everyone else what they saw. Hannah felt as if a knife had been jabbed into her heart. What right did these men have to just eat their food and take up residence in their homes? Some nasty, dirty man was probably sleeping in her bed! She was feeling a loss of faith in humanity. She was feeling completely hopeless and violated.

Daniel said that surely the men knew that people had been living there until recently, so those people could be hiding out nearby. They would probably be scouting around looking, so everyone still needed to stay inside the cave at all times.

On the fourth day, while everyone was inside the cave, they began to hear noises. Daniel snuck outside and told the others to take the rocks that had been stacked up to block off the storage room, and use those rocks to block off the main entrance instead. He then went to investigate.

He didn't come back for several hours. When he did, he identified himself and told the others to take down the rocks so he could get in. Once inside, they stacked the rocks back up, but left enough room for fresh air to get inside. As they were stacking the rocks back, Daniel told them what he saw.

"I guess the commander had sent out a group of about six of his men to scout out the trail leading beside Panther Creek. They followed the trail all the way to Grandpa's old house. I watched as they went inside and rummaged around, but since we had already taken everything out of the house, they didn't find anything. I was afraid they were going to set it on fire before they left, but for whatever reason, they didn't."

"You don't know how scared I was when I watched them walk past the spot where we turned off the trail to come to the cave. But, thankfully we didn't leave any evidence of a trail, so they just continued on back down."

Hannah said "I am so thankful you told us not to bring the animals, Daniel! Can you imagine if we'd brought the horses up? We would've had to tie them down on the trail, and the men would've found them. They probably would've been able to figure out which way we'd gone."

"Yes, it's a good thing in a way. But, now those men have our horses. I wish we'd had time to take the cows and pigs off in the woods somewhere and tie them up. But, it all happened so fast. Chances are, they might have found them anyway."

This went on for several days. Each day Daniel would take either Harding or Albert with him, and they would go spy on the soldiers. Each day they came back with more unfavorable reports. They had killed the other two hogs and one of the cows. They had also begun killing the chickens and cooking them for their meals.

Back at the cave, the bread was all gone now, and all they had left were canned items, a little bit of dried deer jerky and the basket of vegetables that had been stored there last fall. No one had bothered with the potatoes yet, because they didn't have a way to cook them. But, finally, hunger took over enough that they began just eating the potatoes raw.

One day for dinner they all just ate raw carrots, cabbage and beets that were really past their prime and didn't taste the best. The women cut them up into small bits and mixed them together and made a raw salad, of sorts. For supper that day they had some canned corn. Irene told them to eat it slowly, so it would last longer. She told the children to take one kernel at a time, eat it slowly, then swallow, then get another kernel. It would help to take up time, and also would give their stomachs time to tell their brains they were full, before the food actually ran out.

One evening they only had pickles for supper. Irene opened some jars and gave each person two pickles. The next morning for breakfast, they opened some strawberry jam and each person just stuck in their fingers and scooped out some jam, and that was all they had to eat. That night Irene came up with the idea to mix some of the corn meal into the jam to make it go further, and she made little balls of cornmeal and jam to give each person. There was a large bag of flour and a large bag of corn meal in the cave, but Irene said the flour was not safe to eat raw, so it was best they saved it for a last resort.

One day for dinner Irene opened some jars of canned squash. She made balls of dough out of smashed up squash and corn meal, with a little salt mixed in for flavor. Thank goodness they had stored some salt in the cave last year! Although it still wasn't very palatable, the salt helped. However, 5 year old Jonah made a face and said "This is nasty!"

Hannah scolded her little brother and said "Jonah! Apologize to Irene! You don't say things like that!"

Then Harding spoke up and said "But, he's not wrong." Irene looked at her son with pretend shock and hurt. Then Harding grinned sheepishly and said "Not to hurt your feelings or anything, Ma, but this is about the worst thing I've ever eaten."

Irene popped one in her mouth, chewed a moment, then said "Oh, Lord! You're right! It's terrible!"

But, Harding reached his hand out toward his mother and said "But, I'm hungry. So, may I have another?"

Irene handed her son another squash ball, then said "I'm so sorry children. I know the food situation is dire at the moment. I know you are tired of being locked up in this cave. I know you deserve better than this. I'm so sorry! But, be thankful that we have this place to hide, and that we at least have something to eat to keep us alive. This won't last forever."

Each day Hannah said a silent prayer to God and thanked him for giving her grandfather the presence of mind to start storing things in this cave, and for telling her and Joseph about it. Without this cave and this food supply, who knows what would have happened to them when the soldiers came?

Hannah thought it was odd how they had come to fear soldiers. All of their lives, a soldier had been thought of as a hero, someone you could go to for protection or help. A soldier was a man of honor, the cream of the crop of men. But, not any more. Now, with this war, a soldier had become someone to fear, someone you couldn't trust, no matter what side he was fighting for. Hannah was confused as to how this happened. It defied all logic in her mind.

The children were completely ate up with boredom. The women tried everything they could think of to keep them occupied. They were allowed to leave the cave only to go out and relieve themselves. So, most of their time was spent sitting in a dark, cold, hard room. And, they were being told constantly to stay quiet, which was a very hard thing for little children to do.

Hannah came up with an idea for a game they could play. She went outside and picked up 40 small rocks of uniform size and brought them inside the cave. The children gathered around curiously to see what she was up to. She got out her inkwell and her pen and took two rocks and wrote the number "1" on one side of each rock. Then, she picked up two more and wrote a "2" on them. She kept doing this until she'd made two rocks with each number from 1 to 20. Then, she laid all the rocks on the floor of the cave, with the numbers down. She took her hands and mixed them all around, so no one knew what numbers were where. She then taught them the game she had come up with.

Each child was asked to pick up two rocks and see what numbers were under them. If they happened to pick two matching numbers, they could keep them, but otherwise they would have to put the rocks back into place. If the other children were paying attention, they could memorize where certain numbers were, which would help them make matches later on. At the end of the game, after all the rocks were gone, whoever had the most pairs in their possession was the winner. Then, they would put them all back and play again.

This worked to keep the children occupied for an hour or two each day, then the women would have to think of something else to do.

On the eighth day, Daniel came back to report that the soldiers appeared to be packing up to leave. He had watched them until late evening. He figured they were planning on heading out in the morning.

That next morning he and Harding left early to go see if the men were truly leaving. They watched as they finished loading up the horses. It was difficult to see their own horses being loaded up with the rest.

Then, to their horror, they heard the commander give the order to burn down all the houses! What a helpless feeling! Daniel looked at Harding and they both knew there was nothing they could do to stop this. If they ran out and yelled for them to stop, the men would just shoot them. If there was any hope of saving all the others back at the cave, the two of them needed to stay alive.

The men started with the houses and barns on the south side of the creek. Daniel watched in agony as his home went up in flames, followed by Harding's home. The boys had never felt more helpless in their lives. The men then crossed the creek and appeared to be heading to the Casey home to set it on fire.

Harding felt overwhelmed and had no other outlet but to pray, so he bowed his head and silently begged God for help. "Dear Lord, please, *please*, do something! I am desperately pleading for your mercy. I feel helpless in the face of my current circumstances. Please hear my cry! Send help from Heaven. Send your angels down to fight this battle for us, to rescue us from this perilous situation. May your strong right hand lift us to a place of security. Lord, we have suffered so, beyond any suffering any of us could have ever imagined. Why do you seem so far away? Do you not hear our cries for help? Have we failed you in some way? I put my hope in you, and I know you will not give us more than we can handle. But, oh, Lord, please have compassion. We are at our breaking point. Save us from this hell we are in."

Harding opened his eyes again and watched as the men began to light the Casey family home on fire. He whispered "Oh, Father, forgive them, for they know not what they do." It was a strange thing to come from his mouth, but the words had welled up inside him and come out, and just at that moment, the captain of the company came running up and yelled for the men to stop. He was holding some papers in his hand.

"Don't burn this one," he said. "I found these letters inside the house. They have the name of Elijah Casey on them. I think this might be Elijah's home. I fought alongside a man named Elijah Casey at the battle of Arkansas Post. He was a good man. A damned good man! He saved my life when he pulled me from the path of a bullet. I thought this was the home of a rebel, but maybe it wasn't after all. Leave this one. Don't burn it boys. Let's go."

The men grumbled, but followed their leader's orders. They all loaded up and left the area leaving the Casey home unburned. As they rode out of sight, Harding ran from his hiding place and pulled off his shirt and began beating at the fire that had been set at the corner of the church. The men had just begun to set the church on fire when the captain told them to stop, so it only had a small flame going. Harding was able to put the flame out and save the church.

But, as he looked across the creek, he saw that there was no saving his home. His and Daniel's homes were burned almost to the ground. A lifetime of memories, gone in an instant.

They soon saw smoke off to the west and realized that they had set William Bennett's old home on fire, too, as they passed on their way out.

Daniel and Harding stayed there long enough to make sure the fires were died down and were not going to spread, then they made the sad walk back to the cave to give the others the news, and tell them they could come back home, to whatever home was left.

As the group made their way back, Hannah saw another red bird in a tree beside the creek. Was Joe letting her know that he was there, watching over them? Or was it just coincidence? She hardly knew what to think. If he was watching over them, he was doing a very poor job of it! She finally chastised herself for having hopes and beliefs such as that. It was probably just a stupid red bird, nothing more.

The next few days were spent trying to clean up and inventory to see what was left that they could use. The men had taken all their horses and killed all three pigs, every single chicken, and the cows. They had no livestock left. It was such a wasteful slaughter, because all the cows and the Inman's bull had been shot, and only the best of the meat removed for the men to eat, while a good deal of the meat was left to rot. It was no longer usable. It was shameful what the soldiers had done.

The people of Buckeye had to build a fire to burn all the animal carcasses so they wouldn't start smelling and drawing buzzards.

The next order of business was where to put everyone now that most of the houses were burned. It was decided that Sarah and Hannah and the rest of their family would continue to stay in their home. Irene and her children agreed to move into the church for the time being. Daniel decided to take Lucy and their children up to live in his grandparent's old home. He didn't like being a mile away from the others, but for now this was their only choice. There were only three buildings left standing, so their options were limited. The old Harris home was small, with only two rooms, but they would have to make do, just as the Inmans were making do with a church building that was simply one large room with no kitchen or inside walls.

All the blankets were brought down from the cave, and any food that was left up there. At least they could use the flour now, since they were able to cook again. But, that one bag of flour was not going to last long. The families split it up evenly, as they did all of the remaining food.

There wasn't a morsel of meat left, so Daniel came up with

the idea to make a fish trap. He put all the girls to work weaving together some grasses, until they had a large grass mat with small enough holes in it for water to pass through, but not fish. He then tied the mat across the creek in a spot where there were small rapids, and left it there. Each day when he went back to check, there would be some fish trapped in it. This provided a little sustenance for everyone.

Thankfully, the men hadn't touched the garden seeds that Hannah and Sarah had saved to plant this summer, so they were able to plant a garden in hopes of having fresh produce eventually. The Inman's seeds had been burned, so it was agreed all would share what food they were able to grow this year from the Casey's seeds.

It was the second year in a row that the Inman family had lost their seeds. First the flood in the spring of 1863, in which most of their seeds were washed away shortly after planting, and then in the spring of 1864 a fire burned them all up. It seemed they just couldn't catch a break.

After several weeks things had calmed down to a point that Hannah was able to find a moment or two alone again to write. She took her journal down to the cemetery and sat near the graves of her mother, her baby sisters, her brother, her grandparents and Joseph, and she jotted down a poem.

I stand silently among you
I feel your spirits close
I absolutely welcome you
I have no fear of ghosts

I know you are around me
I hear you, but it's faint
I see you, but it's fleeting
I recognize constraint

Possess me if you must!
If that's how I'll get my answers
For turning war to peace

For healing wounds and cancers

Help me understand
Take my brain for just a minute
You may use my body
As long as you are in it

I want to hug my Ma again
To see dear Jesse's smile
I want to talk to Joseph
If only for awhile

A few days later she took her journal and went down to the buckeye tree and came up with another poem as she watched the creek flow across the rocks at her feet.

Before he died
Thinking of death
Could cause me to get obsessive
But, now that he's gone
It's common as breath
It is no longer impressive

Before his death
I was vulnerable
I worried to the point of fragility
But now I find
I'm no longer capable
I've simply lost the ability

I used to have dreams
I had wonderful goals
Tell me... I was ready to hear it
But, now that I've been
Raked over the coals

When the Buckeyes Fall

I've completely lost my spirit

I've learned that worrying
Is all for naught
It will not change a thing
It makes you anxious
And overwrought
And adds venom to the sting

Then, one morning a few days later she woke up in her bed with another poem swimming in her head, so she grabbed her journal and jotted it down.

Why is it so hard
To spread your wings and fly
Yet it requires little effort
To lay right down and die

Why does it hurt so much
To lose the ones you love
When there's knowledge that it's better
Living up above

Why do memories flood
At times when you don't want them
When all you need is a day
When you don't think about him

Why does the sun still shine
When clouds keep you from seeing
But, dreary isn't dreary
For every human being

Why do raindrops fall
Where flood waters are roaring
When somewhere else the flowers die
For no raindrops were pouring

Why do those who work the hardest
Seem to have the least
And those who live by taking
Have the biggest feast

Why is your heart the strongest
When your body is the weakest
And sometimes you're the bravest
When inside you are the meekest

Why do the good die young
While the horrible live forever
And why is being happy
An impossible endeavor

Hannah went downstairs to help Sarah with breakfast. Sarah said "Writing again?"

Hannah admitted that she was. She said "I don't know why it is, but before any of my loved ones died, I only wrote about my daily life or dreams in my journal, but now, I have all these poems just pouring out of me. I wake up at night with an idea for a poem, or I go for a walk and one pops into my head. It's the oddest thing."

Sarah said "I believe that grief brings things like that out in people. Some of the best inventors, writers, painters and poets of our time have been through much grief in their life. The grief brings out the creativity. It's like you cannot come up with these wonderful things until a deep hole has been opened up in your soul to release what you had hidden deep inside you all along."

"That sounds like a line I could work into a poem," Hannah said.

Sarah smiled "Well, anything I can do to help. But seriously, Hannah, you should keep developing this talent of yours. Maybe you could become a published writer some day."

"Oh, Sarah, I appreciate your confidence in me, but I don't really think I would ever be published. I just do it for myself. I'm nowhere near talented enough to be published. My poems are too simple."

"I don't know," Sarah said. "There is a place in this world for simple. You might be surprised at how many people would prefer a poem like yours to those with fancy words that are hard to understand. And, not just the poems, but I know that you've written down a lot of your family history, from your Grandma and Grandpa's stories. There is a big market for historical things, and biographies. I just think you need to keep up with your writing and see where it may lead you."

June

It was now June. Two months had gone by since the occupation of the soldiers. The garden was growing good, and the fish trap was still working. Some days Hannah was so sick of eating fish, but occasionally one of the boys had been able to bring in another source of meat, an occasional squirrel or rabbit. She would give anything for some pork or chicken, but that was not something they had available to them for the time being.

It was decided that it was time for a trip to town, for supplies had become dangerously low. But, without any horses, there was no way to carry a load of lumber to town to sell. And, no way to carry back a large amount of purchased goods. Anything that they would be able to trade would need to be small enough for a person to carry on the long trip across the mountain. And, in order to bring the purchased supplies back, they would need a horse, at the least. But, how would they manage to get a horse? This seemed to be a dilemma at first, but the members of the little community were nothing if not resourceful.

Thankfully, many of their small valuable items had been hidden in the cave when the soldiers came through, so had not been stolen or burned. Everyone retrieved those items and began making hard, but necessary, decisions.

Sarah got her candlesticks, her silver baby cup, and her cross necklace and put them on the table. At first she wasn't going to, but she finally, reluctantly, laid her late husband's pocket watch on the table, too. She knew he would have thought it was more important for his girls to eat, than to have this old pocket watch to pass down to them. Lastly, she went and got her gold wedding ring that she'd worn during her first marriage, and added it to the pile. She wasn't wearing it now, it was just sitting in a box. It was more important that they all be able to eat. But, she felt an overwhelming sadness, for it represented a time in her life that had ended abruptly, and against her will. But, she still had her three girls, and she loved Elijah, and it was time to let the past stay in the past.

Hannah went into the bedroom and brought out her Pa's pocket knife and added it to the pile. She wished she, herself, had something valuable to add, but nothing she owned had any real monetary value at all, only sentimental value. Unfortunately, you can't buy food with sentiments. She asked Sarah if her mother's locket might be of value, but Sarah told her the locket was not made of silver or gold, it was just costume jewelry, so she felt Hannah should keep it. Hannah was so thankful her Pa had not bought her mother a real silver or gold necklace. She didn't care what it was made out of, anyway. It was what it stood for that mattered. So, she was thankful to be able to keep it.

Daniel hated to do it, but he laid his grandfather's sword on the table. This was the sword he had carried with him in the War of 1812, the sword with the Eagle head on it. Joshua had hidden it in the cave, and it was passed down to Daniel after Joshua died. It made Hannah so proud to see him give of himself in such a way.

Seeing this, Isabelle and Charlotte went to their rooms and came back with some jewelry that had belonged to Grandma Harris. The jewelry had also been stored in the cave by Grandpa, and it had been decided that Izzy and Lottie should have it after he died. Hannah was touched that the girls were giving it up. She reached over and took two pieces of the jewelry and handed each girl a piece back. "Keep one thing each, and give up the rest." They willingly took it back and were thankful for their big sister's compassion.

Irene brought over her silverware and an antique brooch that her mother had passed down to her many years ago. She then felt like maybe she hadn't contributed enough. Her thoughts went to the five Seated Liberty silver dollars that Henry had kept hidden away for years. When she and Henry had left to come to Arkansas, his father had given him the five dollar coins. He had told Henry to hold onto them until he was an old man, and they would most likely increase in value, but if there were ever an emergency, he would have the coins to fall back on. They were made in 1840, the first year that particular coin was minted. Henry had held onto them all this time, and Irene had managed to keep them safe by hiding them in the cave for a time. She knew how much they meant to Henry, but she also knew that Henry would not want his family to starve. It was torture to give them up, knowing how heartbroken Henry was going to be, but people had to eat. What choice did she have? Maybe the reason Henry had held onto them all these years was for just such an occasion as this. If this wasn't a time of emergency, she didn't know what was. She went to the church, where she had hidden the coins for the time being, and came back and added them to the pile.

All of the items they had gathered were small enough that they could be carried without a horse. The hope was that, once in town, they could trade some of these items for a horse, and maybe a small cart, and then with the remainder buy enough supplies to load the horse down with to bring home. It was impossible for a man to carry several bags of flour or sugar all the way home over the mountain, but with a horse they could manage it.

It was decided that all three of the older boys, Daniel, Harding and Albert, would make the trip. They split up all the items they needed to carry, and they set off. Sarah ran out at the last minute waving some letters and said "Don't forget to mail our letters while you are there!" One of those letters was from Hannah to her Aunt Caroline, informing her of the death of her parents that past winter. It had been very difficult for her to sit down and write that letter. Because paper was scarce, she had used a page from her journal to write it, and then ripped it out and folded it over. On one of the folds she had written a short poem of condolence, hoping it would be helpful to her aunt.

As they began walking away, Sarah was reminding them not to let themselves be taken advantage of when trading. She told them to go to more than one store and ask what they would give for each item, then compare and sell to the highest bidder. Get as much as possible for each thing. And, do the same when buying the supplies. Find the person who was willing to sell the cheapest, and give them the business.

The boys were gone four days. The girls were getting a bit worried, but when they finally arrived back home with a pretty brown horse, they explained that it had been difficult to find someone who would trade a horse for what little they had to offer. But, they had eventually found a man who was a fan of old war collectibles, and he agreed to trade one of his horses for Grandpa's old sword, especially after the boys told them that he had killed men in battle with it (even though they weren't completely sure if that was true).

Then, they had found someone who agreed to give them two dollars for each of their 1840 dollar coins, and with that money they were able to purchase a small wooden cart with two wheels that could be pulled by a horse. It was much smaller than the types of carts Elijah and Henry had always used, theirs had always been the type with four wheels, but it was all they could afford, and with it they would be able to haul back all the supplies they needed, which was a relief.

When the boys arrived back in Buckeye, the girls were elated to see the bags of flour and sugar, for now they could have bread again, and even a pie or cake from time to time. And, happily, the little girls discovered a familiar sound coming from a little box in the back of the cart. It was the peeping of little baby chickens. Daniel took the box down and opened it and six soft little baby chickens tumbled out. He told the girls to take very good care of them so they could have eggs again eventually. They had all been missing the taste of eggs for breakfast.

The boys brought back a bit of war news, too, and it was not good news. They told everyone, sadly, that Union forces had occupied Clarksville for a time, and the boys had barely missed showing up at the same time they were there. A few weeks earlier the soldiers had left the area, but they had set fire to many buildings in town on their way out. Harding turned to Hannah and said "Remember that pretty Methodist church with the stained glass windows that we saw? Well, they burned it to the ground!" It upset Hannah to hear this. She failed to understand the point in burning up beautiful buildings, and burning people's businesses and homes. She realized they were doing it to punish their perceived enemies, but it just didn't seem morally right to Hannah. She could halfway understand punishing the soldiers fighting on the opposite sides, but why punish the everyday person who was just trying to live their lives in peace?

The thing everyone was waiting for the most, as always, was the mail. Daniel handed it out to each recipient, and they all gathered around to hear the news.

There were only two letters from Elijah that had made it through. The first one was dated March 22, 1864, and stated that he and Henry were getting ready to leave Little Rock to go on the 'Camden Expedition'. They were going to march to Shreveport to join forces with another company. There was no letter to tell them what happened on that expedition.

But, they assumed the worst when they read the second letter. It was dated April 29 of '64. In this letter Elijah said that he and Henry had been captured and sent to a military prison in Andersonville, Georgia. He said it was called "Camp Sumter". He painted a grim picture of the camp. He said there were thousands of Union soldiers there, and that they were all treated miserably, inhumanely, in fact. He said "Men are dying by the dozens every day. There's poor sanitation, overcrowding, malnutrition and disease." He said that the prison grounds covered about 16 acres and was surrounded by a 15 foot high stockade wall, and guarded well. There seemed to be no hope of escape. He said "There's a line around the inside of the walls, about 20 feet away from the wall, that prisoners are told not to cross. They call this the 'deadline'. If anyone even sets one foot across the line, the guards in the pigeon roosts are ordered to fire and kill them."

He went on to say "There are vermin everywhere. You can pick all the lice off you, but the minute you sit down again you will be covered anew. There's a swampy low place where they empty all the filth, and that place is simply alive. You hear a regular buzzing sound coming from it, and it is covered with large white maggots."

It was very difficult for Hannah to picture her Pa in such circumstances. But, even more so, the looks on Sarah and Irene's faces, after hearing the condition their husbands were in, was hard to witness.

After a few minutes of silence, Harding said "Maybe we should all pray."

"That's a wonderful idea son," Irene said. "Let's all gather in a circle and pray for our men. Harding, would you like to do the honors?"

Harding had never been asked to pray out loud for a group before, but he wanted to do it, for his Pa and for Elijah, who, although not blood related, had always felt like an uncle to him. So, he began...

"Dear Heavenly Father,
We ask you to bless Henry and Elijah.
We ask that you watch over them
as they undertake this difficult
journey they are on.
Please provide them with
health of body and soul
and the strength to endure
so they may return home
to their loved ones
safe and sound.
We pray in the name of Jesus,
Amen."

Sarah thanked Harding for such an inspirational prayer. As

they all knew, the power of prayer could sometimes make all the difference, and it is helpful and comforting to those who hear it. It was easy to give up hope during these difficult times, and maybe they had all strayed a bit too far from God lately. It felt good to reach out to him again.

August

The summer of 1864 dragged on, day by hot day. The garden was producing vegetables, so there was food to eat. The chickens were growing, although they probably wouldn't start producing eggs until about October. There was no food to feed the chickens, so they were let out during the day so they could find their own food by going around looking for bugs. At night they would be shut back into the barn to keep them safe from prowling animals. Thankfully, the Casey's barn had survived the burning from the soldiers back in the spring, because the other barns across the creek had not.

There had been no more trouble from soldiers or bushwhackers. The trauma from the last encounter was beginning to wear off and people were beginning to feel more trusting, going farther from home without worrying as much, and allowing the little children to play outside unattended again. They knew that another event could happen at any time, but it was exhausting to live your life in fear constantly. It was much better to put their faith in the Lord and live their lives in the best way they could.

One afternoon after everyone had been working hard in the garden, Hannah told Sarah she was going for a walk. She was extremely hot and sweaty, and just needed some time to herself to think and cool off. She hadn't thought about where she was walking exactly, but soon found her feet going down the road toward where the Owens family had lived. She passed the burned out structure of their home and felt sad about it. She had many memories of coming here and playing with Lucy and Abe when they were all younger. It was hard to believe how much had changed in just a few years' time.

After a few moments of reflection, she found herself continuing on past their homeplace, and heading toward the old swimming hole, where she and her siblings and the other children had spent many afternoons swimming when she was younger. For whatever reason, they hadn't been swimming here in quite a long time. When they played in the water, they tended to do it within view of the house. It just felt safer that way. But, on this day Hannah felt the need to go back and relive the olden days.

When she got to the swimming hole she sat down on the bank and put her bare feet in the water. The coolness of it felt so good. It had to be a hundred degrees today, and it was so wonderful to feel the cool wetness on her toes. It felt so good, in fact, she decided to go for a swim.

She started to jump in, but then decided she didn't really want to get her dress wet, even though it could probably use a good washing. It was hard to swim in a dress, though, and she honestly just craved the chance to really get out there and swim, unencumbered, like a fish. Oh, how refreshing that would be!

She looked around. No one else was about. Why not? She felt a bit naughty as she took off her dress and undergarments. Even though she was alone, she stood behind a tree to undress, as if someone might see her. She stood for a moment and felt the slight breeze blowing across her naked body. It felt wonderful. It was just so hot out!

Finally, she eased herself down into the cool water of the creek and submerged up to her neck. Oh, that was refreshing! She began swimming around, then went under to get her hair completely wet. She came back up and wiped the water from her eyes. Now, this was the life! She was feeling so much better. She then pushed out deeper into the water and began swimming, a little on her stomach, and then floating on her back some.

She was floating on her back, looking up at the billowy white clouds, with her ears just enough under the water that all sound was muffled. In a way it was as if she were floating in another realm. All her stresses were melting away. She felt free.

Suddenly a flash of red crossed her vision. She raised up quickly to see what it was, and that's when she noticed a pretty red Cardinal landing on the tip of a tree branch just above her.

"Amazing!" she thought. "Is that you, Joe? Why are you always showing up like this? Are you trying to communicate with me, or are you just trying to see me naked?" She laughed.

Then she quickly told herself she was being silly. She had seen red birds many times in her life, and only since Joe's death did she suddenly think it meant something. She was just making it represent what she wanted it to represent. Yet, still, she couldn't help feeling that there was a meaning behind this bird's appearance. The way it looked at her! Then, it flew away.

She was still swimming around in the creek, enjoying the cool, thinking maybe it was time to go back home, but not wanting to leave, when suddenly she heard a noise. She ducked down neck-deep into the water, so as to hide herself a bit, while she tried to ascertain what the noise was.

Then she saw them! Two men and two horses, coming down the road!

What should she do? Here she was, totally naked, defenseless. What if these men were out to harm her? But, then again, maybe they were perfectly nice men, but she still didn't want them to see her unclothed. She was frantically looking about, trying to figure out what to do and where to go.

As she did this she was watching them, and she was beginning to feel less and less threatened by what she saw. It was two men, maybe 25 to 30 years old. They had two horses. One man was leading both horses and walking, while the other man was riding one of the horses, and leaning forward as if he were injured or sick. They were walking slowly, as if they were tired and had been walking a long while.

Hannah decided maybe if she just stayed very quiet, they would go on by and not see her. So, she just hovered down in the water, with barely her head sticking out. They had almost made it past, when suddenly the man walking caught a glimpse of Hannah's dress hanging across a tree limb. He stopped the horses and looked around.

"Good afternoon! Is someone here?"

Hannah knew that from the direction they'd come, they would not have seen a house for a good 20 or more miles, so to see a woman's dress hanging on a tree must have been shocking to them, out here in the middle of nowhere. But, Hannah didn't want to be discovered and remained quiet.

The man again spoke and said "Is anyone here?"

He looked around a bit more and then said "I'm not going to hurt you, if you're afraid to come out. I assure you, I'm only in need of help. My friend here is hurt."

Hannah felt a tinge of sympathy for the man. He looked so helpless standing there. Against her better judgement, she decided to speak.

"I ask you, kind sir, to turn your gaze. I am swimming nude."

The man immediately reddened, as he caught sight of her head out in the water for the first time. He turned his head quickly.

"Please, sir," Hannah begged. "Please go ahead on the trail until you are out of sight and wait for me there."

So the man did as she asked and dissappeared down the road. Hannah waited a moment or two and then quickly jumped out of the water and ran and hid behind the tree again. She peeped around to make sure he wasn't in sight, then quickly dressed herself. She tried to brush her wet hair out a bit with her fingers, so she didn't look too frightful, then she began walking in the direction of the men.

She chastised herself for doing this, but something inside her told her that she was safe, that these men were not here to harm her. Maybe it was because she had seen the red bird. It seemed as if it had been a signal to her that something was about to happen, but that it was a good thing. She didn't know why, she just knew she sensed she was safe.

When she stepped into view, the man who had been walking turned around cautiously and said "I beg your pardon, ma'am. I did not intend to come up on you like that. Please accept my apologies for any embarrassment I may have caused."

Hannah felt a bit shy as she said "Think nothing of it. I just did not expect to see another human being strolling along as you were. May I ask what is wrong with your friend?"

"Well, as you can probably see from our clothing, we are soldiers in the Confederate army. Our company was scattered during a skirmish. My friend and I were fleeing on horseback when his horse was frightened by something and he was thrown off. I stopped to help and discovered that his leg was severely injured. He was not able to walk. Our company, not realizing what happened, continued on. We got separated from them. We are now lost, and have just been following this road here for quite some time, for two days now, trying to find someone that could help us."

Hannah said "I just live about a half a mile further. Follow me and I will see what we can do to help. We don't have a doctor around anywhere close, though."

As they walked, Hannah and the soldier introduced themselves.

"My name is Hannah Casey. I live here with my stepmother and my large family of younger siblings. I have an older brother, too, named Daniel, who is married to Lucy, and they live here. Also, my father's good friend Henry Inman's family lives here. We used to have other families, but one moved away and the others died or were killed."

"Killed?" the man asked.

"Yes, we have had some bushwhacker activity up here in these mountains. My father and his friend Henry are both away fighting in the war. They have been gone for two years now. My brother and some of the other boys in our community were fighting in the war, too, but my brother is back home now."

"May I ask which side they were fighting on?"

Hannah wasn't sure if she should say, but something made her trust this man. She said "Well, we had four young boys and men from our community that were in the Confederate army, like you. One of the boys was killed in battle, and two others were killed by bushwhackers after they returned home. My brother Daniel is the only one of the four who is still alive. He was shot, but he recovered, thankfully."

"I'm glad to hear that about your brother. I'm sorry about the other boys, though. There has been too much useless death in this war."

"Yes, there has," she agreed. "I had another brother who was only 15, and he was also killed by bushwhackers, or soldiers, I don't even know what the men were, to be honest. I just know that Jesse didn't deserve to die."

She paused, then said "My father and his friend are both in the Union army." She paused to see if this would cause a negative reaction from the man. But, he didn't seem to find it odd.

"That must be difficult," he said. "I mean, having members of the same family fighting for different sides. Unfortunately, this is not the first time I have heard of it happening. Just because you grow up under the same roof doesn't always mean you develop the same beliefs. I knew two brothers back home who each joined opposite sides."

"Where is back home?" she asked.

"I'm from Charleston, South Carolina."

"That far!?" Hannah asked. "How did you end up here?"

"Long story. I've been enlisted since the beginning, and I've been tossed about from company to company and marched from place to place, until now I find myself here, walking along with a lovely young lady in the middle of nowhere in the mountains of Arkansas."

Hannah blushed at the mention of her being a 'lovely young lady', especially when she knew she looked horrid after working all day in the garden and then swimming and getting her hair all wet.

"I don't think I caught your name..." Hannah said.

"Oh, forgive me, ma'am," he said. "Where are my manners?"

"Let me just tell you up front, you don't have to keep calling me ma'am," she said.

He looked at her out of the corner of his eye. "It just feels like the respectable thing to do."

"Well, I don't feel like a ma'am. That is what you call old married women."

"So, you're not married?"

"No, sir, I'm not."

"Well, if I am not to call you ma'am, then you don't need to address me as 'sir', either," he said with a grin on his face.

"How can I address you otherwise, when I still don't know your name!"

The man laughed and said "Well, ma'am... I mean 'Miss Hannah Casey'.... My name is Jonathan Oakley, but folks just call me 'John'. This here," he said as he motioned toward his friend on the horse "is Samuel Underwood, but you can just call him 'Sam'."

Sam mumbled a greeting to Hannah, but she could tell he was in so much pain he was almost delirious. She said "We will do our best to help you, Sam. I'm sorry that you're hurting so."

She then asked John if he and Sam were both from South Carolina.

"No, I met Sam at Fort Henry in Tennessee. I guess it was about February of '62, early on in the war. My company and his had both been sent there, and afterward we merged together into one larger company. From that time on, Sam and I have been together."

"So, is Sam from Tennessee?"

"No, he's from Jackson, Mississippi."

As they passed by the Owens' old home, John said "What happened here?"

Hannah said "That was the home of Rev. Owens. He was the preacher of our little church. But, after his son Abe was killed in the war, he and his wife decided to go back home to Tennessee, where they were originally from, to be with their children and grandchildren, except for Lucy. Lucy stayed here because she was married to my brother, Daniel. Anyway, the house was sitting empty but bushwhackers occupied it, then soldiers came and burned it. They burned three other houses, too. You will see when we get there. Thankfully, they didn't burn my house, or the church."

Hannah continued to tell John a little more about her little community and the people who lived there as they walked along.

She found John to be very amiable, and easy to talk to, and she couldn't help but notice that he was easy on the eyes, as well. As they came into view of her house, she said "Maybe you should stay right here while I go explain to my stepmother what is going on."

John was looking around at the other burned homes, and noticing the church and the cemetery, just taking in everything, while Hannah disappeared into her house. He could tell that these poor people had been through a lot. He was thinking about the young woman he had just met, and how beautiful she was, a natural beauty, not a made-up one. He was thinking that she seemed so smart and articulate, and he wondered how she got that way being so sheltered up here in these mountains for so long. He certainly had not expected to meet someone like Hannah Casey on a day like today. It had been a pleasant surprise.

Sarah had not been easily convinced that these two soldiers Hannah had escorted home were trustworthy. She came out on the porch, drying her hands on her apron, and glared down the hill at the men. John could feel himself being sized up. He waved up to her in a friendly manner, hoping to win her over.

Sarah was not at all sure, but she finally relented enough to allow Hannah to put the men up in the barn. But, out of caution, she sent Albert running off to fetch Daniel from Grandpa's old house where he was living now. Better to have Daniel here to size things up further.

Sarah and Hannah helped John get Sam off the horse and laid down in the barn. Sarah could see the man was suffering, and her tender heart relented. She went into the house and got a bottle of laudanum that she kept hidden for just such a time. She gave the man a drink of it, and then began to examine his leg. There was a deep gash in it, and she thought that possibly it was broken. She didn't have any idea about broken bones or how to set them, but since the leg wasn't misshapen, she hoped that the bone would heal back on it's own, if in fact it was broken. She doctored up his cut with some of the laudanum. It seemed to give the man a lot of relief, because he relaxed and fell asleep. Sarah wrapped up his leg and told John that it was just going to take time. If it was a break, it could take two or three months for it to heal.

When Daniel arrived, he sent the women back into the house so he could study these two men and make sure they were harmless. Hannah and Sarah prepared supper and Hannah carried some out to the men. She apologized to John that it was only a little bit of fish. They just did not have much meat to speak of these days.

John said fried fish sounded wonderful to him, and he ate it as if he hadn't eaten in weeks. By now Daniel seemed to be at ease with the men, and seemed to even have developed a friendship with John. The two were getting along very well, and swapping war stories. Hannah was happy to see that Daniel approved. With Sam's injury, it looked like it might be awhile before the men could pick up and move on, so if Daniel felt comfortable with them, then it would be nice to have more men around.

John and Sam stayed in the barn that night. Hannah brought them each a blanket, but there was nothing she could do about a pillow for them. John said the blanket was good enough, and more than he even expected.

The next morning Hannah brought them breakfast. Again, she was apologizing because there were no eggs, and she was trying to explain how the bushwhackers had killed their chickens and they had to get new ones but they were still too young to lay. John again said there was no need to apologize. This food was better than anything he'd had in the army for months on end.

Hannah and the others went about their chores that day, and John came out to help. He worked alongside them in the garden, then helped carry water up from the creek when it was needed. He was a huge help to them, and they all appreciated it very much.

At supper time that night Hannah sat in the barn and visited with John and Sam for awhile. It was exciting to have someone new around to talk to. She was curious to find out what it was like where they were both from, what their families were like.

"What is Charleston like?" she asked.

"Well, it's a large city, probably larger than anything you've ever seen. I think the population is around 40,000 people."

Hannah said "I think I remember Sarah teaching us in school that the town of Clarksville had a population of about 300. That's the biggest town I've ever seen, or at least that I can remember seeing. I can't imagine 40,000 in one city alone."

"It's very big," John said. "It's on the east coast near the Atlantic ocean. There's a peninsula of land that sticks out. On the end of that peninsula is the battery. On each side of the battery are rivers that flow out into the ocean. On the west side is the Ashley River, and then on the east side there are two rivers, the Cooper and the Wando, that flow together and join just before emptying out in the ocean. The spot where the three rivers meet is called Charleston Harbor and once you pass out of the harbor you are in the Atlantic Ocean. There are all these beautiful homes along the edges of the battery, looking out into the harbor. You wouldn't believe how opulent they are. They're just magnificent. Of course, you have to be well off to live in one of them, of which my family is not. But, I love strolling through there and looking at them all, and imagining what it would be like to live in one of them. Some of the homes have historical significance. There is one that I know of that was built for one of the signers of the Declaration of Independence. Further inland, there are magnificent plantations with beautiful two-story mansions with wrap-around porches and giant columns going all the way around."

"What do you mean by a 'battery'," Hannah asked.

"Oh, well, the battery is a place where a lot of artillery is kept, like cannons and large guns and such, so as to protect the mainland. It faces out into the water so if enemy boats or ships come up, they can be fired upon. And, out from the battery, in Charleston Harbor, there is an island with a fort on it called Fort Sumter. That's where the first shots of this war we are in were fired. I witnessed those shots myself. It was what prompted me to enlist when war was declared."

Hannah was having a hard time imagining all the scenes that John was describing, but it all sounded so interesting to her.

She asked what his house was like. He said it was what you might call a middle-class home. "My family doesn't own a plantation, or any slaves, but we're not poor either. We fall in line with the merchant class, the ship builders, shop owners, hoteliers and the like."

"Are your parents still alive?"

"Yes," John said. "My father is Jonathan Israel Oakley, but no one ever calls him by the name Jonathan. He's always referred to as Israel. My mother is Mary Katherine."

"So, are you Jonathan Israel, too, after your father?"

"No, I'm Jonathan after my father, but my middle name is Wade, after my mother's family. My mother's maiden name was Mary Katherine Wade. She is very proud of our family heritage. She says my 6th great grandfather was Colonel Jonathan Wade who came to America in the 1600's from England. He settled in Massachusetts Bay Colony. My Ma says that the stories passed down through our family are that Col. Wade knew some of the members of the Mayflower from Plymouth Colony. Supposedly he did business with people like John Alden, William Brewster, John Carver and Myles Standish. She also says he was a witness to the famous Salem Witch Trials, and watched when they hung some of those poor women. I don't know if all that's true, but my Ma has family tree charts and names that show how it goes from Col. Jonathan Wade down to me, Jonathan Wade Oakley. I think my 5th great grandfather was John Wade, Jr., but I can't remember the rest of the names after that. My Ma has them, though, if I ever want to look at them."

"Jonathan Wade Oakley," Hannah said. She liked the sound of it. It was a good, strong name.

"Yep, that's me! My Ma said the Jonathan part of my name is really after my father, but it is an interesting coincidence that it is the same name as my original ancestor. My Ma is proud of the fact that I have that name."

"I think that's really interesting," Hannah said. "I wish I knew more about my family history going back. I only know back to my grandparents on one side and my great grandparents on the other, nothing further. I should have asked Grandma and Grandpa to tell me the names of their family as far back as they remembered. They are gone now, and it's too late. Maybe I could write Aunt Caroline and see what she knows. As far back as I know on my mother's side is to my great grandparents. My grandpa Joshua's parents were Hugh & Sarah Harris. My Grandma Ruth's parents were John & Magdalene Moseley. Grandma Ruth told me that her full name was a mouthful, because she'd been married twice. It was Ruth Ann Moseley Middleton Harris."

"That is a mouthful!" John agreed.

Hannah continued and said "On my father's side, though, I don't know any of the names of my greats, only my grands. They were Daniel & Hannah Casey. I should ask my father if he knows his grandparents' names. I need to write that down if he does. He may not know, though, because he lost his parents very young. My father was their first born. They named him Elijah Warren Casey. Then, two years later they had another boy, my uncle Morgan Daniel Casey. My grandmother died in childbirth with uncle Morgan. I think Pa said she was only about 21 years old. Grandpa Daniel was left with two little boys, a 2 year old and a newborn. I'm not sure who helped him with raising them at first. I need to ask my father that, too! Anyway, I think when my Pa was about 8 years old, and Morgan was about 6, their father married again. I don't remember the 2nd wife's name. She would have been my step-grandmother, I suppose. Anyway, Pa says that his father had 3 more children with this second wife, who would be my Pa's half-siblings. I think it was two boys and a girl. And, then, after only about 6 years of marriage, my Pa's father died young, too. He was in his 30's, I think. My Pa was only about 14 years old when his father died. At only 14, he had lost both of his parents. Isn't that sad? Anyway, I guess his stepmother raised him for a bit after that, but he and uncle Morgan left home pretty early. I think they didn't really like living with their stepmother. I think she treated her own three children better than she did her two stepsons. Pa didn't stay close with his stepmother or his half-siblings, but he and uncle Morgan stayed close, at least at first. They were living near each other back in Tennessee, and saw each other often. But, Morgan didn't move to Arkansas with Pa, so they haven't seen each other in about 13 years. I think it's sad that my Pa lost touch with his family like he did."

"I'm guessing you were named after your grandma Hannah, then, your Pa's mother who died so young giving birth to your uncle?"

"Yes, I sure am!"

"So, what is your middle name, Miss Hannah Casey?" John asked as he gave her a playful wink. He knew she was rambling, but he loved to hear her talk.

"I'm Hannah Ruth. I was named after my two grandmas, Hannah & Ruth. My grandpa always called me Hannah Belle, I guess it was his nickname for me, but my middle name is actually Ruth. My Ma had the same middle name. She was Emeline Ruth."

"I like hearing the history of how people come up with the names for their children," John said. "Most of the time they name them after someone they love or admire, but sometimes they just pick a random name, just because they like the sound of it."

"Yes, most of my siblings are named after someone," Hannah said. "Let's see, Daniel was the first born in my family. He is Daniel Joshua. He was named after our two grandfathers, Daniel Casey & Joshua Harris. And, then came me, who was named after the two grandmothers. So, they got all the grandparents taken care of after only two children. After that came Jesse Thomas. Ma got the name Jesse from the Bible, but Thomas was after one of our uncles, one of my mom's older brothers that she really admired. Next was Albert Joseph. He was given the two middle names of our grandfathers, because Ma's father was Joshua Albert and Pa's father was Daniel Joseph. So, one of my brothers has the grandpas' two first names, and another has their two middle names."

"And, you have your grandmas' two first names, so does one of your sisters have your grandmas' two middle names?" he asked.

"Well, no. They used both of the grandmas' middle names, but they split it between two of their daughters. The next born was Isabel Rose. She was named Isabel because Pa's mother was Hannah Isabel, so Izzy and I are both named after the same grandmother. But, the Rose part I don't think was after anybody. Then, after Izzy it was Charlotte Ann. She was given the middle name of Ann because it was my other grandma's middle name, grandma Ruth Ann. So, Lottie and I are also both named after the same grandmother. I think the Charlotte part of her name was just a name that they liked, though."

"Next came Michael Warren. I think they just liked the name Michael, or it may have come from the Bible, but Warren is Pa's middle name. Then came the twins, Jacob & Jonah. Ma wanted to have biblical names for them, so she picked four boy names from the Bible and put them together to make Jacob Aaron & Jonah Adam. She wanted them to have the same initials, since they were twins. Both of their initials are J.A.C. Pa used to tease Ma and call them 'Jack 1' and 'Jack 2', because their initials sounded like 'Jack'. One of them would toddle up to him and he'd say 'Which one are you? Jack 1 or Jack 2?' and Ma would get so mad at him! She'd say 'They have names Eli!'. But, I guess the novelty of that wore off, because he doesn't call them that anymore."

"And, then after Pa married Sarah they had my youngest brother Jasper. Sarah named him Jasper Elijah. The Jasper part was after her dad, and then Elijah, of course, was after Pa. Funny that with all the boys Ma and Pa had together, they never named one of them Elijah. They only used Pa's middle name for one of them. Actually, they didn't name any of their daughters Emeline, after Ma, either. They only used her middle name for me, which was my grandma's middle name, too, so it was sort of after her as well, but Ma always said I was named after my Grandma, not after her. We were both named after grandma, she said. But, I like to think I was named after my Ma, too."

Hannah seemed to have run out of steam all the sudden, and she stopped talking. Something told her that she was talking too much, and maybe she was boring him. Maybe she should quit rambling so much. He probably didn't care in the least how all her siblings got their names! But, there was just something about this man that made her want to talk and talk and talk. She'd never really experienced what it was like to get to know someone. Her whole life she was always just around people that she already knew everything about, and who already knew everything about her. This was a new and exciting experience. She just found herself wanting to share everything about her life with John, and she wanted to hear everything about his life.

John, on the other hand, was not the least bit bored or annoyed by all her talking. He just kept looking at her lovely face and thinking how easy it was to listen to her, how her voice was soothing to him, and how much he was enjoying it and didn't want it to end. She had filled his head with a dizzying array of words, and he half forgot what all she said because he couldn't keep up. But, none of that mattered. He loved listening to her, and he wanted to keep her talking. If she ran out of words, she might leave and go back in the house, and he didn't want her to leave.

"So, you have a big family, Miss Hannah Ruth. I have certainly been a witness to that. I thought *my* family was big, until I met yours. I suppose you would still consider my family to be somewhat big. Funny thing is, I am the only boy out of seven children. My parents had three girls, then me, then three more girls."

"What are your sisters' names?" Hannah wanted to know.

"Well, let's see, the older three are Matilda, Margaret and Talitha, and the younger three are Doshia, Susan and Ellen."

"Are you married, Mr. Jonathan Wade Oakley?" Hannah asked, silently hoping the answer would not be yes.

"No, Miss Hannah, I am not married."

She looked at him skeptically, and said "How is it you are not married? I mean, you look plenty old enough to be married to me."

He playfully asked "Well, how old do you think I am?"

She thought for a minute and said "Ummm... 30?"

He said "Pretty close! I am actually 29 years old. And, may I take a guess at your age? I know it's not polite to ask a lady her age."

"Oh, I don't mind," she said. "Go ahead and guess."

"I think you might be 25 years old."

She said "Well, you guessed me a little high. I am actually only 19, well... 19 and a half."

John seemed a bit surprised that she was younger than he'd thought. It didn't seem possible that they were ten years apart, because she had an old soul, and the way she talked to him, he would have guessed her much older. Maybe he had just wished her to be older and closer to his age.

"So, you didn't answer me," Hannah reminded him. "How is it you have never been married at the ripe old age of 29?"

He put her off by saying "That's a story for another time."

John and Sam soon began to fit right in with the other members of the community. The children loved them both, and Daniel had especially developed a strong friendship with John. About a week after their arrival, Daniel and John went off on a hunting trip together, and they came back with a large deer. Everyone was excited at the prospect of fresh deer meat, and the rest was smoked for later use.

A week later they went hunting again, and got another deer. This meat was also smoked and put away. Hannah was beginning to see that John was a good asset to have around. He seemed to have a knack for hunting that her brothers did not have. They were good at bringing home small game from time to time, but the bigger game was a struggle for them.

Each day after supper Hannah went out to the barn to talk with John and Sam. Each day she got to know John a little bit more. She enjoyed his company immensely, and was starting to hope the time would not come when he would leave. She had invited them to come inside the house, but John insisted that it wasn't their place to intrude in the house. He felt better if they just stayed in the barn.

On the third week after John had arrived, he and Daniel were out in the woods again when they discovered a bee hive in an old hollow tree. They came home very excited. They said the next day they planned on going back and retrieving some honey. Hannah was very interested in this project and asked if she might go along. Daniel, at first, said no, but John persuaded him to allow Hannah to come, so he relented.

They left about midday, because John said the bees would

be more likely to be away from the hive at that time of day. They made Hannah stand back far from the hive, while the two of them carefully walked up close and placed some branches and debris underneath the tree. Then they lit the branches and got a good fire going. Once the fire began giving off a lot of smoke, John explained that the bees would be subdued, giving them time to come in and take some of the honey without being stung.

John told Daniel to only get about two thirds of the honeycomb out, because they must leave enough for the bees to survive on, because, after all, that was their food source. If they only took some of it, then the bees would continue to make more and they might be able to raid the hive again next year.

After they had stuffed all the containers they brought along with honeycomb, they put out the fire and left so the bees could come back.

At home they squeezed out as much honey as they could from the waxy combs, and put it into jars. Not only was the honey wonderful for putting on biscuits or pancakes, but it also could be used as a substitute for sugar if they needed it.

Then, they took the leftover wax and melted it over a fire and made candles out of it. Hannah found it so interesting to learn this new technique. John told her that when the candles were burned, they gave off a slight aroma of sweet honey, which made the house smell nice. Collecting beeswax and honey was not a skill that Hannah had seen her father or Mr. Inman do. How refreshing it was to have someone new come and teach them all something. The more she was around John Oakley, the more interesting he became.

By week four of their visit, Sam was beginning to put a little weight on his leg, but he still could not walk. Sarah guessed it would still be at least two more weeks, maybe more, before he could put enough pressure on it to attempt walking. Hannah was secretly glad, because she didn't want John to go. John Oakley was the best thing to happen to her in a long time. He was bringing her out of her depression. She was blossoming because of him.

September

It turned out Lucy was correct in assuming her baby would come in September. She had a fairly easy delivery, and it was another little girl. Hannah found it amusing when she was told the baby's name. Lucy said since the new baby girl was so close in age to the other two girls, why not make her name match with theirs? So, she picked the name 'Etta Jean'. Hannah now had three little nieces named Emma June, Ella Jane and Etta Jean, all born within 15 months. It was crazy, but somehow it seemed perfect.

When Hannah visited with John later that day, he asked how the baby was going to be baptized.

Hannah said "Well, I don't see how we can. We don't have a preacher. Lucy's other two babies didn't get baptized either, and neither did my littlest brother, Jasper. All of them were born after Rev. Owens left two years ago. We haven't had a preacher since."

John asked "So, did all of you just stop going to church after your reverend left? I ask, because since I have been here, I have seen no church services being held."

"No, I suppose we just kind of stopped having church. We also stopped having school. Sarah used to teach all of us children, that's how we all learned to read and write. She was a wonderful teacher. But, since the war started it just seems like there is never enough time left in the day for school. And, church, well, I can't explain it other than we just didn't have a preacher to lead us, so we just didn't know what to say or do, so we just stopped having it. And, now, of course, with the Inman home burned, Irene and her children have been living in the church building."

"What's to stop you from having church anyway?" John asked. "God doesn't care how you do it, just so long as you show up."

"I don't have an answer for that, John. I know what you are saying is right, but we just haven't made the effort. I don't suppose we have a good excuse."

"Why don't you stop making excuses and just do it?" he

said. "When Sunday comes next, let's just do it."

Hannah smiled and said "Okay, John, if that will make you happy."

John said "I don't know if it will make *me* happy or not, but I know it will make God happy."

Hannah stared at this man who had so unexpectedly come into her life, and she found herself amazed by him. He had such good character and values, and he wasn't afraid to say what he was feeling or thinking.

"And another thing," he said. "What is being done about rebuilding the homes that were burned?"

Hannah shrugged and said "Nothing. I suppose we are all waiting until Pa and Henry return."

"Well, seems to me you have a perfectly good sawmill sitting over there, and a few strong young men who could very easily cut down some trees and begin cutting some lumber. At least it's a start. I can help. We can at least make a dent in the amount of boards that will be needed, then when your pa comes back, there will be that much less work for him to do."

Hannah was simply amazed. This man seemed to have no end of energy and ideas. He was a person who saw a need and didn't waste any time getting that need fulfilled. She found herself being drawn to him more and more each day, and not just emotionally and spiritually, but physically, as well. Sometimes when their eyes met, she felt weak at the knees and a nice, warm sensation travelled through her body. She sometimes lay in bed at night thinking about the shape of his face, and the line of his mouth, and wondered what it might be like to kiss him. But, then she would chastise herself, because she thought she was much too young for him to be even remotely interested in her. He probably was attracted to more mature, experienced women.

Little did she know that John had been thinking similar thoughts about her. He had told himself to stop thinking about Hannah that way, because there was no way she would want a man who was so much older than she was.

The next Sunday all of the people gathered on the hill in

front of Hannah's home to have church. John had said an outdoor church seemed like a lovely idea on this beautiful day. Everyone just sat around on the grass. Those who had Bibles brought them.

At first, no one knew quite what to say or do. Hannah said "Should we just read something from the Bible?" Everyone agreed, but no one was jumping up to volunteer. Finally, John said "I don't mind reading something, if it's okay with you all."

They all sighed with relief, because no one was very eager to get up in front of everyone else and read. They were more than happy to let John do it.

John flipped through his Bible, for even throughout the war he had carried a small Bible with him. It was getting worn out and about to fall apart, but it had gotten him through many moments of fear and doubt. He turned to Ecclesiastes.

"I'm going to read Ecclesiastes 3. This is a part of the Bible that has comforted me in many troubled times. I know that this little community in the mountains here has seen much suffering, but God promises us that nothing stays the same. There is a time for everything, and your time of suffering will not last. If you continue to have faith in him, he will pull you out of the dark and back into the light."

As John slowly read each line on his page, the group were lost in their own thoughts, comparing each phrase that came from John's mouth with something that had happened in their own lives.

"To every thing there is a season, and a time to every purpose under Heaven."

Hannah noticed immediately that John had a very commanding voice. It was not all hellfire and damnation, but rather forceful and convincing, and calming at the same time.

"A time to be born, and a time to die."

Hannah saw how true that was. How many births had she witnessed recently, and oh, how many deaths!

"A time to plant, and a time to pluck up that which is planted."

Yes, each year she had gone through the ritual of planting and harvesting, like clockwork.

"A time to kill, and a time to heal."

She had wanted to kill more than once. Each time one of these bands of ragged men had come through and harmed the ones she loved, she felt rage and would have killed if she could. But, is there really a time to heal? She wasn't sure if that were possible, but she knew if God said it, it must be so.

"A time to break down, and a time to build up."

Oh, how many times had she broken down in the past few years! Only since John's arrival had she begun to feel a sense of building back up.

"A time to weep, and a time to laugh."

So much weeping, but not enough laughter. But, when there was laughter, it was such a healing thing.

"A time to mourn, and a time to dance."

She remembered mourning for Joe, but she also remembered dancing with him by the fireplace that night, when he put her name into the song.

"A time to cast away stones, and a time to gather stones together."

She smiled as she thought of all the times as children, when she and Lucy had sat in the shallow waters of the creek, turning over every little rock, trying to find the prettiest ones to add to their collections, but then as she got older, she would go down to the creek when she was angry and pick up these same rocks and throw them across the water with such force, as if that act would magically take her anger away. She knew the Bible verse was probably not talking about *real* stones, but the memory had popped into her mind anyway.

"A time to embrace, and a time to refrain from embracing."

She remembered the time she'd stopped Joe from going any further, because it just didn't feel right. Somehow she'd known. If she hadn't stopped him, who knows, she might have a child by now. She wasn't meant to have children with Joe, she saw that now. God must have put the thought into her head to stop herself from going any further. It was a good thing she'd listened.

"A time to get, and a time to lose. A time to keep, and a time to cast away."

Hannah felt she had lost so much lately, and had not kept much of anything. Everything seemed to be cast away that meant anything in her life.

"A time to rend, and a time to sew."

She knew that to 'rend' meant to 'tear', and she remembered when she'd had to tear the curtains from the Bennett house into pieces to use as face masks when William died, and she certainly had done her share of sewing up holes in socks and clothing over the past few years!

"A time to keep silence, and a time to speak."

Hannah remembered being told to stay quiet because the bushwhackers and soldiers might hear her, but she also remembered when she'd felt it was time to fight back and yell at them, and let her voice be heard.

"A time to love, and a time to hate."

Hannah didn't want to hate any more. She wanted to love. She craved being able to love again. As she watched John recite the words from the pages of his Bible, she felt love. She felt love for this man standing before her. But, how could this be? She shook her head, because these crazy thoughts should not be in there.

"A time of war, and a time of peace."

Tears welled up in Hannah's eyes. Oh, how she was tired of war, and how she needed peace in her life.

"What profit hath he that worketh in that wherein he laboureth? I have seen the travail, which God hath given to the sons of men to be exercised in it. He hath made everything beautiful in his time, also he hath set the world in their heart, so that no man can find out the work that God maketh from the beginning to the end."

John paused for effect, and his eyes caught Hannah's in the crowd. He lingered maybe a bit too long in her gaze. He then looked back at his Bible.

"I know that there is no good in them, but for a man to rejoice, and to do good in his life. And, also that every man should eat and drink, and enjoy the good of all his labour, it is the gift of God. I know that, whatsoever God doeth, it shall be forever, nothing

can be put to it, nor anything taken from it, and God doeth it that men should fear before him."

"That which hath been is now, and that which is to be hath already been, and God requireth that which is past."

John's voice raised to a small degree, but was still comforting and convincing, as he said *"And moreover, I saw under the sun the place of judgement, that wickedness was there, and the place of righteousness, that iniquity was there. I said in mine heart, God shall judge the righteous and the wicked, for there is a time there for every purpose and for every work."*

"I said in mine heart concerning the estate of the sons of men, that God might manifest them, and that they might see themselves are beasts. For that which befalleth the sons of men befalleth beasts, even one thing befalleth them, as the one dieth, so dieth the other, yea, they have all one breath, so that a man hath no preeminence above a beast, for all is vanity."

"All go unto one place, all are of the dust, and all turn to dust again."

"Who knoweth the spirit of man that goeth upward, and the spirit of the beast that goeth downward to Earth? Wherefore I perceive that there is nothing better, than that a man should rejoice in his own works, for that is his portion, for who shall bring him to see what shall be after him?"

John realized that he was going on a bit long, and people were beginning to lose interest, so he closed his Bible and looked out at the small crowd of new friends he had so recently made. "I think what we can take from this, is that we are all very small, when you look at the history of the world, and at God's overall plan for his world. Everything will happen just as God has planned for it to happen, regardless of what we do. We are no more important, as humans, than the cow, or the dog, or the bird. Each of us has our place, and that place is a small part of the bigger plan."

"I think we can also take from this that we must do each thing in it's time. When we are sad, we must be sad. When we are happy, we must be happy. It is all part of a greater plan that we will never fully understand while we live here on Earth. We must try not to weary ourselves of understanding it, and simply do the things that we need to do in order to make our own lives better. As each person betters his own life, the accumulative effect is that it will better the whole of mankind. We may think we are small and insignificant, but would there be a beach without the millions of tiny grains of sand? Would there be an ocean without the millions of droplets of water? We may be tiny, but we most certainly are *not* insignificant."

"In summary, if the things we did each day did not have eternal value, then what would be the point? If the planting of a garden today did not have an effect on the outcome of eternity, then why do it? If the hug you give your child did not have eternal value and significance, then why do it? It is because there is an eternal life, that these things are worthwhile. And, God rewards us for the necessary low times. For every hour of hard labor, you get to taste delicious food and feel the warm sun on your face. For every pain of childbirth, you are rewarded with wonderful hugs and kisses, and admiration, and sometimes even ecstasy. For every death, there is a joyous birth. God was a master planner, and he knew just how to even it all out."

"If you are looking at an ant hill, you see a pile of dirt with a few ants crawling around on top. But, somewhere down below there are thousands of ants you don't see, who are wandering around and building a huge underground ant city. If one of those ants dies, it does not change the fact that the ant hill will be built. Therefore, let each ant go about his duty, happy with the knowledge that the hill will be built, even if he drops his grain of sand that day. In the same way, let each of us go about our duty, even if we sometimes fail, and be happy in the knowledge that our hill, which can be called eternity, will be built."

He suddenly seemed to have run out of words. He said "Well, I suppose that is all I have for today." The crowd began to murmur and they all began to rise and say "Amen" and "What a wonderful sermon, John! You have a talent!" Some of them went to shake his hand or hug him. There were choruses of "We needed this. It is good for our souls. We should do this every Sunday. We should have never stopped. Oh, John, you must speak to us again next week!"

And, John did just that. He began to read a passage of the Bible to them each Sunday, and a wonderful spiritual healing began to take place there.

October

Hannah finished her morning chores and sneaked away for a bit to go visit the graveyard. Something had been troubling her all day. She sat between Joseph's grave and her brother Jesse's grave. She was hidden from view by the church building, and she knew Irene and all her children had gone down to the creek, so no one could see her from within the church.

She wasn't sure what she was feeling, but she felt the need to talk to Joseph. "I wrote another poem Joseph. I wanted to share it with you."

"Not long after you died I heard
The story about the red bird
How any time you see one
It's the spirit of a loved one
Coming back to visit you

I was skeptical at first
'Til my feelings got reversed
For birds began appearing
Ever nearing, never fearing
Always in my field of view

Each one brought me peace
And an uplifting release
Too many to be coincidence
Their beauty and their innocence
Helped to pull me through"

"Thank you for the birds, Joe. Or should I be thanking God? Or was it my guardian angel bringing them? I can picture you, Joe, going to God and asking him to send me a bird. I can see him telling one of his angels to make it so. Oh, I don't know the ways of the spirit world, but I know something is happening. I just feel it."

"Oh, Joseph! Today marks one year since you were taken from us. I've been thinking about you all day. I don't want to forget you, or forget what we had, but I feel things changing. I suppose they must if I am to survive. I don't want to let go, but some days I feel myself desiring to let go. I feel myself needing to heal from the loss of you. And, not just you, but all the loved ones that are buried here."

She looked at Jesse's grave and tears came to her eyes. What a loss of potential! He was such a good boy. Jesse had been the sibling born just after Hannah. They were only two years apart. They had been close. She looked across at her grandparents' graves. She felt a ball of sadness welling up in her chest as she remembered the sounds of their voices, and she could have sworn she heard her grandfather's voice saying 'I love you Hannah Belle' in the breeze. Then she looked at the graves of her mother and the two little sisters that she never got to know. She was wondering what they would be like now. Who would they look like? What would their personalities be like? Oh, why did they not get a chance to live? And, then, her mother. Images of her mother began to flood her. What a hard lot in life she had been given, and then taken so young, before she had a chance to see the fruits of all that labor. She never got to see her grandchildren. So many things she never got to do.

Suddenly, Hannah burst out in tears and just sobbed hard, like she hadn't sobbed since Joseph's death a year ago. She was sitting on the ground between the graves, with her head down in her hands, just crying tears from deep inside.

And then she looked up and there was John, standing at the corner of the church, looking at her. She felt a wave of embarrassment that he had shown up and found her like this. She turned her head and began to wipe the tears from her eyes. She could feel John walking toward her. She was so ashamed that she was letting him see this side of her. She wanted to appear strong to him.

But, something truly wonderful happened. John gently kneeled down over her. He put his hands on each side of her head and pulled her face into his chest. He began to pray over her.

"Dear Lord, I beg of you to release this pain from Hannah's heart. I ask that you end her time of suffering. Bring her joy, bring her love, bring her the life you created her to live. I know you have been molding her, teaching her, building her into the wonderful woman that she is today. But, I ask that you release her now. Give her back to us. Give her back to *me*. Open her heart and allow all the pain to ebb away. Give her pain to me if you must! I will gladly take it for her. In Jesus' name, Amen."

Hannah had never had someone pray over her like this before. She was having trouble dealing with her emotions about it. The entire time she was pulled close to John's chest, she had felt safe. She had felt... 'home'. She had no other way of describing it. She had felt like she was home, she was where she belonged. A peace had traveled through her body as he prayed over her, as if the very spirit of God had flowed through them both. She felt an overwhelming love for this man. She didn't think it was possible, but she had opened her heart to feeling love again. She wanted nothing more right now than to be back in his arms, with her head pressed against his warm, strong, comforting chest. But, he had released her, and was looking at her with concerned eyes.

"Thank you, John," she said. "Thank you! No one ever did that for me before."

"Did what?"

"Prayed over me."

"Oh, well, I don't think I ever prayed over anyone before either. I don't know what came over me. I just saw you there and something spoke to me and said you needed to be prayed over. I was compelled to do it."

They sat there for a few minutes, no longer touching, but feeling closer than two people had ever felt, and Hannah kept replaying in her mind how John had asked God to 'give her back to me'. What exactly did he mean by that? Did it mean he wanted her?

It may have been because of his developing feelings for Hannah, or it may have been because Samuel just was not healing as fast as he'd hoped, or maybe it was a combination of both, but at the next Sunday service John informed the crowd that he and Sam had decided to stay for the winter, if they were willing to have them.

Everyone was delighted, for they had all grown to love these two men that came into their lives so suddenly. But, no one was more delighted than Hannah.

That evening she went to the barn to visit John, and she said "There really is no reason why you should continue to stay in the barn. If you and Sam are to be here all winter, you will freeze to death out here! I think it's time you move into the house. We will put some of the children together and give you and Sam one of the upstairs bedrooms."

John finally relented, and so Sarah and Hannah set about rearranging the household. Sarah had seen the glances shared between Hannah and John, and had a feeling that something was developing between them. Her motherly instincts told her that it might not be a good idea for Hannah and John to be close together at night. So, she suggested Hannah move down and sleep in the room with her. Hannah was a bit perturbed at this arrangement, but she knew there was no use arguing, and the more she thought about it, it might be better to share a room with another grown woman, instead of little children, for a change.

Sarah was still keeping little Jasper in bed with her at night, because he was nursing, so Jasper would also be sleeping in their room.

Upstairs, after they'd done the rearranging, the wing on the right side of the house became the girls' wing. One room was to be occupied by Isabelle and Rebecca, who were both 13 now, while the other room held 11 year old Charlotte, 10 year old Rachel and 8 year old Ruby. In the boys' wing on the left side of the house, Sarah had put Albert in with the little boys. He wasn't thrilled with the arrangement, but he felt it was only for the winter and by spring he would have more space again. So, 15 year old Albert had to start sharing a room with his 7 year old brother Michael, and his twin 5 year old brothers, Jacob and Jonah. The other room in the boys' wing was given to John and Sam.

Now that the men were part of the household, Hannah began to learn more and more about them. She learned that Sam was a year younger than John, he was 28 years old. He hadn't mentioned it before, but he now told them that he was married. He had a wife and two little children back home in Mississippi, and his greatest desire was to get back home to them. He had hoped to leave before the winter, but he knew his leg was not healed enough for such a journey, so reluctantly, he had to stay. He hoped that in the spring he would be completely healed and back to his old self again.

Sam told them his wife was named Kathleen, and his little girl was Bridgette and his boy was Nicholas. Nicky had been only one year old when he had left for the war. He hated to think of how much he'd probably grown and how he wouldn't even remember his Pa. Hannah understood how difficult that must be for Sam.

Sam was a nice young man. Everyone liked him. But, Hannah did not have that special connection with him like she did with John. Each evening she and John sat out on the porch talking, and sometimes they went for walks together.

She had never shared her special place with him, her buckeye tree. At first she felt that he was not going to be there long, so what was the point? And, then she went through a phase of thinking she was betraying Joe if she shared their spot. But, now she was coming around to realizing that Joe would have wanted her to move on and be happy. She could feel it deep in her heart. Maybe it was God telling her that it was time to move on. So, on a day in late October she took John to her tree.

The buckeyes were all over the ground. Hannah found it interesting that big things in her life, good or bad, always seemed to happen when the buckeyes fell.

She and John were sitting on the big exposed roots of the

tree, throwing buckeyes into the water, when he suddenly said "The Lord works in mysterious ways."

Hannah said "What are you referring to?"

He said "I thought I was to go through life alone. My heart was shattered once, and I lost all trust in women, and in love."

Hannah realized that maybe he was finally opening up to her. Maybe she was about to find out why, at 29 years old, he was still not married. She knew enough to not push him, so she just let him talk.

"When I was about your age I proposed to a girl that I had known most of my life. We had grown up together. Our parents were friends. I had grown to love her, and all I could think about was a life with her, growing old with her and having a dozen children. I suppose I was infatuated with her, but looking back now, maybe it was for all the wrong reasons. Anyway, I proposed, and she said yes. We were planning the wedding, but at the same time, I felt as if she was becoming very distant with me. I blamed it on wedding jitters. But, one week before we were to wed, I was walking along in town and I rounded a corner and saw her standing in front of a store with another boy that we both knew, a friend of mine that I grew up with. I began walking toward them, because I was happy to see the both of them, but then I was jolted into reality when I saw them embrace, in a very loving way. Then, he began kissing her. I felt like my world had ended. I ran to them, yelling, screaming, threatening to kill them both. She was saying 'You don't understand....' He was saying 'I'm sorry John, it just happened....' Then in the midst of all the yelling she suddenly said 'I don't love you, John! I don't want to marry you!' And, then she ran out of my life."

Hannah took John's hand and said "Oh, John, I'm so sorry."

He said "No, don't be. I spent years running from the pain. I joined the war as an excuse to get away. I volunteered for any assignment that put me in danger, or took me further and further away from those memories. I blamed all women for the actions of one woman. I didn't want anything to do with women, because I thought all they did was hurt you. I let that one girl mess with my head so much, for nearly 10 years of my life. Can you imagine?"

"Yes, I suppose I can."

"Oh, I'm sorry Hannah. I don't mean to compare my jilted love affair with the death of your fiance. That was not what I meant to say at all."

"Oh, of course not, John. I didn't think you did. I don't suppose one person's grief is any worse or better, just different."

She looked into his eyes and felt so much love coming back to her. She wasn't sure if she should open herself up and be vulnerable to him, but she felt the need to at that moment.

"John, my ghosts are gone now."

"What?"

"My ghosts! The things that have haunted me. The deaths of my family members, and my childhood friends. They are gone from me. I feel a lightness of heart that I have not felt in years. It's because of you, John."

She looked timidly into his eyes and felt him squeezing her hand.

He put his hand gently on the side of her cheek and said "Hannah... You have awakened me. I was dying, and you brought me back to life. What I had before, it can't even compare. What I thought was love before was only drama. It was always drama. I walked around scared to say the wrong thing or do the wrong thing. I just assumed that's what it was like when you were in a relationship. But, with you, there is none of that drama. There is an ease with you. I've found I don't want or need the kind of life I used to lead. I've let all the old drop away. I'm free of it now. You have become a part of me. I couldn't separate from you if I tried."

She tried to fight back the tears of happiness that were welling up in her eyes, but it was no use. They came pouring out. He reached up and wiped them with his fingers. He then said "I didn't know love until I met you."

Hannah was thinking the very same thing. Oh, she had loved Joseph, there was no doubt, but it was a childhood love, a love of familiarity and shared history. The feelings she was having right then and there with John were feelings she had never felt in her life. It was a deeper love, a spiritual love, a love that connects two souls through time and space forever. As much as she loved

Joe, she knew in her heart they had not had this type of connection. She hadn't even known it existed.

John said "My past history with women, I see now was more about lust than love. I don't want that kind of relationship any more. That is the kind of relationship I was running from. What I want is..."

He took his hand and gently traced his fingers down Hannah's arm, from the top near her shoulder down to the wrist. She felt chills go through her. As he did that movement with his hand he was saying "What I want is this....."

Then he moved and put his hand beside her cheek again and with his thumb wiped a tear, and said "What I want is this...."

Hannah felt herself coming alive. Everything inside her was screaming "I want that, too!"

He took both her hands in his and pressed them to his chest. He held her hands to his heart and closed his eyes for a moment and said "I want *this*...."

Then he put both hands on either side of her face, and moved his body closer to hers. Hannah could feel his masculine presence, his strength, hovering over her. It was powerful and all-consuming. As he continued to gaze into her eyes, he said "And, I want this...."

He leaned in and gently pressed his lips to hers, ever so lightly. He moved slowly to the left and pressed his lips to hers again, just holding his mouth close to hers, not moving, just pressing close, and allowing the love to pass from his body into hers. Then, he moved slightly to the right and pressed his lips to hers again.

Hannah was lost in a feeling she'd never known. Kisses with Joe had been nice, but nothing like this. She had never felt the Earth moving under her feet. She had never felt as if their bodies were joining together and becoming one. Oh, it was a teenage love, and maybe it could have grown to become something more, but maybe it wouldn't have. She would never know. The only thing that mattered to her now was this man and this time in her life. She was finally letting go. She was finally ready to move on.

She understood now that she had kept a wall up when it

came to Joe. There was always a bit of a wall of protection around her, a wall of uncertainty, a wall of hesitation. But, with John, the wall had come crashing down. She felt no need for it anymore. Her heart was laid wide open.

The feelings in the air were so thick. When they finally stopped kissing, she found herself looking at his chest, and thinking "I want to be there. I want to be right there, pressed tightly against his chest." She knew that was a place where she would always be safe. She pulled him closer to her and pressed her face into his chest as he wrapped his strong arms around her.

She couldn't stop thinking about his kiss, how wonderfully gentle and loving his kiss was! It was so unlike the kisses with Joe. She had enjoyed the kisses with Joe, most of the time, at least she thought she had, but she didn't have anything to compare it to. Joe's kisses had been sloppy and eager, like he was devouring her. She thought that's just how people kissed. She had wanted Joe to slow down and not stick his tongue so far into her mouth, but thought maybe there was something wrong with her for not wanting to be kissed like that. She had been too young and uncertain about herself to speak up and tell him what she wanted. But, here was a man whom she didn't even have to tell, because he already knew. It just came natural with him. It was as if he could read her mind, and knew exactly how she wanted to be kissed. His gentle, slow kisses stopped time, and stirred up a fire in her soul. She wanted more of John Oakley's kisses, now and for the rest of her life.

December

Christmas that year was wonderful, the best one they'd had in a long time. With John and Sam there, everything was more festive and happy. Samuel, since he was trying to stay off his injured leg as much as possible, had spent most of his down time carving something out of wood. The children were curious what it was, but Sam refused to tell them until he was finished. At

Christmas he surprised them all with a game that he told them was called "Checkers".

He had carved a large square piece of wood into a board with many smaller squares on it. Then, he had carved out 24 round disk shapes. John had found some red winter berries growing wild, which he brought to Sam in secret. Sam used the berries to make a red dye. He tinted 12 of the round wooden disks with the red dye. With the other 12 disks, he held them to a flame and charred them, then smoothed them out, so that they became a black color.

John and Sam played the first game with the new checkerboard, so they could teach the children how to play it. Sarah and Irene had both seen a checkerboard before, but it was all new to the rest of them. From that moment forward, any time there was free time, two of the children were playing checkers. They even fought over whose turn it was to play with it so often that Sam finally decided to start carving a second board. Even Hannah enjoyed playing against John, trying her best to beat him.

There had been plenty of good food for Christmas, because John and Daniel had went hunting and found a flock of turkeys. They were able to take down two of them, so a wonderful turkey dinner was enjoyed by all. The women made pies using some of the canned berries and fruits they had gathered that past summer.

Hannah even recited a poem she had written. She had read it to John, and he was bragging to the others about it. "Hannah, please read it to them. It's wonderful! You have a gift for writing."

Hannah said "Well, if you all really want to hear it. It's a little bit sad, but then again, maybe not really. It depends on how you look at it, I suppose. I wrote it in honor of all the loved ones we've lost these past few years."

"I know it's better up there
As you gather 'round God's regal chair
The angels sing better than anyone here
The circle of love exceptionally dear
Joyous hearts without any fear

I know your sparkling Christmas trees rise
So high up into the skies
That the tops can't even be seen
You just stare at its glorious sheen
Unimaginable shades of silver and green

I know the gifts aren't tied up in bows
Stacked under the tree in rows
No, the gifts are somehow bestowed
Into hearts that seem to explode
With a love that has overflowed

I know I can't be part of it yet
My duties on Earth haven't been met
So, save me a place next to you
With an awesome, glorious view
So I can be part of it, too"

Everyone told Hannah that her poem was simply beautiful. But, no one complimented her more than John. He was always asking her to read her poems and stories to him, and he seemed geniunely interested. Each time she finished one he would look at her with misty eyes and say "You have such a talent! I am just amazed at what you can do." And, each time he complimented her like that, she knew that she *was* talented, and she *could* do anything. There was so much power in his words, and she told him so.

He said "Hannah, words *are* powerful! They have the power to heal and the power to harm. I choose to use my words to heal."

What an incredible man! Each day Hannah grew to love him more. She was amazed by him. Each day she would think "This is the most it is possible to love someone! I've reached the pinnacle." But, then the next day she would think "I only thought I loved him yesterday! Today it is even stronger."

Just when Christmas day was almost over, John surprised Hannah with a special gift that he gave to her privately. It turned out he had been secretly carving something as well. It was a small wooden cross. It had intricate carvings all over it in beautiful designs. It was the most beautiful carving she'd ever seen.

"I love it John! I love it so much! I'm amazed that you could do this. You have such talent! I couldn't carve a simple X on a piece of wood without messing it up. This is just really good."

John basked in her compliments. He had been proud of how it turned out, but he wanted her to like it, and that was all that mattered. Just seeing the smile on her face made it all worthwhile to him.

"It is a token of my feelings for you. I know it isn't much...."

"Oh, but it is! It truly is John! It means the world to me, to know that your hands carved every little detail of this. What a work of love!"

"I carved it from a branch that I took from your buckeye tree."

Hannah was taken aback. What did he just say? How could one man be so incredibly thoughtful? Hannah had thought it was special before, but hearing him say it came from her tree, it brought her to tears. Every time she thought she'd seen the best of Jonathan Oakley, he would surprise her with something even better.

All she wanted out of life at this point was to spend it with John. It didn't matter where she was or what she was doing or who else was around, as long as she could be with John.

1865

A new year, and still her father had not come home from the war. Elijah and Henry had been gone for two and a half years.

Hannah was still hiding her valuables in the spot under the floor. She was no longer sleeping in that room, but Izzy and Becky didn't mind if she kept her things hidden under their floor. Hannah was bent over looking at her stash. She had some journals, her mother's Bible and locket, Joseph's tintype and the buckeye he had carried, and now she had the wooden cross that John had carved for her from the branch of the buckeye tree. Until this war was over, she would keep these things hidden away, for fear of some wayward soldier coming and taking them from her.

John and Sam had now been living with them for five months. The past winter had been much easier on everyone than previous ones, partly because of John being there. It seemed he inspired Daniel and Harding, and the three of them together were doing a very good job of keeping the families supplied with meat and firewood and any other necessities they needed.

In their spare time, the men and boys had sawed a pretty good stack of wood boards at the sawmill. Not enough for a house yet, but they were making progress. Hannah didn't like Daniel and Lucy being separated by a mile from the rest of them, so she was really looking forward to a time when they could build a larger house for themselves, and closer to the rest of them. She just felt safer when they were all in visual distance of each other.

John had continued with Sunday services all winter, but it was too cold to have them outdoors, so they gathered in the church. Irene simply moved her family's things to the side of the large room each Sunday so there would be room for everyone. It wasn't that hard to do, because she didn't have much. Her furnishings had all burned up in the fire. Harding had managed to make her a crude table and a shelf, but he just wasn't that great at carpentry, so he was looking forward to a time when his Pa would be home and they could make something better. The family had been using the hard church benches for chairs and even as beds. They longed for something more comfortable.

Ever since they'd started back up with church, though, things had been better. There had been no deaths, and no visits by soldiers or bushwhackers. No one wanted to risk breaking that streak by deserting God again.

Harding had begun to show an interest in the ministry, so John was letting him perform the service from time to time. He felt that once he left the area, they would need someone who could perform the duties of a minister, and Harding seemed to be the obvious choice. He seemed to enjoy it and had a knack for it.

Harding hadn't told anyone, but that day when he watched his house burn, and he prayed so frantically to God to do something, and then the Casey home was miraculously saved just moments later, he had felt that a miracle had occurred. He felt God truly heard him, and from that day on he felt a change within himself, a sort of spiritual awakening.

Harding was now 18 years old. On his birthday he had mentioned that he was old enough to join the war effort now. He was considering it, although half-heartedly. He just didn't want anyone to think he was a coward if he didn't do it. John, Sam and Daniel all talked him out of it. They convinced him that he was not meant to protect them by fighting a physical war, he was meant to protect them by fighting a spiritual war. He was needed as a preacher. Everyone agreed, and thankfully, since his heart hadn't really been in it, it was easy to convince Harding to stay. Hannah had told him that for the sake of his mother, he needed to stay. His mother could not handle losing her second son, too. Losing Joe was enough of a blow.

One evening in early February, as everyone gathered around the fire at Hannah's home, someone mentioned to John that the ministry seemed to be his calling. Someone asked if he'd ever preached anywhere before.

John said "No, I never have. But, I grew up around it, because my Pa is a preacher."

Hannah sat up, shocked. "Jonathan Oakley! Why in all this time had you not told me your father was a preacher?"

"I don't know! I suppose it just never came up."

"Well, this explains so much," she said. "No wonder you are such a natural at it, you learned by example!"

Sarah asked if he had thought about taking up his father's profession.

"I never did even consider it. I suppose as a young man I was rebellious and wanted to be the complete opposite of my father. But, it wasn't a conscious decision, really. I had started working on a fishing boat in Charleston Harbor. We'd go out and deep-sea fish and bring in our haul each day. That's what I was doing when Fort Sumter got fired on and I was able to witness it all. From there I joined the war and have been doing that for the last four years. It wasn't until I happened upon this little mountain community that I suddenly felt a desire to share my spiritual thoughts with everyone. There's just something about this place. It brought it out in me."

"Do you think, after the war is over, you might consider joining the ministry? Or do you think you'll go back to fishing on that fishing boat?" Sarah asked.

John said "I haven't even thought about it. If you'd asked me four years ago if I wanted to be a preacher, I would have said 'Of course not!' But, now I'm not opposed to it. War changes a man. We shall have to see."

Sarah said "Well, not that my opinion means anything, but I think you should."

"I shall keep that in mind," he said with a smile.

All of the children had went up to bed that evening, and Sam was resting in the room upstairs. Sarah got up and took Jasper to the bedroom to put him down. This left John and Hannah alone in the sitting room. They kept stealing glances at each other. The sexual tension was so thick in the room.

Finally, John got up and put his coat on and said he was going to the barn. Hannah could just feel that he wanted her to follow, so she said "I'll be back in a bit, Sarah," and she put a quilt around her shoulders and followed him out.

She made her way in the darkness across the scattering of snow that had fallen that day. Each time she exhaled she could see her breath. As soon as she stepped into the barn and pushed the door closed, John came up behind her and took her in his arms, and any thoughts of being cold vanished when she felt his warmth around her. He began to kiss the back of her neck, then he turned her to face him and began to kiss her in that slow, passionate way of his, but then it became a bit more forceful as his hunger for her grew. He gently pushed her back into the wall of the barn and she could feel his longing as his hands began to roam and his body pressed hard against hers.

She was a twenty year old woman now, not a child anymore, and she wanted this man! She didn't care that they weren't married. She didn't care if she was sinning. She was hungry for him, she was *starving* for him! Her hands began to roam all over his body as well.

She ran her hands up under his shirt. The feel of his skin, and the soft chest hairs growing there, sent feelings of excitement traveling through her body. She wanted to feel her naked breasts pressed up against his bare skin.

He lifted her skirt and ran his fingers up the inside of her thigh. She cried out in pleasure. She wanted him to touch her everywhere. She wanted to be as close to him as you could be to another person.

John gently lowered her to the floor, and the two of them made love right there in the barn, on a pile of loose hay, with only a faint light from the moon shining through the hay loft window up above. It was slow, tender and passionate all at once. He gazed into her eyes, he brushed her hair back out of her face. He ran his hands all over her body. She ran her hands all over his. She had no idea if she was doing it right, but somehow it just felt natural, and they melded together like they were one.

When it was over and they'd calmed down, she cried... not tears of sadness or regret, but tears of happiness, tears of release. They held each other until they began to grow cold, for it was January and there was no fire to keep them warm in the barn. Their earlier passion had been enough to keep them warm, but the cold was now seeping into their bones.

They put their clothes back on, and John wrapped his coat around her. She threw the quilt over his shoulders and they just stood there embracing for several minutes.

John lifted her chin with his finger and when her eyes met his he said "Hannah, I'm sorry. I let my animal urges take over."

She said "Oh, Jonathan! I want more of those animal urges! I was just as bad as you. I wasn't acting very much the lady just then, was I?"

He said "Hannah, there is nothing you could do that would make me think you less of a lady. But, here I am playing the part of a preacher, and then going against everything the Bible says and being with a woman out of wedlock."

"Don't you dare act as if you are ashamed of what just happened!" she said. "I am not ashamed. You should not be ashamed either. And, as for God... well, I think God knows these are troubling times, and I think God forgives us just this once. I think he might make an exception."

"I'm not sure that's how it works, Hannah," he said with a sheepish grin. "But, I know what you're trying to say. How could God bring you into my life, and not expect me to want to know you in the most intimate way a man can know a woman? I am not ashamed, Hannah. Don't you ever think I am ashamed. But, I want to do this right. I want to please God and myself, all at the same time. I think we should try harder to not let things get this far again. We both know in our hearts it isn't the right way."

Hannah said "After five months of wanting and waiting, it's no wonder! We are only human! God made us with these urges, after all!"

"Are you trying to say it's God's fault?" he teased.

She smiled and then kissed him again.

"Oh, Hannah!" he said, as he hungrily kissed her back. "I want you to marry me! Please say you will marry me!"

"Yes, Jonathan... I will marry you. I will marry you today, tomorrow, next year, for the rest of my life. I will marry you over and over again. In my heart we are already married."

"I feel the same. I feel like I know you inside and out. But, God wants us to do this the right way. So, as much as it pains me to say it, we have to stop. You have to stop kissing me now, or I am going to take you again, right here against this barn door."

Hannah found it so arousing to have a man of God talk to her in such a passionate way! She had always imagined that a preacher had a very boring and predictable sex life, only having sex out of necessity, to make babies, nothing more. They were not allowed to enjoy it. But, she had been wrong. With John, she had the best of both worlds.

After she'd crawled in bed that night next to Sarah, she laid there feeling like she was about to explode. The man she loved was right upstairs, but she was not allowed to go to him. She had just lost her virginity, a pivotal moment in any woman's life, yet she couldn't really tell anyone about it. Yes, she had to marry Jonathan Oakley soon. And, she did not care if she had babies right away. She did not care if she had *ten* babies with him. She wanted little boys that were just as kind and as handsome as he was, and little girls that liked to write poetry. She found herself wanting to be a mother for the first time in her life. For John, she would do anything, just so long as she could hold him close like that every night of her life.

But, five days later when she went to the privy and saw that her monthly time had come right on schedule, she couldn't help but breathe a sigh of relief. She wanted children with John, but not until they were married. She didn't want the shame or stigma that would follow her around if she had a child out of wedlock. She vowed that she would try to control herself better until after they were married.

John and Hannah were able to control themselves for the rest of that winter, although it was touch and go some days. They would pass each other in the barn and he would say longingly "How I want to make love with you..." She would blush, but she secretly loved it. "You have the most beautiful body, and I love to watch you walk, you do it with such grace," he would say. "You are the most beautiful woman I've ever laid eyes on!" The things he said to her made her feel so womanly. She had such a strong desire to take care of him, for the rest of their lives. She wanted to cook for him, she wanted to please him in bed. She wanted to go on adventures with him. She just wanted it all.

Some days when she watched him work, whether it be swinging an ax to chop wood, or pulling on the reins of a horse to make it go, when she saw the muscles of his arms flex, she would go all silly inside and wish *she* were that ax, or *she* was that horse, being so effortlessly molded into doing what he wanted.

Sam's leg had healed over the winter, and he was walking just fine now. He had a slight limp, which he probably would have for the rest of his life, because the bone had healed a little crooked, causing one leg to be a bit shorter than the other. But, despite that, he was able to get around as quickly as anyone with two good legs. He was ready to get home to his family, but he and John were just waiting for warm enough weather for traveling.

John had sat Hannah down one evening and told her that he felt an obligation to Sam. They had been together through most of the war. Sam had always been there to support him, so now it was his time to return the favor. It was still dangerous for men to be traveling alone, what with the war still going on and bushwhackers everywhere. It would be safer if they traveled together.

"I want to escort Sam back to Mississippi to his family. It will do me good to know I've seen him safely home."

"I will go with you!" Hannah said.

"Hannah, I love you, and I want nothing more than to have you by my side, but I feel it is too dangerous right now, what with the war going on and all. This is something I need to do for myself, and for Sam. I hope you will understand."

"But, when will you go?"

"We will probably leave in late March or early April, after we are sure of no more freezing weather. We think it will take about ten days to get there on horseback. I may rest at Sam's home for a few days, then start the trip back. So, hopefully no more than a month and I will return to you, then we will get married."

"But, who will marry us?" she asked.

"We can go down to Clarksville and find a minister there, I'm sure."

Hannah didn't want him to leave, but she understood his reasons. If she'd waited this long, she could wait one more month, surely.

April

It turned out that there were some bad storms and cold spells in early April that year, so the trip to take Sam home kept getting put off later and later. Sam was getting antsy, because he really needed to get home to his wife and children. He had not been able to write to them in eight months. They probably thought he was dead by now. It broke his heart to think of what they must be going through.

Finally, on April 24th, after several days of wonderful weather, the two men decided to set off. As it happened, Daniel and Harding decided to travel with them, for supplies had gotten extremely low. They were hoping to maybe find a little work they could do in town to make enough money to restock. The four men would travel together as far as Clarksville, then John and Sam would go on from there.

Hannah and John were having a difficult time saying goodbye. He was holding her close.

"It will only be a month at the most, and I will have you in my arms again," he said.

"I will miss you so," Hannah told him. "Please come safely back to me. My heart could not take the loss of you."

"I *will* come back, Hannah. I promise! A pack of wild hogs couldn't keep me away."

Then he left her with a wonderful piece of advice. "When you get scared or lonely, and feel the need to turn to God, do what I have learned to do, and it makes all the difference. If you truly have faith in God, then when you pray, instead of saying 'Dear God, please keep John safe', you should say 'Dear God, thank you for keeping John safe'. Do you see the difference? The first way of praying is saying that you don't have faith that God is already doing the things you ask, so you feel you have to beg him, but the second way is simply giving him praise because you know he is already doing it. That is the true meaning of faith. I promise you, if you will start praying that way, you will notice a difference."

Hannah was once again amazed at the way John looked at life, and she promised him she would start praying that way.

As they rode off, Hannah waved until they were out of sight. Floating in the breeze she thought she could hear her grandfather's voice say "Fear only makes the wolf look bigger than he is, Hannah Belle....", and in the other ear she thought she could hear Joseph whispering "Fear doesn't stop death, but it certainly does stop life...." She knew they were both right, and it was best not to fear, but it was difficult, after all she'd been through, not to imagine the worst every time someone walked out of her life.

May

The women had expected Daniel and Harding to be gone for longer than usual, because of the fact that they were going to have to try and get some work. So, it was no surprise when they hadn't returned in two weeks. But, thankfully, they showed up 17 days after they had left, on May 11th.

Daniel explained to everyone that they had both obtained two weeks of work helping some men who were building a store building in town across from the courthouse. With their two weeks' pay they had enough money to buy the supplies they needed.

Sadly, they reported that there was no mail at the post office from either Elijah or Henry. This was concerning to all of them. Had they died in that awful prison? Hannah kept telling herself "Don't worry. They are tough men. They will be fine. Just put your faith in the Lord. Remember to thank God for keeping them alive and healthy, don't beg him to do it. Remember what John said."

"We have some news, though, that is very distressful, to say the least," Daniel said. "I didn't want to forget the details, so I brought this newspaper article."

He unfolded the paper and began to read. "On the evening of April 14, 1865, while attending a special performance of the comedy 'Our American Cousin', President Abraham Lincoln was shot."

There was an uproar from all the women and children. "He was shot! Oh, my word. Is he still alive? Who shot him? Oh, how awful!"

"Let me finish," Daniel said. "Accompanying him at Ford's Theatre that night were his wife, Mary Todd Lincoln, a 28 year old officer named Major Henry R. Rathbone, and Rathbone's fiancee, Clara Harris. After the play was in progress, a figure with a drawn derringer pistol stepped into the presidential box, aimed, and fired. The president slumped forward."

Irene put her hand to her mouth. "What does this mean for

our country? Oh, Heaven help us!"

Daniel went on. "The assassin, John Wilkes Booth, dropped the pistol and waved a dagger. Rathbone lunged at him, and though slashed in the arm, forced the killer to the railing. Booth leapt from the balcony and caught the spur of his left boot on a flag draped over the rail, and broke a bone in his leg on landing. Though injured, he rushed out the back door, and disappeared into the night on horseback."

"Who is this John Wilkes Booth?" some of them were wondering.

Daniel said "I heard he was a stage actor." He read some more. "A doctor in the audience, Dr. Charles Leale, immediately went upstairs to the box. The bullet had entered through Lincoln's left ear and lodged behind his right eye. He was paralyzed and barely breathing. He was carried across Tenth Street, to a boarding house opposite the theater, but the doctor's best efforts failed. Nine hours later, at 7:22 a.m. on April 15th, Lincoln died."

Some of the group began to cry. It was a shock to hear of their president being assassinated. This was not something anyone had considered or expected. They were unsure what this was going to mean for the country, and for the men and boys fighting in the war.

Harding then spoke up and said "There was another article in the paper dated about 10 or 11 days later that said they caught up to this John Wilkes Booth. He was hiding in a barn. They shot him and killed him."

"I'm glad he is not free to kill again. What an evil man!" Rebecca said. "Who is the president now?"

Daniel said "The vice-president, Andrew Johnson, was sworn in after Lincoln died."

Then he continued, saying "There is other news that may be considered good news to some of you. We heard that just five days before Lincoln was shot, Lee and Grant had a meeting in Virginia and Lee signed documents of surrender to Grant."

"What does that mean?" Isabelle asked.

"Well," Daniel said. "It effectively means the war is over, and the north has won."

"It's over! Oh, thank God in Heaven!" Irene said.

"They are saying that some of the western troops don't know it yet, so battles are still being fought. But, as soon as word spreads, each company will be forced to surrender. The prisoners of war are all being released."

This news was wonderful to hear! Sarah and Irene both sat down and began to sob. Finally, *finally*, maybe their husbands would be coming home, God willing.

Daniel said "From what I gathered, this Booth character was upset about the Confederate surrender, and thought if he took out the president then the Union would fall and the Confederacy could be restored."

"I'm not happy that the south lost, but I can't say I'm sad either. I have wanted this war to be over for so long, I would take a loss from either side, so long as it ended," Sarah said. "When I think of all the times I've prayed, and how weary I am from praying... Think of how weary God must be, for you know he has been called on so many times from both sides of this argument."

Hannah had not expected, when the boys returned, to be hearing news that the war was over. It had been going on so long, it had become a way of life for her. She wasn't even sure how they would all adjust back to being 'normal' again. But, she was so relieved and thankful.

Daniel then told them he had a bit of local war news to share as well. "So, you know how we call people Bushwhackers? Well, there is another word they are using to describe mostly Union supporters who have been going around causing havoc in the name of war. They apparently call them 'Jayhawkers'. Well, back in February, a bunch of Jayhawkers came through Johnson County's Pittsburg community. With most of the men away at war, the women were home alone and helpless, so they burned down some homes and tortured a bunch of the women, trying to get them to reveal where they may have hidden money or valuables. I heard that they held one woman's legs down in a bed of hot coals. They said her name was Lutetia Howell. The woman's legs were burned so badly, she had to have both legs amputated!"

Hannah cringed at the thought of what that poor woman went through. It was hard to imagine such torture. "Did they catch any of these men?"

Daniel said "I heard that a few were rounded up. They were Union soldiers and deserters from Arkansas and Kansas. But, it seems they were eventually released and not really punished for their crimes."

Then Harding spoke up and said "Also, last fall, some Union soldiers invaded Clarksville again. Remember how on our last trip, we had learned that in early '64 they occupied the town, then burned much of it when they left? Well, in late '64 another group came through. They landed in the vicinity of the Spadra bluffs and came up north to Clarksville. The Confederates tried to hold them off, but couldn't, so they fell back and hid behind fences and houses. By the time they left, seven people were left dead on the streets of Clarksville."

Daniel then remembered another thing. "I was in one of the stores down in Clarksville, trying to trade for sugar and salt, when I heard some men talking to the owner of the store. I went over and introduced myself. They said their names were John Baskin and Thomas Porter, and they lived in Harmony. They were in town to do a little trading, just like I was. They were talking about all the losses they and others in their community had endured. Mr. Baskin said his two oldest boys were lost due to the war. One took sick while being held prisoner in Little Rock, and died. The other was home on leave, visiting his new wife, and was ambushed and killed by bushwhackers. One was 19 and the other 21 years old."

"Mr. Porter said he'd lost two sons as well. One was 18 and the other 21. He said four sons had served, but the middle two didn't come back, both killed in battle in '62. He said that one son had received four marks of the bullet, but never flinched from his post. Even though he is devastated by the loss of his boys, you can still hear the pride in his voice when he talks about them. He went on to say his oldest boy was home visiting his wife, and she was hiding him out in the woods to keep him safe, and bringing him food each day. But, one day soldiers were combing the woods looking for him and his son mistakenly thought it was his wife bringing the food, so he made himself known, and he was captured. He was held prisoner for a time, but at least this son survived."

"Then, Mr. Baskin said that this son Mr. Porter was talking about was married to Mr. Baskin's daughter. It was *his* daughter who had hid her husband out in the woods. This explained why the two men were together in the store, their children were married to each other, and they were both grandfathers to the same grandchildren. And, now they also had a shared history of each losing two sons in the war. Can you imagine the heartache these two men were having to endure? Losing one son is bad enough, but each of these men had lost two of their sons in such tragic ways. So much hope and dreams of the future, just lost in an instant. That's all war is good for."

"Oh, and also, Mr. Baskin said his wife's grandfather, an elderly man named Billy Puckett, was taken from his home and hanged in the woods by bushwhackers. It seemed like everywhere I went in Clarksville, that's all I was hearing, was stories about loss and death and torture because of the war. I heard stories about people having to hide their valuables, just like we did. Some of them said they dug holes and buried their valuables."

"Oh," Harding remembered. "While we were there talking to them, I asked these men if they knew Michael and Thomas Bean or Solomon Martin, remember, these were the three men we had rode along with back in '63 when we went to town, until we found out they had signed up with the Union army. I was curious how they were faring. The men told me that the Bean brothers had both survived the war, but that their brother-in-law, Solomon, did not. They said that people whose families fought on the Union side were being harrassed by the locals, who mostly supported the south. When Solomon heard of this he asked for leave so he could go check on his wife and children, but the leave wasn't granted. So, Solomon just left anyway. They said that he took sick at home and was in bed with fever, when men came up and dragged him from his sick bed, right in front of his children, and took him off down by the creek and shot him and left him there. The women found his body later, laying on a big rock. They said he wasn't recognizable from the waist up, because they'd put so many bullets in him. The women, with no men around to help, had to put his body on a sheet and drag him to the cemetery with a horse and bury him themselves."

Hannah solemnly said "Just like what happened with William...."

Harding agreed. "Yes, that's what I was thinking, too. It sounded so similar to what happened with William. I wondered if it was the same men who did it."

Daniel said "Everybody down in Clarksville seems to have a story about some tragedy with someone in their family." Daniel then paused, and with a sadness in his voice he said "I guess we do, too. We have our stories of the losses of Abe, and William, and Jesse, and of how Harding was almost hung, and how the soldiers burned our homes, and stole from us, and how they raped poor Martha."

Everyone in Buckeye hoped that these were the last of the terrible stories, and that the country was entering into a time of rebuilding and renewal. Hannah thought to herself that someone should go around and interview all the citizens, and make a book or something to record all the events that had happened over the last four years in Johnson County. It would be of great historical value some day.

Hannah began looking for John to return after he'd been gone about three weeks. Each day she caught herself looking down the road to see if he was coming home. It was hard to concentrate on anything else.

She busied her brain by writing poems. She had noticed that the subject matter of her poems had changed since meeting John. Rather than writing poems about grief, she was now beginning to write poems about love. It was a nice change. It was refreshing.

She would sit on the roots of her buckeye tree and read the poems outloud to any little forest creatures that might choose to listen.

Most of her poems came from words that John had said to her. This one was written because he had told her it was worth going through the pain in order to find this kind of love...

When you love with all you have
You grieve with all you are
Your heart comes crashing to the ground
Much like a falling star
The purchase price of love
Is the risk of sudden pain
A hefty price, for sure
But, think of all that you could gain!
If there ever was a gamble
Worth risking all and taking
A fearless bet with all your heart
Is the one you should be making

This one was written because he'd told her that he didn't know love, real love, until he met her...

The gates of my soul are thrown wide open
My sleeping heart has been awoken
Unspoken words are comprehended
Hearts once shattered now have mended
Love overflows the brittle walls
Crashing through like waterfalls
We silently hold fast to one another
We didn't know love until each other

And, this one was written because John had told her one day that he felt as if they were so close, that no light could shine between them...

When you are so close to someone
That no light can shine between you
When the peace becomes so thick
It's like a fog that can't be seen through

When someone breathes your breath
And someone cries your tears
When someone sucks the life
From all your worries and your fears
When comfort becomes the icing
On your cake of discontent
Then you've found that Godly love
That is truly Heaven sent

This one she had written simply because she longed to see John again. She had been sitting on the porch one evening and staring up at the moon, wondering if John was looking at the same moon. She felt as if they were so far apart, they might as well be like the moon and the earth...

The moon loved the earth
He watched her at night
He made sure everything
Was perfect and right
He bathed her in moonlight
And sprinkled the stars
All around her for beauty
That could not equal hers
He whispered with wind
How he loved her so much
But he could only see
He could not touch
The moon loved the earth
But couldn't come near
He loved her from there
She loved him from here

John was her muse, her inspiration. The wonderful words that came out of his mouth would go through Hannah and become a poem. Together, they made beautiful music. Without her, his words had no meaning, and without him, she couldn't even find the words.

But, there were times when she put John away for a moment or two and dwelled on the past, memories from her childhood, and she would write something like this...

Little girl of the mountains
Running barefoot in the hills
Skipping rocks across the creek
And picking Daffodils
Climbing cliffs and finding caves
Collecting pretty rocks
Sun up 'til sun down
Never looking at any clocks
Running down the dusty road
Scarring up her knees
Splashing in the muddy creek
And climbing all the trees
Many called her 'Tomboy'
But, little did she care
As long as she was free to roam
And breathe the mountain air

As she read each poem out loud, she liked the cadence of it. She liked to hear her own voice expressing the rhythm of the words. Reading them silently just didn't have the same effect. So, she escaped often with her little journal, to hear herself reading out loud. Sometimes she would write something in silence, when in a group of people, but she didn't consider it complete until she was able to read it out loud to herself.

Sadly, her little journal was about to be filled up. She should have asked Daniel on his last trip to town to get her a new one, but it didn't seem fair to ask for such a selfish thing, when food was what they really needed.

Of all the poems she'd written about John, the one she always seemed to go back to, the one that had become her favorite, was one she called 'I'm a Tree, You're a Tree'. It went like this...

When the Buckeyes Fall

I'm a tree, you're a tree
Standing side by side
To others we look separate
They don't see what we hide

We are planted near the water
We send our roots out to the stream
We never fear when heat comes
Our leaves are always green

Underneath the soil
We are holding one another
Our roots have grown together
We support each other

If storms bring damage to you
And try to blow you down
It's going to be a battle
Because I hold you to the ground

When you blossom, I blossom
When your leaves fall, so do mine
Together naked through the winter
Pulling strength from our entwine

We hold each other tightly
With such intensity
Amazing others look at us
And only see a tree

It was now May 24th. One month had gone by. Where was John?

It had been a month and a half since Lee surrendered to Grant. Why hadn't Elijah and Henry made it home? Could it be that they were not going to make it home? Could it be that they didn't survive?

After a few more weeks, everyone seemed to have given up

hope on any of them returning. They all had become numb to the fact that Henry and Elijah did not survive the prison camp, and that John must have had a change of heart, and decided not to come back for Hannah.

Hannah couldn't believe that to be true. The love she and John shared was not something that would just die. Even as the others began to tell her how sorry they were that he didn't come back, she knew in her heart of hearts that the only way he would not have come back is if he couldn't come back, which meant something was wrong. She felt completely helpless. After so much loss, she had hoped for a happy ending, but it was beginning to look like happiness was a luxury for her.

She was just numb. She went through the days much like everyone else did. They planted the gardens, they cooked meals and cleaned up. They did the washing every Saturday. They even had church every Sunday, with Harding leading them, but some of them were feeling as if God had abandoned them.

But, every now and then, Hannah would remember John's parting words to her, so she would stop what she was doing and pray "Dear God, thank you for keeping Pa and Henry and John safe. Thank you for continuing to protect them as they make their way back home to us. I know you are watching over them, and it may take time, but you will deliver them safely home."

June

It was the last Sunday in June. Everyone had gathered for church, and now that it was over, they were all sitting around outside the church, just visiting and enjoying the Lord's day of rest.

All the little boys were sitting in a dirt patch by a hollow log that was laying near the creek. They had figured out a way to play checkers in the dirt by drawing out the pattern of the board with a stick, then using rocks for red checkers and sticks for black checkers. The adults wouldn't allow them to bring the wooden checkerboard outside, so they improvised.

Daniel, Harding and Albert were off in the distance down the creek, flipping over rocks and trying to catch crawdads to fish with later. The young girls were all sitting behind the church in the shade, talking and laughing, watching the boys down at the creek and teasing each other about who might some day marry Harding and who might marry Albert, and which one was the most handsome of the two.

The women were sitting on the step in front of the church. Lucy was breastfeeding Etta, while the other three women were entertaining the toddlers.

The first to see them were the little boys. Six year old James Inman yelled to his mother "Ma, there's someone coming!" Irene and the other women squinted their eyes against the hot midday sun, trying to see what the boys were looking at. Far in the distance, slowly coming down the road toward them, was what looked like two men and two horses pulling a wagon. With the war over now, they didn't fear soldiers or bushwhackers any more, but they were still unsure who this could be and what they wanted. The women stood up and called for Albert and the men to come back down the creek to join them.

The closer the men got, the more Hannah thought they must be strangers. She didn't recognize them at all. All she and the others could do was wait until they got close enough to talk with them. So, they just kept watching. As the men came into view of the church, they both suddenly stopped walking. They were standing, looking across the creek at what was left of the two burned out homes and the barns. They weren't moving at all. They just kept staring, until a voice from the back corner of the church timidly said "Pa?" It was Isabelle, who had come around from behind the church with the other girls, to see what the commotion was about.

It took that one word from Izzy to change the dynamic of the moment. Hannah thought to herself, "Oh, the poor girl misses Pa so much, she's wanting any old stranger to be him." But, just as quickly as that thought went through her head, she caught a glimpse of a familiar movement. One of the men took off his hat, wiped his brow with his shirt sleeve, then put his hat back on. Elijah had always done that, in the same manner. Before Hannah even had a chance to scream out "Pa!", Sarah had already yelled "Elijah!" and began running toward him.

Then, Nancy & Elizabeth realized the other man was their Pa, Henry, and they ran toward him crying out "Pa! Pa!" Within seconds everyone was running to them. But, the men seemed to be in a trance. They just kept staring at the burned out homes, not registering that people were running to them. They were in shock, and were trying to make sense out of what must have happened while they were gone.

Hannah stopped short when she got a few feet from the men. She knew this was her Pa and Henry, but at the same time, she didn't recognize them. When they had left three years ago, they were muscular, trim men, weighing a healthy 180 pounds each. They were both men in the prime of their life, mid to late 30's, with thick wavy brown hair. What stood before them all now were two men with graying, straggly hair and beards, who looked 10 to 15 years older, who each weighed no more than 100 pounds, whose clothes were hanging on them, showing every protruding bone of their body. They looked like walking skeletons. Their faces were so gaunt and sunken in.

Hannah felt like crying. She was afraid to hug them, for fear they would crumble and break. It seemed the others felt the same way, or else they simply thought they were dreaming, and if they attempted a hug they would find out that there was nothing there, and it was all a mirage.

Then Henry spoke up and said "What happened to my home? My barn? Oh, dear God! Where is my family?" He turned around and began searching with his eyes. They were standing right there before him, but he was in such a state of shock, it wasn't registering with him. In his mind he was imagining them all burned to death inside the house, so it took a minute to get past that image and realize they were right there standing next to him.

Irene gingerly hugged her husband and he began to come back to reality. He began to search out each of his children, but after three years, he didn't even recognize his youngest two boys, James and Charlie. James had only been 3 years old when he left, but was now 6. He had grown from a toddler to a little boy. Charlie had been a baby of only 8 months old, but was now 3 years old and running around and talking in complete sentences. As he was hugging all the children and standing back and admiring how they'd grown, he suddenly realized one was still missing. "Where's Joseph?" he asked with a big grin. They all watched as that hopeful grin was shattered when Irene pulled him aside to tell him the heartbreaking news that he was never going to see his firstborn son again. Henry's knees gave out and he fell to the ground and sobbed.

As this was all going on, Elijah was also hugging all his family and tears were rolling down his face. He kissed Sarah and told her "I will never leave you again! Never! Oh, Sarah! You are a soothing balm to my weary eyes." He went up to Daniel, who had grown from age 19 to age 22, and shook his hand, man to man. "Son... you are a man now. You have grown into the man I always knew you would be." Then he went to Albert, who had been a scraggly 13 year old when he left, but who was now 16. "You are tall as your Pa now," Elijah said.

He hugged all his many daughters, the little ones first. Then he came to Hannah. "Look at you," he said. "If you ain't the spittin' image of your Ma." Then, Sarah encouraged 8 year old Michael and 6 year old Jacob and Jonah to go hug their father. They stood back because they had been so young when he left, they really couldn't remember him, and felt as if he were a stranger. The realization of it broke Elijah's heart, and he was sad that if he'd seen either of the three on a street somewhere, he would not have known they were his sons, they had all grown and changed so much.

The biggest surprise was when he asked Sarah whose baby she was holding. She turned two year old Jasper around to face his father and said "This is your son, Jasper." Elijah was dumbfounded. He'd had no idea that Sarah was with child when he left.

It was all so much to take in. They had so many questions.

What happened to the burned homes? Why did Elijah's home and the church *not* get burned? Where were William and Martha? Where were Grandma and Grandpa? Where was Rev. Owens and Winnie?

As their questions tumbled out, one after the other, Hannah began to realize how much they'd truly missed, and how much had changed. They were trying to fill them in, but so much of the answers brought sadness to them all. When they heard about all the many tragic events and the needless deaths, both men became quiet and reserved. It was so much to have to process all at once.

Elijah was introduced to his two biological granddaughters that he'd never seen, and to the three adopted grandchildren. Thomas and Isaac had only been 3 and 1 when he left, and now they were 6 and 4. Even though he'd seen them, he had known them as William and Martha's children, so he hadn't really paid as much attention to them as maybe he should have. He barely remembered what they'd looked like. So, he was being told he had *five* grandchildren now! He was simply overwhelmed.

The men were so weak that they had to sit down in the grass. They simply didn't have the legs to stand any more. Someone went down to the creek and brought them both some water to drink. Elijah asked some of the older children to take the horses and wagon into the barn, unhook the horses and get them a drink and put them in the stalls. He said they could worry about unloading the wagon tomorrow, after they had a chance to rest. They'd been walking for too long and they had no energy left.

The women decided they'd been in the sun for far too long, so each wife took her husband home. Daniel and Sarah walked on each side of Elijah and helped him up the hill and into the house. They laid him in his bed and propped him up with pillows. Sarah told everyone to go away and let Elijah rest for a bit. He would be able to talk to them later. So, they all went back outside, while Sarah remained and laid down on the bed next to her husband, holding onto him for dear life.

After several hours of sleep, Elijah was able to get up and

enjoy supper with his family, although he found it hard to eat as hearty as he used to. His stomach could only handle small amounts of food at a time. After being nearly starved to death in the prison camp, his stomach had shriveled up to almost nothing.

Daniel and Lucy and their children had stayed down at the house instead of going back home that night, because Daniel still had so many questions. He wasn't ready to leave his father and be a mile away from him. He was afraid if he did, he might never see him again. He just wanted to stay close. Everyone, in fact, wanted to stay close.

After supper everyone went outside. Elijah was given a comfortable spot to sit on the porch. Sarah and Hannah sat on either side of him, and everyone else gathered around. Daniel wanted to know everything they had been through the last three years. Where had they traveled? What battles had they been in? How did they end up in prison, and how long were they there?

Elijah wanted to know how everyone back home had survived all this time. Were they able to get to town? Did they get any of his letters? What happened to all the livestock, and how did they come up with that brown horse that he saw tied by the barn? How were they able to protect themselves and escape injury when bushwhackers and soldiers came around?

Elijah proclaimed Joseph a hero for what he did, much like he felt Jesse had been a hero to them. He said he felt extreme guilt that he and Henry did not stay to protect them all, if they had then maybe Joe would still be alive, and maybe William, too. He said that he felt he was off fighting for everyone else's sons and daughters for three years, when he now realized he should have been at home protecting his own.

Of course, they all assured him that no one felt that way, and that he did what he felt was the best thing at the time. No one knew how long this war was going to drag on. No one had imagined how long he was going to be gone.

"Pa?" Izzy asked. "Why did it take you so long to get home?"

"Well, they didn't release us from prison until the middle of April. You must understand the condition Henry and I were in. If you think we look bad now, you should have seen us that day. We could barely walk. We were on death's door. We knew there was no way we could possibly make it home in that condition."

"What did you do?" Lottie asked.

"Well, God put the right people in the right places at the right time. There were two other soldiers, Tom Kennedy and Frank Ward, who helped us initially. They said they both were from Atlanta and they were heading north to go home. In healthier times they told us they could make that trip in 2 days on horseback, or 6 days walking, but because we were so ill, and could barely put one foot in front of the other, it took the four of us thirteen days to get to Atlanta."

"We arrived in Atlanta about April 29th, if I remember correctly. Our two soldier friends had a joyous reunion with their families, and Henry and I were so jealous, longing for the day when we would get to do the same. But, Arkansas seemed a lifetime away at that point. Some days I wasn't sure if I could live long enough to make it back."

"Our friends said we could stay with them as long as we needed to, until we got stronger and were up to the trip. I sent you letters during that time, so you would not worry, but I know that you weren't able to get to town and receive them. I tried to write to you from the prison, but it was near impossible to find a way to get paper and pen to do so. I think I only wrote two letters in all the time I was in the prison. I worried every day about what you all must be thinking. I assumed you thought I was long dead."

Sarah said "The last letter I received from you was to say you had been taken to a prison. I won't lie, I truly had begun to believe you were dead."

"Well, I was in that prison for just about a full year. In all that time, I received no letters from home."

"We sent letters each time someone made the trip to town, but I think we only made three or four trips during the whole time you were gone, so we weren't able to send letters often. I had hopes you would have received them," Sarah said.

"I did not receive one single letter from home in the entirety. It was a lonely existence, I can assure you. The mail service was spotty at best. The way they moved us around so much, it was almost impossible to keep the mail going to where it needed to go, and then once we were in prison, I think the men running the prison didn't care one way or another if we received any mail."

"Anyway, we stayed with Tom and Frank for just about a month. Their families fed us well, and we were able to build back some strength. After a few weeks Henry and I took our army pay and went into town to purchase the supplies we would need in order to make the trip back. We bought the two horses, and the wagon, and enough food supplies for the two of us. Then, on June 1st we set off for home. We could not cover as much ground as two healthy men could, but we struggled through it. It took us 24 days to get here."

"We stopped in Clarksville for our final night, and purchased a good deal of supplies to bring up. I assumed you would be very low on food, but did not realize just how low. I feel what I brought will not be nearly enough, but at least it's a start. For now, I am just thankful to be home. My journey has ended. I never want to leave this mountain again!"

Sarah said "Did they pay you everything you were owed?"

"Almost," Elijah said. "From what I've heard, the Confederate soldiers did not make as much as we in the Union did, and had a harder time collecting their pay. But, Henry and I received our pay each month before we were captured and sent to prison, and we just kept it hidden away in our clothing. We figured out a way to cut a small slit in the lining of our coats and stuff the money inside for safe keeping. Every night I used my coat as a pillow, so I could keep it guarded, just in case. We were afraid to try and send money home, for fear it would not arrive safely. As a Captain, I was receiving $115 a month. Henry got much less in his position. He was a sergeant and was getting $20 a month. But, each time we were paid, we would split our money evenly, and each store away half in our coats. We figured this way, if something happened to either one of us, at least the other would have half the money to take home to split between our families."

Daniel seemed shocked, and said to his Pa "You are right

about those of us in the Confederate army not making as much. I only got $11 a month! I was only a private, though, not a captain like you, but I feel like I risked my life just as much, and deserved much more than I got. I feel a bit cheated, knowing how little I was valued."

"For those of us here in Buckeye, you are valued more than you will ever know. And, I thank you, son, for spending a good portion of that money buying food and supplies for the family," Elijah said. "It does me proud to know I raised such a compassionate young man. You absolutely deserved more than you got! There was so much about this war that was unfair."

Elijah seemed tired, so everyone gave him a break for a bit and quit asking questions. His eyelids were heavy and he was dozing a bit. Hannah was watching him, feeling so much love in her heart. She couldn't even put into words how thankful she was that he'd made it back home. Yet, she could see the change in him, and she hoped it wasn't a permanent change. She wanted her old Pa back.

He opened his eyes and saw her looking at him. He smiled, then turned his gaze. He'd slipped down somewhat in his chair and was looking up toward the top of the porch, with his head leaning back against the chair. He began staring upward with a concentrated frown.

"What is it Pa?" she asked.

"Hannah, what is that?"

She followed his gaze, but didn't see anything.

"What do you mean?"

"Right there, near the top of that post..."

Hannah squinted, and finally saw what he was looking at. At the top of the post supporting the porch roof, it looked as if something was carved in the wood. She couldn't make it out, so she got a chair and climbed up on it. It was two names. She suddenly jumped down off the chair in anger and said "That makes me so angry!!!!"

Sarah said "What? Did one of those children climb up there and carve their names?"

"No! It wasn't one of the children. Oh, I could just spit bullets right now!"

"Hannah, whatever has you so upset?" Elijah asked.

"Pa, it says Jeremiah Jones and John Fields! It must have been two of those soldiers that had taken over our home! They must have climbed up there and carved their names, just to be spiteful to us. As if they didn't already do enough to us! Give me a knife or something, so I can scratch it out."

Pa said "Hannah, honey....calm down."

"But, it's so infuriating! I don't want those names there a minute longer!"

Pa then said "Hannah, I want you to leave them there."

"But, why?"

"Don't we all have scars from this war?"

"Yes, but I don't see...."

"Some of our scars are visible, some are hidden, but we all have scars. Now, our home has some visible scars too. We can't remove our scars, so let's not remove the scars our house received, either. Let's embrace them. Let's build strength from them. Every time you walk across this porch and glance up at those names, let it be a source of strength and pride... because the house still stands. Those men did not succeed in destroying it. The house triumphed. I see those names as a good thing. For all we know those two men didn't survive the war. Let's let it drop. Let's leave the names there."

Hannah wasn't sure she understood her father's reasoning, but the longer she stared at the names, the more she began to lose her anger, and she settled down a bit and sat back down by Elijah. She sighed a deep sigh. Maybe he was right. If she tried to scratch out the names, it would just make a bigger, uglier "scar" as her father saw it. It would never look like it did before the names were carved. She looked over at her father again and wondered how he got so smart about things.

She said "I'm going to look up at those names every day and be proud. I'm going to pull strength from them until the names no longer have any power over me. I'm going to let them serve as a symbol of all we endured, and all we overcame."

"That's my girl," Elijah said. "We are Caseys, and 'ol Jeremiah Jones and John Fields did not beat us!"

Then Sarah spoke up, with a catch in her voice, and said "The Civil War did not beat us!"

The next morning after breakfast, everyone went to the barn to unload the wagon. Once all the bags of flour, salt, sugar and corn meal were unloaded, Elijah and Henry then removed a blanket from a pile of things that had been stored at the back of the wagon. The first thing they did was pull out several bolts of fabric. Elijah said "I got to thinking of how the army was supplying me with clothing, yet mine was still wearing out all the time, and here my family was, probably with no way to get material for new clothing in all this time. It's a wonder I didn't come home to find you all running around naked!"

The women were ecstatic to see some fresh fabric to make new clothing with! It was true that they were on their last stitches. Hannah had been wearing the same dress for all these years, and the material was so thin you could almost see through it. She had not complained, but how she had longed for a newer, prettier dress. She had especially wished she'd had a better dress while John was there. At times she'd been embarrassed that he saw her in the same raggedy dress all the time.

The men then pulled out a sack full of candy to pass out to all the children. The children jumped up and down with joy, took their candy and ran off to play. Elijah and Henry had purchased pocket knives as gifts for their older sons. Elijah gave Daniel and Albert their knives, and Henry gave Harding his. He held the one in his hand that he had planned to give to Joseph, and tears welled up in his eyes. He took it and put it in his own pocket. Oh, would the cruel reminders of the loss never cease!

The men had gifts for everyone, including a piece of jewelry for each of their wives, and a small music box for each of the girls.

Pa then pulled Hannah aside and handed her a new journal. "Do you still write?" he asked.

"Oh, Pa! Yes! I have been writing all along. I recently slowed down some because I was almost out of paper, so I only wrote if it was really, really important." She turned the journal over and over and admired the pretty cover, then flipped through the fresh, crisp pages, just waiting to be filled with words. How wonderful it was to have a father who knew her so well and understood what she needed most. She didn't need a music box, she needed a journal. The other girls loved their boxes, and it was a perfect gift for them, but Pa knew Hannah would be happier with a new journal, and he was right.

The final thing they unpacked were a few letters that they had picked up from the post office in town. Pa handed Sarah a letter from her parents, and one from good old Aunt Caroline. He handed a few letters to Lucy from her parents, and letters that Irene and Henry had received from relatives back in Tennessee. Then he held up the last one and said "Hannah, why do I have a letter here addressed to you from someone named Jonathan Oakley?"

Hannah screamed and snatched the letter from her father. Her hands were shaking as she opened it up. She read it silently to herself, and then said "Oh, thank God!"

"What is it, Hannah?" they all wanted to know. "What did John say?"

"Who in Heaven's name is this John?" Elijah asked.

"Oh, Pa!" Hannah said. "He's just the most wonderful man! I'm to be his wife when he returns for me."

Hannah quickly filled him in on how John and Sam had arrived and stayed for the winter, and how she and John had fallen in love, and he asked her to marry him before he went away, but he promised to come back.

Then she said "But, he didn't come back, and oh, Pa, I thought something terrible had happened to him!"

"Well, read us the letter, Hannah! We are dying to know!" Sarah said.

Elijah was still reeling from this news, and not sure he was happy about it, but Hannah was oblivious to his concern as she began to read the letter out loud to them all.

My Dear Hannah,

Oh, how I miss you! All the way on my trip to Jackson I had so many moments where I wanted to just turn around and come back to you, but I knew I must finish what I had started and return Sam to his family. We arrived safely. I am happy to report Sam and his wife enjoy a happy reunion, and his children are overjoyed. I, however, am miserable. I have news to report that you may not find pleasing. Upon my arrival in Jackson, I went to the post office. I had written letters to my parents while in the war, and since I never knew where I would be at any given time, I had asked them to send any correspondence to Jackson, Mississippi. Before I met you, Hannah, my plan had always been to go with Sam back to his home in Jackson after the war, so I thought it was a safe bet I would eventually get my mail there. I did, in fact, receive some mail, but I am sad to report that it was filled with bad news. Hannah, they say my mother is very sick. They beg me to come home, so that I may see her before she dies. Oh, my dear, I sat with that letter, debating what to do, for hours. I was so torn! My love for you compels me to return, but my love for my mother compels me to go to her. She is dying, it may be my last chance to see her in this life. I have made the difficult decision to go home, to see Mother, and to be there to support Father. I will stay only as long as I am needed, until Mother either recovers, or passes. Then, Hannah, I will keep my promise and return for you. I cannot say how long this will be, as I don't know how sick Mother is. I hope to not arrive and find her already gone. Please understand, my love, the reason I must break my promise to you, but only for now. I will return to you. Nothing will stop me from being by your side. Please wait for me. Please, if you can, write to me in Charleston, South Carolina. Oh, how my heart aches to have to make this decision. If only I had brought you along from the start, as you had wished. Please give everyone there my love, and most importantly, do not give up on me. I love you! I cannot live my life without you at my side. I need you in my arms once again.

John

Elijah was shocked, stunned, that he had been gone so long that his eldest daughter had found love, and everyone in his community was familiar with this man, but he knew nothing about him. He felt an extreme sense of regret over all that he had missed, and vowed he would never repeat that mistake ever again. His place was here, with his family. He should have been here to size up this man that his daughter wanted to marry. He should have been here to get to know him, right along with everyone else.

Hannah held the letter close to her heart, and felt so much happiness. Now that she knew he was alive and well, she could wait, however long it took. She knew, without a doubt, that he would return. She had complete faith in him. Her world felt right once again.

Sarah saw the look on Hannah's face and said to her "Just remember, good things come to those who wait."

Hannah said "I know, I know... and 'patience is a virtue' and all that, but it's so very difficult."

Sarah understood, because she, herself, had waited three long years.

July

It was not long before Elijah and Henry began to build their strength back. Daniel and Harding took them to the sawmill and showed them all the boards they had been able to cut, with the help of John. Although Elijah's instinct was to immediately think no man was good enough for his daughter, he kept finding out more and more about this John to make him think maybe he should not be so quick to judge.

It was decided that the first home that should be built was for Henry and Irene and their family, so they could move out of the church and have a decent place to live. So, that hot July, they began the tedious work of rebuilding Henry's home. Sometimes Elijah or Henry would have to stop and rest, because they were still not completely back to normal, but with the help of Daniel, Harding and Albert, and even the women, they began to see the shape of a house forming.

The Inman's old home had been a one-story house with three small bedrooms. There was a partial loft upstairs that you couldn't stand straight up in, that served as a fourth bedroom. And, there had been a porch on the front. Henry and Irene had planned out their new home to be just a bit bigger, but similar. This time they made it have four bedrooms, each a bit bigger than the bedrooms had been before. And, since the children had always liked the loft, they put a loft in this home, too. It was much bigger than the old loft, and you could actually stand up in the middle part of it. They also made the porch bigger this time. Instead of it only going across the front, they had it curve around and cover two sides of the house. It was a little wider than the last porch, as well.

It was wonderful that things were getting back to normal. There was no more fear of danger from a war that was finally over. It was a healing time. Although there had been much loss, there was much to be thankful for.

September

By September, the home was complete enough that the Inmans were able to move in. It was a joyous occasion! A huge dinner was cooked and there was much celebration. Harding even played some of the songs that Joe had taught him on the harmonica, and they all danced and sang. Irene loved her new home. It didn't erase the memory of all that she'd been through, and all that she'd lost, but it definitely soothed the sting and gave her hope for a brighter future.

The church was turned back into a church again. Harding stood in front of the congregation each Sunday and spoke to them all in the way John had taught him. He had seamlessly stepped into the shoes of Rev. Owens. Four years ago, no one would have ever imagined that Harding Inman would one day become their preacher, and a leader of their community, but somehow, at the tender age of 19, he had done just that. You could see the pride in Henry and Irene's eyes each Sunday as they sat and listened to their boy.

The building also regained another of its former uses when Sarah decided it was time to open the school back up. It had been too long that she had neglected the children. So, that September she gathered them all together on a Monday morning and began a new session of school. Hannah agreed to watch little Jasper for her so she would not be distracted as she taught her class of fourteen children.

Sarah made her seating arrangement on that first day. In the front row she sat the four 6 year old boys, Jacob and Jonah Casey, James Inman and Thomas Bennett Casey. On the second row she sat 8 year old Michael Casey, 9 year old Ruby Madison and 9 year old Virginia Inman. On the third row back she sat 11 year old Rachel Madison, 12 year old Charlotte Casey and 12 year old Elizabeth Inman. And, finally, on the back row were the oldest four children, 16 year old Albert Casey and the three 14 year old girls, Isabelle Casey, Rebecca Madison and Nancy Inman.

Albert, being the only boy above the age of 8, balked at first about going back to school, but Sarah convinced him to give her one more year with him, and then he could stop attending school with the other children. Elijah had said "Albert, do as your mother says," and even though Sarah was technically his *step*mother, not his real mother, he knew better than to backtalk his Pa. It was difficult, because Albert had been through so many adult situations in the past four years, he didn't feel like he was a child any more. But, Sarah knew that he needed to be a child for just a bit longer. He needed to regain some of what had been taken from him.

Albert didn't know it at the time, but that final year of school, sitting next to Nancy Inman, brought the two closer and closer together, and eventually they realized they had found love. Nancy had not forgotten the day Albert had saved her from the roaring flood waters, how he had gripped her tight as they floated along in the current, never letting her go. From that day on she had felt connected to him for life. Nancy knew she loved Albert from that day forward, but it took Albert a bit longer to realize it. About two years later, when he was 18 and she 16, Albert Casey and Nancy Inman would be married, and that same year, 20 year old Harding Inman and 16 year old Isabelle Casey would be married. Since the two Casey siblings married two of the Inman siblings, all their future children became double cousins to each other. Harding and Albert would remain friends (and brothers-in-law) for life, much like their fathers had, and they would stay in Buckeye all their lives and raise their families there. They would eventually take over the sawmill and run it together, and Harding would remain 'Rev. Inman' and preside over countless Sunday sermons, many weddings, burials and baptisms.

Sarah was back in her element. She was teaching again, which gave her a sense of worth. She had her husband back, and for good this time. She smiled at her students and said "Welcome back children!" Then, she put her hand on her stomach and smiled to herself, for she knew in a few short months there would be another future student. Sarah was now pregnant again, with her 5th child and Elijah's 13th.

Another improvement was made around this time to the little cemetery behind the church. There were now nine graves. Elijah and Henry both had children buried there now, so they decided they wanted to give it a little makeover. Everyone who was able was sent to find rocks down by the creek that were easy for stacking. It took two days to complete the project, but when they were done, there was a pretty little rock fence going all the way around the cemetery, and each grave was lined with rocks. The headstone of each grave, which was simply a rectangular rock buried upright in the ground, was straightened up and lined up just so. It was a beautiful little oasis in the wilderness when they were done. A peaceful resting place.

Hannah wished there were a way to mark the graves, because she worried that the names would be lost to time eventually. She decided the least she could do was record it in her new journal. So, she opened it up to a new page and drew a diagram of the cemetery. She drew the graves in two rows, just as they were laid out, and filled in each person's name and dates in the correct spot.

Buckeye Cemetery
Johnson County, Arkansas

Robert Madison husband of Sarah died 1858, age 28	William Bennett husband of Martha died 1863, age 26
baby girl Casey daughter of Elijah & Emeline born and died 1855	Martha Bennett wife of William died 1863, age 22
Emeline Casey & baby girl wife of Elijah died 1861, age 36	Ruth Harris wife of Joshua died 1864, age 73
Jesse Casey son of Elijah & Emeline died 1862, age 15	Joshua Harris husband of Ruth died 1864, age 75
Joseph Inman son of Henry & Irene died 1863, age 19	

October

John Oakley had buried his mother in early September. She had held on long enough for her only son to make it home to her. He stayed with her and visited her in her sick room every day, for the two months that she lingered close to death. He was forever grateful, in later years, that he had made the decision to go home to her when he did.

Mary Katherine Oakley was laid to rest in Magnolia Cemetery on a beautiful Saturday morning. John stood next to his father, Israel, and they watched as each of John's six married sisters walked up and tossed a flower into the grave.

John had talked of Hannah continuously upon his return. Both his parents had been happy to hear that he had finally found a woman to settle down with. The two of them had 31 grandchildren, but with all of them being born to their six daughters, there was not a single one to carry on the Oakley name. They had prayed and prayed for John to finally marry and produce some little Oakleys.

John's older three sisters were all in their 30's now. They had 21 children between them. His younger three sisters were all in their 20's. They had 10 children between them. John had turned 30 years old that year, and had yet to have any children. His parents were about to give up hope until they heard about Hannah.

John was anxious to get back to Hannah, as he had promised, but worried about leaving his father alone. With all of his sisters married and moved away, his father would now be all alone in his house after John left. He remained for two weeks after the funeral, but then told his father he was ready to go back. As he was packing up to go, something put a thought in his head. He ran into the house and said "Pa....why don't you come with me?"

At first Israel said he couldn't possibly, but after thinking on it a bit, he changed his mind. Maybe it would be good for him to get away for a bit and not just sit around wallowing in his grief. He was only 57 years old. He still had a bit of life left in him, and a trip such as this, especially since he could spend the time with his son, was sounding more and more intriguing. So, the two packed up Israel's best two horses and set out on September 16th.

On October 8th they arrived in Clarksville. John showed him around the town. They stopped to get candies to take to the children of Buckeye, and John bought an inexpensive wedding ring for Hannah. They each got their hair cut and got all cleaned up and presentable. After one more night, they got up bright and early on October 9th and began the trip up the mountain to Buckeye.

It was around supper time when they rounded the last curve and the little town came into view. The first thing John noticed was the new home that had been built across the creek. He and Israel got down off their horses just as Sarah and Elijah came out onto their porch.

"Elijah! It's Hannah's John!" Sarah said with excitement. "He's back!"

They went out to greet the two men, and John introduced his father to them. As all the children began running out to greet him, John said "Where's Hannah?"

Albert said "I think she went down to that tree by the creek where she always sits."

John jumped back onto his horse and just left his father standing among a group of complete strangers. They all had to laugh as they watched him take off down the road toward Hannah's tree. Elijah patted Israel on the back and said "Come on up to the porch and have a rest. You must be tired."

Hannah was deep in thought as she sat on her favorite tree root, staring out across Mulberry Creek. She had her pen poised above the blank page of her journal. She had been thinking of writing a short story. She had the general plot in mind but was having trouble coming up with a good opening sentence. She was so deep in thought she didn't notice at first that a horse was galloping down the road, coming in her direction.

When it was almost up to her, she finally was jolted from

her reverie. She turned, startled, just as the rider pulled his horse to a sudden, abrupt stop. The horse whinnied and pranced back and forth with impatience as the rider pulled back on the reins, and said "I must say, I'm a bit disappointed. I'd hoped to see a dress hanging from a tree."

Hannah's mind snapped back to a memory from a year ago, of a handsome soldier coming up on her as she swam nude. She jumped up, scattering her writing utensils, and ran toward the man. "John!" she cried out, as her heart soared.

He dismounted and ran into her outstretched arms. He lifted her and spun her in a circle as he held her close. Then he put her down gently and took her face in his hands and just gazed lovingly into her eyes.

"You are even more beautiful than I remembered. You are stunning.... Simply stunning!"

Hannah felt her heart melt, and peace returned to her soul. She was once again complete. When she stood facing John this way, with his eyes looking back into hers, she knew she'd finally found her purpose, her reason for being in this world.

When he brought his lips to hers, she began to cry. It felt as if all the weight of the last few years had finally released from her body.

She said to him, through tears "Sometimes you don't realize the weight of something you've been carrying, until you feel the weight of its release."

He said "That sounds like one of your poems. You should write that down."

"I think I will."

"It's good to let go," he said. "Let no weights be tied to your ankles. If it's heavy, let it go. A shackled bird can never fly."

"Oh, that's good, too!" she said as she wiped her eyes and smiled. "How about this one... These mountains that you are carrying, you were only supposed to climb." Then she motioned with her outstretched hands to the mountains all around them.

"That's amazing, Hannah! I don't know if I can top that."

She was smiling now, and her tears were drying up. But, then he said, very seriously, "I can conquer the whole world with one hand behind my back, as long as you are holding the other." Then, her tears came flooding back again.

"Will you still marry me, Hannah Casey?"

"A pack of wild hogs couldn't stop me," she said, smiling through her tears, because that was what he'd said to her when he left, promising he would return.

They made their way back to Hannah's house, where everyone was waiting. Elijah was eager to get to know this man who was to be his son-in-law. In many ways he already felt he knew him, because Hannah and the others had talked about him so much.

After supper, the men gathered together on the porch to talk war for a bit. Even though they had been on opposite sides, for Hannah's sake they were able to put their political differences aside now that the war was over. When Elijah told John about the conditions he and Henry had suffered through at Andersonville Prison, Israel spoke up and said "I read in the newspaper that the commander of that prison was arrested after the war ended, and charged with murder, in violation of the laws of war. His trial was ongoing last I heard. They are wanting to hang him. But, he says he was only following orders. Others say there are some deeds that can be forgiven in the scope of a war, but this is not one of them."

Elijah said "I hope they do hang him. The suffering I saw will be with me for the rest of my days."

Then Israel added "It might also help you to know that a former prisoner got together a group of people who went back and identified and marked most of the graves. This soldier, I think his name was Atwater, had been put in charge of recording the names of the deceased Union soldiers. He had made a second copy of the records for himself, for fear that the originals would be destroyed. He had wanted to make sure he could notify the families of the men who died. Thanks to this Atwater, over 12,000 of the dead were identified. They say only about 460 of the graves there had to be marked 'unknown soldier'." Elijah said that it was a comfort to him to know that the names were not lost entirely.

When the women were done cleaning up after supper they

came out to join the men on the porch. Hannah was captivated by Israel. He had the same piercing blue eyes that John had. Both of them were handsome men, just one of them had a lot of gray speckled into his hair, and a few more laugh lines on his face. Hannah realized that good genes ran in John's family. She couldn't help but think she would have beautiful children with him.

Just then Lottie asked Hannah when she and John were going to be married. The conversations all stopped as all ears turned to listen. Hannah said "Well, we will have to plan a trip into Clarksville, I suppose..."

Then, John said "Hannah? Have you forgotten? Pa is a minister! He can marry us right here!"

Hannah *had* forgotten. But, once she realized it, she knew it was perfect. What better person to marry them than John's own father?

"Well, I suppose we could get married right away then," Hannah said.

"So....when?" Isabelle prodded.

"How about this Saturday?" Hannah asked, as she looked to John for approval.

"I think Saturday is perfect," he said.

It was currently Monday, so they had five days to prepare. The girls set about making flower bouquets and planning the menu. Hannah had planned to wear the one new dress she had, which had been made from some of the cloth that Elijah had brought back from Clarksville. It was blue with a white flower print on it. But, Sarah surprised her by asking her if she would like to wear the fancy purple dress that she had worn when she married Elijah. It had come all the way from Virginia, and was nicer than anything they had there in these Arkansas mountains. Hannah said she was honored to wear it, and when she tried it on, she realized that she *was* capable of looking pretty like those fancy women she saw in town. She couldn't wait to see the look on John's face when he saw her in it.

On Saturday, October 14, 1865, 20 year old Hannah Casey and 30 year old John Oakley were married in the little church in

Buckeye, Arkansas. It was perfect timing, because, yes, the buckeyes were falling. The girls had even worked some buckeyes into Hannah's flowers that she carried, and the flowers that were hung inside the church.

Hannah's heart raced as she stood outside the church door with her father. Everyone else was inside waiting. She had not wanted anyone to see her in her dress until the moment she walked down the aisle.

Elijah looked at his daughter and said "Hannah, you are just beautiful. You are so like your mother on the day I married her. I wish she could have been here to see you on this day."

Hannah said "She *is* here, Pa. She is here. I feel it," and she tried to not start crying. "They are all here; Ma, Jesse, Grandma and Grandpa, even Joseph. They are all watching today. I believe they can see us from Heaven."

"I believe they do, Hannah. I certainly do."

Then he swallowed his emotions back as he said "You make me proud. Every day of my life you have made me proud."

"Stop it, Pa!" she cried. "I'm not supposed to cry just yet." She bent forward and kissed him on the cheek.

Then, the door of the church opened and Harding motioned for them to come in. It was time. They were all ready.

Hannah slowly walked down the short little church aisle with her hand through her father's arm. It was completely quiet in the little one-room chapel. Hannah saw all the people that she loved and had been such a part of her life. She thought of all the hardships and struggles they'd all shared together. She felt so much love coming back at her.

Then her eyes fell on John, and everybody else just faded away into the distance, and it was just the two of them, standing in front of Israel as he took them through their vows and prayed over them. When it was time for the ring, Hannah had fully expected there would not be one, but John pulled out the ring he'd purchased down in Clarksville and she was pleasantly surprised.

When it was time for the kiss, Hannah knew John wasn't kissing her for all those other people who were watching. He was kissing her because he loved her. He was projecting all his love into her. He was taking a moment to impart everything he was feeling. There was no rush. And, when everyone cheered after, they didn't even hear it at first. They were that much absorbed in each other.

The celebratory dinner after the wedding was one to remember. It was a beautiful fall day. The children ran around in the crunchy leaves, throwing them up into the air and laughing. The food was all delicious and everyone kept going back for more. It seemed to Hannah as if everything in her life had finally, for the first time since she was 16 years old, become what she had imagined it could be. She was truly happy. No longer did she have to feel she was going through life alone, bearing all her troubles alone. She now had this handsome, smart, strong, spiritual, wonderful man that she could always turn to for strength and love. Just knowing that he was there, to take care of her forever, was a comforting feeling. She had been strong for so long, it felt good to release some of that control, and allow someone else to be strong with her.

In the middle of her thoughts, Isabel walked over to her and said "I was thinking about that day when we were talking to Grandma, when she was dying. Remember what she said? She said 'The Lord will provide', and then she said 'You are going to marry a preacher man'."

"Oh, I forgot about that, Izzy! She *did* say that, didn't she? How did she know?"

Isabel said "Well, we are always told we should listen to our elders, because they are wise. Even Grandpa knew about things. Like how he was hiding things in the cave, and he told you about it. It was as if he knew that we would need it. He may have saved all our lives by doing that."

"I think you're right," Hannah said. Then, she caught something in the corner of her vision. She turned and said "Oh, Izzy! Look!" She pointed at the church. Izzy turned and saw that a bright red bird was perched on the window sill of the church. The girls stood and watched it until it flew away into the trees.

Izzy said "Do you think that was Grandma's spirit? Since we

were talking about her?"

"I don't know," Hannah said. "I used to think it was Joe every time I saw one. But, maybe it was Ma, because earlier I told Pa that I thought she was watching today. Or maybe it was Jesse. Or, maybe all along it has simply been God, and nothing more. Maybe it's just God's way of giving me hope."

"Still, how wonderful that you got to see one on your wedding day," Izzy said. "That's a good sign, I think."

"I think so, too, Izzy. I think so, too."

After the celebration had died down, everyone headed back to their homes. Hannah was beginning to feel a little strange. Earlier that day, Sarah had rearranged the household again, moving some of the children together, so that Hannah and John could have their own room for their honeymoon night. Hannah was feeling very odd about taking a man into her room for the night, knowing her father was just below her in the house. She knew John was probably feeling the same, maybe even more so than she was.

Once everyone began to retire, Hannah and John excused themselves and went upstairs to their room. They stood and kissed for a bit, until they had become very aroused. John began to remove her dress, and she, in return, began removing his clothing. Once they were down to their underclothes, they crawled into bed. But, that's when things stopped. They just couldn't relax, knowing that any noise they made might be heard by all the others in the house. Not only was Hannah's father in the house, but John's father was also there. There was absolutely no privacy.

John said "I feel so awkward! I feel like I can't just be myself with you, knowing there are so many people in this house. I want our first time as husband and wife to be special, something we will always remember, and this isn't feeling very special all the sudden."

Hannah was afraid that her wedding night had been ruined, until an idea popped into her head. She whispered to John "Let's sneak out". He was a bit taken aback, but immediately realized what she was thinking, and his heart raced with anticipation. The two of them quietly put their clothes back on. Then, Hannah took the quilt from her bed and folded it up and put it over her arm. She took John's hand and they quietly began to sneak through the house.

They gingerly began creeping down the stairs, trying not to make any creaking sounds as their weight pushed down on the wooden steps. About halfway down they heard a loud "creeeaaakkkk". They froze! Hannah stifled a giggle by putting her hand over her mouth. She turned and saw John was doing the same. She put her finger to her lips and said "Shhhhh". It was so thrilling to feel as if they were teenagers sneaking out without their parents knowing it.

When they got to Hannah's parents' bedroom door, they stopped and held their breath for a moment. Hannah let go of John and quietly tiptoed past the doorway. Then, she turned and motioned for John to do the same. Once they were safely past that door, they then only had a few more feet to go to make it to the front door. Hannah quietly turned the handle and they snuck out onto the porch. They tiptoed across the porch, and when they were just a few feet from the bottom step Hannah grabbed John's hand and took off running down the hill toward the church.

John had thought she was taking them to the barn, where they had first made love. But, when she yanked him the other direction, he just followed. She could have led him anywhere! They ran along in the dark, laughing and touching, and stopping to kiss here and there, until they came to Hannah's tree.

The moon was full and shining bright in the sky and reflecting on the water. Hannah spread out her quilt on the ground next to the tree. Then she stood in front of John and slowly undressed herself as he watched. Soon, she was standing in the moonlight, completely nude. He was entranced with her beauty. She was amazed at how free she felt. He then removed all his clothing, too, and the two embraced and became lost in each other.

John lowered her to the quilt and they made love, over and over again, for hours as the moon moved across the sky. Afterward, they lay there staring up at the stars, holding each other close to stay warm in the cool night air.

John said "Hannah, you make me a better man. I can't explain why, but I find myself wanting to be better. I want to make you proud of me. I want to be your protector. I want to have children with you, and take care of you and the children, giving you a good home, and all the things you need to be happy. And, I also find myself wanting to be a better servant for God. I haven't given myself to him like I should."

"Oh, John, I know just how you feel, because I feel those same things. Did you know, before I met you, I actually thought maybe I didn't want to have children, but as soon as I realized I was in love with you, I completely changed my thinking, and it became the one thing I wanted more than anything! I want to create beautiful babies with you, and raise them the right way. I want to one day sit on the porch with you in our rockers when we are in our 80's, and smile as we look out at the nighttime stars, and listen to the whippoorwills, and get lost trying to count how many grandchildren we have."

"I am never letting you go," John said. "You are a part of me forever. Everything I do now, for the rest of my life, will be for you."

"Oh, John! From you I get comfort, I get strength. I feel like I can do anything as long as I have you there backing me up."

John pulled her closer to him and said "When I left you to take Sam home, I had the most awful feeling. I don't know how to explain it, other than I felt like I'd been uprooted. You know, like a tree that has been pulled up out of the soil. Like a giant hand reached down and yanked me up. I felt like I was dangling there in the air, with my roots no longer in the ground, like I no longer had a way to pull the nourishment from the soil, and I knew if I couldn't get my roots back into the ground, I would die soon. It wasn't until I pulled you into my arms when I came back, that I felt like I'd been replanted, and I felt my root system start working again, breathing life back into my veins. When I'm away from you, I feel uprooted, but when I'm with you I feel replanted."

He paused, then said "Does that sound a little too mushy and romantic?"

She turned to him and kissed him gently and said "No, it sounds exactly like what I feel, too. I even wrote a poem about how we were both trees, planted near each other and drawing strength from our roots that are entwined together under the ground where no one can see. I suppose I was thinking the same thing as you, just expressing it a different way. Funny, we both made reference to a tree, though. I suppose a tree is a symbol of strength. Even after the big flood we had here, my buckeye tree still stands. A little more dirt has been washed out from under her roots, but she still stands, strong and true. Our love will be that way, too. When hard times come to us, it will just be a bit of dirt washed away from our roots, but we will still stand, strong and true. We just have to stay planted and not let ourselves be uprooted."

John thought for a minute as he gazed over at the buckeye tree, standing there next to them in the moonlight, and then he said "I see what you mean. A few more exposed roots is not a bad thing. It gives us character. Like your tree here. You like her because of the roots sticking out, so you have a place to sit and reflect. If the roots weren't exposed, you would think of her as just any old tree. But, because this tree has character, and isn't perfect, you chose her. The hard times she has been through gave her character, and drew you to her."

John's mind began working and he was starting to imagine a Sunday sermon on just this topic. It was amazing to him how he suddenly was always thinking of topics for a sermon. Maybe Sarah was right, and he should become a preacher, like his Pa. He realized that Hannah had this way of opening up his mind to spiritual thoughts. He had never associated life's events with sermons before, until he met Hannah. She brought it out in him. She had changed him. Oh, he had always believed in God, and talked with God, but it had always been a private thing. Now, with Hannah's love, he found himself wanting to share all of his spirituality, to help others see what he was seeing, to open up the minds of others so they could find strength and comfort in God's word, just as he always had.

Hannah's mind was also working, and she was thinking

about how John had just said this tree had character. She thought back to the soldier's names etched into the post at her home, and she realized that her house now had character, too. It had a story to tell. And, the little church in Buckeye, with the burnt spot at the corner where the soldiers had set it on fire, but Harding had put it out... the church had character, too. It also had a story to tell. There was something about the way John spoke, the way he looked at the world, that opened up her eyes as well, and helped her to see things differently.

Hannah said "John, will you make love to me again?"

He said "Hannah, honey, I haven't made love to you yet. I don't want to ever make love to you. I only want to make love with you."

They made love again, and held each other for a bit longer, each of them crying tears of happiness, never wanting this night to end. But, then, finally John said maybe they better get back home. It was getting a bit too cold out. So, they made their way back to the house, moving much slower this time, for they were worn out and bathed in contentment, and they snuck back upstairs to their room.

Hannah fell asleep that night feeling like she was the luckiest woman in the world.

The next morning, when she opened her eyes, John was gazing at her from his pillow. He said "I can't believe I had to travel halfway across the country to find you!"

She snuggled up against his chest and said "God must have brought us together."

John laughed to himself and said "Maybe this whole terrible war was just God's way of bringing Hannah and John together."

She rolled her eyes and said "I don't think I'd go *that* far, John!"

It was Sunday, and Harding had already prepared a sermon for that day, so they all went to church to listen. But, John couldn't stop thinking about an idea for a sermon about trees and their roots, so he spent the following week preparing something, and the following Sunday, with Harding's permission, he gathered everyone together in the little church and talked to them, in a very personal way.

He first welcomed everyone to church and said an opening prayer. Then, he said that today he wanted to talk mostly to the children. What he had to say would be important for the adults, as well, but he wanted all the children to come up close in front of the congregation so they could pay close attention today. After they all moved up close and grew quiet again, John said "I'm going to read a sentence from the Bible, and I want you to tell me what you think it means."

"And there shall come forth a rod out of the stem of Jesse, and a branch shall grow out of his roots."

"Can anyone tell me what they think that means?" John asked.

Izzy spoke up and said "Well, I think it means that whoever this Jesse person is, he maybe had lost his way, but when finding God in his life, he finds a way to grow back again."

"That's very good, Izzy, you are close. This verse is talking about a man who produces great offspring, even though he himself may have appeared to be a mere stump of a tree. Something was still able to sprout from that stump, with God's help," John said. "Does anyone know who Jesse was?"

They all shook their heads. Then, Izzy said "I only know that Ma named my brother Jesse, after someone from the Bible. Is this the same Jesse we are talking about?"

Elijah spoke up and said "I think it is, Izzy."

"Well, I think your mother chose wisely in naming your brother," John said. "Jesse was a simple farmer and sheep breeder in Bethlehem. He was nobody famous, just a simple man with a simple life, but because of his existence, we have Jesus. You see, Jesse had eight sons, the youngest being a boy named David. Does anyone know who David grew up to be?"

The children all shook their heads, but a few of the adults knew the answer. However, they were staying quiet so the children could enjoy this lesson.

"Well, David was a young shepherd and harpist. You may

remember the story of David and Goliath? Well, that is this same David. He seemed to be the last person who could defeat the giant Goliath, because he was so small and frail compared to the giant, but because he had faith in the Lord, he was able to find a way by picking up a stone and slinging it and hitting the giant in the head, killing him. All the stronger men had tried killing him with brute strength, but God gave David the wisdom to use his brains and come up with a better way."

"David was a teenager, like some of you, when he slayed the giant. But, later in life, when he was a grown man, he became 'King David'. From humble beginnings he became a king. And, through the line of King David, we eventually get Joseph, who was the father of Jesus."

"But, I thought God was Jesus's father," Nancy said.

"Well, he was," John admitted. "But, because Jesus was born to Mary, who was married to Joseph, he became the legal adopted son of Joseph. Just like it is today, if a man adopts a child, he becomes that man's child, in all respects, just like his blood children are. So, Jesus is of the line of King David, although not by blood, he is still of that line because the man who raised him and called him 'son' was of that line. He was legally of that line. Think of it this way... God could have chosen any woman to be the birth mother of Jesus, but he chose the one who was married to Joseph, a man of the line of Jesse and King David. He chose Joseph for a reason. He chose the line of Jesse to be Jesus's family, for a reason."

"Think of how Daniel and Lucy have adopted the Bennett children. Do they not call Elijah and Sarah "Grandma and Grandpa"? They are not blood related to them, but I am sure Elijah would have no problem saying they are "of his line". Do you see what I am saying? Sometimes love makes you part of a family line, even if blood doesn't."

"Oh, I see!" Nancy said. "So, the verse you read is saying that the branch that grew from the roots of Jesse was Jesus."

"Yes, that is so. But, why do you think the verse says *A rod shall come from the stem of Jesse*, instead of saying *from the stem of King David*, which would sound more impressive?"

Nancy said "I suppose because it would seem natural that Jesus would come from a King. But, the father of that King was Jesse, a simple farmer, and Jesus also comes from him. It sounds less believable, but more impressive, to say that Jesus came from a simple sheep farmer."

"Yes, I think it shows that greatness can come from even the most humble and simple person. You don't have to be someone famous or of a high position. Anyone is capable of creating great things, and even the most highly thought of may have come from humble beginnings."

John continued "So, my sermon today is about trees, and roots and seeds. Jesus came from the roots of a simple farmer, named Jesse, but even though Jesse may have seemed not all that important of a man in his time, he was the most important in the grand scheme of things."

"That last verse was from Isaiah. But, the Bible is full of references to trees and roots, and always it comes back to faith. For instance, John 15 says *Remain in me, and I will remain in you. No branch can bear fruit by itself; it must remain in the vine. Neither can you bear fruit unless you remain in me.* What do you think that verse means?"

Albert said "If you don't have faith in God, and accept him in your life, you don't have the foundation to bear fruit in your life."

"Exactly! The vine represents your faith in God, it's what connects us to God. A grape cannot grow into a grape unless it is hanging from the vine. It needs the vine to bring nourishment to it, just as we need God to bring nourishment into our souls. Think of it this way children. Think of yourselves as the grape, and Jesus as the vine. But, God is the gardener. John 15 goes on to say *I am the true vine, and my Father is the gardener. He cuts off every branch in me that bears no fruit, while every branch that does bear fruit, he prunes so that it will be even more fruitful.* What do you think that means?"

Elizabeth spoke up and said "I think it means that if we believe in God, then when we consider sinning, that sin is like the branch of the vine that isn't producing fruit, so with God as our gardener, he will cut off that bad branch. But, if we don't give ourselves to God, that branch will continue to grow, and maybe someday overtake all the good branches, and turn us evil."

Then Charlotte said "Oh, I see! So, Jesus is the vine. God uses the vine to help us grow into grapes. He keeps Jesus (the vine) healthy and strong in spirit, so that through him, we can draw nourishment and grow. Without God (the gardener), Jesus (the vine) wouldn't be a strong, healthy vine for us to grow on, because he prunes out the bad branches. But, without Jesus (the vine), God would have no place for us to hang from and grow from. Jesus is not God, but he is what connects us to God. God works through him to reach us. It makes so much sense to me now."

Hannah was amazed! John was getting the children to really think about things, and this was spilling over to the adults, as well. She realized that he was a very good spiritual teacher to the little ones, and that meant he would probably be a good teacher to their own children when they had them some day.

John told Elizabeth that she was exactly right in her thinking. He said that faith was so important in every aspect of your life.

Then he said "I want to read to you all a poem that Hannah wrote."

Hannah perked up. He had not mentioned to her that he was doing this. What poem is he talking about?

He began reading it out loud to them. He had copied it down from her journal when she wasn't looking.

"I'm a tree, you're a tree
Standing side by side
To others we look separate
They don't see what we hide

We are planted near the water
We send our roots out to the stream
We never fear when heat comes
Our leaves are always green

When the Buckeyes Fall

Underneath the soil
We are holding one another
Our roots have grown together
We support each other

If storms bring damage to you
And try to blow you down
It's going to be a battle
Because I hold you to the ground

When you blossom, I blossom
When your leaves fall, so do mine
Together naked through the winter
Pulling strength from our entwine

We hold each other tightly
With such intensity
Amazing others look at us
And only see a tree"

John noticed some of the children giggling a bit under their breath when he read the part about being together naked through the winter. He said "I heard those little snickers...." He smiled at them and said "In Hannah's poem, she doesn't mean the literal form of naked, I don't think. Do you, Hannah?"

She shook her head no.

"What do you think she means?"

Rebecca said "Well, the naked part could mean two different things. In one way, it could just mean how the trees have no leaves in the winter, so they are naked, in a sense, like people without clothes. But, in another way, if you look deeper, it could mean naked in the sense of not hiding anything, being completely open to someone else and sharing everything you have with them."

John glanced at Hannah and she said "Yes, Becky. That's kind of what I was trying to say."

John said "Does anyone notice something in Hannah's

poem that pertains to the Bible?"

The children all shook their heads.

"In Jeremiah 17 God says that *cursed be the man that trusteth in man, and whose heart departeth from the Lord. But blessed is the man that trusteth in the Lord, and whose hope the Lord is. For he shall be as a tree planted by the waters, and that spreadeth out her roots by the river, and shall not see when heat* cometh, *but her leaf shall be green; and shall not be careful in the year of drought, neither shall cease from yielding fruit.*"

"The 5th through 8th lines of Hannah's poem are taken from those words in the Bible," John said proudly.

Rachel spoke up and said "I think Hannah's poem could be interpreted two ways. It could be about two people loving each other, but also about a person and their love of God."

"Yes, it could be interpreted either way," John said. "When it says *sending our roots out to the stream,* it could be simply talking about trees reaching toward water, but if you think deeper, it could be talking about people praying and *reaching* toward God for the nourishment they need to survive."

"Now, there is one other thing I wanted to mention from the Bible. This part is not so much about trees, but about planting seeds. Can anyone think of a part of the Bible where they talk about seeds?"

Charlotte said "In the Parables!"

John said "Yes, in the Parables. When Jesus was sitting in the boat by the edge of the sea, and talking to his followers, he spoke in parables, which are sort of like thought-provoking comparisons to things, like little stories that make you think. Can anyone think of a parable about seeds or growing things?"

Charlotte said "There was the one about the mustard seed."

"That's right. In that parable, Jesus was trying to describe what the Kingdom of God was like. He said it was like a mustard seed, which is the tiniest of seeds, yet when you plant it, it grows and becomes the greatest of all the herbs, shooting out great branches so large that birds can rest in the shadows of it. In much the same way, the Kingdom of God seemed small, until Jesus went around planting the little seeds in everyone's heads and spreading the word, so that it could grow into a giant movement."

"There is another parable about seeds. It goes like this... *Behold! There went a sower to sow. And it came to pass, as he sowed, some fell by the way side, and the fowls of the air came and devoured it up. Some fell on stony ground, where it had not much earth, and immediately it sprang up, because it had no depth of earth, but when the sun was up, it was scorched, and because it had no root, it withered away. And, some fell among thorns, and the thorns grew up and choked it, and it yielded no fruit. And, others fell on good ground, and did yield fruit that sprang up and increased, and brought forth some thirty, and some sixty and some a hundredfold."*

"So, what do you think Jesus was teaching with this parable? What did he mean by the seeds that just fell on the ground?"

Nancy said "Those seeds just blew away and never took root, because it's like a person who hears the word of God, but doesn't listen or believe."

"And what about the seeds that fell among the rocks?"

Izzy took this one and said "I think that one is talking about a person who hears the word and believes at first, but then quickly forgets it, so when trying times come, they have lost their way, they can't survive the hard times, much like the seed couldn't because it didn't have enough soil. It only had enough soil to get started, but not enough for the long term."

"Great! I like to think of that part as like the person that only goes to church on Christmas and Easter. They don't have enough soil in them to take root and grow properly. They can get started, but they can't sustain in the long run. Now, what about the third part, about the seed that fell among the thorns?"

Rachel said "I think that represents someone who goes to church and hears the word, but then they surround themselves with bad people, and hang around in bad places, so they let the evil things in life grow around them and choke the word back out, just like the thorns choked the seed out."

"That's right, Rachel," John said. "But, the seed that was sewn in good soil is the seed that prospers and makes a hundredfold of itself. The *good soil* is the word of God."

"Now, has anyone noticed the trees down by the creek that have roots showing, because the water has washed the dirt out from under them?" John asked.

The children all nodded yes.

"Those trees are still standing, aren't they?"

They all nodded.

"That is because they had a good strong base, a lot of roots running through the soil for many feet, giving them a strong hold. So, even if some of the dirt got washed away, they still had enough left to survive and hang on. Remember when you had the big flood a couple of years ago? Well, some trees were uprooted and washed away in that flood, weren't they? Their roots weren't quite strong enough. But, some held on, like Hannah's tree that she likes to go sit by when she writes. That tree lost a little more of the dirt that was holding it in place, but it still held on, because it had enough dirt to make it. It could afford to lose a bit of dirt, because it had so much."

"I want all of you children to learn as much as you can about God, because each thing you learn is like another root growing out from your tree. Each little bit of faith that you develop is like more dirt that your roots can attach itself to. If you keep doing this, then when hard times come, for instance, when you suffer through the loss of a loved one, or you get sick or injured, then those times will be like the floods are to the trees. Maybe some of your dirt will get washed away, but you will still have enough roots wrapped around enough dirt to hold you in place, so you can weather that storm. That's what the love of God is, it's like that strong root system and all that dirt, holding you where you need to be, so you can stand tall and true."

"I know all of you have been through a great deal," he looked up from the children and scanned the crowd of adults as well. "But, you all have character now. You all have a few exposed roots. You may look a little different now, but the flood didn't take you down. So, keep growing. Don't be ashamed of your exposed roots. Let people sit on them and write poems..." He turned to look at Hannah and everyone smiled and laughed a bit. Tears came to Hannah's eyes.

Israel had been watching with pride, seeing his son following in his footsteps the way he was. He had hoped, in younger years, to maybe see his son become a man of God, like himself, but had lost all hope of it after John's teenage years. It just didn't seem to be the path he was going to take. But, now, there was hope again. Israel only wished his wife had lived to see it.

Israel had left his own church back in Charleston in the care of his assistant pastor while he took this trip with his son. He was eager to get back to it, and hoped that maybe his son would join him and take over the church some day.

John closed out the sermon and everyone went back to their respective homes. Hannah walked toward her house with her arm entwined with John's, and she looked up at him and smiled with such pride. Oh, how she loved this man! She wasn't sure what she did to deserve his presence in her life, but she was so thankful that God brought him to her. She loved how he took their loving words to each other and turned them into a sermon. It made her feel like their love was a Godly kind of love, and she had always wanted that.

John was also thinking about Hannah in that moment, and how she had brought out the spiritual side of him. He would never be able to come up with sermons like this without her input and her love. He had been pulling away from God before he met her. He was like the tree about to be washed away in the flood, but just in time she pulled him back and replanted him. As long as he had her, he would never be uprooted again. He would grow and thrive. He needed her, he needed her so much.

After some discussion over the next few days, it was decided that John and Israel would stay the winter in Buckeye. But, when spring came, John wanted Hannah to leave with him, so they could go out and start their lives together. They would start by traveling back to Charleston, so everyone in his family could meet her. They would spend some time there, and then eventually decide where they wanted to live and raise their future children.

Maybe Hannah would love Charleston, and they would decide to stay, or maybe they would decide to come back to Buckeye. Or, just maybe there would be some other place that would call to them. But, for now, they would winter with Hannah's family.

1866

As the winter of 1865-66 passed by, John and Israel melded right into the group and got along wonderfully with everyone. Elijah, especially, was very fond of Israel. The two sat up late many nights talking and smoking their pipes.

John and Daniel resumed their friendship. There were many evenings when Hannah and John walked the mile to Daniel and Lucy's house, where they would visit and talk and make plans for the future. On one of these trips, Hannah decided she wanted to share the cave with John, so she took him up to see it. He stood there looking around inside the cave, and felt so much sadness when he thought of everyone having to hide out in there, for fear of their lives. "You are a strong woman, Hannah," he said. "Each day I know you I see more proof of that."

Every Sunday, Harding, John and Israel took turns giving the sermon. Sometimes all three of them would speak. They planned the services together, and Harding & John were both learning a great deal from Israel, since he was an actual preacher. The little church in the woods had never had such lively sermons as it did that winter.

Hannah turned 21 years old at the end of January. Everyone kept telling her 'happy birthday', but she couldn't help feeling a bit sad. She just kept thinking about how this could very well be her last birthday ever spent in Buckeye. She didn't like to think about such things.

John had wanted to leave at the very beginning of April, as soon as the last chance of snow had passed. But, Hannah begged John to wait just a few more weeks, because Sarah was due to have her baby in May. She promised, if they could just wait for that event, so Hannah could see if she had a new baby brother or a sister, then she would be ready to leave any time after that. She just had a fear that if she didn't wait those few extra weeks, it could be months before she'd learn about the details of the birth. She didn't think a few weeks was too much to ask. John agreed that it would be cruel to ask her to so narrowly miss such a special time, so he relented.

One morning in early April, after church services, Daniel stood up and told the congregation that he had an announcement to make. Hannah immediately thought "Oh, Lord! Lucy's pregnant *again*! Etta is only 1 year old!", but it turned out that was not what the announcement was about.

He began, rather timidly, "I know that we were supposed to be rebuilding Lucy's and my home this year. I was looking forward to moving out of Grandpa's little house and moving down here closer to everyone..."

Everyone began to stir and murmur. What was going on?

Daniel continued "But, I don't think that will be necessary after all."

"What are you talking about, Daniel?" Elijah asked.

Daniel took a deep breath. He didn't think his Pa was going to like what he had to say.

"It's just that... Lucy and I have been talking. Lucy is missing her family very much. She has no one from her immediate family that is close any more. They don't even know our children, and our children don't know them. Lucy wants to go back to

Tennessee to be near Rev. Owens and all the rest of her family."

Everyone began to talk all at once.

"Do you mean just for a visit, or for good?" Elijah wanted to know.

"I'm not sure, Pa. It might be for good."

"I would be lying if I said I didn't worry about something such as this," Elijah said. "When a man has children, most of them generally do move away. But, I just had hopes that my oldest boy would stay around. And, if you think of it from my point of view, I may never know my grandchildren, or they me. Rev. Owens may be getting to finally know his grandchildren, but I am just beginning to know them, and my time is going to be cut short."

"I know Father. I have thought of all this, and turned it over in my mind. But, after being off in the war, and seeing other places, I have become stifled here. I've seen larger towns and places that seem so much more exciting, places where I can work and make money to support my family. I was okay with living here before, but now that I've seen some of the world, I feel so locked away from everything here. I'm not saying I don't love it here. I will always think of Buckeye as home. But, if my children grow up here, I don't see that I have much to offer them. And, when it's all said and done, a man wants to see his wife happy. If going back to Tennessee will bring my wife happiness, then that is what I want to do. I can be happy anywhere, so long as Lucy is happy. That is most important to me. She is my life."

"I see. When did you plan on leaving out?" Elijah asked.

"Well, I was thinking that, if Hannah and John don't mind, we could leave out with them after Sarah has the baby. Maybe we could all travel together until we get to Lucy's family in Tennessee, then Hannah, John and Israel could go on to South Carolina from there."

Hannah was almost afraid to answer. She loved her brother, and the thought of having him along for part of the trip was exciting. She wanted that. But, she also knew that either way, she probably was not going to see Daniel much, if at all, for the rest of her life. She was resigned to the fact that she wasn't going to see him, but hated to think of Pa not being able to. She didn't want to make it easy for Daniel to leave, but she knew, even without her and John's help, he would still find a way to leave. So, she told him that she would be more than happy to have him along.

Sarah said "Have you thought about how difficult it will be to travel with five young children?"

"Yes," Daniel said. "We know it will be rough going. But, the way we see it, if we wait until these children are older, there will just be more children born. No matter when we go, there will be little ones. There really is no good time to go."

Elijah sighed. "I was finally beginning to get used to the idea of *one* of my children leaving. Now I find out it will be two of them. I don't like it, but I know that I was supposed to raise you to be able to fend for yourselves, not to depend on me for the rest of your lives. So, this just means I did my job."

May

On the morning of May 7th, Sarah woke up with labor pains. As was the usual, the men were sent outside, and the children were taken across to Irene's house where Lucy and the teenage girls kept an eye on all of them. Hannah and Irene stayed with Sarah all day as she suffered through her pains.

"Do you hope for a girl or a boy this time?" Hannah asked.

"I don't know," Sarah said. "I just want it to be healthy. But, everyone says that, right?"

"Yes, they do. But, keeping in mind that it *will* be healthy, you must have a secret desire for one or the other."

"I think I really hope it's another boy. I know that Elijah has 6 living sons, and only 3 daughters, so for him, it might be nice to have another girl. He told me the other day that his youngest girl is a teenager now, and he kind of misses having a sweet little girl to come sit on his lap and give him butterfly kisses. Also, his youngest four children are all boys, so seems like the odds are against it being a boy again. But, the way I look at it, I already have

3 girls, but only 1 boy. I'd like to have another boy. And, wouldn't it be nice for Jasper to have a little brother close to his age?"

Hannah said she was kind of hoping for a girl, but she, of course, would be happy no matter how it turned out.

Hannah's mind began to drift to her own prospects of motherhood. She counted up the months and realized it had been almost 7 months now since her wedding, yet she was not pregnant. She was glad, in a way, because she didn't relish the idea of traveling while pregnant, but sometimes late at night, as she lay beside John, watching him sleep, she worried that maybe she was going to be one of those unlucky women who couldn't get pregnant. What if God had taken her too seriously all the times she said she didn't want to have a bunch of children! She told herself that it was too soon to worry about such things yet. Her time would come when it was supposed to come. She was only 21. She had many childbearing years ahead of her still.

"Hannah, I'm glad you're here," Sarah said, snapping Hannah back to reality.

"I'm glad I am, too," Hannah replied. "I didn't want to miss this for anything. I am so very happy that you and Pa have each other now. It would have been difficult for me to leave if I thought he was alone, especially with all these children to look after!"

"I loved Robert," Sarah said, speaking of her first husband. "But, sometimes now I feel like that was somebody else's life. It doesn't seem real that I was married to him. I feel like I've always been married to Elijah. I know I was meant to be with Robert so I could have my girls, but I realize now that Elijah was always supposed to be my life partner. Maybe God sent Robert to me to guide me to Elijah. It was Robert who wanted to come to Arkansas, after all. Maybe God knew Robert was going to die young, so he put the thought for him to come here in his head. Do you ever think about things like that, Hannah?"

"Sure I do!" she said. "It could very well be that God knew my Ma and your Robert would both die young, and that Pa and you would be perfectly suited for each other, so he brought the two families together. Life has an odd way of working itself out. Just like with me and John. God may have sent him my way knowing that he would be just the one to heal me from the loss of Joseph."

"I'm going to miss you when you go, Hannah. In many ways you have become my daughter, I mean my *real* daughter, not just my stepdaughter."

"I feel the same about you," Hannah said, as her eyes teared up.

"Hannah, when you get to wherever life takes you, if it's Charleston, or wherever it might be, I want you to seriously think about trying to get some of your writing published. Most bigger cities have publishing houses. Just take your work there and ask them to read it and consider it. You may get rejections at first, but one day someone will like what they read. I just know it is your calling to write, and not just for yourself, but for others to benefit from, as well. Promise me you will look into that. There is so much you can make of yourself after you leave here. I know you have what it takes."

"I will try, Sarah. If not for me, then for you."

"I'm glad."

Hannah looked at Sarah and said "If it weren't for you, none of it would be possible for me. You were my teacher. You were the one who taught me how to read and write, how to take my thoughts and put them to paper. Without you, none of it would have happened."

"Well, then you can dedicate your first book to me..." Sarah teased.

"You tease, but if I'm lucky enough to have a published book, I most certainly *will* dedicate it to you!"

Sarah smiled, then grimaced with pain as another contraction siezed her body.

When it was over, Hannah said "Sarah, I feel guilty about leaving here."

"Hannah, I would like nothing more than for you to stay, but I don't want you to feel guilty."

"But, I'm just leaving you! I'm leaving Pa! I'm leaving all my brothers and sisters!"

"You are no different than any other woman of your age.

Think about it! I also left my family and moved far away. Your Pa and Ma left their families and moved far away. We all felt guilty, but it was something we all felt we needed to do. It is natural for a child to grow up and move away. Don't feel guilty. Just follow your dreams! Make a life for yourself, and make it good. Don't waste it."

Late in the evening of May 7th, Sarah Casey gave birth to another little boy. Hannah held her new baby brother and marveled at how much he looked like Jasper had when he was born. She told John how thankful she was that he'd agreed to let her stay so she could hold her baby brother. She knew that there was a chance it could be years before she'd ever hold him again, so this meant the world to her.

Everyone gathered around and gazed at the new little human being. What a miracle it was, the way a woman and man could create a life that way. What a blessing each baby was to a family!

There were six doting half-sisters looking down at the precious bundle of joy. There were Sarah's three daughters from her first marriage, Rebecca (15), Rachel (12) and Ruby (10), and Elijah's three daughters from his first marriage, Hannah (21), Isabelle (15) and Charlotte (13). All six of them already loved the new baby and couldn't wait to hold him and play with him.

And besides his own full brother, Jasper (3), the new baby also had 5 older half-brothers on his father's side, Daniel (23), Albert (17), Michael (9) and the twins, Jacob and Jonah (7).

He had 6 brothers and 6 sisters. He had a built-in fortress of love and protection. What a lucky boy!

And, this wasn't even counting the three siblings that were buried in the little graveyard. Counting them, the new baby had *fifteen* older brothers and sisters!

When the baby was 2 days old, Sarah and Elijah announced what they were going to name him. Sarah said "We decided to name him after two of his uncles. His first name will be 'Silas', after one of my brothers, and his middle name will be 'Morgan', after Elijah's brother. Silas Morgan Casey."

That evening, as she and John were in their room getting ready for bed, Hannah got her mother's Bible and opened it near the candlelight. She began writing something.

John said "What are you writing at this late hour?"

She said "I'm adding Silas's birth to my records in Ma's Bible. Come to think of it, I never put down our wedding day." She recorded both things, then said "Oh, and I should put *your* birthday down, too." She wrote John's birthday in. Then, she said "Your birthday is almost here. You're going to be 31 years old this year. And, I never realized *this* before!"

"Realized what?" John asked.

"Listen to this..." she said, then she read off some dates. "May 18, 1835, Jonathan Wade Oakley is born. January 31, 1845, Hannah Ruth Casey is born. October 14, 1865, Hannah Casey and John Oakley are married."

"Yes, that all seems correct."

"But, don't you notice anything?" she asked.

"Uhhhh, not really..."

"Look at the years....1835, 1845, 1865. Everything seems to happen for us in years ending in five."

"Oh, I guess you're right. Only *you* would notice such a thing!" he teased.

"I'm just saying... maybe five is our lucky number."

"Maybe it is, Hannah. Maybe it is," he agreed. "Now come and give me five kisses."

She put her Bible down and blew out the candle and crawled into his arms.

Now that the birth of baby Silas had come and gone, John said it was time to pick the day of departure. Hannah and John walked up to Daniel and Lucy's house one afternoon and they all sat around and discussed it, and it was decided that they would leave on Saturday, May 12th.

The two couples began making arrangements. John and Israel had arrived there last fall on two horses, with no wagon or cart of any kind to haul things. They'd only traveled with necessities in packs tied to the horses' backs. It would have been possible for John, Israel and Hannah to take the horses down to Clarksville and purchase a wagon there, but now that Daniel and Lucy were going, it seemed they needed a wagon to haul their five children as they went along.

Elijah and Israel talked, and they agreed that Israel would purchase Elijah's wagon from him. This way they could make the trip much more comfortable for all of them. Elijah said he would go to town at a later date and purchase a new wagon with the money Israel had paid him, so everything would work out in the end.

On the morning of the departure, Daniel and Lucy loaded up all their household items and belongings into the wagon. They'd taken several of the children with them to carry everything down the creek so they could load it up. Now Grandma and Grandpa's old house sat empty again. It made Hannah feel sad to see it that way. She wondered if anyone would ever live in it again.

Now it was Hannah's turn to pack up. She went to her room and put everything on her bed. There was her one extra dress, a set of extra undergarments, her journals, ink and pen, her mother's locket and Bible, the cross John had carved for her from the buckeye tree, the tintype photo of Joe, and the buckeye that she had given him before he went off to war.

She picked up the tintype and touched Joe's face. So many childhood memories flooded through her. She remembered how happy she'd been when he gave her the photo. She then picked up the buckeye. She held them both for a moment, then made a decision. She laid the buckeye back down on the bed, then took the photograph and walked out of the house.

She made her way across the creek to the Inman's home, a trip she'd made so many times in her life. She stepped on all the stepping stones as she crossed, so she wouldn't get her feet wet, and with each step she could hear Joe's laughter, and the laughter of all her brothers and sisters, and all of Joe's brothers and sisters through the years, as they splashed across this creek.

She went up onto the Inman's porch and announced her arrival. Henry met her at the door.

"Hi, Hannah," he said.

"Hi, Uncle Henry," she said. Even though he wasn't *really* her uncle, he had played that role in her life for so long. She and her siblings had called him 'uncle' on and off through the years, as a term of affection. "I came to give you and Irene something."

Irene walked into the sitting room, drying her hands on her apron. "What is it Hannah?" she asked.

Hannah had never showed the tintype to Joseph's parents. She had always felt it was her gift from him, meant for her and no one else. But, now she realized how selfish she had been, and that it would mean so much more to them. She had moved on and married someone else. Joe would never be her husband, but he would always be Henry and Irene's son. So, she handed the picture to Irene.

"Joe gave me this when he came back from the war. I thought I would keep it forever. But, now, I know that it would not be right to carry around an image of an old love, as I enter into my new life with John. I know that Joe would want you to have it."

Irene and Henry both broke down in tears as they lovingly held the picture.

"That's our boy," Irene sobbed. "Seeing his face again breaks my heart, yet heals me all at the same time. I was afraid I would forget what he looked like. Now, I never will. Oh, Hannah, thank you! Thank you for this wonderful gift! You will never know what it means to us both."

"I think I do. I just felt strongly that Joe would want it this way."

She left them gazing at the picture of their precious son, and she went back home to her packing. She picked up the buckeye and looked up toward Heaven and said "But, Joe, I *am* keeping this. There are a million buckeyes here. One buckeye wouldn't be any more special than another one to anyone else here. But, this one.... I know that you carried it with you in the war, and I know the meaning behind it. So, I am going to carry it with me for the rest of my life, not only as a memory of our friendship, but also as a memory of this place."

Just then John walked into the room. "Do you have everything?" he asked.

She looked down at her belongings and said "Yes, I think so. But, John, look at this!" She motioned toward the meager pile. "I have nothing much to show for my 21 years of life. I have *nothing* to take with me!"

"Well, it's not what you take with you that determine's a person's worth. It's what you leave behind you when you go," he said.

Hannah thought about all the people who loved her that she would be leaving behind, and how much she had affected their lives, and they hers, and how a little piece of her would be left behind in each of them. She thought of her beloved buckeye tree, the swimming hole, the waterfall, the cliffs, the cave, the little church that had also been her school, and the cemetery that held so many of those that she held dear. She realized that she was leaving behind so much more of herself than she was taking with her.

She turned to John and said "That was very profound, what you just said."

He smiled and said "Maybe you'll turn it into a poem..."

"Maybe I will," she said, as she went to him and pressed her face into his chest and felt his strong arms wrap around her.

She told John that she wanted to go visit the cemetery one last time. He understood that it was something she needed to do by herself.

She walked down and stepped inside the little rock wall and sat down in the grass amid all the graves. On the walk there she had thought she would cry, but as she sat there the tears didn't come. She realized that she was in a different place now, a place of acceptance. So, rather than cry, she just talked to them all, as if they were sitting around in a circle in the grass having a chat.

"William," she began. "I didn't know you as well as I should have, but the way you died, it will stick with me forever. I hope that I brought some peace to your soul by bringing your body home. No one should have to die the way you did, or witness the things you witnessed. I know that your children will be in good care with my brother, and they will be loved. I hope it brings you comfort to know that."

"Martha," she continued, as she turned to the next grave. "It seems your life was doomed from the start. I'm sure you didn't really want to come here, but you followed William because you loved him. I know that Thomas and Isaac were your life, and I'm sorry you weren't able to connect in the same way with Ella. But, she is a beautiful little girl. I know you are proud of her and the boys, and happy to see they have a good life. I'm sorry that we were not better able to care for you after what happened. I know that, mentally, you were not well. I wish there had been more we could have done for you."

"Grandma... All of the advice you gave me over the years, I wrote down and recorded. I value everything you taught me. And, I'm thankful that you and Grandpa came here with us when we left Tennessee. It was wonderful having you close by as I grew up. I love you more than you will ever know."

"Grandpa... I know that John loves me the way you loved Grandma, and I hope we will have a long life together, just as the two of you did. I understand now why you died so soon after Grandma. I understand that you wanted to be with her. I'm proud to be your granddaughter, and I will take a piece of you with me wherever I go in life. I will always be your 'Hannah Belle'."

She turned to face the other row of graves and began again.

"Mr. Madison... I have a hard time simply calling you 'Robert'. I was only 13 when you died, and 'Mr. Madison' was what I always called you back then, out of respect. I want to say thank you for bringing Sarah and moving here. I'm sorry that you died so young, but thankful that I got to know you, and that you gave me the gift of Sarah, and the gift of Rebecca, Rachel and Ruby. I didn't know back then that they would one day become my sisters."

"My dear little sister that I never knew... I was 10 years old when you were born dead. It was my first experience with death. I can still remember Ma's sad crying for days after, but she was strong, and she eventually put the sadness away and moved on.

But, I know deep in her heart there was always a missing piece. I get comfort knowing that the two of you are together now in Heaven. I wish I could have known you. I wish you had been given a name. You would have been 11 years old now if you had survived. I wonder what you would be like."

"Ma, and my other unnamed baby sister... This sister would be 5 now if she'd lived. Again, I wonder what she would have been like, and what you would have named her. I'm glad she rests forever in your arms. I know that so much of myself came from you, Ma. There was so much you taught me. But, I didn't have enough time with you. A girl needs her mother! There are no words to describe how much I love you, and how much I miss you. I hope I will make you proud in my life. I'm glad I was given your middle name. I'm glad I can carry that piece of you with me wherever I go."

"Jesse... My little brother. You would have been 19 now. I wonder if you would have chosen to go with me on this trip, like Daniel did. You had an adventurous spirit. I feel like you wouldn't have stayed here in Buckeye. Albert will stay, I'm almost certain of that. But, you wouldn't have. And, you didn't. You're in Heaven now. I wish I could go back in time and grab your arm and keep you from running off like you did and getting shot. But, I know we can't live in the past. I love you little brother, and I am sad that we never got to know what you could have become."

"Joe.... My childhood memories will always have you front and foremost in them. You were my partner in every game we played growing up. You were my confidant when I had secrets to tell. You were my willing accomplice any time I came up with a crazy scheme. I know you would have followed me to the ends of the Earth. I know how much you loved me. In some ways I feel I didn't return the love to the degree you deserved. But, I hope you know that you meant the world to me, and you helped shape me into the person I am today. Your love and support were so important to me. I will always wonder what path my life would have taken had you lived. I know you are happy for me as you look down from Heaven. I hope I live a life worthy of the one you wanted for me. Goodbye, my friend."

Hannah thought she was done, but then she realized that there had been one more death, one that didn't have a grave to represent it, and that was Abraham. She remembered how infatuated she had been with him. He was her first crush, and even though the feelings weren't returned, she still had many childhood memories that included him. It truly was sad the way he had went off to war and died and never came back. Her heart ached for Lucy and her parents. She felt it was such a shame that he didn't have a grave here as well, that he didn't rest along with the others.

"Rest in peace, Abraham," she said.

She stood up and brushed the dirt off the back of her dress. She took one last look at the little cemetery, and felt a sadness, knowing there was a good chance she might never see it again in her life. She hoped that would not be the case.

After the visit to the cemetery, Hannah walked down to her buckeye tree one last time. She didn't linger long, but she just needed one last look at everything. She wanted to take a mental picture of the tree, the view of the creek, the sound of the water flowing over the rocks. If only she could take this place with her. But, like everything else, she had to let it go. She held the wooden cross in her hand that John had carved from a branch of the tree, and she felt happy knowing she could carry a piece of her tree with her always. And, she had one of the tree's buckeyes, Joe's buckeye, to keep as well. In so many ways this tree would be traveling with her through life.

She was a little sad that it wasn't autumn, because she would have liked to see the tree one last time when the buckeyes had fallen, because like she was always telling everyone, that was her favorite time of year. She felt a bit sad that she might never see it again in the fall. But, as she stood there reminiscing, a thought suddenly came to her. *The people of Buckeye were the buckeyes!* What else would you call people who lived in a community called Buckeye? The people were buckeyes, and over the last few years, too many of them had fallen. Maybe it was time to put that time of her life away, to stop clinging to the past.

Back at the house, Sarah and Elijah had gathered a few things to send along with them. There were some jars of honey, some salt pork, some smoked deer meat, five fresh baked loaves of bread, some canned jellies, pickles, and various vegetables, a skillet and a large spoon for stirring, and a little coffee and sugar.

Elijah had also pulled Daniel aside and given him one of his guns that he had inherited from his own father. Hannah was pretty sure that that gun was the one Joseph had loaded for her in the barn that day, when she had to shoot at the soldiers. She could tell that the gesture meant the world to Daniel.

Then she saw the women of Buckeye walking toward her carrying a quilt. They spread it out for all to see, and they presented it to Hannah. Sarah said "This is for you and John. We all worked on it in our spare time, as a 'going away' gift to you. The pattern of it is called a "wedding ring" pattern. We used bits and pieces of some of our old clothes to make it."

She pointed at a blue piece of cloth and said "This was from one of Jesse's old shirts." Then she pointed at a flowered print and said "This was your Ma's old dress." Then, she continued showing Hannah different pieces and prints. "This one was a shirt that Joseph used to wear. This one was Izzy's. This was your Grandma's apron. This was your Pa's old handkerchief. This piece was from Harding's coat, and this one was from Albert's pants. This one was from a baby blanket that I used for Jasper when he was little and I didn't have any clothes to dress him in. This one is a piece of the curtains that were in the Bennett's old home, the ones you tore up to make face covers when you went to get William's body. This is a piece of that old dress that you wore for so long during the war, because we didn't have money for new material. And the white pieces that tie it all together are from an old tablecloth that we used to spread out to serve the dinners on after church every Sunday."

Hannah broke down in tears as she gathered the quilt in her arms. It was the most special gift she'd ever received, a little piece of everyone that she could take with her. Saying goodbye to her family was one of the hardest things she'd ever had to do. But, when faced with the choice of staying with them forever, or leaving with John, there was no question in her mind. She wanted to be with John. But, having this quilt to cover herself with at night, a quilt that held so many pieces of her past, was a wonderful blessing.

Hannah's younger step-sisters, Rachel & Ruby, had made her a necklace out of yellow dandelions. They made her bend down so they could put it around her neck. Hannah was touched. It hadn't been that long ago when she, herself, was the little girl making necklaces out of dandelions. She hugged all three of her step-sisters and told them how much she was going to miss them.

So many memories were flashing before her eyes. She saw Izzy laying on the other side of Grandma holding her hand as she lay dying. How special it was that she and Izzy had shared that experience. They were both holding Grandma's hand when she passed on to the other side. She saw Lottie holding the gun in the barn and crying because she didn't think she could "shoot nobody". Dear sweet Lottie. She would miss Izzy and Lottie the most, because she'd slept in the same bed with them most of their lives, and had countless late-night conversations. She saw how they were trying to be tough and not cry, and she felt pride. She knew they were made of strong stuff.

She went up to each of her little brothers and hugged and kissed them. She looked at Michael and the twins and remembered all the times she had to play the part of mother to them after their own mother died. She was afraid they might not even remember what all she'd done for them. She looked at Albert and remembered the boy who had to act like a man so many times while the war was going on. She remembered how he'd saved their lives by firing at the soldiers from two different sides of the house. She saw him helping her carry William's dead body, and all those times he struggled to dig a grave for someone they had lost. She remembered him sitting on the porch in the dark, holding his dead brother's hand so he wouldn't be alone. But, she also remembered how fast he could swim, and how high he could climb a tree, and all the other times when he was simply being a boy. It made her sad to think that her half-brothers, Jasper and Silas, would not remember her if she wasn't able to come back soon. She wished she had a tintype photo of all of them to take with her, or one of herself to leave behind. But, unfortunately, she didn't.

She saw the Inman family standing off to the side, waiting to say goodbye. She hugged Henry and Irene. Then she went to each of their children and hugged them; the little boys, James and Charlie, who were 7 and 4 now, and the girls, Nancy, Elizabeth and Virginia, who were 15, 13 and 10. Last she hugged Harding. Oh, Harding.... So much she had been through with him. He'd always been steadfast at her side when things were rough. Looking at him now, she realized how much he looked like his big brother Joe. She realized that she had grown very fond of Harding, he was like a little brother to her, and she was so proud of him for embracing his calling. The young man standing before her was Rev. Inman now, not the little boy that used to follow Joe around like a puppy. She hoped that maybe one day he and Izzy might get married. She'd always thought they were a good match, and they got along well. Izzy was ony 15 right now, to Harding's 19, but Hannah had already begun to see some stirrings of affection between the two.

Lucy and the children loaded up into the wagon. Lucy was 21 years old now, but had so much responsibility with her five children. She was a wonderful mother, though. It just came naturally to her. Thomas was 7 years old now, and Isaac was 5. They had adjusted well after the loss of their parents, and an outsider looking in would never know that Lucy and Daniel weren't their biological parents. Emma and Ella would be turning 3 years old in a month, and Etta was 1 ½.

Lucy and the children would be riding in the wagon, but Hannah, John, Israel and Daniel were going to be walking alongside the wagon, at least for now. The four of them stood next to the wagon, looking back at everyone. Daniel was holding the reins of the horses. John was holding Hannah's hand. Israel thanked everyone for being such wonderful hosts to him all winter long. He said he'd enjoyed his time here very much, and it had been a healing journey for him after the loss of his wife. John also thanked them, for the two winters that they had taken him in.

Just as Hannah and Daniel were about to both turn and

start walking away, Elijah blurted out "Don't ever forget that you are a Casey!" He choked back a tear, then continued. "Be proud that you carry the Casey blood in your veins. Always carry yourself with dignity, and keep God in your life." Daniel let go of the reins of the horse and ran and hugged his father. Then, Hannah did the same. The two of them clung to him with everything they had. They loved this man more than life itself! It was so hard to leave him.

The goodbyes could no longer be dragged out. It was time to go. Daniel pulled on the horses' reins and they began walking away down the road toward town.

Hannah looked back and said "This is not a sad occasion everyone. I want to remember you happy! Harding, play something on your harmonica."

Harding remembered a song that Joe had taught him called "Wait For the Wagon". As he watched the wagon go further and further away, he began to play the song, and the others joined in singing...

"Will you come with me, my Phillis, dear,
To yon blue mountain free
Where the blossoms smell the sweetest,
Come rove along with me
It's every Sunday morning
When I am by your side
We'll jump into the wagon,
And all take a ride

Wait for the wagon
Wait for the wagon
Wait for the wagon
And we'll all take a ride

Wait for the wagon
Wait for the wagon
Wait for the wagon

And we'll all take a ride"

Hannah saw all their smiling, singing faces, and she smiled and waved one final time as the song faded away in the distance and they made the last bend in the road and disappeared out of sight.

Hannah turned and faced her uncertain future, and fought back tears. She felt so odd, a feeling she'd never really felt before in her life. It was a feeling of loss, mixed with a feeling of anticipation. She felt a bit faint. She put her hand to her heart, pressing it against the slightly wilted dandelion necklace. She inhaled a deep breath, hoping to get oxygen into her lungs so she wouldn't pass out.

John was holding her other hand. When he saw what she was doing, he said "What's wrong, Hannah?"

She said "Oh, John! I feel as if I'm standing at the top of a high cliff, with my toes hanging over the edge. What if I fall?"

He looked at her with those sparkling blue eyes of his, and that heart-stopping smile, and said "But, what if you fly?"

She suddenly had an image of the hawk she'd seen soaring freely among the cliffs above her waterfall.

John squeezed her hand tight and with a feeling of excitement, he said it again...

"Hannah, what if you fly?"

These mountains that you carried
You were only meant to climb
This man that you have married
Was sent for you through time
By God, from up on high
To release your heavy weights
So you could learn to fly
On your way to Heaven's gates

by Hannah Oakley
May 1866

About the author.....

Joanie Lynn (Bean) Long was born in Clarksville, Arkansas, and lived there for the first half of her childhood. She then moved to the mountains north of Clarksville, to a little community called Catalpa, where she lived from age 10 to age 15. From here she moved to Tulsa, Oklahoma, where she graduated from high school. While living in Tulsa she met and married her husband, Chris, and together they had three children; Codey, Justin & Wade, all born in the 1990's. She moved to Sperry, Oklahoma when she was 25 years old, and raised her children in that small town, where she still lives today. She is now the proud "Nana" of two precious souls; Morgan & Silas.

Joanie has always enjoyed reading books and writing, but it wasn't until a terrible tragedy happened in her life that she began to explore writing to a fuller extent. In 2013, when her son Justin was 20 years old, he died suddenly and tragically in a motorcycle accident. This event devastated Joanie and all her family. The only thing that seemed to give her some relief was writing. If she was writing then she wasn't concentrating on her grief as much. She began by writing poetry, mostly poetry about grief and loss, but then began to graduate to happier poems. She then wrote and published several articles about her family history for a historical society journal from her hometown. With the help of her granddaughter, she wrote and published a couple of children's books, and then she decided to write her first official novel, of which you hold in your hands today.

Made in the USA
Middletown, DE
27 October 2022

13589911R00234